PRINCE OF THE FALLEN

RECORD OF THE SENTINEL SEER: 1

M. H. WOODSCOURT

True North Press

Cover design by Whimsy Book Cover Graphics.

Published by True North Press

www.mhwoodscourt.com

Paperback ISBN: 9798481317021

Hardcover ISBN: 9798481317946

To everyone who feels different, outcast, alone.
You're seen. You're loved. You're worthwhile.
Don't give up.

Also to Heidi, Lekore's first fan.

The World of Erokel

CONTENT WARNING

Dearest Reader,

While I never intend to write gratuitous violence, sometimes a story calls on an author to pen difficult and distressing scenes.

Contained in these pages is a blood rite that more sensitive readers may find highly disturbing. If you're among these beautiful souls, please be aware and consider skimming or skipping chapter 12 of this book.

Also contained herein are brief mentions of rape, scenes involving death, the theme of slavery, political intrigue, religious zealotry, family trama, and similar sensitive topics. I try to handle these themes with tact, but they still exist and are critical to the story.

Proceed with due caution.

—*M. H. W.*

PROLOGUE

S hards of glass sparkled red around the king's shattered body. Nerenoth's torch sputtered and hissed in the deluge of rain as horror speared him in place for one eternal second, then he moved before his mind could give the command. He knelt before King Adelair.

Blood pooled around his knees and boots.

Night's shadows painted gruesome lines across the corpse's pale face.

"My liege?" Nerenoth's voice hung low, faint.

The king didn't stir.

It was far too late. Nerenoth knew that already. King Adelair's rich raiment clung to his broken frame, golden threads glistening under the torrent. Lifeblood puddled around him, too much of it.

Nerenoth lifted his eyes against the pelting rain and sought the height from which the king had fallen. Two tiers up. The king's study, judging by the broken window.

Bowing his head, Nerenoth raised his hand to trace the arc of the rising sun in a silent prayer to the Sun Gods. Stood. Gripped his sword hilt and strode toward the courtyard's inner doorway. His boots left watery tracks as his long, midnight blue hair clung to his sopping white cape.

Grief. Vengeance. Such must wait. Prince Adenye needed him.

He strode along darkened corridors, steps muted under the storm's protection and the ornate tapestries lining the walls. Thunder growled overhead. It was late; too late for servants and slaves. But where were the guards? Fearing Prince Netye's growing madness, Nerenoth had left strict instructions before he'd ridden to his ailing father's bedside at the Irothé plantation: Keep the man in sight at all times.

Surely the king's brother wouldn't harm little Adenye.

You're jumping to conclusions. Netye might not be involved in this.

Fear pressed Nerenoth onward. He didn't feel the marble beneath his feet.

The way was familiar. In broad and happier days, this same route had brought Nerenoth pleasure to tread. Now, he moved among the shadows, keeping a steady, quiet gait. He mustn't draw notice to himself, in case the assassin lurked nearby.

A faint scuff in the darkness ahead halted Nerenoth's steps. His ears hummed with the strain to hear beyond the wrathful song of rain outside.

A distant rumble, but not thunder. Nerenoth lifted his hand to the wall. It throbbed beneath his fingers. He frowned.

Did someone escape using the hidden passageway? Friend or foe?

Nerenoth's eyes lingered on the corridor for another heartbeat. Prince Adenye's chambers lay ahead. Did the little body lie beneath the coverlets, bleeding out its lifeblood, too late to rescue?

A tiny cry drew Nerenoth's gaze back to the wall and the hidden passage.

"Ank! Dark."

"Hush, my boy." Netye's cooing tones wafted through the air. "This is a great new adventure for you. Hold my hand and I will keep you safe."

Fire teemed inside Nerenoth. His grip on his sword tightened and he started forward—but paused. Why hadn't Netye murdered his nephew yet? Where did he intend to take the child?

You're making assumptions again. He might be protecting the boy.

A hiss and a whispering snip sounded as the passage panel slid shut. Nerenoth held still for a long moment. They must have gone far enough down the steps by now. He could enter the passage undetected.

Best watch and wait. If Netye was innocent, Nerenoth couldn't risk accusing him.

He covered the distance to the panel in a few bounding steps, pressed the space just beneath the single, smooth black plate set into the glittering white stones of the wall. The panel slid aside. Abandoning his torch, Nerenoth stepped into darkness and took care as he descended, one step at a time.

The stairs plunged deep beneath the palace before the ground gave way to a level floor of rock. Nerenoth paced himself, knowing Prince Netye's progress would be slow with the three-year-old in tow. The child's soft murmurs drifted across the shadows ahead.

Would Netye murder the boy?

He might have murdered his brother, but King Adelair and Netye had never been close. After Netye's wife died in childbirth, his mind had cracked. Only little Adenye had broken through his uncle's grief over the past fortnight, and then he'd kept vigil as much as a three-year-old could.

No one approached Netye without the toddler prince's sanction, nor would Adenye leave Netye alone except to sleep.

Netye loved the child. But did he remember that now, in the dark of night and the madness of his soul?

Reaching level ground, Nerenoth heard the two ahead of him, steps scuffing against stone and dust. Shuffles echoed off walls, and soon, a torch flickered into life. Adenye laughed and clapped his hands. His uncle didn't quiet him. Netye thought himself safe from discovery.

Their noise would cover Nerenoth's soft steps and the faint clink of his armor.

If the man was guilty of murder, he might've paid off the guards or they'd been disloyal from the start. This morning, Nerenoth received word that Netye had struck Prince Adenye across the face in a fitful rage. Only the toddler's calm intercession had prevented the king from imprisoning his brother.

Now King Adelair is dead.

Searing fury flooded Nerenoth's veins, but he held himself back with gritted teeth, keeping beyond the torchlight. Patience had always been his ally. He would wait until he knew Netye's purpose. Knew his guilt beyond all doubt. Wait, and then rescue the little crown prince before harm came to him.

The tunnel led outside the city walls. It was the king's private escape route in the event he must flee from danger.

King Adelair would never need it now.

The walk through the dark barraged Nerenoth's frame. Every sound stretched his nerves tighter. Sweat slickened his sword grip.

At last. A familiar bend appeared in the tunnel ahead. One Nerenoth had known since early childhood when he and the king had played in the hidden passageways, shadowed now by storm and true night.

He peered around the bend.

Netye's lean frame blazed against the flash of lightning as the sky rumbled beyond the tunnel's round maw. There stood the toddler prince, wrapped in a golden night robe: staring bravely up at his uncle, unaware of danger, oblivious to treachery.

Nerenoth's heart pitched. He started forward, caught himself, set his jaw. *Stay a moment longer.*

Netye crouched before his nephew, adorned in scarlet sleeping robes, a fond smile on his lips. "My dear boy, are you tired?"

Adenye nodded, pale blue hair bobbing against his shoulders. "Much farther, Ank?"

"Only a little. Take my hand." Netye rose, blue hair falling away from his gaunt face. He guided Adenye through the doorway, out into the storm.

Nerenoth swept after them but allowed Netye to close the passage before he reached the exit. He waited in the darkness as long as he dared, then slipped out the door.

Though thunder still rumbled in the distance, the rain had tamed into a drizzle. Against the gray promise of approaching dawn, Nerenoth searched the grasslands before him. There, near a stand of boulders, Netye knelt before the little prince again.

Nerenoth bent low in the tall grass and raced across the muddy earth, sword hand throbbing for action. He drew up and crouched before a large rock, just near enough to hear, and sank to his knees.

"It is very important, do you understand, Nye?"

"Yes, Ank. Wait."

"That's right, dear boy. Wait until I come for you. Trust me as you always have. Wait for your Ank."

Adenye raised his fingers and pressed them against Netye's face. "Ank, I'll wait."

"Brave, clever boy." Netye seized those tiny fingers and kissed them. "Say uncle just once for me. Uncle."

Adenye laughed. "Ank!"

Netye's shoulders fell as he released the prince's fingers. "I shall miss you, but it's too late, my boy. Too late for retreat. Life is cruel. I must be crueler. You understand, don't you, Adenye? You understand better than anyone. You always understood me. Dear boy. You're too good for this world." He rose. "Stay among the rocks, little Nye. Wait for me."

"I'll wait, Ank," said the toddler. "Bye, bye."

Netye strode toward Nerenoth, toward the passage. Nerenoth crouched lower behind the rock, letting Netye pass him by. *He's leaving him here to die?*

So, the man was too much the coward to slay his nephew. Instead, he would leave him to starve in the grasslands, if the emockye didn't devour him first. Nerenoth waited, eyes riveted on Prince Adenye, until the passageway rumbled shut. Prince Netye would return to Inpizal, return to the palace, and declare King Adelair and his successor killed by assassins or slaves. He would rule as king—so he thought. But Nerenoth would not stand by and allow the rightful heir to die; nor would he let Netye inherit the throne.

Nerenoth stood up and started toward Prince Adenye, who had seated himself on a large rock beneath the shelter of a leaning boulder. The toddler buried his face in his knees to shield against the windy drizzle, golden robe darkening as droplets penetrated the heavy brocade.

"Hold fast, Lord Captain."

Nerenoth spun, sword half-drawn, before he found the source of the stranger's voice. His breath caught. He sheathed his sword and dropped to one knee. "O Holy One, what is thy will?"

He knew he should lower his eyes, but the wondrous figure before him snared them. It was but a child in appearance; a boy, perhaps eight or nine years of age, with hair of golden-yellow and eyes of sky blue. Ears, long and narrowing into a point, framed his fair face as rain dripped down his rosy cheeks. He wore opulent gold and white raiment, as well as a smile of kindly wisdom far beyond his outward years.

Lifting a hand, the Sun God spoke. "Leave the child."

Nerenoth started. "Holy One—"

"I shall care for him. You must return to Inpizal and continue to serve as Lord Captain under the new king."

Nerenoth stared, a lump growing in his throat. "But Holy One, Netye is a traitor and a murderer—" Was he arguing with a Sun God? Was he seeing one, or had grief and anger tainted his mind?

The childlike Sun God's smile shone as radiant as the Zen-hour sun itself. "This boy cannot be raised among your people. Let Netye rule for now and hold your peace in these matters. Have patience, knowing that a greater will is at work here."

Warmth spread across Nerenoth's cheeks, and he pulled his eyes to the ground. "As thou wilt, O Holy God."

"There's a good lad. Return to your father's plantation. Make haste, for he will not last the night, I fear. He has grown worse in your absence."

Nerenoth rose as the pinprick pain of alarm stabbed his lungs. "At once, Holy One." He offered a sweeping bow, his cape rustling in the tall grass as droplets rolled off his silver breastplate. He started for the passageway, but halted after several feet, and glanced back.

The divine being approached the tiny crown prince while the toddler stared up at the Sun God with widened eyes and a glowing smile. The ache in Nerenoth's heart deepened. He loved Adenye. Would he ever see those earnest, knowing eyes again in this life?

Trust in the Sun Gods.

It was all he could do.

Once inside the passageway, he would take another underground route to the Royal Garrison, and from there he would ride to Irothé Plantation and pay his last respects to his dying father.

By then, word of King Adelair's death would already have spread; and soon afterward, Nerenoth Irothé, Lord Captain of the Royal Army, would be obliged to bend the knee to a mad usurper.

CHAPTER 1

Eighteen Years Later

The sun pennants rode the wind in a jaunty dance, crisp and proud above the gleaming armor of the Kel procession. Princess Talanee peeked through the velvet curtains of her carriage window, hoping for a glimpse of Lord Captain Nerenoth in the column ahead. So far, she'd had no luck. Hopefully, that wasn't an ill omen.

Today must be perfect.

The Lighting would signify the beginning of the Fire Month and the first of three pivotal ceremonies in concurrence with the Sun Festival. Not that she felt especially honored to signal the start of the festivities, for this wasn't her first time. In fact, the event had become tedious after performing the rite these past four years.

But the Lord Captain had joined the procession this year, rather than send the Lord Lieutenant alone. Unrest in the westlands had set the court's nerves against a blade's edge, and Father had insisted Lord Captain Nerenoth oversee the Lighting.

Talanee allowed herself a smile, pleased by the turn of events despite the rumors of a brewing war with the heathen Tawloomez tribes on the northwest coastline. How dangerous could the savages be in their leather armor, anyway?

A cloud of dust swelled ahead of the line and Talanee dropped the curtain with a sigh. Another twenty or more minutes must pass before she would reach the ancient tower amid the Ruins of Halathe to perform her duty to the Sun Gods. Couldn't the procession march a *little* faster?

"My lady?"

Talanee lanced her willowy lady-in-waiting with a scowl. "Yes, Keerva?"

The young woman blushed until her complexion matched the bloodred color of her irises. "Forgive me, but..." She drew aside the curtain on her half of the rolling carriage even as the conveyance slowed, "...a messenger has arrived from one of the western cities. Erokes, I think. At least his insignia suggests..." She trailed off, lines appearing between her brows. She caught a strand of light blue hair and twisted it. "What do you think it means, my lady?"

Talanee scooted across her seat with a whisper of silk to peer outside. Her heart stuttered.

It was him.

The Lord Captain met the messenger on the edge of the procession, and the two men conversed in muted tones, expressions grim. A few clipped words: that was all. Then the messenger saluted, wheeled his reptilian pythe around, and took off at a quick lope.

The equine creature's deep green scales flashed in the sunlight, its black mane like a streamer in the air as its long, scaled tail kept the creature's balance. It beat its useless stubs where wings might have been in another age.

Nerenoth Irothé brought his pythe around and cantered to the carriage as the conveyance came to a full stop. His long, midnight blue hair settled across his white cape, highlighting the strands of lavender that declared his noble lineage.

Talanee stuck her head out the window, locks of long blue hair sliding over her shoulder to stir in the faint breeze. "What did the messenger say, Lord Captain?"

Nerenoth Irothé was a man impossible to read. If he looked grim now, it was no different from his usual gravity. Yet as she met his red eyes, a biting fear chilled her arms despite the heat of the midzen hour.

"Erokes is under attack, Your Highness," he said in measured tones. "I must gather a force to march there at once. I shall leave you with my lieutenant, though I don't wish to abandon you so far from Inpizal."

Talanee lifted her chin to hide the horror ripping through her frame. "Don't waste another thought on me, Lord Captain. See to our people. Out here, who can harm me? Lord Lieutenant Rez is a capable man besides. We'll be fine. Go show those spiteful heathens the wrath of the Sun Gods."

The Lord Captain lingered a heartbeat longer, searching her face. He offered a grim nod, then flicked the reins of his stallion pythe and nudged it into motion. The pythe's long, powerful legs loped to the front of the column, talons digging into dirt.

"Rez!" Nerenoth's voice straightened the spines of every soldier along his path. A brief conversation between the Lord Captain and his right-hand man ensued, then Nerenoth wheeled south as he barked a last command. "Carrack, Dilhar, with me!"

Two mounted officers split from the column to race after their commanding lord. Talanee watched their departure with a plummeting heart as the carriage lurched and rolled on.

Not a word parted any soldier's lips, nor any priest's riding with them to witness the upcoming holy rite.

Talanee's mind strayed far from the Ruins of Halathe. She bowed her head. "O Sun Gods above, by thy glorious light, protect the Lord Captain and preserve the people of Erokes against our vile enemy."

"Amen," murmured Keerva in her timid voice.

The next twenty minutes gnawed at Talanee's nerves. Every jolt in the road fortified her anger. Why carry on this silly rite, rather than return to Inpizal to organize relief efforts for the citizens of Erokes?

"We've arrived, my lady," said Keerva in soft tones. Perhaps she could read Talanee's growing agitation. It wasn't as though she'd tried to hide it.

Talanee pulled the curtain aside to find the familiar tower stretching toward the sun at its zenith. That glistening white stone stabbed the cloudless blue sky. Talanee's chest constricted.

Of course. I must do this. This rite is exactly the best way to aid Erokes and Lord Captain Nerenoth.

The princess stepped down from the carriage with Keerva's aid. She smoothed her heavy skirts, drew the white hood over her blue hair, and turned to her handmaids, who had journeyed in a second carriage behind her own. "Prepare the holy instruments."

Two priests removed a large, gilt trunk from its place between the back wheels of the royal carriage, stirring puffs of cloud that clung to their white and gold vestments. Talanee's handmaids opened the trunk and extracted a long wooden rod soaked in oil and pitch. A sprig of golden leaves adorned the torch's tip. The handmaids sprinkled phials of holy water along the base of the torch as the priests chanted ancient prayers to the Holy Sun Throne.

Soldiers fanned out to create two columns leading to the base of the tower, armor flashing, sun pennants snapping in the hot wind. The remaining priests looked on to witness and approve the auspicious event.

Despite the encircling grasslands, the ruins held no weeds or brush: An ocean of wild grass surrounded an island of stone and dust. The fragments of buildings jutted up like broken teeth, weathered by time, crumbling and whistling with the wind's endless music.

Casting her eyes skyward, Talanee smiled, noting the sun at its highest point. They'd arrived just in time. At her nod, her handmaids built up wood for a fire and lit the blessed kindling with flint and a piece of steel. As the flames grew to consume the dry wood, Talanee took up the sacred torch and began her chant.

"Most Holy Sun Gods above, accept this thy servant as thy handmaid. Behold the fire of the world, captured and delivered unto thee at the foot of thy Sun Throne; a return of what is borrowed from thy everlasting light." She dipped the torch's tip in the fire, and it caught flame with a brilliant flash of red and blue. The golden leaves glowed and then turned black as they curled in the smoke and flame.

She lifted the torch and began the long climb up the cracked granite steps to the tower's great height.

No procession followed her. She must go the path alone, a willing servant of the Sun Gods. It was a beautiful ceremony, and now that she performed it, her fears vanished as the pull of duty and faith settled upon her like a comfortable weight.

"Lend thy people thy light through the dark days of the coming gray. Let the sun burn beyond the clouds of water sent by the cursed Moon Throne. Bless thy people with great abundance, that the rain of the wicked may be turned to a purpose of good. Let the crops thrive rather than drown. Cultivate the land that in thy glory it shall not shrivel."

She took careful steps, focused on the chant to forget the strain of carrying the weighty torch. Acrid smoke curled around her face and tears welled in her eyes, but she moved with stubborn determination toward the tower's tor, hair bobbing against the small of her back.

"Upon thy faithful, deliver the light of day even in the dark cracks of the night." She stumbled on the hem of her pearl-seed gown but steadied herself and kept going. "Unto those who serve the Star Gods, bring destruction and forgive them not, for they have chosen the path of the night."

Someone shouted. Talanee whipped around, heart beating against her ribs. From thirty feet above the troops, she spotted a swarm of brown-clad warriors charging the three dozen armored men with blood-curdling screams.

Lord Lieutenant Rez's sword flashed silver as he pulled it from his scabbard.

Talanee dug her nails into the torch. Tawloomez, here? They'd never dared to step upon the sacred ground of this holy ruin; not since the War of Brothers five hundred years ago.

As the Kel soldiers clashed with the enemy, Talanee found herself mesmerized by the beauty of the soldiers. The Tawloomez fought with savage aggression, spears and scimitars and daggers lashing in an ugly, wild dance. Rez's men formed themselves into triangles and ovals to take on their adversary with calculated grace, shields and swords winking under the high sun.

A new cry ascended, and a second flood of Tawloomez appeared from the shadows of boulders and broken structures. A hundred or more Tawloomez now battled against three dozen Kel. But the Kel wore steel and the Tawloomez didn't.

The odds favored the Royal Army of Erokel.

With a jolt, Talanee remembered her duty. Her eyes flicked between the sputtering torch and the tower's top, and she climbed again. Her mind sought her place in the chant. She must do her part to please the Sun Gods.

"Unto those who serve the Star Gods," she said, then growled under her breath. She'd already intoned that part. Path of the night...path of the night...what came after that? She tripped on the hem of her white gown again and staggered forward.

The torch clattered from her hand as she caught herself, scraping her palms. Gasping, she groped around for the holy instrument. The torch remained lit but had rolled down several steps. She scurried after it, smearing blood from her hands on the steps. She snatched up the guttering torch and glanced again at the battle waging below.

Several Tawloomez had freed themselves from the fight and sprinted up the steps toward her. She gritted her teeth, pushed to her feet, and quickened her pace as much as she dared in her heavy gown.

I'm dead either way. But she wouldn't die without completing the ceremony, even if she broke every bone in her body doing it. *For Erokes. For Nerenoth.*

The shouts and clangs of battle rose like a song from the cruel Moon Throne. Talanee muttered the chant under her breath, trying not to picture the carnage. "Guard thy people from the grip of darkness and when time ends, bring us unto thee and shelter us beneath thy beaming face."

How appropriate.

"Let thy light consume thy people in the eternal flames of thy divinity and let not thy people falter in the way to thee." Her breath rasped, her heart pounded against her ribs, and she stumbled again. She could hear the slap of feet close on her heels.

I won't make it. I wish I'd been allowed to wear my sword!

But the ceremony was an act of faith; to bring a weapon up the steps signified doubt.

"O ye Gods of the Sun, let thy glory encircle us within thy mighty bosom."

A hand snatched her arm and jerked her around. She stared into the grinning face of a dark-skinned, brown-haired Tawloomez. Paint in shimmering green patterns, beautiful and hideous at once, adorned his cheeks and forehead. A grotesque snake-bone necklace hung over his brown-leather battle garb. Two more Tawloomez stood behind him.

"*Vatakay owi?*"

She didn't know what he said, but his tones dripped with mockery. Talanee gripped the torch with white knuckles and spat in the Tawloomez's face. "Release me, heathen scum."

The Tawloomez's brown eyes flashed. He snatched the torch's haft and tried to wrench it away. Talanee swung with it, refusing to let go.

"Gods protect me!"

As though in answer to her prayer, the flame of the holy torch leapt into a brilliant, churning arc. Intense heat and a deafening roar scored the air near her face. Flames encircled her without touching her skin, then stretched fiery fingers toward the

Tawloomez warrior, who cried out as he and his fellows stumbled backward. They turned tail and dashed down the steps as the flames gave chase.

Talanee stood stunned, enthralled by the unending flame shooting up and out from the torch she held in trembling hands. She turned her eyes upward and found nothing but the brilliant sun in its sky to signify divine intervention. Could her prayer have worked? A breeze tugged at her hair, and she glanced down at the battlefield. The arc of fire had reached the bottom of the tower, and all the Tawloomez warriors cowered, corralled within it.

Talanee started down the steps, gripping the torch in her hands as it poured forth the terrible wrath of her beloved Sun Gods.

At the bottommost step, she stopped. The Kel soldiers had flinched back, even Lord Lieutenant Rez, though he held his sword before him.

A breeze breathed across Talanee's neck, but the fire of the torch maintained its vigil over the trapped Tawloomez, unerring despite the rising wind that tossed her hair. She resisted the urge to release the blazing torch with even one hand. Her eyes followed the trail of her hair in the sky—and she spotted him.

A figure perched on a ruined wall across from the tower. He was slender, barely a man, with the palest, longest blue hair she'd ever beheld, and eyes of red like all the Kel race, but these eyes blazed as though they held the wreathing fire. A tattered black cloak billowed behind him in the growing windstorm. One arm rose before him, hand splayed.

As she watched, he snapped his fingers into a fist. The fire of the torch died. The wreath of flame wisped into smoke and vanished.

The Tawloomez had seen the young man, too. With a cry, one heathen jabbed his finger toward the stranger. *"Akuu! Nu jas Akuu-Ry!"*

The Tawloomez stumbled backward, eyes wide, nearly wild, some dropping their weapons. They fled from the young man, racing northwest. One stumbled on grit and struck his knees, then dragged himself upright and sprinted on.

The Kel soldiers, still stunned, didn't rally to cut off their retreat.

In the ringing silence that followed, Lord Lieutenant Rez dragged long strands of blue hair from his perspiring face as he found his voice. "See to the wounded!"

Talanee released a low breath and let her numb fingers drop the cold torch. Her eyes returned to the young man upon the ruin. His gaze met hers across the wide space. His brow creased, and he threw out his hand as the slap of feet sounded behind her.

She whirled to face a lone, charging Tawloomez, scissor knife in his hand, its several blades glinting under the dazzling sun. Her fingers gripped the torch, prepared to brandish it like her missing sword.

The wind changed direction. The strange young man from the ruin landed on the packed earth beside her, as though he'd taken flight upon the breeze to reach her.

He lifted a narrow, curved sword against the Tawloomez. Metal sang across the air as their weapons struck.

The Tawloomez gritted his teeth and spat out the same foreign phrase, this time like a curse word: "*Akuu-Ry!*"

The young man took a single step forward, and the Tawloomez's brown eyes widened, the green paint of his face shimmering as though to reflect his fear.

"Leave, *Tauw-Nijar*, and I shall not do you harm," said the young man in lilting tones.

The Tawloomez snarled and threw a long sliver of metal at Talanee. She yelped and tried to dodge as the young man shoved her aside. The tiny, glinting object caught his arm. A hiss was all the noise he made, but he sank to his knees and the sword clattered from his hand.

The Tawloomez sneered and swiped the scissor knife at the boy's throat, but an arrow pierced his chest before he met his target. He grunted and fell, his swinging arm catching the young man's shoulder, biting into the flesh in three distinct stripes.

A second arrow sank into the heathen's chest, and the warrior crashed backward against the white stone stairs. Blood bloomed across his snake-bone necklace and down his front. He offered up a last gurgling breath, then his eyes turned to glass.

Talanee allowed the satisfaction of his passing to shiver across her skin, then she turned to the young man kneeling beside her. He looked up to meet her stare, and for a moment Talanee couldn't move. His eyes still wielded that strange light like a fire burned within him, yet the clarity there made her feel as though he had stripped her bare to see every thought, every lie, every desire, every fear.

His eyes flicked to the dead Tawloomez. His hand snaked out for his sword near the fallen warrior.

"Don't touch it. Don't move." Rez's voice rang through the ruins as he raced across the field, red cape flowing behind him, to join Talanee and the strange young man. An archer ran with him, another arrow nocked and aimed at the stranger.

The young man's fingertips brushed the sword. As Talanee looked on, the weapon vanished. Gone, as though the very air had swallowed it!

The stranger staggered to his feet. His pale hair, long and straight, rippled like water as it settled down his back and against his ankles. He offered a strained smile and raised his arm into the air. The wind howled, drawing his hair into a whirlwind, carrying the scent of wild things. He bounded upward, and the wind lifted him into the sky, above the tower, above the armored soldiers and Sun Priests, above Talanee and the grasslands. He leapt impossibly high and moved away in an arc, as though he could fly.

"Halt!" Rez slowed his pace and came to a stop beside Talanee, eyes lifted heavenward as the archer's second arrow missed its mark. "By the Sun Gods, what is it we've seen?"

Talanee shook her head. "The very will of the Sun Throne, Lord Lieutenant. What else could it be?"

"Was he real?"

Talanee's eyes lowered as she sought an answer. Blood stained the scissor knife lying beside its dead owner. "I think he was." She traced a rising sun before her chest. "Sun Gods be praised. I think he was."

Rez stirred from his watch of the sky. "Should we...try to complete the ceremony again, Your Highness?"

Talanee glanced at the fallen torch. "I don't think we have to, Lord Lieutenant. The rite was already accepted, or we wouldn't be alive." She glanced around for the priests and found several slain, blood staining their white robes, while the rest cowered beneath the carriages. No one protested her assumption.

Next time, the Holy Hakija had better send his Sun Warriors rather than these cowards.

Rez eyed the priests and nodded. "Then we should return to Inpizal, Your Highness. There are wounded to tend, and we must report all that's happened."

"Of course." Talanee stooped to pick up the torch. "The king needs to know. And we should consult the Hakija." She picked up her hem and glided toward her carriage, where Keerva and her other handmaids huddled inside, waiting. Talanee glanced back toward the tower. Her gaze drifted north, where the young man had vanished in the air.

Would she ever see him again, or had he traveled from the very Sun Throne to aid her and her people?

CHAPTER 2

"Lord Captain Nerenoth has arrived, my lady!"

Princess Talanee looked up, letting her fork clatter onto her plate. "Where is he?"

"Bearing toward the throne room," said Keerva between breaths, her lean frame shuddering as she slouched against the doorframe. At Talanee's behest, the lady-in-waiting had been on the lookout for the return of Nerenoth and his troops all morning. Talanee had expected them since word reached the king yesterzen evening that the fortress city of Erokes had been overrun.

A few hundred refugees rode with Nerenoth's troops back to Inpizal. The king and Hakija had withheld further news of the Tawloomez invaders from public knowledge; and infuriatingly, that included Talanee. But now she would get answers.

She rose, tugged her pale green skirts free of any wrinkles, and swept across the dining hall. "With me, Keerva."

Her lady-in-waiting followed at a respectful distance as Talanee conquered the corridors leading to the throne room. Servants in green livery bowed, Tawloomez slaves dressed in grays and browns scurried out of the way, and soldiers in silver armor saluted as she whisked past.

At last, the great doors to the throne room loomed before her, made of ornate wood, lined with swirls no Kel artisan could craft: a relic from the Sun Gods in another, holier era. Guards drew aside the doors to admit the crown princess of Erokel. The chamber stood nearly empty.

The king had summoned none of the nobility and gentry for the Lord Captain's report, but nor had he kept the church out of this matter.

Lord Father sat stiff and scowling upon his sun-crowned throne, while the Holy Hakija, Dakeer Vasar, stood in ceremonial dignity beside him upon the raised dais. Both illustrious men appeared small in contrast to the imposing grandeur of the hollow chamber, with its high vaulted ceiling and graceful stone columns, the fluttering green pennants of the Royal House of Getaal, and the festooned white and gold accents.

Before them, taller than the Hakija, taller still than the king, Nerenoth Irothé stood in the gleaming silver armor and white cape of his unmatched military rank. His dark hair hung long and straight down his back.

Talanee studied the Triad of Erokel representing the branches of government: civil, spiritual, and protective. A tingle swept from the crown of her head down to her toes, not unlike the feeling she'd had when that strange young man sailed down from a ruin to rescue her from death. An experience she'd intended to report to Lord Father, but he'd been too preoccupied with Erokes to devote himself to any other alarming news.

Now she could tell him, or at least Nerenoth, of what had transpired.

"What is *she* doing here?"

Talanee flinched as Lord Father's voice rang across the throne room. Keerva stepped back. Talanee lifted her chin and swept forward. "Lord Father, I came to hear the news of Erokes."

Lord Captain Nerenoth inclined his head; it was all the deference he need show, as he wielded more power than she did at present.

"Princess," said Dakeer in his rich tones, "a formal report will be issued to the public soon."

"I've a right to know ahead of the public—"

"Get out, daughter. You're not needed here." The king's voice rolled over the chamber, savage as an emockye's growl. His sallow complexion matched the yellow hems of his velvet green tunic, and his thinning hair wisped against his shoulders as he waved her away.

She squared her shoulders to fight against recoiling. *Don't back down.* She would permit herself to feel the sting of his barb later. "Were the Tawloomez pushed back?"

Nerenoth spoke. "They retreated before we ever arrived, Your Highness, their deadly work accomplished."

"Now go," said Lord Father. "Or should I have you escorted out?"

She strode nearer, hands clutching her skirts. "They attacked us at Halathe."

The Triad stared at her.

"Your Highness, do you mean the Tawloomez?" asked Nerenoth.

She nodded. "Lord Lieutenant Rez requested an audience with you, Lord Father, but you turned him away—as well as me." She scowled at the pout in her voice. Why should now be different from any other point in her life?

"How many, Princess?" asked Nerenoth.

"To attack at Halathe?" said the Hakija at the same time. "The boldness of it!"

Talanee fastened her eyes on the Lord Captain. "Over a hundred, my lord; by your lieutenant's reckoning, as well as my own."

Nerenoth's eyes narrowed. "Against so few of our own troops, how are you still alive, Princess?"

Talanee pinched her pale green gown. How could she form the words to describe all she'd seen? Her prayer to the Sun Gods, answered with fire spewing from her torch; the young man who had directed its course before he flew down to save her; and then, wounded, had flown again out of reach, back into the heavens, perhaps to the Sun Throne itself.

"There's so much to tell." Her heart pounded. She thought she could smell smoke in her hair, though the ceremony had been yesterzen, and she'd bathed upon her return to Inpizal. Drawing air, she allowed the words to pour out as they would. Let the Triad unravel her images to make sense of them. Let the Holy Hakija make of them what he would with his divine authority.

Her eyes held onto the Lord Captain's. He most of all must believe what she'd witnessed; he, who had no love of the church nor a firm belief in the Sun Throne. Let him believe her.

Silence clung to the air when her words died. Nerenoth wore a frown.

"This stranger," said Dakeer Vasar. "He truly flew?"

"As though he had tamed the very wind to his will, Your Holiness." Talanee wrenched her gaze free of the Lord Captain's. "He was wounded. There was blood upon the blade that cut his shoulder. The Lord Lieutenant will testify to all I've said."

"By the glorious Sun Throne," murmured Lord Father. "What does all this mean, Hakija?"

Hakija Dakeer Vasar was a slender man, young for his office but older than he appeared, as though the Sun Gods had removed age from his countenance. He and Nerenoth had both taken their respective offices far younger than any other in recorded history, save the Heretic himself.

Dakeer's prowess, his knowledge and steady temperament, and his sober character had garnered deep respect within the Sun Tribunal, and culminated in an early rise to the head of the church. He was perhaps ten years older than Nerenoth, handsome, but not as handsome—though none were. His hair was light, reaching past his shoulders to frame the white and gold vestments of the Holy Hakija. Atop his head he wore a gold-threaded miter.

Talanee had heard all her life that Dakeer Vasar and Nerenoth

Irothé did not like one another, but both were difficult to read, careful in public, and quiet in their dispositions.

The Hakija sighed. "I must meditate on this matter, my king. There are accounts of Kel who were sun-touched in the past—those who wielded the very might of the Sun Throne—but nothing of its kind has occurred since the days of King Erokel the Second and his heir. However, it's doubtful that the Moon Throne deceived the princess and Rez Kuaan. We should burn offerings to express our gratitude for their safe return and the harm that befell our enemy."

"That makes two attacks," said Nerenoth. "A third will happen, my lords."

The Hakija's mouth quirked into a humorless smile. "No thoughts on the miracle Princess Talanee has described, Lord Captain?"

"That is your province, Hakija," said Nerenoth, "just as the defense of our people is mine. If you will excuse me, Your Holiness, Your Majesty, Princess, I will take my leave. We must tighten the borders around our country or risk greater tragedy than we now face." He clicked his heels, bowed, and whirled to march from the room.

Talanee tracked him with a plummeting heart. She'd hoped he would ask her more questions, or anything... Anything for the chance to speak with him further.

"You're still here, daughter?" Lord Father's bitter voice sundered her thoughts.

Talanee pressed her face into what she hoped was a neutral expression, curtsied, and retreated. Keerva lingered in the corridor —as did the Lord Captain. Talanee's breath hitched as her heart tripped.

The guards shut the double doors to the throne room.

"Would you mind accompanying me for a moment, Your Highness?" asked Nerenoth.

With Keerva present, it was perfectly proper. Talanee allowed herself a smile as warmth spread through her. "Certainly, my lord."

25

They traveled the long gallery, passing the portraits of her ancestors, the royals of House Getaal, silence between them. Keerva trailed behind at a respectful distance.

"This young man you saw," said Nerenoth after a while. "How would you describe him?"

Talanee reached back to recollect everything she could of the strange young man. "He was...beautiful, my lord. He appeared otherworldly, yet he could bleed. His hair was the palest blue I've ever seen, and terribly long, and he bore the faintest hint of pale lavender locks, unless the sun tricked my eyes. His irises were red as any Kel, yet they blazed like fire and...and I felt like he could see *inside* me. *Beyond* me. I should have been frightened, but somehow, I felt calm. He moved like water, rather silvery and lithe. He wasn't quite...not *quite* Kel."

Nerenoth nodded, a crease between his brows. Talanee studied him, glad of the chance to admire the angles of his comely face. Her favorite feature was the scar vivid against the bridge of his nose; somehow it added to his wealth of pleasing attributes. Apart from being one of the three most powerful men in all Erokel, he was considered its most handsome and, though he was promised to Lady Lanasha, the most desirable above any other nobleborn man.

Talanee scowled. Were it not for the unfulfilled attachment to that primping, simpering, cold-hearted creature, Nerenoth would be the best-suited choice for Talanee upon her coming-of-age celebration next Rainy Season.

"Did he speak?"

She blinked. Her mind seized on the present subject again and she nodded. "Yes, he spoke to one of the Tawloomez. He called him...Tow Na... I don't quite recall."

"*Tauw-Nijar.*" Nerenoth nodded. "It means 'honored warrior' in the Tawloomez tongue."

She frowned. "To show respect to our enemy—"

"Is no crime, Your Highness. I am more interested in his knowledge of their tongue. Or at least of an obscure term primarily used among the upper echelon of Tawloomez warriors, rarely among their common folk, and almost never among the Kel." His hand cut across the air in a dismissive wave. "Perhaps it matters not. I am glad you're safe, Princess. On the heels of Erokes, your loss would have been a crushing blow to our people."

Talanee's smile threatened to deepen, but she caught the flash of pain in the Lord Captain's eyes. Revelation dawned like a spear of lightning. "You had family in Erokes, didn't you, my lord?"

"I believe my uncle and aunt and their children were killed, Your Highness." Always the stoic face, the grim but detached tone. She admired his composure.

"With your permission, I will pray to the Sun Throne for their souls, my lord."

"You're most kind, Your Highness. You said the young man was wounded defending you?"

"Yes, Lord Captain. Twice. The first was a long slender pin meant for me. The second, the bite of a scissor knife, here." She pawed her shoulder.

"I see." Nerenoth clapped a hand to his chest and made a faint bow. "Thank you for your time, Princess. I will leave you now."

She dipped into a curtsy as her lips pressed together. She took a breath. "I hope I've helped in any small way."

He strode toward the distant double doors leading to the courtyard outside. Guards saluted him, admiration bright in their red eyes. When he reached the doors, a guard pushed the great barriers aside. The Lord Captain turned one last time, inclined his head, then disappeared into the light funneling in from the zenhour sun. His cape slithered out last. The doors swooped shut.

A third attack will happen. She clutched her skirts. What was she doing, yearning for the Lord Captain's attention when war brewed on the next horizon? She must prepare. The Sun Festival had begun. People flocked to Inpizal in droves; at first for the month-long celebration for the Sun Gods, now for the safety of her great walls. With these droves would come crimes, mayhem, even Star Worshipers.

Talanee wasn't the king, but her province was large enough. She set the standard for ladies, not just in fashion, but also decorum, and even faith. She would keep in the public view. Demonstrate her faith. Remain calm and demand order of all within her sights. She'd already begun organizing relief efforts, and she would continue to oversee them.

A last glance at the door was all Talanee allowed of herself before she swept down the corridor toward her wing of the palace. Lord Captain Nerenoth would do his part as well. None were more composed or competent than he. And if he lacked faith, if he didn't appear at the Cathedral of the Sun for Zenday sermons, well, no one was perfect. He scorned no one else's belief.

Still, at this hour, when the Tawloomez boldly poured into Kel lands, when a strange young man could wield fire from the very heavens, would the Lord Captain's questionable religious standing not threaten the very favor of the Sun Throne? Would the gods not demand his conviction?

She shuddered. Best not to overthink matters. The province of other souls lay in the hands of Hakija Dakeer Vasar. She must see to her own.

CHAPTER 3

Nerenoth Irothé strode into his lieutenant's sparsely decorated office, not bothering to knock. There wasn't time.

Rez Kuaan looked up from sharpening his sword, keen eyes bright in the light from a narrow window, then slid from sitting on his unadorned desk to clap a fist to his breastplate. "My Lord Captain?"

"Rez, come with me. We have several things to discuss en route."

"En route, sir?" Rez pocketed his whetstone, wiped his blade free of metal dust, and sheathed the weapon at his hip.

Nerenoth nodded. When the Lord Lieutenant joined him at the door, Nerenoth swept out of the chamber and down the barracks corridor. Rez followed on his heels.

"I heard Princess Talanee's report regarding the incident at Halathe," Nerenoth said, keeping his tones low. "I would like your version as we ride toward the ruins."

"Of course, sir."

"I've ordered your pythe to be saddled. Speed is crucial right now."

"Yes, sir. Thank you."

Neither man spoke again until they reached the stable yard. Nerenoth mounted his pythe and glanced behind him to find Rez upon his own reptilian beast.

Nerenoth signaled. They rode from the yard and into the triangular courtyard joining the palace gate, garrison gate, and the gate to the Cathedral of the Sun. In the courtyard's center, a massive fountain burbled. Nerenoth's eye caught the glinting light of gold reflecting sunlight, and he glanced at the shining dome of the cathedral as he batted down a scowl.

Turning his back on the three towering landmarks that set the Holy City of Inpizal apart from its lesser sister cities, Nerenoth guided his pythe into the thriving thoroughfare running northward beyond the Sun Courtyard. Garrison soldiers saluted and passersby paused to watch the Lord Captain and Lord Lieutenant ride past.

A straight shot took Nerenoth and Rez through Inpizal and its uniform townhouses to the Sunburst Gate, a grand, enormous, two-door barrier set into the high, white walls of the holy city. The doors stood open as they always did during the zen hours at festival time, but now, soldiers in the copper and silver armor of the City Watch searched every cart and parcel with a grimness that punctuated the tense mood.

Instead of a routine inspection for hidden contraband smuggled in by sketchy traders, the road beyond Inpizal now stood littered with refugees, nobleborn and peasantry alike. Everyone sought the sanctuary of Inpizal.

The Lord Captain couldn't blame them. Erokes had been among the strongest of the Sun Cities, renowned for its defensibility against the Tawloomez, who often stole down the northwestern coastline to strike at the Kel. Now the city and nearly all its inhabitants were but crushed stone, decaying flesh, and bleaching bones. The Tawloomez had never been so bold nor so victorious before.

Nerenoth's fingers tightened over his reins. What a pitiable, unforgivable waste. He set his jaw and signaled two guards, who rushed ahead to clear a path between the refugees and merchant wagons. Both riders loped through the gate and out onto the highway. The line of incoming Kel murmured and pointed as Nerenoth raced past them, headed north toward the ancient hills beyond the grasslands. There, at the roots of Nakoth, the gray mountain range, lay the ruins of Halathe.

He slowed his pythe enough that Rez could ride beside him to relate his perspective on the incidents of yesterzen. Nerenoth didn't interrupt but mulled over every action with a growing hunger. He glanced at Rez as the young soldier finished his story.

"This stranger. How old did he appear?"

"Perhaps nineteen? No more than twenty-one or two, sir."

Nerenoth flicked his eyes ahead as the road curved northwest. His heart swelled.

The age is right.

"Sir, I understand we're heading for Halathe, but why the urgency?" asked Rez. "Not that I don't appreciate a moment to escape my festival duties, but it *is* festival time, and after everything at Erokes, we're, well, we're needed in Inpizal. Sir."

"If this were not of utmost importance, Lieutenant—"

"Forgive me, sir. I spoke without thinking. I know you well enough to understand nothing would take you from your duty unless it *did* matter."

Nerenoth allowed himself a smile. "Then, let us discuss nothing further. We ride with all haste to Halathe."

Their pythe carried them to a crossroads outside the city of Sadal, and they took the higher road toward the ruins as the afterzen sun sank toward the western horizon. Two hours more brought them to the outskirts of the ruinous site.

Nerenoth threw himself from his pythe's back and strode toward the tower. Rez's soldiers had been thorough, and no bodies remained to mar the earth. No sign remained of the wreathing flame either. Only browned stains of blood revealed yesterzen's battle.

He reached the tower steps and turned to view the ruin across from the monolith. "Is that where the young man first appeared?"

Rez followed his pointing finger. "Yes, sir. From there he swooped down on the very wind and landed just here, in time to save the princess."

Nerenoth marched to the spot and stooped. "This blood. Tawloomez?"

"I think so, sir. That bit there, that belonged to our rescuer. This was the weapon that nicked his shoulder." Rez drew it from a pouch. "I'd thought to present it to the Hakija for his verdict on what we witnessed, but he hasn't yet granted an audience."

Nerenoth stood and accepted the scissor knife. "I saw the handiwork of these, and of the slender darts, when I reached Erokes." He pinched the weapon's trigger and the scissor knife snapped out into three separate blades. "A useful tool for gutting one's victims." He eyed the bloodstains. "The darts are equally nasty. Poison-tipped. Not meant to kill quickly, but to slow one down in order to capture and torture. From what I could surmise, the poison enhances pain rather than numbing it."

"That sounds just like Tawloomez filth."

Nerenoth looked north toward the Nakoth mountains. "He went that way?"

"Yes, sir."

Nerenoth handed the scissor knife back to Rez. "Keep that for now. We ride north."

"Sir?" Rez drew a breath. "Yes, sir. You intend to find the young man?"

Nerenoth swung into his saddle. Leather creaked beneath the weight of his armor. "I do."

"Yes, sir." Rez mounted his pythe, and they started north, kicking up dust to cover the blood in Halathe.

THE PASS THROUGH THE ROCKY MOUNTAINS SNAKED UP A narrow, ever-steepening incline. Here, the sun filtered down patches of light, but shadows had long conquered the natural road.

Few travelers came this way. Shrubs and branches hung in the path, grasping at the pythes' scaly ankles, spooking the stub-winged creatures.

A moaning wind rose and fell along the road. Between its cries, Nerenoth caught snatches of Rez's muttered prayers. He couldn't blame the man. This territory harbored an unholy feeling, not unlike the Star Worshipers tucked within Inpizal's slums. Nerenoth sank his heels into the pythe's flank to hurry the animal along.

Although my destination is no better than the road leading towards it.

He knew well what waited on the other side of Nakoth Pass. No Kel ventured into the Charnel Valley; not outlaw, nor cartographer, nor scout. But now Nerenoth steered his mount there, despite the chill spidering up his arms, despite Rez's earnest chants, despite the shouting wind.

The sun dipped beyond the far-off horizon, drawing the last golden rays of day with it, painting the pass in dark grays and blacks. Rez's prayers grew more audible. Nerenoth's muscles tensed. The wind fell into faint whispers.

The walls of Nakoth gave way as the ground sloped. A pebble-strewn path rolled down into a blasted dale littered with gnarled scrub, dusty armor, and bleached bones. Nerenoth's pythe tossed its head and let out a faint grunt, rolling its slitted eyes. The Lord Captain patted its neck as he nudged it forward.

"Sir?" Rez's voice toned low and faint.

"Remain here, Lieutenant. If I do not return by dawn, leave me behind and return to Inpizal."

Whatever protests Rez meant to say, they died on his tongue as the howls of an emockye pack sang upon the twilight air.

Nerenoth drew his sword and urged his pythe to pace faster. As the reptilian animal loped into the Charnel Valley, the Lord Captain's eyes darted to every stretching shadow. The howls sang out again somewhere beyond the natural walls of this blighted realm. Did the canine creatures, too, fear entering here?

I can't blame them.

A grinning skull glinted up at him from under a golden helm. Nerenoth danced his pythe around the fallen god and followed a beaten path that meandered across the wide valley floor. Countless bones spread before his view; some in golden armor, others in the armor of Kel worn five hundred years ago, still others with naught but bone daggers to bear record of their Tawloomez heritage.

"Gods stand with me," Nerenoth whispered, chest tightening.

The howls swelled, closer now, perhaps hunkered among the lower mountains. Nerenoth scanned the crags and crevices. His gaze halted on a gaping hole lodged atop a steep incline, not halfway up the roots of Nakoth's northern heights. Did a fire flicker within that cavity?

He aimed for it along the pathway. Each loping step brought him closer, and his heart stuck in his throat. Could this be right? Had he found what he sought?

At the base of the slope, Nerenoth swung down from his mount. He sheathed his sword and started upward on foot. Twice, he slipped, and pebbles rolled and bounced to the valley floor. Halfway up, he glanced at the cave's mouth. No question: A fire burned inside.

The Lord Captain allowed himself a smile. *The moment of truth has come. Is this Adenye? Gods, bear me up.*

He crested the slope and drew his blade, then slinked toward the maw of the cave, and faltered as a growl welled up from within the sheltering cavity. The lambent fire against the dark interior painted his vision orange.

"Hush, Lios. Shh."

That voice. Soft, lilting.

The growls heightened.

Faint laughter answered. "What teases you so?"

Tension bled from Nerenoth's shoulders. His heart eased back into his chest. He'd found what he sought after eighteen years. *Do not build your hope too high. Are you so certain?*

Something lunged over the fire. Nerenoth raised his sword, but the canine beast landed short of him, fangs bared, hackles raised. Pale green eyes glowed against the mounting night.

"Down, Lios. Hold fast."

Nerenoth's eyes flicked past the half-grown emockye to find a young man leaning heavily against the cave mouth. White-blue hair twisted down his shoulder and past his knees, and red eyes glittered in the fire's glow, while a sheen of perspiration shone against his brow. In his hand, he clutched a sword whose curved blade and ruby-bedecked hilt gleamed and flashed in the sparking flames.

Lowering his own weapon, Nerenoth glanced between the emockye pup and the young man. "I mean no harm. I have come to aid you."

The young man searched his face. Though so many years had passed, those deep red eyes held the same secret, penetrating fire, peeling back layers to burrow and probe into Nerenoth's soul. He canted his head, a motion so familiar, so like little Adenye.

He is my king.

Nerenoth's heart throbbed. Would the Sun Gods stop him from taking the rightful heir back to Erokel?

Guide my steps, O Gods.

The fire popped and hissed. Wind breathed against Nerenoth's neck. The young man's hand released the sword, and the weapon disappeared into the air as though it had been a trick of the faint light. Princess Talanee hadn't imagined it.

"You are Kel," said the young man.

Nerenoth dragged his eyes from the air where the sword had been. "I... Yes, I am. I rode here from Inpizal."

The emockye growled.

"Lios." The young man winced and leaned harder against the rock. His plain garb sported several rips, blood staining the coarse cloth at his shoulder. "Why have you come to aid me?"

Nerenoth slid a look toward the emockye and took one step forward. The canine's growls deepened. Ignoring its warning,

Nerenoth searched the young man's face for any hint of recognition.

Will he remember me? Does he recall his life in Erokel at all?

"Lios, come here."

The emockye's ears pricked up. It wheeled and trotted to the young man's side, tail wagging. In the dark, its gray fur tipped in pale pink looked almost black.

Nerenoth shook himself free of forlorn memories. "I've never seen a tame emockye before."

The young man's lips lifted in a faint smile. "He is not tame. He is a friend. We have saved one another from many perils." He clicked his tongue, and the animal folded himself at the young man's feet, tail thumping as one pale green eye stared hard at Nerenoth.

"It is still an impressive thing. I am Nerenoth Irothé, Lord Captain of the Royal Army of Erokel."

The young man slanted his head to press his cheek against the rock. "I am called Lekore. This is my home. Be welcome." He swallowed hard and squeezed his eyes shut. "Forgive me. I do not feel quite well."

Lekore. So, the Sun Gods had given Adenye a new name. "It's the poison. My lieutenant informed me you took the dart meant for my princess."

The young man called Lekore opened his eyes. "So I did. I have attempted to cleanse the wound, but this poison is new to me."

"If treated swiftly, it isn't fatal. But you've already suffered from its effects since yesterzen. A day or so more and you will be dead."

"That is not good," murmured Lekore.

"Let me bring you to my physician in Inpizal. It is the least I can do for one who saved the king's daughter."

Lekore slid down the rock to crouch beside the emockye. He whispered into the animal's ear and stroked his fur. The canine whimpered and licked Lekore's face until the young man chuckled.

Lekore tried to rise, but swayed, then slumped against the cave wall.

Nerenoth started forward, but the emockye sprang up and growled again, ears flat against its head.

"Lios, I said to be polite." Lekore stumbled to his feet. "You must remain here until I return. Let Skye know what has happened, if you please."

Skye. Nerenoth lifted a brow at the heretical name but asked nothing. There would be time to learn the wonders of this young man's life on future days. He sheathed his sword. "My lieutenant waits within Nakoth Pass. I doubt you can walk so far on your own. Will you let me support you?"

Lekore's gaze probed him again. He smiled. "Yes, Lord Captain of Erokel. I will let you support me." He padded forward, steps silent, and reached Nerenoth's side.

He stood several inches shy of Nerenoth's height, a slight figure for his twenty-one years. In the growing light of the rising moon, Nerenoth noted the pallor of Lekore's face as he sought the similarities between this young man and his dead father. He looked more like his mother.

"Do you recall how you came to dwell in this valley of bones?" asked Nerenoth.

Lekore's smile grew. "I am waiting for someone."

The words struck like a dagger point. "Someone?"

"Yes. Someone named Ank." Lekore wavered.

Nerenoth caught the young man's arm and wrapped it around his neck. "This Ank. Do you expect them soon?"

"I have waited for him these eighteen years, yet I know he will come. If not soon, then someday." Pain filled Lekore's eyes. "Forgive me, Lord Captain of Erokel. I feel very faint."

"No need to speak further." He strode toward the steep slope, Lekore's weight a slight burden.

Eighteen years. Such a long time. When last Nerenoth had seen this youthful man, he himself had been nineteen years old, younger than Lekore was now.

Lekore. A strange name. Nerenoth had never met another Kel called by anything like it. Yet now, attached by years to this identity, how much of the toddler prince remained? What had the gods wanted with him?

And what fate awaited Crown Prince Adenye Getaal, the rightful king of Erokel, who still waited, so many years later, for his deranged and underhanded uncle?

PALE-FACED, REZ STEPPED FROM THE SHADOWS OF THE PASS AS Nerenoth rode his pythe up the trail. Lekore slumped against the Lord Captain's back, dozing.

Nerenoth smiled grimly. Few soldiers under his command would have the courage to stay near the Charnel Valley for such a long time. He'd chosen the right man.

The Lord Lieutenant exhaled and managed a wobbly grin as he pushed long hair off his shoulder. "You've found him, Sun Gods be thanked. Is he well enough to travel, sir?"

"Well enough or otherwise, he must travel. The poison runs deep. We ride through this night."

Rez chewed his lip but nodded. "As you command, sir." He cast a glance overhead. "Those clouds promise rain."

Nerenoth followed his lieutenant's gaze. Dark clouds gathered above the Charnel Valley, low and grumbling, inching across the moon to take it hostage. "Then let's not delay."

"Yes, sir." Rez trotted to his pythe and swung up into the saddle.

They loped into the pass as lightning painted illuminations across the heavens.

Nerenoth glanced skyward. *Do the Star Gods rage against my actions?* It was sign enough that the Sun Gods approved of his choice to find his prince and bring him to Inpizal.

CHAPTER 4

'*It comes from the north.*'

'*Do you hear? Do you listen?*'

Lekore cracked his eyes open.

'*Hush, he is sleeping!*'

'*Rest, Lekki. Shhhh.*'

The ground thundered somewhere below him, far away.

'*Not now. No time. You must awaken!*'

The wafting scent of wild grass taunted his nose. He had traveled far from his vale. The wind howled as its myriad voices clambered for his attention. He sat straight, then flinched as midnight blue hair whipped into his eyes. Swatting aside the tangle of the Lord Captain's tresses, Lekore leaned away from the wind's assault and craned his neck to look behind him, northward.

Clouds swirled from the Wildwood east of his vale, dark, louring, mounting in strength. A wind spirit flung the fragrance of rain and lightning at him.

He drew a heady breath and looked ahead. "Cease a moment, Lord Captain of Erokel. Please."

The pythe slowed to a lope. "What is it?" asked the Lord Captain.

"Something I must see to, if I can." Lekore slipped from the pythe's scaly back and turned toward the coming storm. "It is not a natural wind, nor has it mustered its full strength. I may yet tame its rage."

The lingering gaze of the stranger pressed into his flesh, but he fastened his eyes on the burgeoning clouds. As he lifted his hands, dizziness bled into his vision, darkening it. He inhaled long and dug his feet into the dewy ground until the earth spirits rooted him in place.

"Come," he called to the wind.

Wind spirits answered, gathering from the hollows and roots of the rolling hills and dipping paths hunched against the night.

'*What do you need, Lekki?*'

"Calm the storm, please. It is out of its season."

The wind eddied around him, then raced into the sky toward the clouds. Lightning answered the spirits with a challenge, but the wind only laughed. The spirits rose in a spear and pierced the black covering until it split apart to reveal the night sky winking and glimmering above.

Lekore sighed and smiled down at the earth spirits, their shapes flickering between rodents and birds as they released his feet. He wavered as his shoulders drooped.

A hand grasped his elbow. "Have you finished?"

"Yes. The storm will break apart now. It was not too far along." Lekore glanced at the Lord Captain. "We may go on."

The man nodded. "Is this taming something you've done before?"

"Not I." Lekore smiled. "I merely ask the wind."

The Kel nodded again, a fleeting smile catching his lips before it faded. "As you said, we must go on." He led Lekore to the pythe.

Once both had mounted, the man urged his pythe on to catch his lieutenant, who waited several yards ahead with wide eyes. They rode southeast toward the dazzling lights of the Jewel City.

Lekore leaned over the Lord Captain's shoulder to better watch the approaching wall. "I have often imagined traveling to Inpizal."

"Now you do so."

44

Lekore settled back and rested his forehead against the cool of the Lord Captain's armor beneath a white cape. "So I do."

He shut his eyes and listened to the whispering wind spirits. One lighted on his shoulder to tell him about the brooding storm as it skulked out to the western coastline. He let himself fall into a quiet place between dreams and wakefulness, the beat of his heart a counterpoint to the steady rhythm of the pythe's long gait.

Time slipped beyond thought. Deep murmurs throbbed beneath the earth.

The sun rose, spreading warm fingers of light across the grasslands, stirring Lekore. He straightened and pulled tangles of pale hair from his face and shoulders. Ahead, the walls of Inpizal glittered beneath the golden pink cast of dawn.

Lekore smiled as his heart pressed against his ribs. He had never ventured here before, yet these walls, those enormous gates, beckoned like his bed of ferns after a long hunt. He searched the battlements, then dropped his eyes to find a line of Kel standing outside the fastened gates.

Eyes turned to watch as he and the Lord Captain passed them. Lekore shifted and lowered his head to hide. So many eyes. So many people. Many more than he had ever imagined. He pressed closer to the Lord Captain's back and hunched away from the crowd.

"Do not fear," said the Lord Captain. "I will let no harm befall you."

Lekore gripped the man's waist tighter and focused on breathing.

A loud noise blasted over the sky. Lekore jerked his head up as the gates rumbled open.

"Hail, Lord Captain!" The noise blasted out again.

Lekore caught sight of something gold glinting in the hands of an armored man. "What is that?"

The Lord Captain glanced up. "A trumpet, welcoming us home."

Lekore craned his head to catch another glimpse, but the pythe crossed under the archway and into the city. He dropped his gaze to look ahead—and his spine stiffened as he inhaled a sharp breath.

People. Bustling. Bumping. Shouting and laughing. Smells bombarded his nose with the potency of a bog within the Wildwood. Yet these scents were far more numerous and strange. Lekore clamped his hand to his nose as his eyes watered. Gazes darted toward him, and he flinched away from the gaping looks and jabbing fingers; the probing, questing thoughts.

Too many people.

"Steady, Lekore," said his rescuer. "You are safest where you are."

Lekore glanced at the rooftops, uncertain he believed the Kel Captain. Yet the wind here wasn't strong. Could the spirits lift him to the heights, or might they drop him into one of the carts, or upon the head of some staring Kel?

Daren't risk it. He pressed his forehead to the Lord Captain's back and willed himself not to look around as the pythe's talons clicked against the cobblestone path. Sweat trickled down his back. The roar and bustle of Kel—so many, many Kel—filled his ears until the noises wrung together to become a droning clamor. His ears might bleed. He clutched at the armor and squeezed his mind against the din.

"We've arrived."

The waving pulse of panic rolled away as sights and sounds settled down around him. Lekore lifted his head and blinked against the sunlight.

"This is the garrison stable yard. You may dismount."

Lekore glanced into the stoic face of Lord Captain Nerenoth Irothé, and his insides settled into a quiet calm. He let out a soft breath and slipped from the pythe's back.

The Lord Captain swung down after him. "Rez, call for my physician."

"Yes, sir." The man trotted off, and Lekore tracked him until he disappeared inside a stone structure.

"Come with me, please." The Lord Captain motioned to a second structure; this one taller and narrower than the long, squat building his companion had entered.

Lekore padded behind his strange protector, careful to keep his feet within the man's footprints across the dirt. Inside, the Lord Captain shut the door behind Lekore, then led him down a narrow hallway. Lekore crept across the smooth floor, taking in every angle and shape. He had learned about buildings. His mentors had explained their construction, and he'd often wondered what it might be like to sit at a table to dine; to rest upon a raised bed; to study the flawless white stones fitted together to form walls and floors. Lekore smiled despite the knot in his stomach.

The Lord Captain opened another door and gestured for Lekore to enter the chamber: a square room, furnished with a wide block of carved wood polished smooth. Behind the block, a square window revealed gardens beyond. Weapons adorned the walls, along with a rectangular white cloth embroidered with a golden sunburst.

"Take the chair, if you would, please."

Lekore considered the object Nerenoth gestured to, crept to it, and eased himself onto the smooth wood. It held him, despite its slender limbs. "Chair." He ran a finger along the leg. "I have heard of these."

The weight of Nerenoth Irothé's gaze pressed against his shoulder, and he looked up to meet the man's eyes across the room. Heavy, probing, yet not dangerous like a predator in the wilds.

Lekore started to ask why the man watched him so, but his mind teetered. He caught the edges of the chair to hold steady until the faintness passed. Inhaling, he closed his eyes and let silence envelop him. Questions must come later.

The door swung open. Lekore tensed but didn't look up.

"My lord, you called for me?"

"Yes, Masar. You've treated patients suffering from Tawloomez poisons before, have you not?"

"I have, yes."

"This young man took a dart. Please see to his arm."

"Yes, Lord Captain."

Lekore pried his eyes open to watch the Kel newcomer. He sat straighter, fingers prickling as he reached for the space where *Calir*, his sword, hovered within another sphere.

"Be at ease. Masar will help you."

Glancing toward Nerenoth Irothé, Lekore let his shoulders slump, and he dropped his fingers. "Very well, Lord Captain." He couldn't say why the Kel Captain invited such trust. Something in his scent; his calm, piercing eyes; the timbre of his voice, settled Lekore's nerves.

The physician, a man of slight stature and middle years, pinched Lekore's flesh near the red pinprick where the dart had lodged itself. Lekore had removed the dart, yet the pain grew, and the skin itched. Now, as Masar prodded, a wave of queasiness rolled over Lekore like the waves of the lake near his cave. He gulped in a breath to beat back the sensation as he swallowed bile.

"One day longer and this might have been beyond my skill," the physician said. "Luckily, I can extract the poison. He'll be weak for a few days. Very weak. I hope you did not wish to induct him into the ranks of your army soon, my lord."

"No, I didn't."

"Good. Bed rest. A great deal of bed rest. I'll recommend a few dishes to lend him strength as he recovers. Will he remain here?"

"At my estate."

Masar rose and straightened his yellow tunic. "Ah. You caused a commotion as you entered the city, my lord. Rumors arrived ahead of you. Many are asking what would call the Lord Captain and his lieutenant away at such a time. Is this the culprit?"

"He is."

Lekore looked between the two Kel. "Forgive me." His voice cracked. "Might you extract the poison soon? I feel very faint."

Masar blinked. "Yes, of course. You're on the cusp of losing consciousness, I expect. Yet that might be best. It's a painful process. Let me just...find..." Masar bent out of view to rummage in something at his feet.

Through hazy vision, Lekore fiddled with his hands as the distant clink and clatter of something like pebbles striking one another filled his ears, though the pitch sang a higher refrain. His mind teetered again, and his thoughts drifted.

Is Ank in the city? Will I find him here? The thought sent a giddy shiver through his limbs.

"Ah. Here. Breathe this in, please."

A cloth pressed against Lekore's nose and mouth. He inhaled, and the potent aromas rushed through his head, heady and stringent. As he slumped forward, hands caught him.

CHAPTER 5

Talanee whirled from the window, brushing against the burgundy drapes as the door swung open. Across her chamber, Keerva entered and curtsied, plain blue gown billowing around her as she gasped for air.

"Well?" asked Talanee.

"It's true, my lady. The...Lord Captain has returned. Rumors claim he brought back a young man fitting...the description of the one we saw at Halathe." Keerva leaned against the doorway, small chest heaving.

Talanee stared. "He *found* him?" A smile slipped onto her lips. "Of course, only he could. Don't stand there idly, Keerva! My lord father will demand to know more. We must hasten to the throne room." She lifted her skirts, gold today, and trotted over the wine-red rug, past a settee and tea-service, to the door.

Keerva puffed after her princess, and Talanee let herself laugh as she raced down the corridor, past the servants and guards, dress rustling as her white slippers padded against the glittering marble floor. The wide archways shone in the midmorning sunlight pouring in from stained glass windows set far overhead. Tapestries fluttered as Talanee hurried by, and the sunburst pennants hanging from the decorous ceilings danced as though they shared her excitement.

Yesterzen, all the servants in the palace had hummed with the news of Nerenoth's sudden departure, along with his lieutenant. Had the Tawloomez attacked another city? Had the Lord Captain argued with the Hakija? Though each man treated the other with proper deference, the Hakija had often warned the Lord Captain that his soul was in peril. What manner of Kel showed no public worship for the Sun Gods?

He must have his reasons. Nerenoth does nothing without a good reason. Talanee simply knew it. She would never feel so strongly for a heretic.

Voices rolled forth from the open doors ahead. Talanee slowed her pace as she approached the throne room.

"...cannot simply leave during the Sun Festival! It's unfathomable how you thought this an acceptable action."

"Please, Hakija. Not so loud." The king's voice. "Close the blasted doors."

Talanee sprinted forward and slipped inside the throne room, a finger pressed to her lips. The guard looked right through her and shut the doors as she lurked in the shadows of the columns surrounding the grand chamber. Keerva hadn't made it inside. That was just as well. The young woman would only give them away with all her wheezing.

Lord Father sat upon his throne, raiment rumpled, probably from a sleepless night. He rarely slept during festival season. He rarely slept at all, which had aged him prematurely. Lines fanned out around his eyes and mouth.

Meanwhile, Dakeer Vasar stood beside the throne, immaculate in his elaborate festival vestments, all white with embroidered golden suns running along his hems. He loomed above Lord Captain Nerenoth, who remained standing before the raised dais, pristine in his silver armor, white cape spilling down his back, hair smooth as though he hadn't ridden through the night to return from Halathe—or wherever he'd found Talanee's rescuer.

Nerenoth spoke in clear, carrying tones. "Had it not been important, I'd not have left amid your festival, Your Holiness, I assure you."

"*My* festival? This is the Sun Festival, a festival of the *gods*, Lord Captain." The Hakija's tones thundered, and his eyes flashed, yet his frame remained still. In all her years observing the Triad of Erokel, Talanee had never witnessed the Hakija or the Lord Captain lose their tempers. Both men kept their composure as the king never could, especially when the other two bullied him in their political debates.

"As you say," Nerenoth answered, dipping his head. "Yet my urgency remained."

"Then you had best explain, my lord," said the Hakija. "What called you away? Tawloomez?"

"No."

"What else could be so critical?"

Nerenoth angled his gaze to the king. "Your daughter's report, sire. I could not separate my thoughts from its significance."

Dakeer Vasar's eyes narrowed. "It was indeed a miracle from the Sun Throne. Yet I fail to see why this prompted you to depart Inpizal." He paused. "The gossip is that you returned with a boy."

"Not a boy. A grown man: The one who rescued our princess from the Tawloomez attack. I found him."

Lord Father stirred in his throne. "Found him?"

"Yes. From Halathe, I traveled north and took Nakoth Pass into the Charnel Valley."

The king and Hakija stiffened as the latter traced the rising sun in the air before his chest.

"You entered that accursed place, Captain?" asked Dakeer Vasar.

"Yes. There I found him, wounded, but well enough to speak. I brought him to Inpizal to be cared for. My physician has removed the poison that afflicted him and cared for his injuries."

"A bold move, and rather a curious one." The Hakija stepped from the dais to stand level with the Lord Captain.

Talanee tiptoed closer, hesitating behind pillars as she made her way across the throne room. Her heart pattered. That strange young man had been brought here.

So, it's true.

Curious, indeed, that the Lord Captain should go to such lengths to retrieve him.

"Not so curious, Your Eminence," Nerenoth said. "There is no reason to doubt the reports from Princess Talanee and my lieutenant regarding the unique qualities of their rescuer. I myself witnessed another miracle as we returned from the Charnel Valley."

"Oh?" Dakeer Vasar raised an eyebrow.

"Yes, Hakija. A storm rose despite the dry season. It chased us through the pass, across the hills, and into the grasslands. Something about it unsettled my spirit. We raced as swiftly as we dared in the darkness until the young man asked me to stop. I adhered to his request and watched him tame the very elements to his will. The storm broke apart despite its ferocity, and drifted away, its malice abolished."

The king and Hakija stared at Nerenoth. Talanee paused behind a pillar to weigh the Captain's words. How could anyone tame the elements? *And yet, did I not see him wield the fire of the Sun Gods?*

"Is this a messenger from the gods?" whispered the Hakija. "Where is the young man now? What do you know about him?"

"I've taken him to my town estate. He rests within a guest chamber where he must remain while he mends. I know he is called Lekore and has dwelt in a cave above the Charnel Valley for eighteen years. He also bears the purple locks of Kel nobility." Nerenoth traced the lavender locks threaded through his own dark tresses.

Lord Father let out a choking cough. He shot to his feet. "We must see this, this rescuer. I shall go ahead. Guards! Guards!"

The guards stationed at the doors trotted forward.

"Bring me my carriage. Make haste!"

They bowed to their king and raced from the room.

The Hakija caught Lord Father's arm. "Calm yourself, my king. We shall journey together to see this wondrous figure. You're not well this morning."

Talanee swallowed as her chest tightened. Was Lord Father ever well?

The Lord Captain strode to stand between the king and the doorways. "Lekore is also unwell. Can this not wait until he has regained his strength? My physician warned against excitement."

"No," the king said. "No, it cannot wait. I must...must thank this stranger for his service to my only daughter."

The Hakija pulled against his arm. "Of course, sire, but *think* a moment. To act in haste in your present condition could cause *complications*. Consider your position, *Your Majesty*."

The king blinked, and his shoulders slumped. "O-of course. You're right. Always right, Dakeer. I will...do nothing to jeopardize... I shall act with decorum. Of course I shall. Unhand me, please. I'm not some child."

The Hakija withdrew his hand. "We shall calmly journey to your house and pay our respects to this Lekore. Please lead the way, Lord Captain. We'll not stay long."

Nerenoth inclined his head. "Very well, Your Holiness." He marched toward the doors ahead of the other two men.

Talanee wrung her hands together. How could she make herself part of this meeting? She inhaled a deep breath and darted from the shadows. "Please, let me come! I wish to thank my rescuer."

The three men whirled, Nerenoth sliding his sword loose. They stared at her.

She folded her hands before her and stood firm, lifting her chin. "I'm coming."

The Hakija nodded. "It is your right, Princess Talanee. Be welcome."

Talanee's eyes flicked to the Lord Captain, and she thought she glimpsed the faintest hint of a smile on his lips.

THE CARRIAGE LURCHED TO A STOP OUTSIDE HOUSE IROTHÉ, and Talanee glanced out the window at the manicured grounds. The Lord Captain also owned a large plantation twenty miles outside Inpizal, but he rarely visited that estate. Instead, his younger brothers saw to matters there, working hand in hand as twins were wont to do.

Nerenoth dismounted his pythe and opened the carriage door to help Talanee out. She accepted his hand with a smile. Lord Father and the Hakija followed, boots crunching pebbles.

They proceeded up the steps and entered the house as a servant bowed them in. Nerenoth strode to a sweeping staircase as Talanee glanced around. It was a tasteful home, if gloomy. Curtains covered the windows and the entryway looked unlived in, though she found no hint of dust.

Feet padded overhead, and Talanee paused midway up the stairs, as did the rest of the company.

Two young men appeared at the top of the staircase, identical, with matching grins. Long blue ponytails highlighted with lavender locks ran down their backs, and swords hung at their hips. Their apparel was indistinguishable, save for the colors of their tunics. Jesh and Jeth Irothé, home for the festival. They'd grown nearly as fetching as their elder brother while they'd been at their family plantation, though their hair was lighter. Their smiles faded as comprehension filled their widening eyes.

"Your Majesty! Holiness! Princess!" Their voices rang out in unison.

Nerenoth started up the stairs again. "They've come about our guest."

"Ah," said the twins and danced out of the way.

The procession mounted the last few steps and strode down the hallway until Nerenoth halted before a wooden door. He swung it open and entered the chamber beyond. The Hakija stepped in next, followed by Lord Father, and Talanee slipped inside last. Within the semi-darkness of the curtain-drawn room, she made out the bulk of an enormous bed but little more.

The Lord Captain moved to the window near the bed, silent despite his light armor. He pulled the curtain aside to let in a sprinkle of sunlight, illuminating the figure in the bed.

Talanee tiptoed forward. Sure as the Sun Throne, here lay the young man from Halathe, caught in dreams that tossed his head from side to side.

The Lord Captain moved to the bedside. "As I said, he is unwell. Masar assures me the fever will burn out soon, yet he will remain weak for a few days."

Lord Father drifted to the vanity lurking in the shadows and slumped into its chair. "Dakeer. Oh, Dakeer." He covered his face with his hands.

Talanee stared. *What a bizarre reaction.*

"Now, there's no cause to feel overwhelmed, Your Majesty," said the Hakija. He strode to the king's side. "The Sun Gods bless us with this miracle, but we are worthy."

"Your Holiness?" Talanee asked. "What *is* he?"

"I've yet to pray for answers, Your Highness, but all signs point to him being a messenger of the gods. We have but one question beyond that to learn: From which gods does he hail?"

Lord Father pulled his hands away and stared up at the Hakija, eyes wide. The ghost of a smile brushed his lips and a spark ignited in his eyes. "Indeed. Indeed, Dakeer. From which gods. Of course, naturally. Yes." He stood and straightened his shoulders. "This is a profoundly serious matter, Nerenoth. Surely, under the circumstances, this...creature...cannot remain here. It's too dangerous."

"Nevertheless, sire," said Nerenoth, eyes bright in his shaft of sunlight, "he shall not move until he is mended."

The Hakija's hand caught Lord Father's elbow. "Best not to upset any gods in this moment, sire. I will pour out my heart for answers. Let us leave, for the present."

Lord Father inhaled and nodded. "Always right. Yes. We'll

depart for now. Good day, Lord Captain. I'll see you this evening for the Sun Dance, yes?"

"Of course, sire." Nerenoth inclined his head. "I will be prompt."

Talanee waited for the Hakija and the king to stride from the room before she turned to the Lord Captain. "I don't understand quite what's going on, but I know you're playing some sort of game. Be careful, my lord. This is a matter of the gods."

"Yes," said Nerenoth Irothé. His eyes caught fire in the sunlight. "So it is."

CHAPTER 6

Glittering gold and sparkling gems filled the throne room.
Talanee glided across the marble floor. Her gown of white rustled and hissed as she moved, embroidered golden sunbursts, crushed diamonds, and teardrop pearls flashing and glinting in the flames of three hundred candelabra. She smiled and waved her fan as she spied familiar faces. Courtiers dipped into bows and curtsies even as she moved on.

Her target stood across the chamber, tall, lean, imposing in his dress armor of silver ornamented with a golden sun upon his breastplate. The Lord Captain wore a white cape trimmed in a golden hem, not elaborate against the ostentation of his fellow Kel. Yet despite his simple garb, Nerenoth Irothé stood out with no effort on his part.

He conversed with Uncle Elekel, the king's brother, one wrist draped over his sword hilt in a casual attitude. No one else hung close to listen in. No one would dare. Even as Uncle Elekel laughed, his unaffected, carefree chortles climbing to the white stone ceiling, lookers-on and dancers didn't lean in. When the Lord Captain smiled his quiet, secret smile, those nearest leaned away.

The Hakija alone matched such command of his surroundings.

Talanee glimpsed the throne and found Lord Father communing with Dakeer Vasar, both in striking finery, their heads close together. Lord Father's hands sliced the air with curt gestures, eyes wild.

She glanced toward Nerenoth again. His gaze had followed hers to the throne, but now it flicked toward her, and he tipped his head in greeting. As good an invitation as any. She drew her shoulders straight and approached.

"Lord Captain. Lord Uncle. I offer warm greetings."

"Hello, my dearest niece," said Uncle Elekel. "Oh, I suppose this is all very formal. Greetings, Your Highness." He tossed his head in an almost pythe-like nod, teeth flashing as he grinned. He looked little like his brother, with a full face; thick mane of blue hair; and keen, narrow eyes. His evening raiment boasted of his eccentricities, starting with the over-large sun pendant hanging from a fat cord around his neck, and a surcoat of gold over a golden shirt and breeches. No doubt, he'd chosen his ensemble to irk the king—a favorite pastime.

Talanee pulled her gaze back to the man's face. "I didn't expect to find you in attendance, Lord Uncle."

His grin stretched into an approximation of an emockye's hungry smile. "What? And miss all the fuss and bustle? Never!"

She arched an eyebrow. "You've missed all the fuss and bustle these past six years. Is this occasion more remarkable than past Sun Festivals, my lord?"

A glint sparked in Elekel's eyes. "No fool, this one. Not like her doddering old—ouch. Thank you, Lord Captain. I nearly forgot myself."

Nerenoth slid his foot off the other man's boot and inclined his head. "Not at all, my lord."

Elekel laughed and sipped from the wine goblet in his hand. He swallowed and licked his lips. "The refreshments are almost worth the agony of these affairs, you know? *Almost.*"

"If not the wine, dear uncle, what entices you from your hermitage this night?"

"Ah, if my niece isn't a charmer, eh, Lord Captain?" Elekel bared his teeth in a sneering smile. "Hermitage, indeed. As though her own father didn't have me ousted from court and placed under house arrest forthwith and always afterward, etcetera, etcetera." He swallowed more wine.

Talanee rested a hand on her hip. "As I remember the affair, it was a mutual agreement that court didn't agree with you, nor did you agree with court. My lord."

He chuckled. "Perhaps so. Yet time and, em, shall we say *age,* does alter one's perspective. Ah! There you are. I'd nearly given up."

Talanee turned around to track Elekel's gaze as it flicked past her shoulder. Before her stood a young man with a smile made to banish sorrow. His short hair of ocean hues, traced with locks of purple, fell in a deliberate mess, adding to the allure of his fair, aristocratic face and lively, knowing eyes.

"Allow me to introduce you," said Elekel, slipping up beside her. "This is Princess Talanee Getaal, as you've undoubtedly guessed. Lady Niece, this is Ademas, my—eh, ward. Yes. Ademas, manners now. You do have them, I presume. Ra Kye didn't keep you from a proper education, hm? Never can tell with these island folk."

The young man bowed at the waist. "Your Highness, it's an honor to meet you. Despite my island upbringing, I assure you I'm perfectly civilized." As he straightened, mirth danced in his eyes. "When I have to be." He extended his hand. "Now that we've dispensed with formal introductions, might I have the honor of dancing with the Princess of Erokel? I've secretly aspired to this quest all day."

Talanee let herself smile as a trickle of pleasure ran up her fingers. "Of course, Ademas. I'd hate to disappoint such deliberate dreams." She took his hand, then stole a glance over her shoulder to catch the Lord Captain's expression. Or lack of it. Did he ever react to anything?

He did smile when I warned him about playing games with gods, she thought with a shiver.

"Are you all right, Princess?" asked Ademas, leading her toward the dancers floating around the center of the ornate chamber. His tasteful wardrobe was a brocaded green tunic and gray breeches, accented with a brown leather belt and polished boots. An elegant sword hung at his waist.

"Yes, perfectly," she answered. "You come from Ra Kye?"

He slipped his hand around her waist and drew her close. "Indeed."

"I've never traveled there, but its beauty is legendary."

"I recommend it for any who enjoy beauty, Princess."

She lifted a brow. "Do you mock, sir?"

"No, never quite. I merely hint at mockery, always. It's a condition."

She lifted her other brow. *This is no mere sycophant. He's far too deliberate.* Sweeping backward to the steps of the intricate Naalis dance, she steeled herself. "I hadn't any idea my lord uncle had taken a ward."

"Ah, that. You don't stray long from important matters, hm, Your Highness? As for Lord Elekel Getaal, he's...a startlingly delicate man in moments."

Talanee stifled a snort. "Is he?"

"Yes. As I said, it's startling, but he actually can be discreet."

"I see. Have you known him all your life?"

Ademas's lips curled into a sardonic smile. "Of him, yes, but we met only yesterzen."

Talanee blinked. "Have you never left Ra Kye before?"

"Well, technically, yes. I visited the smaller isles around it often. But never the mainland."

"Why ever not?"

"There was so much else to do." He stepped into the more complex patterns of the dance, gliding as well as Talanee. Impressive. They moved together, beat for beat through the rising and falling melody.

As the music shifted into a new strand, slowing the dance to a crawl, Talanee spoke again. "I've always known my uncle to be a frivolous man, not prone to generous gestures. Why did he choose to sponsor you?"

That grin widened, brightening his eyes. "Are you certain you'd like to know, Your Highness?"

"Of course. I believe it's my duty to know."

"Duty." He flung her out as the music twirled, then drew her back in. "That word is a perfect excuse for nosiness, isn't it?"

She almost missed the next dance step. "Are you calling me nosy?"

He grinned. "No doubt you wonder why I know your lord uncle to be discreet upon occasion, if I met him only a day ago."

"The thought crossed my mind." She weaved into the new sequence.

"Upon our introduction, Lord Elekel failed to offer my surname."

"I did note that."

"Well, it's Getaal."

Her shoe snared the fabric of her dress. She snapped her eyes up to meet the young man's gaze. "What?"

"As I said. Cousin."

She shook her head. "But that's..."

"Unlikely, yes. Yet, I submit it's not impossible. And after all, your lord uncle has taken me in as his ward."

Heat crawled across Talanee's face. The implications were clear enough, yet Uncle Elekel had always expressed a stalwart aversion to matrimony and, indeed, women in general. She cleared her throat and swallowed, centering every thought on the placement of her feet. Ademas chuckled as the dance took them into a new intricate arrangement, but she abandoned her embarrassment as she threw herself into the steps. Another five minutes passed before the music ceased and the musicians laid aside their instruments for a brief respite.

Ademas offered his hand, and she took it. He led her toward the Lord Captain and Uncle Elekel, moving at a comfortable gait.

"You don't seem ashamed at all of your predicament," Talanee said before she could stop herself. Then again, it was an accurate statement. Why not state it?

"Should I be ashamed, Princess? Have I done anything to offend the Sun Gods?"

"Of course not, but to boldly—"

"I've stated nothing, merely implied. You picked up my threads. What will you do with them, Cousin?"

They reached the two waiting men.

"You make a handsome couple on the dance floor," said Uncle Elekel. "Indeed, they may give you and your lady fair some competition, Lord Captain."

Nerenoth inclined his head. "As you say, my lord."

Elekel rolled his eyes. "Ever the diplomat. One of these days, Captain, you'll speak your mind bluntly and stun everyone with the thoughts lurking in your sinister head."

"Perhaps." The Lord Captain's eyes traveled to the throne and narrowed. Talanee stalked his gaze and found the king and Hakija striding toward the door reserved for royal entrances and exits. The armored sentinels moved aside to let the two men slip through the door, then stepped back to their place.

"Go on, Captain," said Elekel. "I'm quite certain I can entertain myself. You needn't chaperone."

Nerenoth glanced at him, arching a brow. "I've never bothered to take responsibility for you, my lord." He inclined his head. "Princess." His eyes flicked to Ademas. He tipped his head again, then strode toward the same shadowed exit, dodging dancers and revelers with the deft certainty of a seasoned swordsman.

Talanee sighed and turned back to Elekel and his...his...ward. "Well, Ademas. What do you think of the mainland now that you're here at last?"

"Dry." Ademas offered a smirk. "Please don't tell me the fair princess busies herself at dances by asking after trivial matters? I'd heard you've quite the wit."

"Have you?" She bared her teeth in a grin. "Perhaps it depends upon the quality of the company."

Elekel snorted into his goblet.

Ademas slipped his hands behind his back. "I wasn't referring so much to conversation as circumstances. Aren't you the least bit curious why the Triad has dodged the most grand and significant party of the year? Or is it that you know *why* they've trotted off to discuss something somehow more important? Could it be the fall of Erokes?"

"Ah," said Elekel. "If you want my wager, it has more to do with the captive Nerenoth brought to Inpizal."

"Captive?" said Ademas, with the faintest hint of curiosity in his tone.

"Mm, yes." Elekel sipped his drink. Swallowed. "Evidently, a young man from somewhere north of Halathe."

"Halathe. That's a ruin, isn't it?"

"Not just a ruin, sir. A monument, carved by the Sun Gods, then broken by the Star Gods during the War of Brothers, so the priests say. It is at the ruins of Halathe that each year Princess Talanee lights a beacon atop the last remaining tower. It marks the high month of the Sunny Season and the start of the Sun Festival in the name of the holy Sun Throne."

Ademas nodded. "Ah, yes. That ritual. We light our own beacons to celebrate the Sunny Season, though not at any ruins. But that doesn't say much about the Lord Captain's captive."

"He's not a captive," Talanee said, then blinked. She'd not meant to say anything about the young man resting at the Irothé Estate.

"Oh?" asked Ademas.

She sighed. "I don't think I should say anything yet. This is a matter for the church."

"Come, come." Elekel swirled his goblet. "There were a lot of Kel soldiers at that ruin, Your Highness. Rumors have spread far and fast these past two days. By all reports—an impressive feat in itself—this boy came out of the sky and rescued you and your soldiers by harnessing the very fires of the sun."

Talanee snapped her fan open. "First of all, one shouldn't heed the rumor mill of Inpizal, especially where soldiers are concerned. Second, Lord Uncle, he's not a boy but a grown man, which only emphasizes the first point. Rumors are rarely truth. Beyond that, I'll say nothing more. It's a topic for the Triad alone, and I'll not risk blaspheming."

Elekel and Ademas shared a glance.

"But there is someone," said Ademas.

Talanee sighed. "Yes."

"Who isn't a captive?"

"Yes."

Ademas took a step closer, eyes shining in the candlelight. "Yet the church *and* the state *and* the military band together to discuss this non-captive who allegedly descended from on high, commanding fire. And Your Highness will say nothing or risk possible blasphemy. The case of the mysterious young man grows ever more intriguing, eh, Lord Elekel?"

"It certainly does. Perhaps we should eavesdrop on matters of state—"

"Don't you dare!" Talanee threw her hands to her hips. "If you so much as twitch toward any exits from this chamber, I'll *skewer* you with my diadem!"

Elekel chuckled. "She'd do it, too. As feisty as her fair mother, Sun Gods preserve her spirit."

Talanee's cheeks warmed as her stomach clenched. Few spoke of Lady Naveena, who had died before Lord Father ever took the throne. So many family tragedies within a few weeks. First Talanee's mother fading as she gave the princess life, followed by King Adelair and his toddler son assassinated by a mad Tawloomez slave, leaving the Royal House of Getaal in shambles. Since then, servants shied away from talking about that time or anything surrounding it.

Talanee knew only two facts about Lady Naveena Getaal. A portrait hung in the Hall of Kings, showcasing the fair lady's flawless appearance; Talanee knew her mother had been beautiful. She also knew that it was *her* fault the beautiful lady had passed.

Never, in these eighteen years, had Lord Father let her forget it. Not by words. Never those. King Netye wasn't fond of speaking to Talanee. It was by his glances, his sneers, or far worse, the days and weeks between those looks when he'd not acknowledge her at all.

Sometimes, Talanee wanted to scream in his face. Just scream. Long and shrill until the man gave her his undivided attention.

She never could. She was afraid of what that attention might cause him to say or do. Could she blame the king for his heartbreak? For censuring the cause of his wife's end?

A hand fell on Talanee's shoulder, and she blinked and lifted her eyes. When had she lowered them? She met Elekel's gentle gaze.

"I apologize, Talee. I shouldn't have brought her up."

Talanee sucked in a breath. "No, it's fine. I don't mind. I enjoy hearing about her."

Uncle Elekel's soft frown stretched into a broad grin. "That's the spirit. You're her spitting image: you should know that. Only one lady contested her beauty, and that was Adelair's wife, Zanah. But they weren't alike at all. Queen Zanah had a frigid beauty, like a lake's mirror surface or the high frosts of the Rainy Season. But Naveena. Ah, she was a thing of fire and stormlight. You're her daughter, make no mistake."

Talanee knew her face flushed as red as her eyes. Her cheeks burned like the candles flickering across the broad chamber as she glanced at Ademas, who eyed her back with mild amusement.

She scowled. "Enough nonsense, Lord Uncle. We weren't talking about me."

"Indeed, not. You're right. We were discussing blasphemy and death threats."

Her eyes narrowed as the heat doused in a flash of cold wrath. "Do you enjoy galling people?"

"Yes. Why are you asking redundant questions?"

She rolled her eyes. "I really must go now, Uncle. I have other, more deserving guests to entertain."

He chuckled. "So you do. Don't be a stranger now, Talee. Visit me while I'm in Inpizal for the holiday."

She started away, then bobbed a last curtsey, risking a glance at Ademas. "Until next time, my lords."

"Farewell, Cousin," Ademas said.

Elekel laughed into his goblet. *Laughed*. As though his ward's choice of words didn't imply a past indiscretion.

Talanee whirled away and lost herself in a sea of gowns and jewels and frivolity. Just once more, several long moments after she'd escaped her uncle and his strange companion, she allowed herself a surreptitious glance in their direction. She'd expected to find them laughing and downing more wine but, while Lord Uncle still had a goblet in his hand, he stood alone and glassy-eyed— indeed; he looked almost like he brooded, eyebrows pinched, a frown straining at his usually merry lips. Talanee looked around for Ademas. No sign.

The princess weaved her way through the vast crowd of nobility and gentry; past the Tawloomez slaves in their plain livery; around a cluster of priests debating the alignment of the stars.

"I tell you, it's a new one. That star has *never* been in the sky before!"

"I say, impossible. This is the season of the Sun Gods! No god of the night would dare to—"

Talanee moved on as a shiver trailed up her back.

The young man was nowhere in the crowd. She ambled up one side of the throne room, then crossed to traipse the length back the other way. Ademas Getaal—if that really was his name—had vanished.

She had an inkling she knew where he'd gone.

CHAPTER 7

A sliver of moonlight brushed the bed as Lekore sat up, heart racing. Something slinked into the shadows near the open window. He held his hand aloft and let the heat from his blood roll into his fingertips. A flame sprang into the air above his palm, reflecting in a mirror set against one wall.

The light illuminated a figure against the night, wide-eyed, stooped before something stretched across the shadowed floor. Moonlight glowed against the metal of the figure's sword, except where darkness polluted the tip of the blade.

The figure straightened, eyes flitting to the floor, then back to Lekore. The sword fell to the stranger's side. "Forgive me for waking you." A soothing, male voice drifted across the air. "I had to dispose of an intruder."

He tipped his blade toward the corpse on the floor. "Someone has taken an apt interest in your welfare." The figure sighed and bent down. Wiped his blade against the body, then rose, and sheathed his blade at his hip. "I'll clean this up. Please return to your slumber. My brother was adamant that we not disturb you, and this intrusion will be unpleasant enough to explain without your fever growing worse."

Lekore's stomach churned as he eyed the shadowed corpse,

then he glanced again at the figure standing above the lifeless Kel as his chest constricted. He lifted the flame higher to better see the stranger before the bed. "Who are you?"

The young man lifted his hand to rub the back of his neck. "My name is Jesh of the House of Irothé. Lord Captain Nerenoth is my elder brother."

Lekore willed the flame to stay aloft as he lowered his hand to his lap. "Your brother aided me before."

"Yes, he did."

"And you aided me just now?"

Jesh cast a look toward the floor. "Well, yes."

"This man upon the ground. He meant to hurt me?"

"It looked that way."

"Why?"

Jesh's eyes speared the flame hovering before Lekore. "Well, I don't know precisely why. I can only make guesses. Didn't get the chance to ask." He shifted his arm to reveal a torn sleeve and deep cut.

Lekore shifted his feet under the plush coverlet. "How did you know I was in danger?"

Jesh puffed out a breath as he shrugged. "Well, that's because..." He scratched his cheek. "This may be uncomfortable to hear, but Nerenoth believed your life might be in peril. He asked my twin and me to take turns guarding your room. I pulled the short thread tonight. Jeth is at the Sun Dance."

Lekore canted his head. "I am sorry. Some of your words make no sense to me."

"Right. Yes. Nerenoth said that might happen. He said you're from—well, he said you lived in the Charnel Valley."

"Yes, that is so. But I call it the Vale That Shines Gold."

The young man stared. "That paints a vastly different image. Does it really shine?"

Lekore nodded. "Yes, each dawning sun pours its light upon the armor riddling the vale floor, and all therein flashes and shines in golden hues."

"You paint a pretty picture. I'd love to see it, but I doubt the church would sanction it. Is it true...do fallen gods lie there among the mortal dead?"

Lekore wrinkled his brow. "I do not know if gods sleep there. But there are many who slumber forever in the vale."

Jesh stared, then cleared his throat. "I'd best get back to removing this—this lump. If you'll excuse me..." He stooped and hefted the body over one shoulder. "Please try to rest. The Lord Captain isn't a merciless man, but he is exacting. He left no room to doubt his preference that you rest undisturbed." Jesh straightened and inclined his head. "I wish you sun-blessed dreams."

The young man tromped toward the door, and Lekore flinched as the dead man's head swung from side to side. Jesh paused at the doorway. Turned to glance back at Lekore. He opened his mouth to speak but hesitated. His curiosity was a palpable, hungry thing.

Lekore tilted his head to one side. "You wish to ask me a question."

Jesh's eyes flicked to the airborne flame at Lekore's side. "Is it true...? Did you command the very fires of the Blessed Sun to rescue Princess Talanee? Forgive me if my question is disrespectful."

Lekore frowned. "I...do not know if the fires came from the sun. I borrowed the flames of the torch held by that Kel woman and encouraged its spirits to increase their numbers. I enlisted their aid to prevent needless death. If those flames came from the sun, that is the working of another, stronger than I."

Jesh stared. "Another? Please, my lord. Another of what?"

"Elementalist," said Lekore, smiling. "I sensed no other present, yet I am still in training. It is possible a master could hide his talent from me. Know you a master of the art?"

Jesh shook his head. "I can't say that I do." He drew a breath. "Are there many of you? Many, er, Elementalists?"

"Yes, many. Though I am acquainted with but two. They are my masters, Ter N'Avea and Skye Getaal." Against the flames,

Lekore thought the young man's face lost a shade of color as he backed toward the door.

"F-forgive me, my lord." Jesh's tones rang hollow. "I must remove my, uh, work." He shifted the body. "Please rest."

Lekore nodded as a wave of dizziness swelled over his mind, lulling him back against the feather stuffed pillows. "I am weary." He closed his eyes and listened to Jesh's soft retreat.

In the silence that followed, a familiar tingle crept up his limbs. He opened his eyes to find Skye Getaal standing in the room, translucent body shimmering in the crossing light of the moon and the single flame. His ancient Kel armor glinted in his private, otherworldly light.

"How do you feel?" asked the specter, red eyes searching Lekore's face.

"Very weak but improving."

"Good." His mentor smiled, but his lips fell fast. "The days ahead shall be hard for you to bear, Lekore. Be brave. Not all Kel will be your enemies."

Lekore shifted and let the flame above him flicker and die. "Was I right to come here, Skye?"

"For your sake, I cannot say. For the Kel race, yes."

Lekore sighed. "Yet I know not what to do."

"You will find your way. And perhaps, just perhaps, you will help the Kel to find theirs."

Lekore blinked and found the room empty. He smiled. Ghosts came and went as they wished; he had long ago stopped reflecting on Skye's wandering roads.

Better to rest. He would learn his own path soon enough.

And perhaps he would find Ank.

CHAPTER 8

"There is a simple solution to our difficulty, sire."

Netye let out a fluttering breath as he watched Dakeer Vasar pace. "I've already solved the problem."

The Hakija's look could flay flesh. "You think sending an assassin into House Irothé will have any effect? Only one twin entertains himself at your dance this night. The other remains behind. Can you guess why, Your Majesty?"

The king slumped back in his chair within the War Room, eyes gliding over the maps spread across the oval table. "But why would the Lord Captain go to such trouble over one boy?"

"There might be a half-dozen reasons, none of which will matter if we handle things with *delicacy*. Your methods tonight will likely fail. I hope they do, or you risk the life of a skilled and faithful son of the church. Jesh Irothé shows promise. I would hate to lose him to one of your impulses."

Netye set his teeth together. His fingers curled over the arms of his chair, tightening until his knuckles whitened. "This...cannot be real..."

"Nothing can be gained by denial, sire. The boy lived. He has become a man. By some bizarre happening, his—shall we call them gifts?—have transformed into something great. And perhaps something terrible. Give him over to the church. Let us work out the source of his," Dakeer whirled his wrist, "abilities."

"He called down fire from on high, Dakeer!" Netye's heart slammed against his ribs like the heathen drums of Tawloomez warriors. "He rescued Talanee."

"So he did. Yet the Moon Throne uses deceit and trickery to its ends. I warned you before, long ago, that the boy was dangerous to you and to the future of our people. I meant what I said. I saw it written upon his heart. You saw it in the brightness of his eyes."

Netye buried his face in his hand. "Is that what I saw?"

"You doubt, after all you fought to attain?"

Netye wrenched his hand away. "Of course not! I did all that was necessary for the kingdom of Erokel. I have no regrets." His heart twisted. His tongue burned against his lie. The memory of little Adenye fluttered into his mind's vision like a petal upon the surface of a royal pond. Those bright, trusting eyes; those tiny fingers caressing Netye's larger hand as the man wept over his wife's still-warm corpse. Somewhere far away, the cry of his infant daughter struck against his soul like cruel stars falling from the firmament.

"There, there, Ank," the little prince had cooed, stroking his hand over and over. "Nye is here. Nye won't leave you."

"Sire?"

Netye pulled his eyes from his trembling hand as the War Room tumbled back into place around him, with its pennants and war instruments hanging from the walls. Dakeer Vasar pinned him with a stony stare until Netye sat straight in his chair and sucked in a steadying breath. "I recognize our plight well enough, Hakija. We can't let this—this imposter prowl the streets of Inpizal, risking all we've built."

"I fear the Lord Captain may use the young man to thwart our efforts otherwise."

Netye wrinkled his brow. "How? Nerenoth has no ties or aspirations to church matters."

"Not to their good, certainly." The Hakija's eyes blazed. "It begs the question: What *does* the Lord Captain aspire to? Always, he bars our path to purge the Tawloomez lands of corruption. Why? Shouldn't military-minded men best see the state of things? Every day the heathen swine grow bolder—"

Netye grimaced and held up his hand. "I know, Dakeer. I've heard enough of your speeches to finish every statement with as much eloquence as you. Yes, I agree we should conquer the Tawloomez. But if we destroy the whole of their race, where do we turn for slaves? You can't expect Kel to take on menial labors."

The Hakija pursed his lips, then sighed, and swiped the miter from his head. "I have little love of using slaves at all, my king. Shackled or otherwise, why encourage our heathen enemy to stand at our very backs? Does it not fill you with unease? At any moment, they might feel the call of their snake gods and stab your heart through."

Netye shifted in his chair. "Not those we've raised to serve us, surely."

"You think they don't feel their rightful lineage, Your Majesty? The call of their underhanded deities? You think they will perpetually accept our right to rule them over their inborn wanderlust?"

Dakeer leaned over the table and rested his hands on the maps outlining the boundaries of Erokel. "Were our roles reversed, and you and I enslaved, sire—never having tasted of freedom or prosperity—always laboring beneath the whims and gluttony of Tawloomez overseers, would we unerringly endure it? Or would we see our Kel brethren in some distant land, our ancient kin, and hunger for a single day free upon the grasslands like the pythe and emockye roving chainless?" Flames burned like the fires of the Sun Throne within Dakeer's eyes. "Surely, our Kel brethren bound in the north ache for freedom."

Netye shifted again as a bead of sweat trickled down the back of his neck. An itch caught in his throat, and he started to nod but halted. A laugh choked out. "Oh, Dakeer. Enough of your melodrama. We Kel are an enlightened and elevated people. The Tawloomez are slow-witted; barely more than animals themselves. It's too much to think they would behave as we might, raised as slaves all their lives. We make them comfortable enough. Most are treated almost like, like, well, like family."

"More a favored pet, which is worse," Dakeer said with a grimace. "No, sire, I cannot agree with your nonchalance. The sooner we rid ourselves of slaves—indeed, the sooner we wipe their foul race from the land—the sooner our Sun Gods will return to us in glory everlasting.

"Meanwhile, I will not allow the Lord Captain in his lethargy, nor *you* in your indulgences, to stay my resistance toward all who would stain our great kingdom and its surrounds in blackest night. That includes the lost prince of Erokel. We must do something about him, or I fear the Star Worshipers will use him to their ends. He is doubtless benighted and therefore malleable. Give him to the Sun Tribunal, and we shall make an end before all is chaos and moon-shadows."

Netye shrugged his hands. "How is your method of disposal different from my own, Dakeer?"

The Hakija sighed. "Your method evokes a kind of martyrdom, especially if harm comes to the beloved Lord Captain's kin. My methods ensure a pagan messenger's death and the symbolic falling of a blighted star. Which would you rather encourage, Your Majesty?"

"Oh, very well. Have it your way. The church always does. But how will you collect your prize from the Lord Captain's estate? I can't command him to hand the—the *imposter* over. This is between church and military might."

"But you *can*, Majesty, and you must." Dakeer's eyes narrowed. "This is exactly the circumstance that requires the judgment of the king. Yes, the Lord Captain could claim he owes the young man for saving his men, as well as your daughter. Yet, if the church insists the power used was tainted by the Moon Throne, it is your responsibility to override the Lord Captain's wishes and hand over a dangerous threat."

Netye scowled at the tabletop. "You wish me to risk the wrath of the most skilled warrior in all Erokel."

Dakeer leaned closer. "I wish you, sire, to grow a spine and recognize the precarious perch upon which you balance. The Lord Captain may or may not yet know the blood of whom he hosts, but should he discover Adelair's child still lives...do you believe he would stand at your side over another's direct claim? The child of his dear friend, in fact? And what of the questions that might follow that discovery? Or how much the restored heir might in fact remember? Where do the threads end, sire? Once, long ago, you put an end to the weakening of our people, while I glanced away. Do not think the church won't glance away again, should powers shift another way."

Blood burned in Netye's cheeks. "Do you threaten your king?"

"No," Dakeer said in a low tone. "I caution one king concerning another. No matter who sits upon the throne of Erokel, the church shall remain." He straightened and rested the miter on his head. "And *I* am the church, sire. Don't forget."

No, Netye wouldn't forget. He knew that the kingship, for all its pomp and wealth, was little more than a mediator between two genuine powers: church and military forces. Netye kept the royal guards, a private force meant to protect the palace and its residents. But his paltry force was nothing to the might of Nerenoth Irothé's Royal Garrison, with its thousands and thousands of trained soldiers. And then there was the Sun Church, outfitted with as many Sun Warriors cloaked like priests; armed with the faith of the Sun Throne, and the steel of mortal-kind.

Once, five hundred years ago, King Erokel the Second ruled as king, Lord Captain, *and* Hakija of the Sun Throne. Long gone were the days of such a sight. Now, between factions, uprisings, and politicking, Netye held onto his throne with threads like spiders' webs.

"What if my assassin succeeds tonight?" Netye's voice rang through his ears, sullen and low.

"Then you won't have to order the Lord Captain to hand him over to the Sun Tribunal after all. But I suspect your hopes stretch thin, sire. Nerenoth's brothers are skilled in their own right."

A knock sounded on the door. Netye's heart leapt into his throat.

Dakeer glanced at the door with a faint frown, then sat in a chair and reached for a bottle of wine. "Who is it?"

The door swung open. Nerenoth Irothé strode into the War Room, one hand draped over his sword hilt. "Forgive me, my lords. I didn't know a meeting of state had been called."

"It hasn't been, Lord Captain," Dakeer answered. "King Netye needed to step away from the crowds. It's been a long day, and tomorrow's ceremonies will be twice as taxing." He sipped his wine, calm as the hottest day of the Sunny Season. As he lowered his goblet, he licked his lips. "We've also been discussing your guest."

"Ah." Nerenoth strode forward. "In what regard, sire? Holiness?"

Netye pulled the golden circlet from his brow and ran a hand through his thin hair. "You must give him to the church, Nerenoth. He needs to be examined. Should Dakeer find him in good standing with the Sun Throne, he'll release him back into your care. Rumors are already flying across Inpizal. A day or two longer and all of Erokel will guess and wonder at the miracles surrounding this stranger's appearance. I'd rather we had facts to counter any exaggerated accounts, wouldn't you?" He met Nerenoth's gaze and willed himself to keep it.

Nerenoth smiled in his cool, stoic fashion. "Certainly, sire. I'll bring my guest to the cathedral at the end of the Sun Festival. I imagine, Your Holiness, that you'll be much too busy for his examination any sooner. And under these circumstances, I suspect you wouldn't want a lesser Sun Priest to attempt it himself. There is also the matter of my guest's recovery. One more week should give him sufficient time to stand before you with a sound mind, Hakija."

Netye's stomach twisted as he shot a glance at Dakeer.

The holy man's eyes had narrowed into slits, but his smile remained tacked in place. He nodded. "A reasonable request, Lord Captain. But you'll forgive me if I make one request of my own?"

"Which is?"

"I would like to place six of my Sun Warriors outside your estate, to better protect the young man. I have every reason to fear Star Worshipers might claim him as their own herald or a threat to their cause. During this festival, it would be a timely device."

Nerenoth inclined his head. "That, too, is reasonable, Your Holiness. Indeed, I welcome your aid."

A throb started in Netye's head. His heart quickened. "Why all this fuss over a single, albeit remarkable stranger? We have more pressing concerns, like the Tawloomez attacking Erokes and Halathe! By your own report, Lord Captain, it's a short matter of time before those barbarians strike again."

"Quite right, Your Majesty," said Dakeer. "Yet the two might be related. One question I intend to put before the Lord Captain's honored guest is how he knew to be at those holy ruins to protect the princess. It is either a tender miracle of the very Sun Throne... or hostile duplicity."

Netye slapped the table. "Then let the church handle the boy, allowing you, Lord Captain, to carry out more important matters."

Nerenoth shifted his wrist against his sword hilt. "I've already set in motion certain measures to ensure we aren't taken unawares a third time, Your Majesty. Keeping the young man abed in my estate meanwhile is no trouble. I will bring him to the Sun Cathedral in one week's time."

Netye slumped back in his chair as a shadow settled across his vision. A weight pushed against his lungs. "Very well. Do as you please, Lord Captain. You're always efficient, aren't you?"

Dakeer hurled a disapproving glance at him, then rose. "Well, then. With these matters settled for now, I feel it's time to return to the Sun Dance. If you're too fatigued, Your Majesty, I shall make your excuses for you."

"Nonsense. I've rested quite long enough." Netye dragged himself to his feet and watched the cloaking shadows fall away in the candlelight. "Besides, there are better spirits in there, and this is a festival: my one chance to imbibe to excess, yes?"

Dakeer offered a laugh, while the Lord Captain nodded agreement. Stuffed shirts; both of them. Dakeer rarely drank at all. Even now, his goblet sat full, but for the single sip he had taken earlier. If Nerenoth Irothé drank, it must be in private. Netye had never seen him drunk in all his nineteen years of service as Lord Captain. Perhaps longer.

These two tall, fit, skillful men loomed before Netye now, censorious, superior, always making him feel small. Yet who was king?

I am. I am the ruler of Erokel. I fought for this throne, and no man stands as my equal. Adelair alone held that position, and I ended his reign with my own hands. None can call me a coward. I won my place.

Yet now, resting in the Lord Captain's house, dear, innocent Adenye lay in oblivious rest... The greatest threat of all.

I won't let Dakeer have his way. I'll show him that his politicking isn't necessary. I'll rid myself of Adenye's ghost once and forever before this festival ends.

Netye was king. No one else.

NERENOTH STRODE BEHIND NETYE AND DAKEER AS THEY strolled toward the throne room and the lilting music cresting the air. As he walked, the Lord Captain's thoughts flitted between events near and far gone, as though he stepped back and forth between two rooms. His memories of King Adelair hadn't dimmed with time. His friend, reckless, bold, unflinching—and the king's small, gentle, contemplative heir—had been so fiercely alive. So much like blazing torches against a chilly night.

"Adenye isn't like other Kel," King Adelair had said more than once in those lost days gilded in the golden hues of hope. "He'll change things, Nerenoth. Search those penetrating eyes of his and tell me I'm wrong."

Nerenoth never could. He knew his friend's son for the odd child he was. The tiny legs, as soon as they were strong enough, had carried the little prince across the expanse of the palace each day. Adenye ministered to everyone—from the Tawloomez slaves to the kitchen staff, from the priests in chapel to the guards stationed in doorways. He knew the name of every soul who crossed the threshold of his childhood home. Most startling of all had been the crown prince's solid bond with Netye.

While Nerenoth had harbored no fondness for the middle Getaal brother, with the man's sullen moods and open disdain for the king, none of this had mattered to little Adenye. The boy attached himself often to his uncle, dislodging the dark curtains of the man's narrow mind, bringing out a smile here, a bark of laughter there, until Netye sought out his nephew daily.

Though leery, Adelair had insisted Nerenoth leave the matter alone. "If anyone can bring my brother's mind some peace, it's Nye."

So it had seemed. All had been well.

Until Netye's long-suffering, fragile wife had died giving breath to Princess Talanee. Netye had been inconsolable. Servants had feared he might harm himself or his infant daughter. He'd barred the door to his wife's room, letting none enter. As Talanee's cries haunted the air, and Netye's silence filled hearts with dread, only one small voice could penetrate the prince's heightening madness.

"Ank, let me in please. It's Nye."

That tiny voice, spoken in the muddled tones of a toddler, had unbarred the door. Only the crown prince entered. A few hours later, the door opened again, and Prince Netye allowed servants to sweep in. A nursemaid took the infant away, while Adenye sat on Netye's lap and stroked the man's hair.

All that, yet in the weeks that had followed, even Adenye's

kindness hadn't been enough to drive away Netye's pain. A cloud had settled over Inpizal, and soon, Adelair was declared murdered. The child, the rightful heir, had been captured. Killed somewhere in the wilderness. Only his bones were recovered, by the official report.

Afterward, word reached the streets of Inpizal: King Adelair's wife, Queen Zanah, who had been in confinement far away, had also died in childbirth. The child hadn't survived. The line of Adelair Getaal had ended, and Netye became king of Erokel.

But not all is as it seemed to be, Nerenoth thought with a grim smile.

After nearly two decades, waiting, hoping, struggling to bend the knee to this treacherous king, Nerenoth would now witness the will of the Sun Gods. All would be righted; he would see Adenye—now called Lekore—on the throne.

No matter what must be done to accomplish the task.

A smattering of color caught his eye. Nerenoth halted just shy of the throne room and glanced left. Leaning against one wall, a crystal goblet balanced in one hand, his other wrist settled across the sword at his hip, Ademas Getaal nodded toward Nerenoth with a carefree smile beneath vehement eyes.

Nerenoth inclined his head and moved on to follow the two other leaders into the swirl and pomp of the Sun Dance. A shadow stretched over his thoughts, clouding his hope a shade or two. Matters would not be simple to sort out. His fingertips tingled like they always did before battle.

The will of the Sun Gods matters most of all.

As he moved into the crowd of revelers, he glimpsed Jeth bobbing among the flash and glitter of tittering nobles. Nerenoth halted, letting the crowds drift away to give him space. Jeth surfaced again and passed by with a cheery smile as his hand brushed Nerenoth's. Away the young man strode, dressed in his finest raiment, waving at some passerby, while Nerenoth clutched the note his brother had slipped him.

Nerenoth retreated to the refreshment tables and plucked up a slice of fruit at random. He ate it without tasting a thing, then slipped into the shadow of a column to read the message:

'Intruder reached L.'s room. Nullified. —J.'

Nerenoth tucked the note into his glove, then made his way back into the merry crowd. He spotted Jeth speaking with Princess Talanee, joined now by Ademas who offered a clear, carrying laugh, eyes sparkling. Nearby, King Netye sat on his throne, a goblet in his hand. Dakeer Vasar stood beneath the dais, speaking with his High Priest, Lithel Kuaan, who had dressed in gaudy shades of gold and yellow.

"There you are, my lord."

Nerenoth stifled a cringe and turned to bow. "My lady."

Lady Lanasha Jahaan stood in a gown of diaphanous yellow. Her long blue hair had been curled and threaded with pearls. Her smile didn't reach her eyes. "I've sought you all evening."

"I apologize for my inattentiveness, lady. It couldn't be helped."

She sighed. "It never can. I suppose I shouldn't complain. You are a most wanted man. But this dance is among my favorites, and I insist you lead me to the dance floor."

Nerenoth accepted her arm. As they positioned themselves among the other dancers, he let his eyes wander the chamber again before his gaze returned to his betrothed.

Lanasha eyed him with a viperous smile. "At least pretend you enjoy my company, my lord."

Nerenoth inclined his head. "As you wish." He stepped into the dance as Lanasha's skirts rustled towards him. Back and forth the couple wove in and out, around, back, back. He released her hand for a turn, then recaptured her slender fingers as they ducked beneath a tunnel of arms. Sweat and perfume teased Nerenoth's nose. He straightened.

The music droned on, and Nerenoth's feet carried him on through the familiar paces, until at last the final piping notes faded, and the crowd of dancers broke up to find refreshment. The Lord Captain guided Lanasha to the food and offered her a plate of delicacies.

She picked at her fare with a faint scowl. "Is it true you're sheltering a suspected heretic, Nerenoth?"

He paused in pouring a glass of wine for her. "What an interesting accusation."

"I'm not accusing you. Gossip falls like unwelcome rain this night, claiming you've offended the church by offering sanctuary to one aligned with the Moon Throne." Her voice fell low and dark.

Nerenoth finished pouring. *So, this is how the Hakija responds to my move.* It didn't surprise him. Dakeer Vasar had as clever a mind as Nerenoth had ever seen. Even when Adelair had held the throne of Erokel, Nerenoth and the Hakija had never agreed on matters of state, but they had a healthy respect for each other. Nerenoth smiled. Let the cunning man counter him all he liked. Let him lift the voice of the people against Nerenoth's actions. In the end, truth and the Sun Gods remained on the Lord Captain's side. He feared nothing.

His gaze settled on Lanasha. "Last week, rumors insisted the Hakija at last intended to take a bride, yet when pressed, His Holiness repelled any thought of such a thing. I hardly think it necessary or prudent to heed every idle tongue, my lady."

Her cheeks colored. "Why are you so cruel to me?"

He handed her the glass of wine. "Am I cruel, my lady?" His voice held even as he met her eyes in a gentle challenge.

She looked away. "No." Bitterness laced the word in venom. "Yet, you cannot conform to our faith to tie the knot of matrimony. Why?"

Nerenoth glanced at the revelers surrounding them. "This is not an appropriate place to discuss delicate matters, Lady Lanasha."

She cast him a dark glare. "Nor is any place. Always formality. Always decorum. Never anything more. I...I despise you, sir."

He inclined his head to accept the censure. "I cannot change your feelings."

She sucked in a hissing breath, then looked away and plastered on a smile. "You won't ruin this night for me. I won't let you."

"I do not intend to ruin your merriment, lady. To that end, I bid you farewell." He bowed.

"You will not leave me. What would people say—"

"Many things, some true, others mere rumor. Good evening, Lanasha." He turned and strode through the parting crowd, feeling her eyes on him. He never glanced back.

CHAPTER 9

L ord Lieutenant Rez Kuaan found Nerenoth twenty minutes
later.

"Captain, we may have a problem," he said, tugging his gold
brocade surcoat straight and straightening his hair.

Nerenoth followed the man to a less frequented corner of the
throne room, even as a crowd gathered in the center of the
chamber for a new dance. A sharp glance toward a group of
stragglers sent them scurrying off to some other bit of floor.

"Go on, lieutenant."

"Reports of a storm brewing have reached me. I went outside
to investigate. It's a dreadful storm, sir. Traveling from the north
like before. Strong winds are buffeting the city walls even now.
Even if it's nothing out of the ordinary, it's got all the signs of an ill
omen. Star Worshipers could react. There might be a need for
crowd control."

Nerenoth nodded as his chest constricted. "With me."

They marched away from the music, out into a corridor where
their boots clicked against the polished stone floor. A few nobles
sticking near the tapestried walls, deep in conversation, slid
glances at the Lord Captain and his lieutenant, but none asked
after their destination. Instead, they turned back to their hushed

discussions, necks arced, backs pinched like scavenger birds feasting upon the misfortunes of others.

The Captain and his Lieutenant reached a north-facing balcony. Wind snatched at Nerenoth's long hair as he trekked into the howling gale. The sky rumbled and growled. Lightning scored the plumes of acrid clouds, staining the darkness with blinding colors.

A bolt of lightning struck the ground just outside Inpizal, and Nerenoth winced. "Gather a troop to see to the plains, Rez. We can't let any wildfires reach the crops."

"Yes, sir. But if this storm doesn't let up, we might have more fires than we can contain."

Nerenoth shook his head. "Not if I can help it." He turned and marched back inside, steps clipped and rapid. He conquered corridor after corridor, ignoring the faces he passed, as he made his way toward the palace's main doors. Nerenoth threw aside the doors and downed the steps three at a time as rain pelted the ground. He waited for the page, who scurried across puddles to claim his pythe. The reptilian creature loped into view as Rez Kuaan joined Nerenoth and waited for his own mount.

The page halted Nerenoth's pythe, and the Lord Captain swung into the saddle, hair thrashing. He glanced at Rez. "I'll join you as soon as I'm able."

"Yes, sir. You're going to fetch that young man, aren't you?"

Nerenoth kicked the pythe into motion without a word. His town estate lay only a block beyond the Sun Courtyard, and soon the clack of talons against the paving stones changed to a crunch on wet gravel as he charged past his gates and into his manicured grounds. The stone edifice rose before him, black against the raging storm. He flung himself from the saddle and up the front steps.

"Jesh!" he called as he threw the front doors aside. Rain hurled water across the marble floor.

A mere moment passed before the young man dashed into view at the head of the staircase, dressed in his training tunic and breeches. He gripped his unsheathed blade and a lit candlestick. "Nerenoth, what in the name of Blessed Naal are you doing here?"

"Is our guest recovered at all?" Nerenoth started up the flight of steps.

Jesh's mouth hung open as he sought the right words. "Well, he seemed lucid enough. But I don't know if he's up to much—" The booming clash of thunder above the roof stole the last of his words. As the sound died away, Jesh shook his head. "What a storm!"

"It bodes ill." Nerenoth reached the landing and stole past Jesh to slip inside Lekore's bedchamber. He stalked to the bedside and stared down at the shadowed features of his slumbering prince. With a soft sigh, he caught Lekore's shoulder with dripping fingers.

The young man's eyes fluttered open.

"Forgive me," Nerenoth said, "but I'm in dire need of your aid, if it's possible. How do you feel?"

Lekore squinted up at him, then blinked several times. "I do not—" The wind screamed outside as rain lashed the windowpane. His eyes narrowed, and he struggled to sit up. "This is not a natural storm." His gaze flicked to the far bedside, as though listening, then he turned to Nerenoth. "If you would, please, I must see to this. Will you help me stand?"

Relief poured through Nerenoth, warming his sodden bones. He hooked his hands under Lekore's arms and lifted the slender young man with little difficulty.

As Lekore found his feet, he swayed but set his jaw. "I must be outside to do this."

"I will take you wherever you need."

"Thank you." Not bothering to change from his silken nightclothes, Lekore started for the chamber door where Jesh looked on from the hall beyond. Nerenoth followed, and they brushed by Jesh to start down the hallway. At the staircase, Lekore gripped the railing and made his descent, trembling yet graceful as he moved. His hair, long and flowing, danced away from his legs and long nightshirt as if to avoid tripping him.

Nerenoth had left the front door ajar, and water pooled inside the entrance. The storm's reflection flashed in the puddle as lightning seared the sky outside. Lekore swayed near the last step but righted himself.

The Lord Captain took his arm. "Use me."

Lekore gripped his elbow, nodding. "I thank you. We must make haste."

They stepped into the deluge. As rain struck the earth, Nerenoth squinted under its icy fingers and guided Lekore toward the gates. Lekore limped forward a few paces, clothes already sopping, hair plastered to his cheeks, then stopped. Nerenoth halted beside him and dragged limp strands of dark hair from his eyes.

"Lord Captain, the storm is much fiercer than before. I must address it from a high place. Might we climb to the heights of your city's outer walls?"

Nerenoth nodded. "My pythe is just there. I'll take you where you must go."

After he helped Lekore to mount, he swung up in front of the prince and urged his pythe on. The creature made no complaint as it lurched through the growing storm. Wind snatched and tore at Nerenoth's hair and cape. The ride took too long, yet he dared go no faster in the slick blackness. Despite the lanterns blazing in the empty streets, he could barely make out the path before him. Instinct alone drew him closer to the walls scraping against the low clouds.

A chanting drone rose above the whistling gale as Nerenoth guided his pythe along a prominent crossroads. He glanced right and spotted a group of black-robed Kel clustered together outside a shuttered townhouse, their arms raised to the storm, their chant the sound of nightmares come to life.

He grimaced and looked ahead as buildings blurred past. There would be time enough to deal with Star Worshipers after the storm had lost its fury.

Minutes dragged by before the townhouses gave way to the dark shape of the city wall.

Nerenoth slowed his pythe, then brought it to a halt. He dismounted and helped Lekore, shivering, to the ground. The young man craned his head to look toward the stairs outlined against a bolt of lightning. Thunder crashed a heartbeat later.

"Our danger will be great when we climb to the top of the wall," Nerenoth shouted above the shrieking wind.

Lekore shook his head. "All shall be well." He started for the stairs.

Nerenoth followed. He expected their progress to remain slow, yet Lekore's feet were certain, and he never slipped against the wet stone. Once, Nerenoth thought Lekore said something, but the storm snatched away his words. After that, the wind died a little on the stairs, and they moved without threat of falling off the wall.

At the top, Lekore padded barefoot along the battlements. A few soldiers huddled on the wall, tucked against the merlons to avoid the worst of the wrathful deluge, the hoods of their cloaks obscuring their faces. They sprang to their feet as Nerenoth approached.

Lekore stepped past them, and Nerenoth raised a hand to halt their questions.

"Let him go."

Lekore moved as near to the Sunburst Gate as he could along the battlements, then halted and faced north. He hefted himself onto a crenel, then up onto a merlon where he lifted one hand into the blasting storm. Lightning struck a building behind him. Nerenoth whirled as flames sprouted on the rooftop of the dark house. Screams rose from inside.

The Lord Captain turned on his men. "Aid them."

"Yessir. Straight away." The soldiers sprinted for the stairs.

Nerenoth turned back to find Lekore speaking, though his words were lost in the downpour. The young man's attention remained pinned on his hand, high above his head, finger extended like a bird rested upon it, yet nothing perched there.

Lekore nodded. Smiled. Flung his hand out like he'd released the invisible bird upon the worsening storm. Moments passed. Lekore dropped his arm and remained still but for his long hair thrashing in the windstorm. Water poured off his face, unchecked. His nightshirt clung to his slender frame. Thunder ceased its grumbling, and the lightning died as though it had never been.

A sigh drifted from the raised merlon. Lekore lowered himself to sit against the white stone, a faint smile etching lines of weariness into his youthful face. "It is done, yet I fear the trouble will rise again, good captain."

The wind quieted. The rain softened to a drizzle.

Nerenoth let out a soft breath as his shoulders loosened. One disaster averted. "What is causing these storms? You called it unnatural."

"It is. It seems, somewhere in the heart of the Wildwood, something holds captive those who cause the storms to rise."

"Someone is holding *others* captive...where?"

Lekore pointed north as the clouds gave way to a starlit night. "In the Wildwood. The corrupted trees where the emockye make their homes."

Nerenoth followed the path of his finger. "The Lands Beyond."

"Yes, so you call it. The tangle of trees holds...what you might call creatures, whose imprisonment is a torment. It causes the wind to rage in protest. I have been uncertain what has inspired these outbursts, but tonight the storm told me."

Nerenoth studied the young man's face. A memory scudded across his mind of Prince Adenye playing in the garden. The toddler had laughed and rushed to his father's side while Nerenoth conversed with the king.

"Look, Fa! Look. So many." The prince had raised his arms as though they were full of something divine—yet nothing had been there.

"How wondrous," King Adelair had said with a grin. "What are they called, Nye?"

"Spirits!"

Neither king nor Lord Captain had known quite how to respond, though the prince scurried off before he noticed their silence. On a later occasion, Adelair had confided to Nerenoth that twice more Adenye had spoken to things that weren't there, and once the little prince had been found upon a tree limb far too high for a toddler to climb.

"Spirits, Fa," had been Adenye's explanation as he laughed about the occurrence.

Now Nerenoth leaned against a merlon and faced Inpizal. He spotted the lightning-struck building whose flames had been doused. Minor damage had been done, and the family appeared hale as they stood outside their home, speaking with the wall guards.

"Spirits," he whispered.

"Captain?"

He met Lekore's probing gaze. "These creatures. Are they spirits?"

Those red eyes searched his face as hunger leapt like a flame in their depths. "You know of them? Do you see them, Captain?"

Nerenoth shook his head. "I knew someone once who could see them, though few of my people would have believed it. It is what you mean now by creatures, isn't it?"

Lekore fingered his thin sleeve, tugging on the wet material. "They are the Spirits Elemental, so my mentors say."

A shiver crawled over Nerenoth's damp arms. *Skye.* "Your mentors."

"Indeed. They are clever and wise." He blinked and glanced over his shoulder. "Who are *they*?"

Nerenoth followed his gaze and stiffened, eyes narrowing. Coming along the street, an awning raised to protect against the remnants of rainfall and followed by a parade of sun-crested priests cloaked in white, Dakeer Vasar neared the wall.

99

The Lord Captain shifted back to Lekore. "I will be brief. The man who is coming will attempt to hold you prisoner in the clutches of the church. He wishes to question you, and perhaps harm you. I will do what I can to keep you safe, yet they may tie my hands for the moment. Rest assured, if he takes you away now, I'll fight to reclaim you."

Lekore shook his head. "I do not understand. Why does this man wish to question me?"

"Because you are different, and that is a frightening thing for most."

The young man tilted his head to one side. "Different from what?"

"Kel." Nerenoth's hand fell to his sword. "Remain here, please."

"Very well."

The Lord Captain strode along the slick wall toward the stairs as the Hakija climbed them. An attendant carried a torch at Dakeer's side, the awning and priests remaining below. The rain had stopped. Dakeer's eyes shone bright in the torch's light as he crested the last steps.

Nerenoth halted a few paces from the top step. "Your Holiness. How unexpected."

Dakeer's gaze flicked past him to light on Lekore waiting upon the merlon. A line appeared between his brows. "He commanded the storm to cease, didn't he?"

"He did, yes, Your Holiness."

"He must come with me now. I must examine him."

Irritation flashed through Nerenoth, quick as lightning. "Lekore is still recovering and ought to have his wits before he's questioned by your Sun Tribunal."

"He'll be cared for, but I shan't rest until I unveil his...gifts. Please, Lord Captain. Surely you see this falls under my province and not yours."

"As our conflict with the Tawloomez falls squarely under mine, yet I don't bar you from my councils."

The line in Dakeer's brow deepened. "Meaning?"

"I request to be present during his examinations. He saved the life of my lieutenant, as well as the princess, Holiness. We owe him much."

"Not if he is of the stars, Captain."

"If you find irrefutable proof of such, I will personally light the torch that burns him. Yet, I doubt that will be his end."

"Such faith, Lord Captain. It's not quite like you." The Hakija's words toned softly across the damp air, yet his eyes held Nerenoth's with a narrow, searching look.

Nerenoth set his shoulders. "Allow me to take him back to my estate tonight. On the morrow, I will bring him to the cathedral for questioning. It's far too late to begin tonight, and we're all cold and soaked through."

Several heartbeats passed before the Hakija sighed and nodded. "Your words are sensible, Lord Captain. Very well. I shall send Lithel after breakfast to escort you and your guest."

Nerenoth bowed his head. "It will be as you say."

Dakeer waggled his fingers across the air. "Blessings." He turned and started back down the steps, attendant beside him, boots scraping the steps.

Nerenoth waited until the two men reached the bottom of the wall before he returned to Lekore's side. "We have much to discuss before dawn. Shall we return to my house?"

Lekore slid from the merlon. "Yes, Lord Captain. Gladly."

CHAPTER 10

"What can you tell me about your mentors?" Nerenoth asked as he placed a cup and saucer in Lekore's hands. "Take care. It's very hot."

The young man sniffed the steaming cup of tea and smiled. "I do not recognize this blend of herbs." He touched the cup's rim and ran his finger along its perimeter to make a full circle. "What do you wish to know?"

Nerenoth eased into a plush chair opposite Lekore wrapped in soft woolen blankets on a silk settee. The curtains in the parlor were drawn for the night, and a servant had placed an elegant candelabrum on the decorative table between the Lord Captain and his guest. Its soft light illuminated the otherwise shadowed chamber. The servant had departed, and all hummed with stillness, but for the faint whispers of the burning candles.

Nerenoth brushed back his wet hair as a chill nipped at his bones. Despite a warm bath and having changed into a thick velvet dressing gown, he doubted the chill would pass until morning. "They raised you. You call them your mentors. What did they teach?"

"Many things." Lekore stared at the candles, then looked up into Nerenoth's eyes. "It would take weeks to summarize."

"Did they teach you much about your fellow Kel?"

"In some ways, yes. I know a little about Inpizal, and about your buildings and furniture. I know of tamed pythe and carriages —which I should very much like to see. I know that you have a vast army to defend against the Tawloomez, though I do not understand what disagreement rests between you." His gaze held a question.

Nerenoth sighed, batting down a desire to shift. Why did this subject fill him with discomfort? "I'm not certain anyone knows what began it. The church claims it is their heathen beliefs that set us apart, yet the Tawloomez feel as strongly as we do about destroying what is different: namely us. For my part, I wish to defend my people against any threat. That includes them."

Lekore nodded, eyes fastened on his cup. "There is a bold hatred within them towards you; so I felt upon the heights of Halathe and at previous encounters. It is deep as the fires of their mountains."

"That I can believe. Whatever might have begun our disputes, now they must hate us all the more, for we use their people as slaves to do our bidding... Though they are guilty of similar actions." Nerenoth scowled at a polished knot in the low table. "I don't use slaves myself. Upon inheriting my father's plantation, I freed those who wished for it and sold those who desired to remain in service."

The settee Lekore sat on creaked, bringing Nerenoth's gaze up until he met the young man's wide eyes.

"You sell people?"

Nerenoth grimaced as shame crawled over his flesh. "It is an unfortunate fact. Many of my family's slaves have been in bondage for generations. The idea of returning to their people is often abhorrent to them. They would rather remain among the Kel, no matter in what capacity. Freed Tawloomez are not well liked in Erokel. Truly, slaves are treated better than them. Many slaves are very comfortable. I don't mean to justify the trade. It simply is what it is. Had the previous king of Erokel lived long enough, he intended to free every Tawloomez slave and set up a separate province for them, if they chose not to return to the Firelands. The idea wasn't popular in his court."

"Would not the present king consider such an action?"

Nerenoth's lips twitched upward in a thin smile. "Never." He pushed his damp hair back. "I suppose we must use our time tonight to better purpose, though I'd like to know more of your mind and the way you were taught. More pressing, you mentioned spirits held against their will somewhere in the Lands Beyond. Will these storms continue while they remain imprisoned?"

"Yes, likely so." After balancing the saucer on his lap, Lekore scooped up his cup in both hands and sipped. "But I do not understand what could cage them. The Wildwood is an unnatural realm, yet those of whom I speak are hard to keep in one place. What could snare them so, and in such a state, that the world rages against their crisis?"

"If you sought them out, could you find them?"

"Yes. The wind would guide me."

"Then I shall help you once we deal with the Hakija and his tribunal. It is to that end I must speak with you. The situation is delicate." Nerenoth rubbed the back of his neck as his stomach knotted. "Please forgive me, but I must be forthright in this matter."

Lekore lowered his cup. "Please do so. I am willing to learn."

"Thank you." Nerenoth marshaled his thoughts. "Tomorrow, our Holy Hakija, a man named Dakeer Vasar, wishes to examine you. He is a very important man, and his decision will affect your fate. Your actions, your talents, are strange to the Kel. As I mentioned earlier, some may perceive such gifts as dangerous. I fear the Hakija might be biased against you and will therefore make a poor judgment call." He pressed a fist to his lips, seeking the right words. "Forgive me. I'm still being too vague. In short, your life is at terrible risk. It's possible the Hakija will condemn you to suit his own purposes, and might even execute you as a symbol of the stars."

Lekore canted his head. "But I am not a star."

"No, yet he might claim you are like one, if he feels threatened."

"I do not pretend to understand all you say, but you seem in earnest. By telling me all this, might I learn enough to protect myself from death, Captain?"

Nerenoth frowned at his hands. "I do not wish to presume, but if you might mention—if you think it would be acceptable..." He inhaled. "To share with him the true nature of your mentors might aid your case. If you feel otherwise, forgive me. Whatever the Hakija's decision, in the end, I will let nothing happen to you."

"Captain."

Nerenoth looked up to meet Lekore's gaze.

The young man smiled at him, eyes shining in the candlelight. "You cannot promise such a thing. *Something* shall happen to me each day, and to fight that is folly. But I thank you for your concern and for your kindness. I had not known what to expect among the Kel, yet you have shown me enough to quiet the loudest of my fears. No matter what I might face next, I shall not forget what I have seen in your soul. I am less afraid now. Let tomorrow come."

CHAPTER 11

Lord Lithel Kuaan nodded to his young acolyte, who turned and knocked upon the main doors of the imposing Irothé estate.

Moments later, a manservant dressed in the blue and silver colors of House Irothé answered, revealing a dreary interior swathed in shadow. "The Lord Captain and his ward will be down soon, my lord," said the servant, impeccably groomed despite the early hour.

Lithel nodded and sighed as he shifted away from a puddle of water on the stone step. The dawn air cradled the dewy green and syrupy musk of wet soil, while birds chattered at each other in the manicured trees beside the large house. The sun slipped soft rays of pale gold across the water-stained drive.

If I must wait on the Lord Captain, at least it's a pleasant kind of morning.

Small comfort. He hated waiting on anyone.

It won't always be so. Someday I'll succeed His Holiness and wait on no one.

He blew out a breath and tapped his fingertips together, then glanced toward his carriage as one of the harnessed pythe let out an impatient snort.

Eloquently put, he thought with a faint smile. Even the beasts of burden felt inconvenienced.

Nerenoth Irothé really must think himself superior to make the High Priest of the Sun Church wait on his front porch like this. Did the man's arrogance know no bounds? Lithel sighed and shuffled his boots again. The Irothé manservant eyed him with perfect blankness—a trait all the staff in this stuffy, insufferable old house must share.

Likely, it's a requirement. Gods forbid anyone show what they're thinking.

It wouldn't be in keeping with the somber estate.

"Good morning, Lord Lithel."

The priest yelped and spun to face his assailant as his acolyte grasped at his own chest, wrinkling his vestments. Young Lord Jesh —or was it Jeth?—stood upon the gravel drive, face flushed from what looked like a run. Tousled hair and sweat spots upon his rather plain tunic and breeches attested to Lithel's supposition.

"Good morning, young lord." Lithel managed a stiff smile. "Out for a stroll?"

"Practice," the twin said and lifted his hand to showcase his blunt-tipped saber. "Jesh is around here someplace, likely sulking. I trounced him once again."

Ah, so this is Jeth after all.

"Wonderful. I hear many praises concerning your sword skills, Lord Jeth. Do you intend to follow your elder brother into military service?"

Fire ignited in the young man's eyes. "Indeed, I do, my lord. Perhaps one day, I'll take his title from him."

Lithel's smile widened. "That is something I should dearly enjoy watching." Perhaps not *all* of House Irothé was somberness and stone. The twins contained ample ambition, and they wore expressions he could read. That was a sight better than their brother and guardian.

"There you are!" called a voice across the green lawn. Jesh, identical to his brother in all but the color of his tunic, jogged across the damp grass, a saber gripped in his fist. "Good morning, my lord." He bowed to Lithel. "Here to collect our guest?"

"Yes, if the Lord Captain chooses to unveil him."

"I do choose it, Lord Lithel."

The priest's heart twisted as he and his acolyte whirled to face the Lord Captain. Clad in full armor, face the stoic mask of a statue, Nerenoth Irothé considered Lithel from the front steps of his estate. Not a strand of long hair strayed in the faint breeze. Not a line appeared on his chiseled visage.

Lithel rolled his shoulders back. His eyes lighted on the slender form standing beside the Lord Captain, and his eyebrows shot up. *This* was the man everyone had made their business? *This* was the daring hero who had rescued the princess from the savages at Halathe? *He* had summoned fire from the heavens? Why, he was barely a man at all!

The strange young man wore a brocaded tunic of gray silk, with brown breeches, and gray boots. His hair was a rare pale blue shade; incredibly long, tickling his ankles, loose and stirring as though a private breeze caressed it.

"This is Lekore," Nerenoth said, brushing his gloved fingers against the young man's shoulder. "Lekore, this is Lord Lithel Kuaan, High Priest of the Holy Church of the Sun Gods. He answers directly to the Hakija."

Lekore dipped his head, causing his hair to ripple like water. "Good morrow to you, Lord Lithel Kuaan."

Nerenoth angled toward Lekore. "He is also the cousin of Lord Lieutenant Rez Kuaan, if you recall him?"

"Yes, I do. Cousin means kin of some kind, does it not?" Lekore's eyes flicked from Nerenoth to fix on Lithel. Despite his slight frame and his sickly hue, something in his mien sent a jolt through Lithel's body. His eyes, even in the shadow cast by the looming mansion, dug into the priest's flesh and reflected all the secrets he kept hidden.

Lithel tried to look away, to break free of the young man's hold...but his eyes probed deeper, searching. Finding. Knowing.

How does he see them? How does he know?

"Lord Lithel?"

He sucked in a breath and blinked at the Lord Captain.

"Shall we?" Nerenoth asked, motioning beyond Lithel.

The priest shook himself and cleared his throat. "Yes. His Holiness awaits us." He tugged on his gold-trimmed surcoat and spun to trot to his carriage. As he brushed by the twins, he dared not meet anyone's eyes. His acolyte scrambled ahead to open the carriage door, and Lithel dragged himself inside to claim a spot away from Lekore's penetrating stare. The Lord Captain and his charge entered and sat without words.

As the carriage rolled and bounced down the drive, and passed the Sun Warriors positioned at the gates, Lithel held very still and looked outside.

TOUCHED BY THE HAND OF THE SUN GODS, THE CATHEDRAL OF the Sun's interior glowed like sunlight on clear water. Every marble surface reflected the light from stained glass sunbursts set along the wide corridor leading to the chapel where the faint song of priests in worship drifted toward Nerenoth and his ward.

For the first time in years, Nerenoth welcomed the atmosphere of the holy cathedral.

Lekore had walked from the carriage with leaden feet, but upon entering the cathedral, his steps lightened, and his eyes darted from alabaster vase to window to the carved crossbeams overhead, then back down to find some other fresh sight. A smile hovered at his lips, shy, perhaps nervous, but blooming. His pace slowed until he halted and turned in a slow revolution to take in the grandeur. Lithel allowed it, triumph bright in his red eyes.

Moments passed, and Lekore finally turned back to the priest. "It reminds me of my vale. What you call the Charnel Valley, I think."

The priest's smile dropped like a bird with a broken wing.

"This way. The Hakija waits in the Tribunal Hall." He strode on, then turned left toward a door near the chapel. He knocked, pulled it open, and motioned Nerenoth and Lekore inside.

Sunlight flooded the chamber through an open eastward window. Plush chairs circled the room, all of them empty but for the single chair resting on a raised dais where Dakeer Vasar sat in lavish festival vestments, his miter in his hands, an absent frown drawing lines in his angular face.

He looked up from his study of the floor, eyes unseeing, then blinked. "Ah, come forward. Please." He motioned to the motif of a sunburst built into the center of the floor. "Stand there." His gaze flicked to Lithel. "That will be all. I shall examine the young man alone."

Lithel bowed, but not before his eyes betrayed a flash of disappointment. "Come, Lord Captain. Refreshments are in—"

"Lord Nerenoth will remain here," said the Hakija.

Lithel's mouth snapped shut. His fingers flexed. "Of course, Your Holiness. Though it may appear odd to some that the military is represented under these circumstances."

"Whether or not it appears odd matters very little to me, High Priest. I am the mouthpiece of the Sun Throne, and my will shall not be questioned."

"Of course not, Holiness." Lithel bowed again, then retreated, footsteps clipped against the polished stone floor. The door snicked shut behind him.

Dakeer waved a hand toward one chair in the outer circle. "Please sit, Lord Captain. You may witness this examination, but I ask that you not interfere."

Nerenoth strode to a chair near the open window and sat. Against the morning's glow and a faint breeze, Lekore's pale hair stirred like water. He resembled a slender tree, lithe, straight-backed, every bit the prince he'd been born. Yet did this man, young and strange, know his heritage? Had the gods taught him to take the throne back, or had they raised him to something greater?

The Lord Captain's hands found his chair arms and gripped them. *He stands mere feet before me. Why does he feel so far away?*

Hakija Dakeer Vasar shifted in his chair. It creaked. "You are called Lekore, are you not?"

"I am," said the young man. "And you are called by many names. I cannot remember them all. I apologize for that."

Dakeer offered a smile. "That is all right, my son. You needn't use them all."

Lekore started and took a step forward. "Am I your son?"

The Hakija's smile tumbled. "Ah, no. It is a religious expression. All the Kel are as sons and daughters to the church, for the Sun Gods created us in their very likeness. I also refer to the Lord Captain as a son of the church."

"Oh." Lekore backed up to stand in the center of the sunburst motif, the light in his eyes dimmer.

Clearing his throat, the Hakija leaned forward. "You may call me Hakija or Holiness."

Lekore nodded. "Hakija, may I ask what this examination is for?"

"Yes, of course. Several reports have reached me concerning your unique...well, frankly, I know not what to call what you do. In Halathe, it appears you called down fire to thwart the Tawloomez attack, and twice you tamed a storm that came from nowhere during the Sunny Season. These feats are strange to us. Even frightening."

"You are afraid of me," said Lekore.

"I am *cautious*. Tell me, Lekore, how did you summon fire?"

Lekore glanced toward Nerenoth, then returned to Dakeer. "I did not summon it. I asked the fire spirits within the torch already burning, and they aided me in saving the Kel about to die."

Dakeer tapped his chin. "Spirits?"

Lekore inclined his head. "They are guardians of the elements; they purify and protect all life. Some are fire, others are water, wind, and earth."

Dakeer frowned. "You can see these...spirits?"

"Yes."

"Always?"

"Yes. There is a wind spirit upon your left shoulder, Hakija."

Dakeer glanced at his shoulder. "I see nothing."

"Few can see them."

"Do you know of others besides yourself who *can* see them?"

Lekore nodded. "My mentors."

"Mentors?" Dakeer rubbed his chin. "You live with others in the Charnel Valley?"

"No, I live alone. But my mentors visit."

"These mentors. Are they Kel?"

"One is. The other is not."

Dakeer's spine straightened. "If not Kel, what is your other mentor? Surely not Tawloomez."

"No. He is Ter. He calls himself an Ephe'ahn. I think that is his race."

"No such race exists, my son. What does he look like?"

Nerenoth drew a breath as his heart quickened. He leaned forward despite himself.

Lekore tilted his head. "He is small, and looks to be a child, though he is ancient. His eyes are the blue of a cloudless day, and his ears are long and pointed. They twitch when he is in a teasing mood—which is often." Lekore grinned. "He is wise, though, and grave when he must be. His hair is the yellow of sunshine. He often dresses in earthen tones."

Tensing, Nerenoth pinned his eyes on the Hakija, whose face had paled. The holy man stared at Lekore with lips parted, hands gripping his miter. His eyes darted between Lekore's, searching.

He blinked and uncurled his fingers. "Is...is that so?" Dakeer cleared his throat, fingers drumming his chair arms. "How did you know to go to Halathe? Did your spirits warn you, or did your *mentor*, this, this, *Ter* tell you to go?"

"Neither, Hakija. I dreamt I must go, and so when I awoke, I went."

"I see." Dakeer sat in silence. Outside, a bird trilled.

Nerenoth studied the Hakija's profile, nerves gnawing at his flesh like emockye picking bones clean. *What will you do, Dakeer? Will you heed the rightful king's witness or will you bury truth to sate your prejudice?*

Lekore glanced toward the window. "Forgive me, Hakija, but might I ask how much longer this examination may be? I must attend to an urgent matter."

Dakeer arched his brow. "What urgency is this? Something you dreamed?"

"No, it is something the wind spirits told me."

Another pause. The Hakija sighed and set his miter on the dais near his feet. He straightened and eyed Lekore for several heartbeats. "Your words concern me, Lekore. Either you are indeed sun-touched, or the stars have gravely deceived you. Your other mentor, the Kel. Is he from civilization? Or does he cower in shadows and boneyards?"

Lekore glanced toward Nerenoth, though his eyes lingered beside the Lord Captain rather than upon him. "He does not hide. He is often among the Kel of Inpizal and other cities. Even now, he is very near."

Dakeer shot a narrowed look at Nerenoth. "Yet, he allowed you to live alone in the Charnel Valley all these years? Or do I misunderstand your upbringing?" He leaned forward, spearing Lekore with a steely stare. "Do I know the man?"

"You have never met him," said Lekore, calm as a windless day. "But perhaps you have heard of him. His name is Skye Getaal."

The Hakija jerked backward as though Lekore had flung a bucket of foul water in his face. Nerenoth glanced between them as his skin crawled against the vile name. Skye Getaal. None since the founder of the Star Worshipers had ever been called such. To speak the name outside of scripture signified the deepest offense. Yet twice now, Lekore had used the name without malice and without church sanction.

The Lord Captain set his jaw and waited, muscles taut, fingers itching to grip the sword strapped to his hip. *Watch and wait. What will Dakeer do?*

Nerenoth reeled against the profane name, himself. Yet had he not witnessed the mentor Lekore called Ter, undoubtedly a Sun God? Could Nerenoth dare to refute his own eyes?

Who am I to understand or make judgments? I already knew the young man to be different. I already knew the tenets taught by the priests to be altered from our first faith.

How far had doctrine strayed? How many lies had been woven into the church to blot out ugly or uncomfortable facts?

What does Lekore know that we have forgotten?

Dakeer Vasar rose. "Your words trouble my soul. I must pray concerning them. Your examination isn't over; indeed, it has only begun. After what you've said, I must call my priests to witness all further proceedings. In the meantime, you must remain here in the church's custody."

Nerenoth stood and strode onto the motif. "That isn't possible while he remains under my protection."

"You cannot be serious," said Dakeer, scowling. "After all you have heard, can you deem it wise to stand against me in this, Captain? Lekore is either deceived or deranged, if not both. Do not press me in this—I am unmoving. Lekore is under arrest by my order. Fight me, Nerenoth, I dare you."

Nerenoth kept his arms at his sides and fastened his gaze on the Hakija. "I shall not resist you. *Yet.* But I must have your word that I remain present at all further examinations, and that between each hearing, Lekore be kept in a comfortable room, well protected, rather than in some dungeon."

The Hakija waved a dismissive hand. "You can make no further requests, Lord Captain. This is fully a matter of the church; a holy war, if that helps you to understand it. The military has no further sway on this subject unless you should like the church to be privy to all military matters in future. The call, my lord, is yours. Will you set a new precedent?"

Nerenoth smoothed his face until it felt like stone against his bones. "Your point is well made, Hakija. I shall leave him to the church." He nodded his head and turned to leave, blood roiling.

"Captain?"

He glanced back to find Lekore's bright eyes aflame with the golden sunlight. Nerenoth smiled faintly, though flames also burned in his stomach. "I will keep my word."

The prince nodded once. "I am not afraid for myself. Look south. The wind is restless for your sake." He turned back to Dakeer. "Shall I not be allowed to answer the urgent call of the Spirits Elemental, Hakija?"

Teeth gritted, Nerenoth strode from the chamber and out into the hall. The last words he heard within were Dakeer's, ringing across the chamber like cold thunder.

"No, my son. Far more pressing matters must keep you here."

The door shut with a rumble that rattled Nerenoth's soul. *You won't win, Dakeer. I won't let you bury your sins.*

CHAPTER 12

The Sun Courtyard rang with merriment as Talanee sat inside her rolling carriage for the brief ride to the Cathedral of the Sun. Her personal guards flanked her conveyance on their pythe, controlling the crowds with steely looks and hands on their sheathed swords.

The princess held the curtain aside to watch the milling revelers, amused by Keerva's nervous glances. Why did the handmaid always look so nervous? Aside from the incident at Halathe, nothing ever threatened Talanee. Her soldiers remained vigilant. No one within Inpizal could touch her.

And during the Sun Festival, the Kel were far too caught up in their own celebrations to entertain ridiculous plots against the throne.

The cathedral loomed close as the sun neared its zenith. Talanee smiled and dropped the curtain into place. She always looked forward to this day of the festival. Even Lord Father looked happy on Blood Day. He'd gone ahead for the ceremony, leaving Talanee to catch up. Just as well. She must look pristine for the occasion. She'd heard from Keerva, who'd heard from a soldier, that Nerenoth would attend this year. Could it be that his faith had grown since matters at Halathe and the young man who harnessed fire?

The princess shifted in her seat.

"Please, my lady," said Keerva. "Don't wrinkle your gown so."

Talanee ran a hand over the skirts of her scarlet and gold ensemble and reached up to check the intricate golden diadem atop her head. Blood Day. She pulled the curtain aside as the carriage rolled into the cathedral grounds. Atop their mounts or within their carriages, nobility waited for her to pass. With a giddy headrush, she draped her handkerchief out the window and let it stream in the breeze, bloodred in the bright sunshine.

Today is a wonderful day.

WITHIN THE CATHEDRAL, LORD LITHEL KUAAN GREETED Talanee. "Your Highness, you look magnificent."

Talanee offered a smile and caught up her skirts to rustle them, sewn jewels flashing. "My tailors outdid themselves, didn't they?" She glanced around at the throng of priests dressed in their best vestments. No sign of the Lord Captain or Lord Father. "Where is the king?"

"Ah, he and the Holy Hakija are in council, but I'm certain they'll finish soon. The sun nears its peak. Shall I escort you to your seat, Princess?"

She stifled her disappointment behind another smile. Of late, the High Priest had been singling her out. Should she be surprised? Few held such influential positions, and few could match his right to win her hand. She supposed Lithel was a handsome man. Indeed, unless she compared him to the Lord Captain, he stood apart in his own right. But Talanee didn't care for his self-important airs and grand apparel. He liked himself altogether too much.

"I give you good day, Cousin."

Talanee's hand froze midair before Lithel's gloved fingers. The

High Priest frowned as his eyes drifted behind Talanee to land on the newcomer.

The princess turned to Ademas Getaal. "Hello, Lord Ademas. I didn't expect to see you here this morning."

The young man's eyes glinted as his smile stretched wider. He wore a different green tunic from last night, this one a richer hue, with gold threaded brocade hems, and white breeches. A sword remained strapped to his hip. "I wouldn't miss a single moment of Inpizal's Sun Festival. I hear today's events are very moving. Lord Elekel was kind enough to secure me an invitation to these more private functions."

"How fortunate for you."

He stepped closer. "I had hoped you might accompany me today and perhaps play my guide." His smile crooked. "If you don't have your heart set on the company of another, that is."

Something in his look, in that sparkling glow of his sly eyes, inspired her rigid smile to thaw into something warm. She took his proffered fingers. "How could I refuse so earnest a request?" She glanced at Lithel. "You'll excuse me, of course."

The High Priest dipped his head as his mouth tightened. "Of course, Your Highness."

Ademas guided her away from Lithel and followed the crowd as it trickled toward the chapel. Talanee glimpsed Keerva in her best yellow gown drifting ahead to join other finely dressed servants at the back of the vaulted chamber.

"What was that all about, *Cousin?*" she whispered.

"What, that? Why, I came to rescue one who looked like an ocean fish lured near a flashy hook. A very reluctant fish who knew better than to take the bait but had no excuse to swim away." He chuckled. "That might be a weak metaphor, but you'll forgive me, I'm sure."

She eyed him without turning her head. "I suppose you thought your actions quite gallant."

"Quite."

"I needed no help."

"Likely not. Yet I did make things easier on you."

She sniffed. "Perhaps you shouldn't be so loose when speaking of your lineage. Calling me cousin openly could mar your reputation before you can make it your own."

"Ah. If I were concerned by such things, I'd thank you for your unsolicited advice. As it stands, I'm not concerned."

She halted and dropped his hand. "While indiscretions may occur among nobility, it isn't something one speaks of."

Ademas shrugged. "Why is that my problem? I've done nothing wrong."

Talanee started forward again as her cheeks burned. "I think we should speak of something else."

He caught up with her. "Very well. What would you like to discuss?"

They reached the door to the chapel and paused. Talanee glanced at him and lowered her voice. "You've never been to Inpizal before. What do you think of the Cathedral of the Sun?"

His eyes darted around the domed chamber filled with wooden pews. An ornate pulpit stood high above the floor. The arched ceiling, held up by golden beams ornamented with sunbursts and runes etched by the gods themselves, shone in sunlight streaming in from high windows. Walls made from white stone glittered and winked as Talanee paced forward again.

"It's very impressive," said Ademas, shaking his head. "Nothing else quite like it, not even the palace."

"Naturally not. This *is* the home of the Sun Gods."

She led him to her cordoned-off pew, guards trailing behind her to stand beside the pew as she sat. Ademas sat with her.

"Is this all right, Cousin?" he asked.

"I'm allowed to invite whomever I please to sit with me."

He hadn't looked ready to move, anyway. Talanee's gaze flicked to the altar at the head of the chapel, beneath the golden sunburst device stretched across the enormous wall behind the pulpit. A priest draped in golden vestments, his face hidden behind a veil, stood beside the altar with a ceremonial knife clutched in gloved hands.

A thrill rushed over Talanee, warming her skin. In past years, she'd given only cursory thought to the rituals of the Sun Festival, but now, facing the threat of Tawloomez warriors, and after the wonders she'd seen Lekore perform, her soul craved the divine wisdom of the Sun Throne. These rituals mattered as they never had before. She wanted answers. *Needed* answers.

The flow of nobility thickened. Talanee glanced to her right to find Lord Father in a crimson tunic of fine silk and royal robes of velvet seated in his customary place apart from everyone else and facing the pews. Despite his impressive wardrobe, he looked sickly and thin. The throne glittered with gold inlays, winking in the shifting light as Kel bowed to the king before filing into their seats around the massive chamber. The king inclined his head, but his dark-rimmed eyes strayed to somewhere above the crowd.

Talanee traced his stare to an enclave on the chapel's second story, where the priestly choir sat between chants on Zendays. Did someone lurk in the shadows? She shifted and craned her neck to spot three figures standing above; two were Sun Warriors of the church, judging by their golden breastplates winking in the gloom. The third stood too far back to identify.

"What are you looking at?" asked Ademas, angling to view the enclave.

"People. Up there. Three, I think."

He glanced at her. "Isn't that normal? It's the choir loft."

"But today the choir won't chant or sing until after the ceremony. That's when they enter the loft. And I'm confident they wouldn't wear armor."

Ademas lifted his eyebrows and turned again toward the enclave. "So they wouldn't. How interesting." He dropped his eyes back to her, a gleam in their red depths.

The droning murmurs surrounding Talanee dipped into a lower hum, then rolled away. She tore her focus from the loft and turned to find the Hakija climbing to his pulpit.

He looks grim.

Odd, considering the nature of the event. Yes, solemnity mattered, yet in years past the Holy Hakija had exuded a kind of quiet pleasure as he began the Rite of Blood. Now, against the heavy silence, he looked...distracted? Perhaps troubled?

This isn't like other years, after all. War looms like a storm cloud upon the horizon.

Hakija Dakeer Vasar lifted his hands, and all whispering ceased. Silence drifted across the assembly like a wave over the shore, heavy and strong. "'O ye Kel children, blessed of the Sun Throne to inherit these hallowed roads and palaces, forget not the sacrifice made in thy behalf. Forget not the great pains of my afflicted soul as I laid down the life of a once beloved brother.'"

Talanee shifted. Rarely did anyone quote the heartbroken lament written by Holy King Erokel after the War of Brothers. How odd to recite them now on Blood Day.

The Hakija bowed his head, then hoisted his gaze. It drifted toward the ceiling—no, he paused upon the loft. His eyes lingered there as his lips dipped into a frown.

"Throughout history," he said, voice low, "we Kel have made tremendous sacrifices for the greater good of our blessed kingdom. As the Holy King once cut down the Cursed One to silence the mortal Voice of the Stars—his own brother, *his own blood*, who had betrayed the Kel to the very Moon Throne—so, too, we have the responsibility to silence what may be precious to us, to prevent the moral destruction of our race.

"War is ever upon our threshold. Not only the threat of Tawloomez at our door, though that must never be forgotten. But even more important, we cannot let cunning words or even our own blood ties keep us from holding fast to our faith in the Sun Gods. Deceit creeps close to every soul. Let us, as Erokel of old, cut it down no matter its form. No matter its power.

"Today, we are gathered to offer sacrifice to the Sun Throne. Let us reflect, let us inspect, and thrice over, let us examine our hearts, our very souls, as we deliver this Rite of Blood unto our gods in deep respect and soberness." He lifted his eyes to the domed ceiling. "O Gods of the Sun, hear my plea and guide us through our weakness as a most fallible people! Let not the shades of night darken our minds and hearts with doubts. Let us look upward to thy Throne through all our trials and adversities. Let us not take pity upon those who would drag us into the shadows of the Moon by their deceitful actions. And please, O Sun Gods, protect us from our enemies, even those fearsome and heinous Tawloomez; they who art vile in thine eyes. Amen!"

His fingers danced across the air to trace the symbol of the rising sun as the chapel rang with the echoed "amen" of the crowd.

Talanee's gaze flicked across the chamber. Despite the rumors, the Lord Captain hadn't shown up. She scowled and settled into her seat. *Oh well, something important might have come up. Or perhaps he's staying in the back of the chapel.*

She'd never known another man of high rank who less enjoyed standing in the public eye. She wasn't certain humility was a virtue, yet the way Nerenoth Irothé wore it, it might soon become a crowning fashion.

Priests in silk hoods streamed from a door left of the pulpit.

Talanee smoothed her skirts. *Pay attention. This is sacred, for Light's sake!*

Watching the priests file in, robed in gold, hooded in white, candles flickering in their gloved hands, Talanee let the hallowedness of the event seep into her bones until she shivered.

The hooded figures circled the altar, footsteps mere scuffs against the marble floor. Their voices lifted in a chant, words even and drawn out until they became an almost inaudible hum. But Talanee knew the chant by heart.

"Praise the Sun Throne. Praise the Gods in the Sky. Smite thine enemies. Bring Light to the Night. Praise the Sun Throne. Praise the Gods in the Sky..."

Talanee mouthed the words, the chills spreading down her limbs.

On the chant went, climbing to the rafters to chime across the ancient chamber, until she thought the Sun Gods might appear. Could they *feel* the faith floating to the steps of the Sun Throne? Were they pleased by the devotion of those assembled here in worship?

A woman gowned in white silk glided from the side door, an infant cradled in her arms. A Tawloomez infant.

Talanee's blood flamed hot. She leaned forward as the chant flooded her mind like a heady wine. Shivers danced down her arms.

"*Smite thine enemies. Bring Light to the Night...*"

The woman reached the altar as two priests parted to let her into their circle. She stooped and laid the infant on the altar. Its cries rose to join the unending chant.

"*Praise the Sun Throne. Praise the Gods in the Sky...*"

From his pulpit on high, the Hakija gave a single nod as bloodlust filled the chapel.

One hooded priest stepped forward and lifted a dagger. The blade flashed in a shaft of sunlight before it plunged downward.

The infant let out a last cry.

Talanee licked her lips. Ademas shifted beside her.

Someone shouted overhead and the chant faltered.

Talanee blinked. *Have the Sun Gods descended from their Throne?* She looked up and twisted around.

Motion in the choir loft snared her gaze. Despite the restraining hands of two Sun Warriors in golden armor, the young man named Lekore leaned over the balcony balustrade and stared at the altar with wide eyes, blood drained from his face.

"Proceed." Dakeer Vasar's voice thundered across the chamber, stilling murmurs as they started.

"*Smite thine enemies...*"

Lekore sank down until his guards caught him and pulled him into the concealing shadows.

Talanee turned back to the altar as the woman carried the bloody infant out through a door on the chapel's right side, blood staining her gown in crimson shades. At the same moment, a second woman gowned in white strode from the first door, another heathen baby toted in her arms.

"No!" cried Lekore from the enclave. "Please stop!"

Mutters cut across the chant as the priests faltered.

The Hakija raised his arm. "Remove him." A faint clatter drifted from above, and shadows swallowed the gleaming armor until all fell still in the loft.

Talanee frowned but dropped her eyes back to the ceremony. Why had the young man interrupted the Rite of Blood? Didn't he understand how crucial it was?

Does he hold Tawloomez sympathies after all?

The chant drifted heavenward once more, and the second infant lost its life in the same swift motion. Even hooded, Talanee suspected the executioner was Lithel. How must it be to carry out the will of the Sun Gods so directly?

It must be sublime. She tried to smile, but her hands curled around her handkerchief, as a shiver rushed through her.

A third white-clad woman emerged from the left side door, a toddler in her arms, as the second lifeless child was carried out.

CHAPTER 13

"South, my lord. Near the brushfire that bloomed up in last night's storm."

"My scouts have seen nothing," Nerenoth said, frowning. "And the brushfire is miles out."

"Yes, my lord," said Jasu'Hekar, dipping his head. "Yet, it is rumored in the slums that hidden there, among many boulders of stone, a door leads down into a tunnel and into the city. It is also rumored that the heathen scouts seek this door by which to enter the city and murder a nobleman's heir during the darkest hours of night."

The Tawloomez lifted his brown eyes and grinned as he brushed floppy brown hair from his face. "They think to protect themselves from the Sun Throne in this way, but it is not possible to sneak beneath the notice of the Light. So your honorable brother has told me." His smile slipped. "My lord, these rumors are from before last night's storm. It is possible the door has been found if it is there to be discovered."

Nerenoth nodded and turned to face a westward window. He stood with the Tawloomez spy in an empty garrison corridor, the man still dressed in the plain slave garb disguise he had donned to carry out Nerenoth's orders. Lord Lieutenant Rez guarded the

131

path to this corridor, redirecting any stray soldier who might pass through.

Look south, Lekore had said.

Nerenoth nodded and turned to Jasu'Hekar. "Show me."

"Now, my lord, during Blood Day services?"

The Lord Captain grimaced, stomach twisting at the thought of the bloody sacrifices. "Could there be a better time?"

He must get away from Inpizal, to clear his thoughts and plot his next move, before Dakeer Vasar silenced Lekore forever. The Hakija had an image to maintain, and so the examinations would not be swift to end. Should the southern threat take more than a day to thwart, he would still have time to rescue the rightful king.

Besides, Lekore had said to look south.

WATER DRIPPED FROM THE CRACKED STONES ABOVE. LEKORE eyed the seam from his chosen corner in the dank, unfurnished chamber, knees drawn to his chest, long hair draped across his shoulders and down his back like a cloak against the dim glow of his prison.

He lifted a hand to wipe tears from his cheeks. His heart wrenched as the images poured into his mind again; all those children, killed, *killed*, like it was nothing at all. He pressed his hands to his eyes, longing to banish the memory forever, eager to dislodge the taint of bloodlust that had inundated the cathedral air.

How could the Kel do such a horrible thing? Did the differences between them and the Tawloomez justify the murder of innocent children?

"I cannot believe it." He buried his head in his arms. "Skye, where are you? What am I to do in this place? Why am I to live among Kel?"

No answer swelled up from the gloom. Only the rhythmic *drip, drip, drip* of water against stone made any noise. No water spirits, no earth spirits, drifted through the tiny chamber to offer solace. No one had come since guards shoved Lekore into this forsaken cell after his display at the cathedral ceremony. Bruises throbbed on his skin where he'd struck the moldy, straw-strewn floor.

Am I to live in this fell place until my end comes?

He dragged in a shuddering breath and straightened to lean against the cool stone wall. The fever from his earlier poisoning still burned his flesh.

It is too soon to despair. Am I to surrender to destruction after only one hour? Have I no greater fortitude than that?

He wiped the last tears from his eyes, then lifted his arm to investigate the bruise on his elbow. Blood smudged his skin, but the cuts would heal without lasting damage. As he shifted his leg to prod at another scrape, the scuff of feet sounded beyond the barrier of his prison. Lekore flinched and pressed against the wall. Had the Kel returned to offer him to an altar next?

Do not be a fool.

Keys brattled together; the lock shrieked; the door swung inward. Torchlight poured across the uneven flagstones, and Lekore winced until he could make out the form of a man against the light.

"You caused me no slight embarrassment in my cathedral," said Dakeer Vasar. "Why did you reject the Blood Ceremony, my son?"

Heat shot through Lekore's blood, lending him strength. "How can you sacrifice children?"

The dripping water reclaimed the room's attention as the Hakija stood unmoving in the doorway. A sigh fluted from his mouth. "How can I explain this to someone so nearly heathen? The Tawloomez are filthy. They worship false gods and prey upon our innocent people. Recently, they cut down every man, woman, and child within the fortress of Erokes. Is this the action of one deserving of mercy?"

Lekore stood, ignoring the pangs of a dozen damaged muscles. "Did they first kill your people, or did you first kill theirs? Might not their actions feel justified, when you slaughter their children in your very churches?"

"It is necessary," came the sharp reply. "The Tawloomez slaves breed too many of their own. If we do not keep their population in Erokel down to a certain number, they will rise up to overthrow us. Turn us *all* into slaves. Heap destruction upon us!"

"And so, you strike first?" Lekore's voice reverberated on the stones.

"Yes!" The Hakija's tones thundered over Lekore's dying echoes. "Too long we have suffered them upon our borders, carrying off our children to be eaten, or worse! I will do whatever it takes to instill fear into their very souls, if it shall keep them at bay!"

"Has it?" asked Lekore, words feather soft.

Anger rolled through the chamber to press against Lekore's heart, palpable, seething. The Hakija stepped into the cell. "Were it not for those like you, those weak-hearted fools who feel so ardently that these lesser creatures deserve our—our *pity*—then, yes, it would have the proper effect."

The notes of anger pitched into hatred, dark, guttural, running through Dakeer's veins like the fires of the northern mountains.

A score of memories pierced Lekore's mind; not his own, but those of a boy tied to a well, screaming out as his home burned. The remains of Kel littered the ground around him, three women and a man, while warriors clad in hides and masked in green paint chortled and threw more torches onto the flames. Acrid smoke curled against his nostrils and sank into his lungs until he choked. On he screamed, on and on and on and on...

Lekore staggered back. Tears blurred his vision. *Block it out. Keep out his emotions.* He rubbed a hand over his face and swallowed down a sob. "I...I am sorry, Hakija. I cannot judge your pain and hatred. I cannot understand your suffering."

Ringing silence filled the chamber. Lekore pulled his head up to find the Kel staring at him, eyes wide and wild in the torchlight.

"What can you mean?" Dakeer's words scraped over his lips. "You know nothing of my—"

"No," said Lekore. "I cannot know it; I have only seen it for a moment. I will not pretend to understand the anguish of one whose family has been massacred. I do not wish to know it. But I can better understand the cause of your blind wrath, and I pity you."

Dakeer's stillness held the pall of death. Moments passed. The torch sputtered and shrank, spiritless. The Hakija drew himself to his full height. "Thou art the spawn of darkest night. Never shall you again see the glory of the sun, nor taste the freedom of wind upon your brow. I condemn thee to spend thy days in this pit."

Chills wracked Lekore's flesh. He stumbled forward. "Please, you cannot leave me here, Hakija."

"Say no more, Vile One! I know thy true self." He whirled and stalked from the cell, taking his torch with him. The door slammed shut, and the keys clanged as the lock screamed again.

"No!" Lekore raced to the door. He slammed his hands against the wooden barrier. "Please! Do not shut me in this terrible place. Please! Do not abandon me!" His lungs hitched. His breaths shortened. The room spun around him, until he sank to his knees, and struck his head against the door. Tears splashed against the floor as he gasped for air.

"No. No, please. Please, Ank. Don't leave me. Don't leave me. Please please please."

CHAPTER 14

Ademas listened in silence as Talanee relayed what she knew of Lekore. It had taken little to probe details out of her, following Lekore's outburst during the Rite of Blood. She'd been dying to speak of it as they traipsed from the chapel and along the cathedral hallways. Out in broad daylight, she'd only awaited a passing comment before she unleashed all the facts upon her audience of one.

They sat now upon a bench in one of the cathedral gardens, where a fountain splashed nearby, and the wafting fragrance of flowers tickled Talanee's senses.

She eyed her alleged cousin with a growing scowl. "Well?"

He dragged his eyes from the fountain. "Well what, Cousin?"

"Well, doesn't it seem odd? He's obviously sun-touched, yet he interrupted a sacred ceremony like it horrified him."

"Perhaps he's unaccustomed to watching blood spilled so freely."

"But he's lived in the wilds, for Light's sake. Surely, he's hunted for his food. How is this different?"

Ademas's smile held an edge. "I suspect it's because these were children."

"*Tawloomez* children."

He shrugged. "He has no reason to dislike them as we do. Has he gone to war against them? If he really has lived away from people most of his life, his perspective must be vastly different from yours or mine. Honestly, it's fascinating. I'd relish the chance to speak with him." Ademas's eyes caught fire.

Talanee arched an eyebrow. "*That's* what captures your interest most? His perspective? What of his powers? His ability to *fly* in the air and rain down *fire* from the heavens? Do you even hear yourself?"

A grin flashed across the young man's face. "Certainly, that's incredible. Utterly unbelievable. It's really the entire picture that snares my attention. What manner of man are we witnessing here? What kind of figure did the Hakija silence in the chapel? What justifies his actions?"

"His actions? Do you mean Lekore's or our Holy Hakija's?"

"Well, both, if I'm honest. Don't you see, Cousin? There are politics at play here."

Talanee snorted. "When are there not politics at play in Inpizal? Perhaps in your quaint island climate, there's little to do besides splash in your pleasant waters and sip lukewarm wine, but *here* we wrestle with daily living and managing an entire country on the cusp of open war."

She expected Ademas to color and sputter an excuse, but instead he leaned close, teeth bared in a grin that brightened the flames in his eyes.

"Cousin," he said in low tones, "I dearly crave the portrait you paint of this fair city. Indeed, I drink in the very notion of wrestling your politics, even with war so near. And, if I might be so bold, I relish doing so *while* I sip my lukewarm wine and—" He sprang up and loped to the fountain, bent, and swiped his hand through the water to send droplets across the lawn. "I might even find time to splash in the water."

She sat frozen on the garden bench, then a smile slipped over her lips unbidden. She laughed. "Well, if I had doubts about your heritage, they're quieted now. You're as odd as my lord uncle."

"Thank you, fair lady," said Ademas, dipping into a bow, one hand on his sword pommel. He straightened. "If only that would —" Mirth died in his eyes as his gaze strayed past Talanee. "Will you excuse me for a moment?" He strode past her.

She shifted to follow his gait across the lawn. He stopped before a man in church livery; a servant of Lithel or some other priest, perhaps. They conversed, then the servant bowed, and trotted back to the cathedral.

Ademas returned, brow creased, arms folded.

"Is anything wrong?" asked Talanee.

He blinked, then his expression melted into affability, light igniting in his eyes. "Oh, no. Lord Elekel just sent a message that he won't be joining me tonight for dinner. He has some other engagement, I suppose. I confess, I'm relieved. We get on well enough, but there's still a tension born from unfamiliarity. Our relationship is new, after all."

She searched his face. *He's lying. His expression doesn't match the trouble inspired by the servant's message.* She tacked on a smile. "Well, I'm sure you'll find comfortable ground with one another. Perhaps slow pacing is the wisest approach."

He tapped a finger against his folded arm. "Is that your approach to your own problem, Your Highness?"

Heat climbed her face. "What do you—"

"It doesn't take a prodigy to recognize family issues, Cousin. Nor do the streets of Inpizal keep silent on matters of royalty. Ask anyone, anyone at all, and they would say the same as I do now: You and your father are not on the best of terms."

She leapt to her feet and batted her scarlet skirts smooth. "I'll thank you to leave that matter alone, *sir*. Good day." She marched past him, but his hand caught her wrist.

"Not so swiftly, Princess. Tantrums don't become you."

She whirled as she lifted her hand to strike his face—but he caught her arm, still smiling.

"Truth may hurt, but that doesn't make it a lie, Talanee. Now, you can stomp your foot and walk away, but that only tells me I'm right. If you wish to defend yourself against my comments, look me in the eye and tell me I'm mistaken. Just that, and I'll believe you."

She stared, trembling as blood pounded in her ears. He didn't move. His hands clutched her arms, not tight, but firm enough that she couldn't break away. Lifting her chin, she pinned him with a look hot enough to burn, steeled herself, and opened her mouth to speak. Words failed. Against the glow of his gaze, against the calm of his demeanor, and the censure of his words, she couldn't speak her lie.

"Fine!" She tugged away as he released her, and she staggered back. Whipping aside strands of her long hair, she leveled her shoulders. "Think what you please. My father is too busy a man to spare his daughter much time. How is that wrong? He's king. Of course he can't pay attention to one girl's needs."

"His own kin?" asked Ademas, tone neutral.

"I, least of all. Aren't his subjects most important? Doesn't the kingdom demand his unwavering attention?"

"Perhaps." Ademas shrugged. "I will answer better when I sit upon a throne."

She rolled her eyes. "I despise flippancy."

"You're entitled to your feelings."

She scoffed. "Am I?"

"Aren't you?"

"Oh, never mind. You're a fool." She spun and trotted off, glittering skirts whisking across the grass. Halfway to the gravel drive, she slowed, then stopped. Drawing deep breaths, she wrestled back tears. Why did he upset her? She had better control than this.

"I apologize, Cousin."

She yelped and spun. Ademas Getaal stood behind her, calm and unruffled as though he'd strolled along the grounds rather than raced to catch her.

His smile crooked. "I had no cause to upset you. Please forgive me, and I'll do my best to be a better companion through this festival day. If I fail, you may flog me senseless."

Talanee shook her head. "Flog you? Are you actually insane?"

"Mad as a six-legged pythe."

"What does that even mean?"

His grin stretched wide. "It means, my dear cousin, you shan't rid yourself of me so easily as all that."

THEY SPENT THE AFTERZEN HOURS STROLLING THROUGH THE market squares, a fleet of soldiers on their heels. Though Ademas had arrived in Inpizal only days before, and claimed to need a guide, he took the lead upon the streets and showed Talanee wares and festival foods she'd never heard of in her life.

At length, they sat beneath a shade tree in a city garden to rest. Talanee nibbled a sweet-cream pastry and studied her cousin. "Are you certain you've never been to Inpizal before?"

"Definitely, but my mother grew up here. How do you think she met my father?"

Talanee blushed as she imagined Uncle Elekel meeting his lover in this very garden. "Did she describe the wonders of the Holy City in such detail?"

"Not all of it, but she gave strict instruction to try certain foods, wander certain thoroughfares, and if I could, to dote on certain princesses." That gleam brightened his eyes again as his smile widened. "How is your pastry?"

Talanee swallowed a bite. "Delicious."

"My mother's favorite."

"What brought you to Inpizal at last, Ademas?"

He leaned against the tree trunk and stared into the branches above as the shifting leaves painted dark shadows across his green tunic. "Several things. Most of all, the time felt right to strike out on my own. I'll turn eighteen soon. I thought this a good season to stretch my wings."

"You're lucky. You've not got responsibilities tying you down, keeping you from taking flight."

He dropped his eyes to hers. "Unlike yourself, Princess?"

She looked away. "Every decision I make affects the kingdom. Pressure is being applied right now to choose a husband who will one day be king. Why does marriage have to be political?"

"Is there no one suitable who quickens your heart, Cousin?"

She grimaced and shot him a look. "Do I detect mockery in your voice?"

Ademas shrugged. "Always. But that's not important right now. I did notice a certain preference for a tall, stately, impressive Lord Captain at the Sun Dance, or did I imagine that?"

Talanee's grimace grew. "Aren't you observant? Of course, I prefer him to most others. He's exactly the ideal man. But, perhaps you don't know, he's betrothed to another."

"Betrothed. Is that common practice in Inpizal?"

"Not anymore. But I understand Lord Captain Nerenoth's father was very traditional, and he wished to connect two powerful houses together. Upon his deathbed, he ordered his son to agree to the alliance. That was eighteen years ago. He and Lady Lanasha Jahaan have been betrothed since, though she won't agree to wed him until he aligns his beliefs more with the church."

Ademas shifted his position in the grass. "Is the Lord Captain apostate?"

"*No.* He just doesn't express himself publicly in his beliefs the way others want him to."

"Hm. Yet I heard he and the Hakija have decidedly different views on church doctrine."

"Rumors." Talanee ripped a bite of pastry with her teeth and chewed it with fervor.

Ademas chuckled. "Your opinion is obviously fixed." He stretched his arms over his head and yawned. "It's getting on toward evening. Shall I escort you home for the palace festivities?"

Talanee swallowed her food. "What will you do?"

"I have some business after dinner."

She frowned as her heart dipped. Had she hoped he might stay near throughout the evening? *Ridiculous.* She popped the last morsel of food into her mouth and brushed the crumbs from her gown. Swallowing, she stood. "Well, I'll leave you here then. I've affairs of my own to manage. Thank you for a diverting afterzen."

He jumped to his feet with the grace of a dancer and bowed at the waist. "I give you good evening, Cousin."

She offered a curt nod and whirled to stride to the carriage waiting at the edge of the manicured garden. Keerva opened the door, and Talanee slipped inside, dragging her heavy skirts after her, throat burning as though she might cry. *I'm not going to. Ademas is just another sycophant. I'm better off alone.*

She didn't need friends. Hadn't she long ago reconciled herself to that fate?

"Drive on," she said in tones as cold as the highest mountain snows. She drew aside the curtain and watched Ademas stroll across the lawn toward the edge of the garden park, where the grand townhouses shrank into more modest versions, and then... She pressed against the window. There wasn't much more in that direction before he reached the slums!

Why is he going that way?

"Stop!"

The carriage rocked to a halt.

"My lady? Is anything—"

"Hush." Talanee chewed the inside of her mouth as she stalked the young man's progress. "Keerva, tell the driver to follow Ademas, but keep at a safe distance. He mustn't see us."

"Your Highness, is—"

"If you're about to question me, reconsider, then do as I say."

Keerva scrambled from the carriage, tangling her legs in the layers of yellow dress. Her voice rose and fell as she relayed the message. A moment later, she batted down her skirts and slipped back inside. "He said he'll wait a few minutes, then follow, my lady."

At least one servant has some intelligence.

Talanee sat back to wait.

* * *

ADEMAS LED THE WAY TO THE SLUMS, JUST AS TALANEE HAD suspected. Here, beneath the leaning townhouses and refuse-strewn alleyways, the young man strode with the confidence of a soldier. No one molested him as he passed by vagrants and gangs.

The carriage could go only a few streets into the unhallowed sector, or it would become too conspicuous. Talanee gathered her skirts, commanded Keerva to lend her the handmaiden's plain white cloak, and, donning it, stepped from the contraption to follow.

"You mustn't," whispered Keerva.

"I'll be fine."

Two soldiers on pytheback dismounted to join her, their capes slithering down their pythes' scales.

Talanee scowled. "You'll give me away."

"Please, Your Highness," one guard said. "Let us go in your stead. We'll report what we find."

Talanee stared after the figure of her cousin, nearly out of sight. "Oh, very well. Only one of you. And try to be discreet!" She turned to the carriage, then glanced back. "Oh, never mind. It's not my business. Let's return to the palace." As the guards bowed, she stepped back into the carriage.

Keerva's relieved expression annoyed the princess.

She clamped a hand to Keerva's mouth as the carriage began to turn around. "On pain of death, say nothing."

Talanee tugged her ruby-studded diadem from her hair and shoved it into Keerva's hands. She drew the hood of the cloak over her head, released Keerva's mouth, then cracked open the other carriage door just as the vehicle rolled in front of an alley. No guards rode on this side, to give the carriage a wide enough berth to change course. Talanee sprang from the carriage and slipped into the shadows of the reeking alley as the carriage swayed and jolted down the narrow street.

The princess smiled, then turned and hurried after her peculiar cousin, holding her red handkerchief to her nose. In the dim light of the street, she worried she wouldn't find him. But as she turned a corner, she spotted the young man nearing the next intersection. He didn't hide his rich raiment or the saber hanging from his hip, yet passersby shrank back as he approached. How did he manage it?

Talanee mingled among the peasant revelers. Bawdy songs climbed the air in warbling voices, and laughter erupted behind closed doors. Cheap streamers flittered on the breeze where they hung from sagging balconies.

A toothless crone dressed in tattered rags staggered toward Talanee. "Be Sun-blessed. Be Sun-blessed!" She cackled a laugh and stumbled sideways to crash into a pile of trash as the princess dodged her.

Reaching the next crossroads, Talanee turned right to follow her cousin, then hissed and ducked into a doorway as she spotted him only a few feet away. From the darkness of the abandoned house where she crouched, she peeked out. Ademas Getaal stood in company with three men in black cloaks.

Her eyes widened. Star Worshipers.

Ademas gestured as he spoke, then he slipped a pendant from beneath his tunic, clutching its chain in his fist. A black starburst. Talanee flinched and traced the rising sun in the air before her, heart hammering. White fury framed her vision. He was one of *them*. A slithering, conniving, blaspheming traitor. How had she ever come to like him, to think of him as family, to *enjoy* his company?

Her hands trembled. What should she do? Could she sneak away unseen, or should she wait until the meeting ended?

Ademas slipped his pendant back under his silk tunic and spoke again. Amid the commotion of the beggars and drunkards staggering along the street, she could hear nothing that passed between him and his companions. She didn't dare slip closer.

One of the cloaked figures pointed west, then crept away, his shrouded fellows following. Ademas remained stationary until they disappeared in the crowds of filth and ruffians, then he turned, a smile etched into his face, brows drawn.

His gaze met Talanee's. She flinched back. Had he seen her in the shadows?

Moments passed. Feet scuffed close, and Ademas appeared in the doorway to lean against the frame. "Hello, Cousin."

Talanee glared at him, a bitter taste on her tongue. "You scum. You filthy scum."

Ademas's lips twitched up. "I'm not the one who stalked me to the slums of Inpizal, you know."

"You're a *Star Worshiper*."

He shrugged. "Perhaps. Perhaps not. That doesn't change the fact you spied on me."

"I'll report you to the church."

"If I let you go."

A chill crept into her veins. "You wouldn't harm the heir of Erokel."

He chuckled and snatched her wrist. "Come with me, Princess."

She staggered after him, blood drumming in her ears. "Let me go! Help!"

No one stepped in.

She patted her skirts for the hidden dagger stowed in a clever pocket, but Ademas's step quickened, and she stumbled. With a growl, she swiped her nails at his face.

Ademas twisted her wrist and spun her around, pinning her back to his chest. "Don't be a fool. Kill me here, now, and you'll be alone in a place where no one cares what your bloodline looks like." He pulled the dagger from her skirt pocket. "I'll be keeping this for now."

Talanee bit her lip as her arm strained. "Let me *go*."

"Keep walking." He jerked her straight and marched on.

He dragged her through the streets, forcing her to trip through garbage, weaving his way around the residents who did nothing to save their princess—though they couldn't know who she was beneath her cloak. Yet Ademas had seen her.

He might not have known it was me until he reached the door.

Twilight darkened to a velvet haze of lanterns against the stars. Music and merrymaking drifted upward to mingle with bonfire smoke and the vapors of ale and wine. Ademas kept walking, ignoring any protests Talanee tried to make. She lost a slipper somewhere along the dimming route. The festival sounds faded. They'd left the slums for the west end of Inpizal.

Her chills returned. People didn't come here.

Not even riffraff.

Burned-out buildings loomed on either side of the road, and a heavy stillness settled like fog in the streets, repressing the last distant noises of Inpizal's populated sectors.

No one will look for my corpse here.

She wrenched against Ademas's grip. "Let me go right now!"

He jerked her close and clamped a hand to her mouth. "Be quiet, or you'll murder us both. Nod if you promise to keep silent."

She bobbed a nod against the warmth of his hand, fighting back tears. *I won't cry. I won't give him that satisfaction!*

He drew his hand from her lips, then tugged her along after him. Their westward progress slowed again as they approached a hunching shape against the night. Talanee's soul quaked. Her limbs trembled. Not here. Why would he bring her here?

He turned, the burned-out temple rising before him like a looming monster. "Stay here. Hide yourself. You can flee, but you won't make it far without encountering Star Worshipers, and without me, you won't get past them."

She opened her mouth.

He held up a hand. "You think they'll care that you're the princess? Think twice."

"Where are you going?"

"I've some urgent business inside."

Her lungs tightened. "You're sacrificing me to them, aren't you? That's what your meeting was about?"

He smiled. "That implies I knew you stalked me to the slums. No, Princess. This isn't about you. This is about saving an innocent life."

She blinked. "What—"

"Time is precious. Could I answer your incessant questions upon my return?" He glanced to her right. "That's a nice dark spot. If you wait there, I'll return as soon as I can." He pressed her dagger into her hands, then strode toward the temple.

Talanee's heart sank into her stomach. She didn't want to huddle in a dark corner in this evil place, waiting outside the grounds of the ancient temple of blaspheming Star Worshipers.

Nor did she want to go inside with Ademas.

I'll wait. She tiptoed to the shadows her cousin had indicated and hunched down. *As if he left me with any other option.*

CHAPTER 15

Lekore sat up, blind in the cold, dark chamber, heart beating against his ribs. Footsteps banged down the corridor beyond the door. He scrambled to his feet and backed away from the barrier, nerves taut and humming in his ears. The feet neared, scuffing and scraping against stones. They halted outside his cell.

Lekore's heart clattered in his ears. Hadn't the Hakija left him for dead?

Is it the Lord Captain?

His heart jolted as hope surged like blood through his limbs. *Of course! Did he not promise he would protect me?*

Something slammed against the door. The wooden barrier shuddered as splinters littered the floor. Again, the door quivered as something struck it. The process repeated several times, loud and thudding against the stones, until the door flung open, bits of debris scudding across the room. Chunks of wood settled at Lekore's feet. He lifted his eyes to find several cloaked men in the doorway, silhouetted against the light of a torch.

"Come, quickly. There is little time." Not Nerenoth's voice.

Lekore hesitated. "Why do you rescue me?"

"I will explain all, but only after we are away from this foul quarter. Please."

The urgency of the man's tone spurred Lekore forward. He reached the door, and a hand seized his wrist.

"Come," the voice said. "This way."

He slipped his boots off and abandoned them in a corner, to stay quiet. Then he allowed the figure to pull him down the damp corridor running beneath the Cathedral of the Sun, his mind stumbling through questions too rapid to catch. Adrenaline surged through his limbs, carrying him along despite his bruises, despite the weakness of his joints from his recent fever, despite the hunger rumbling in his belly.

On the cloaked figures moved, three, perhaps four of them, clambering along the walkway, loud in the stillness of night. In the wilds near the Vale That Shines Gold, these men would long have been tracked down and eaten by emockye or worse things prowling in the night.

They guided him up a flight of stairs and along dark corridors flanked in shadows until at last they reached a wall. One figure slid his hand along the stones until, with a rumble, the wall slid aside. The band emerged in a dilapidated courtyard. Here, under the bright moon, a garden of weeds stretched before him. A broken statue stood headless in its center.

Chills spidered up Lekore's spine. "What is this place?"

"The grounds of the Holy Temple of the Moon," whispered the man clutching his wrist. "Come. Not much further now." He tugged until Lekore's feet followed.

The head of the statue lay in a clump of flowering weeds whose barbs nestled the statue's face. Lekore shrank away from the clump, then staggered as his rescuer pulled him on. Ahead, a square building hunkered against the night, pillars broken, stone surface dark and scarred. Did Lekore imagine the lingering scent of smoke as he neared the cracked and crumbling steps?

"Lekore!"

He whirled. "Skye?"

The hand gripping his wrist tightened. "Come, hurry now. We must seek shelter before your disappearance is discovered."

Had Lekore imagined the voice calling out to him? The courtyard stood empty. No spirits, no ghosts, roamed its ruinous splendor. He turned back to the edifice, nerves taut. "I think...I would rather not go in."

Scraping metal whispered on the air. Lekore stared down at a dagger pointed at his gut.

"I must insist," said the man.

Heartbeat rapid, Lekore looked up into the moonlit face hooded under a cowl of black. "Do you mean to harm me, after all the trouble you have undergone to rescue me?"

"I would much rather avoid it if you would be so good as to cooperate. Please, my lord."

Lekore stiffened as the dagger pressed nearer. He swallowed and nodded. "I will come."

The stairs gave way to a stone landing before the wide archway to the building proper. No door barred the way into the black maw. As Lekore stepped across the boundary and into the building itself, a heaviness fell over him, smothering like a thick fur. He drew a quaking breath and pressed on, lips trembling. His steps, and those of his rescuers, echoed through the darkness, suggesting a vast chamber hung over them. The single torch did nothing to illuminate the temple beyond a few paces ahead of the company. Grit crunched beneath Lekore's bare feet, and twice, chunks of rubble nipped at his toes.

Minutes stretched on until the company halted before a door sagging on its hinges. The figure holding Lekore's wrist yanked, and Lekore tripped after him as the man swung the door aside. The hinges made no sound of protest.

Flames danced in a hearth against the opposing wall of the small chamber, painting the room in hues of red. Despite the dilapidated state of the temple, this room appeared as whole as any of the Lord Captain's apartments, with ornately framed portraits and a single wide mirror. Plush chairs circled an altar of black stone. Lekore shrank back.

"Don't fear, my lord," said his captor, and tugged him into the chamber. "You are among your fellows now."

As his feet sank into a plush rug, Lekore sought the man's face against the shadows of his cowl and found red eyes. Kel eyes. "What do you want with me?"

"I saw you," the man said. "You calmed the storm yesternight. I witnessed you upon the wall as you tamed the wild winds to your will—just as the Voice of the Stars did, many years past. Please, my lord. Sit. You must be hungry."

The other three in the company fanned out and took seats around the altar where they drew back their cowls to reveal faces perfectly Kel-like. Had he expected something different?

The man beside him released his wrist. "Please, my lord. Be welcome and rest." He brushed the hood from his face, revealing the youthful features of someone little older than Lekore. He wore a smile, but his eyes glittered like the high frosts.

Lekore flinched, mouth going dry. "I would rather depart."

The smile stretched as the man's eyes frosted more. "I'm afraid we cannot allow that just yet. There is much to discuss. Please, sit."

"I will not. I must go. A matter of urgency calls me away."

"And go you shall, but not soon. I must examine you, as the Sun Church failed to do. Please allow this graciously, my lord. It will end long before daybreak."

Lekore backed toward the door but struck something solid and breathing. Gasping, he whirled and stared up at a man almost as tall as the ceiling. He was adorned in the white and gold of the Sun Church.

"Ah, Teon, welcome," said the man of frost.

The man-mountain inclined his head. "I've completed my task, my Hakija."

Lekore jerked his eyes back to his captor.

The man's smile softened. "Yes, I too am Hakija, though my province is the night. I am the mouthpiece of the Moon Throne and all its gods—those who were betrayed and abandoned by their brothers. We are like you, Lord Lekore. We strive to purge the corruption and lies of our fellow Kel. Their heinous acts of barbarism, their petty squabbles with the Tawloomez, sear my soul like a terrible fire. They besmirch the name of our Founder and call him fallen. Yet I heard you on the steps of our temple. You called out to him. You spoke his name, not as a fearful Kel or a faithful follower, but as an equal."

Chills danced across Lekore's arms. "Do you mean Skye?"

"Yes!" The frost turned to a cold flame, and the man stepped nearer. "The very one you name! Have you communed with him?" Craving hunger pounded over Lekore like ocean tides until he thought he might drown. He stepped away but found the bulk of the man called Teon. Pinned between stone and water, he shut his eyes and willed the raging emotions to back away.

Skye, where are you?

The Hakija sighed. "We've frightened you. That was never my intent." He gestured, revealing a flash of elegant clothes beneath his cloak. "Teon, bring him near the fire."

Hands seized his shoulders and pushed him from behind toward the fireplace. Against the might of those hands, he could do nothing but obey. Teon steered him around a chair set before the flames, and he sat Lekore down with a nudge that might buckle a pillar. Sinking into the cushions, Lekore sought the fire. No spirits danced in its embers.

The Hakija sat in a chair next to him, eyes probing, but Lekore wouldn't meet that searching gaze.

"Tell me, Lord Lekore. Tell me of Skye Getaal."

Lekore fastened his eyes on the flames and held still. What could he say of Skye that this man would want to hear? He craved something vastly different from truth.

The man leaned closer. "Are you sent by him? Are you as he was? Do you See as he did?"

Starting, Lekore found the man's frost-rimmed eyes.

"Do you?" The man's voice hung low. "Do you See truth, my lord?"

A shudder racked Lekore's bones. He dragged in air. "Please release me."

The man shot from his chair and stood before Lekore like a bird of prey, smile wide and wicked, eyes bright with ice. "It must be true! You, who commands wind, who defies the Sun Church and its lies, who speaks the name of our Founder as an intimate friend —you must See true! Krett, bring me the box."

The scuff of boots moved away. Shuffling noises sounded near the far wall. The feet stumped close and halted beside Lekore's chair.

"Holiness."

The dark Hakija reached beyond Lekore's view, then turned to face him again, a rectangular black box clutched in both hands. Runes adorned its exterior; as Lekore studied them, fingers of fear clasped his heart. The box exuded a miasma, reeking of blood and cruelty. Dark tendrils of magic dripped through its restraints.

"What is this?" he gasped.

"A gift from our gods, my lord. You feel its full potency, don't you?" The man knelt before the chair. "Teon, hold him still."

The vise-like grip clamped down on Lekore's shoulders. His heart leapt into his throat, and he pressed back against his chair as the Hakija held the box closer.

"Please, I do not wish to see..."

Those frosty eyes gleamed. "It appears you do not know what you are, Lord Lekore. I should have expected as much. The words of the Star Gods implied it, and their Voice declared it in prophecy. You know not what you are!" His eyes flicked to something behind Lekore. "Krett, hold up his arm."

Gloved fingers slithered into view and plucked up Lekore's arm to keep it steady.

The Hakija drew a dagger from his cloak. The firelight reflected off the blade as he tipped it near Lekore's arm and tore the delicate fabric of his sleeve from wrist to shoulder, revealing Lekore's bandages from his fight against the Tawloomez at Halathe. "This needn't hurt too much. Hold still, my lord."

Lekore wrenched against Teon's grip, but the man never budged. His fingers tightened. Lekore's muscles throbbed. "Stop," he whispered, voice cracking.

The blade bit into his flesh. Dug in. A bead of blood swelled up and spilled down his arm to drip onto the slick fabric of the chair. The Hakija dug deeper and sliced toward himself, drawing a line along Lekore's skin. The pinprick pain danced up his arm. He flinched and sucked in a hissing breath as the blood soaked into his torn sleeve. His heart pulsed against his skull.

The Hakija pulled the dagger back and tucked it away in the folds of his cloak. He bent down, retrieved the black box, and opened it with a click. His fingers plucked up something within its velvet confines. He held up a polished stone, black but for a purple flame burning in its center. This, the Hakija lowered to Lekore's bleeding arm.

The taint of the miasma rushed over Lekore's flesh, nauseating. He struggled against Teon's grip, but the man's fingers dug in harder until he cried out.

"A moment more, my lord. Only a moment." The Hakija's eyes met his. "To be alive for this...to be among the chosen... It is almost intoxicating."

Lekore ripped his eyes from the man's face and stared at the flaming stone. "Do not do this. Please. It is evil." He swallowed bile.

"You beg in ignorance, chosen one. But you will soon learn." The man pressed the stone to the wound.

The flame within brightened, and a pulse rushed through Lekore's frame, chilling his bones until they ached. He gulped in air as tears pricked his eyes.

The Hakija leapt to his feet. "Do you see? We have summoned them! The flame burns with such radiance." He clutched it to his heart, then found Lekore with his hungry eyes. "They are coming for you, Lord of Starlight. Krett, is our guest's room prepared?"

"Yes, my Hakija."

"Good. Teon, make certain he reaches his room unmolested. Krett, lead the way, if you please."

The man-giant pulled Lekore to his feet and steered him around his chair. Chilled as he was, Lekore found his limbs sluggish and heavy, though his mind raced. He must escape. He must flee Inpizal and all its horrors. His eyes flicked about the chamber, but only the door provided any kind of exit. Teon guided him toward it. Just as well. Outside the stifling chamber, more possibilities might present themselves.

His stomach heaved.

Krett entered the vast space outside the room. Teon pushed Lekore out next. In the hollow hall, the shriek of the distant wind rattled above the roof.

He canted his head. *Why can you not come in?*

Krett turned left. Teon forced Lekore to follow.

Shadows drew closer, drawing the impression of an archway made of black stone; beyond that, a corridor stretched further into the temple. *I cannot go in or I shall never come out.*

He tried to halt, heart pounding in his ears, but Teon shoved him onward.

"Hold a moment," said Krett. He slipped into the darkness ahead. Voices murmured, then silence descended. Steps approached. "All right, it's clear."

"Who were you speaking to?" asked Teon.

"His guard. All is well."

A door creaked open in the darkness. Within the chamber, Lekore glimpsed a narrow bed draped in black blankets. A torch nestled in a sconce on the wall.

"Enter," said Krett.

Teon pushed Lekore inside. Far overhead, the wind screamed, unable to find a way in.

"That will do," said Krett.

Teon hesitated. "I can guard him."

"Unnecessary. You need to return to the cathedral and help search for him. Otherwise, you'll be suspected."

Teon let out a huff. As Lekore risked a glance at the large man, flesh prickling, he noted the hungry look of an emockye in his eyes. The man retreated from the room.

Krett drifted to the door. "I'll bring food. Try to get comfortable. You'll be here for a bit."

Lekore stepped toward him, limbs quivering. "Please. Your Hakija said I might leave by daybreak."

"Things have changed. Rest well." The man slipped out and shut the door behind him. Voices rose, then fell away. No sound of keys in the lock followed. Seconds later, the door groaned as it opened.

"Now would be a good time to slip away, friend," said a voice, unfamiliar, lined in sardonic mirth.

Lekore stiffened and stepped back. "Who are you?"

"One who would rather cut introductions short while we stand in a nest of vipers, if I'm being honest." Warmth curled around those words, welcome as the dawn.

Lekore sprinted to the door and found a friendly face smiling back at him. A young man, barely grown. His eyes held the cunning glint of Lios, Lekore's emockye pup. Despite the ache of his muscles, the chill of his bones, and the blood crusting on his arm, Lekore grinned and gasped out, "Lead on. Please."

"This way." The young man disappeared into the shadows. As Lekore trailed him, he glimpsed the shape of a body sprawled across the corridor floor before his prison.

⸻

LEKORE'S RESCUER LED HIM TO STAIRS PLUNGING DOWN, AND from there, into a hidden network of tunnels reeking of earth and stagnant water. The young man lit a torch, revealing his short, mussed hair, and strode on through the gloom. Walking along the musty earthen corridor, old memories stirred, but Lekore couldn't catch and hold them in his mind. He clutched his arm where he'd been cut and shadowed his rescuer.

Will this end as before? Is he someone I might trust?

Lekore's foot sank into a puddle of water. He glanced down as he withdrew it and sucked in a breath. The sleek form of a water spirit clung to his toes.

"What is it?" whispered the young man, hand falling to the sword hanging from his hip.

"Oh, I...stepped in water. It startled me."

The young man considered him, then nodded. When he started on down the tunnel, Lekore stooped and plucked up the liquid spirit. It flickered between the shape of a fish and a Kel, shimmering and rippling as it giggled without sound.

"Where have you all been?" Lekore asked as softly as he could manage.

It sent the impression of waves against the shoreline, beating, pounding, never breaking free.

"Is the Temple of the Moon beyond your reach?"

The spirit flickered into Kel form and nodded, then turned into droplets, and slipped between Lekore's fingers to splash the dirt floor and seep away.

Lekore rushed to catch up with the young man. The ground sloped upward.

"Soon we'll reach stairs, then the exit," said the young man. "It brings us near the outer walls of Inpizal. I know of a safehouse where you can hide for a while and recover your strength. After that, you'll have a few decisions to make. I imagine they won't be easy ones." His eyes flashed as he glanced back at Lekore. "Did they harm you?"

"Of whom do you speak? Those of sun or moon?"

A pause. "Both, I suppose."

"Yes." Lekore squeezed his arm, chills spidering through his blood. "Both did."

"I'm sorry for that."

"Why do you help me?"

The young man drew a breath. "I don't believe innocent souls should suffer most in political squabbles. Princess Talanee explained your part in all this, and I couldn't stand by and let them tear you to shreds. Whatever the source of your—well, of *you*, your actions have only been kind." He shrugged. "There. See the stairs?"

Lekore dipped his head. The torchlight flickered, and he glanced up to find a fire spirit waving at him among the flames. He smiled, but his lips grew heavy, and he let his thin smile die. So much had happened. His body burned with fatigue, and his mind spun with weariness, but his soul screamed to flee. Disappear. Return to his home far away from Kel.

He shadowed his rescuer up the stairs.

When the hidden door slid aside, a cool breeze stirred Lekore's hair, and a half dozen wind spirits tumbled into his tresses to untangle them. Their presence soothed his soul a little as he followed the young man guiding him along a street. The torch had been left inside the tunnel, doused in another puddle. The moon overhead lit the street well enough.

A wind spirit detached itself from his hair and settled on his shoulder. It fluted an inquiry. He shook his head. No, he wasn't well.

'Come away, Lekki,' the spirit chimed. *'We will carry you.'*

Lekore eyed his guide's tousled head of hair. The young man didn't glance back.

Flee. Run. Escape. His instincts screamed at him to cave to the wind's temptation. His arm throbbed. His bruises twinged.

Lekore nodded. "Thank you," he called.

The young man turned. His eyes widened as the wind spirits lifted Lekore into the air. He arced toward the wall of Inpizal, hair fluttering, heart soaring. Nearly free!

He glanced down as the spirits fleetly carried him over the boundary of Inpizal and into the grasslands west of the highway. No guards looked up. Why would they?

Free. He arced down, and the spirits dropped him in the tall grass. Lekore raced north, toward home.

CHAPTER 16

Talanee shivered. *Did he forget about me, or did he run into trouble?*

She brushed back stray strands of hair and hugged herself to fight off the growing cold. The weather was so odd for the Sunny Season. She shifted her chilled feet, angry at herself for getting into this mess.

Why hadn't she listened to Keerva?

Wait for Ademas. Just wait. If he's not back by dawn, at least you'll have the protection of the Sun Gods then.

The clack of talons pelted the street. Talanee raised her head. Had the Lord Captain sent soldiers to find her? She stood but remained hidden in the shadows of a leaning building, straining to see down the moonlit road. Two pythe soon appeared, one bearing a rider. Behind the pythe, three more reptilian mounts appeared, two of which also bore riders.

Her heart took wing, and she scurried from the shadows to hail her champions; two of them, at least. As they neared her, she rushed past Ademas and his mount to approach the twin brothers of Lord Captain Nerenoth. Jesh and Jeth Irothé smiled down at her, adorned in brown leather travel clothes rather than festival finery.

"Princess," said one of them. She didn't know which. "Are you well?"

"Hardly. How did you meet up with...?" She tossed a dirty look at her cousin, who only grinned.

"We didn't. He met us," the other twin said. "Forgive us. We didn't know you were in trouble."

"It doesn't matter now." She glanced at the riderless pythe. "Which is mine?"

"This one," said Ademas, holding the tether for his spare pythe with its sidesaddle. He also wore travel garb, still green, but plain compared to his earlier ensemble. "Please hurry. The twins and I have somewhere to be, Your Highness, and little time to dawdle." Though his tones held the frank friendliness he often wielded, an underlying rumble punctuated his request.

She frowned, then hoisted herself onto the pythe and arranged her soiled gown around her legs. "What urgency calls you away now, Cousin?"

A grin crossed his face, showing teeth. She colored. Drat. She hadn't meant to give him the satisfaction of acknowledging his heritage. Glancing at the twins, she found them trying to apply the stoicism their elder brother carried so well. They were failing as they stared between Ademas and Talanee.

"The same urgency that calls the twins away," Ademas said, letting his grin settle into a smirk. "The sun-touched Lekore has escaped from the Cathedral of the Sun, and all the Sun Warriors and royal garrison search for him."

Talanee's lips parted. "But *why?*"

Ademas shrugged. "Perhaps incessant questioning didn't agree with him, or perhaps another faction carried him off."

Her eyes narrowed. Did he guess, or did he know something? *He went into the forbidden temple to rescue someone innocent. Is it possible he knew Lekore would be taken?*

The liveried servant at the Cathedral. The Star Worshipers in the slums.

What are you trying to accomplish, Cousin? She didn't dare ask him aloud. Not in front of Jesh and Jeth. Talanee turned to the twins. "I'll help in the search as well."

"I'm sorry," one twin said. "That's not wise, Your Highness."

"Why not?"

The twins exchanged a look. "Well," said one.

"We're not staying in Inpizal."

Talanee folded her arms. "Again, why not?"

They slid their gazes to Ademas. She glared at him.

The young man shrugged. "He flew over the wall." His hand arced over the air to demonstrate.

Her mind tripped over the vision, recalling his exit at Halathe. "I see. Then you did rescue him?"

He sighed. "Time is of the essence right now, Princess."

"But why chase him if he wants to escape?" Talanee asked. "Just report him to the Lord Captain and let the Triad decide how to proceed."

"Well," said one twin, rubbing the back of his neck. "We are, Princess Talanee. That is, we did. Our elder brother gave us strict instructions to protect him should anything arise. Lord Ademas informed us that he helped Lekore to escape from the Temple of the Moon, and that he fled afterward. Our oath demands we follow and protect him."

"And I intend to help," said Ademas. "Which means we can only escort you to the king's soldiers, and then we must be on our way. Lekore was wounded and frightened, and I suspect he's ill. Right now, he might not survive in the wilds, no matter his skills."

Talanee looked between the three young men, noting their grim frowns, their eyes gleaming in the moonlight, the swords strapped to their hips. *I want to go. I want to help him too. But they won't let me; they'll escort me home if necessary.* She lowered her eyes and gripped the reins of her mount. "Fine. Escort me out of this sector and be on your way."

One twin let out a breath. "Yes, Your Highness."

They trotted away from the temple, away from the evil silence of the street, toward the growing hum of the celebrating city.

Talanee scowled. *Are they still celebrating? Or is everyone now looking for Lekore? Or even me. I ran off without giving a thought to what might happen once Keerva reaches the palace and I'm discovered missing.*

How Keerva would be punished.

Talanee slipped her hand into the hidden pocket of her gown and fingered the sheathed dagger. *Let them fret a while longer. Perhaps for once in his life, Lord Father will feel some stab of concern for me—if only because I'm his heir.*

Clouds blanketed the moon, carpeting the road in shadows. Soon the company reached a crossroads where lanterns flickered before a line of comely townhouses. Talanee's nerves relaxed, and she traced the rising sun before her. *Praised be the Sun Throne. We're safe.*

Her eyes fell on Ademas. Was he a Star Worshiper, or had he pretended in order to save Lekore from that vile order of blasphemers? She longed to ask him. Until she knew if he was a traitor to the Sun Throne, she couldn't ignore his potential danger to Lord Father.

She drew a breath and pushed a smile to her lips. "Leave me here. I can make my own way. Lekore's safety is far more pressing a concern."

The twins eyed each other. "Are you certain?" Their voices rang out in unison.

She felt Ademas's narrowed look and tossed her head. "I'm capable of handling myself, or have you forgotten I hold my own in every ladies' sword competition?"

"That doesn't change the fact that you're the princess," said one twin—probably Jeth, the more outspoken of the two.

"No, it doesn't," she said. "And as your princess, I order you to leave me here. I'll return to the palace and make some excuse for my disappearance. Meanwhile," she cast a look toward Ademas, "I'll withhold my judgment of tonight's events until I've had the chance to weigh everything."

Ademas quirked a smile as wind snatched at his tousled hair.

"As you wish, Princess. Come along, my lords. Feels like a storm is brewing. We don't want to miss our chance."

The young men turned, guiding the riderless pythe as they loped north toward the Sunburst Gate. Talanee wheeled south and trotted down the street until the clatter of pythe talons faded behind her. She slowed. Halted. Glanced back.

Safe. She yanked the reins and brought the pythe around. Overhead, the sky darkened more as low clouds circled the city. With Lekore's disappearance, and the impending storm, who would even notice the absence of their princess? Certainly not the king.

"*Ha*." She dug her heels into the pythe's flank and sent it speeding down the street, heading north.

"STICK HIS HEAD ON A PIKE, JASU'HEKAR."

The Tawloomez spy bowed his head to Nerenoth. "As you command, my lord." He stooped, sword in hand, to decapitate the head of the fallen Tawloomez leader. Strewn across the ground, the remains of six Tawloomez warriors would never rise again. Nor would they report they had discovered the south hidden passage into Inpizal.

Nerenoth slipped a cloth from under his breastplate and wiped his sword clean. Upon discovering the party, he and Jasu'Hekar had chased them away from the boulders and cut them down. Now, Nerenoth must return to the hidden door and seal it forever beneath the rocks. Under the full moon, Nerenoth sheathed his blade and turned north. Wind stirred his hair. Clouds gathered over the distant city of Inpizal.

Another storm.

"Hurry, Jasu'Hekar."

"It is done, my lord."

Nerenoth glanced at the grotesque sight and nodded. "Very good. It will serve as a fair warning to any others who venture this far south. We must make haste. A new storm is growing." He swung up into the saddle of his pythe and wheeled north.

Jasu'Hekar sprang onto his own mount.

They rode hard against the rising wind as it howled over the grasslands. Clouds hid the moon. Nerenoth must reach Lekore before the storm grew worse.

CHAPTER 17

Lor'Toreth of the Flame pounded hard against the strange white door, leaving a streak of blood against the gleaming surface. His knuckles throbbed as he sank to his knees and let out a sob.

No answer. No sound beyond the impenetrable barrier that had swallowed his companions in the darkness, shutting him out.

Alone.

He rocked back against his snakeskin wrapped heels and listened to the call of the cheos in the close-knit trees surrounding him. Their song echoed through the hollow of his soul.

Lor scrubbed at his face and staggered to his feet. He stared up at the overgrown structure holding his companions prisoner and pressed his hand against the blood-soaked bandages wrapped beneath his open leather vest. His vision wobbled. His lungs hitched. A cheos took flight somewhere overhead with a warning note. Lor lifted his eyes to track its progress, but the dense canopy of leaves soon swallowed the bird.

The foliage behind Lor rustled.

He stumbled around to face the unseen threat. He already knew what it was. The fierce tree-nesting cheos paid homage to few predators in the Wildwood. Within the treeline, lavender eyes glowed under the large magnos leaves. A faint growl rumbled.

Lor reached for his bone knife, fingers slick, heart trembling.

The emockye lunged. Knocked Lor to the ground.

As the canine beast sank its claws into Lor's shoulders, sharp teeth dribbling with drool as its jaw stretched wide, Lor shoved his knife into its breast. The beast staggered off him with a yelp and sprang into the dense undergrowth, issuing a cry to its pack. Did it demand revenge, or warn them off?

Either way, I am soon dead.

Lor sat up and glanced at his shoulders. Blood oozed from the wounds, thick and slow, poisoned by the emockye's claws. He grimaced and wavered to his feet, dragging his snake-patterned shoulder wrap loose to press to the wound. The ground teetered and he slumped against a tree trunk.

Must get help. Must tell the emockye that the strange door ate my protectors. Ate them like vermin.

Something in his mind told him his thoughts weren't quite hale, but he couldn't worry about that right now. *Must find someone to open the cage.*

He staggered and dodged trees, heading away from the sun. Toward the deepest stretch of the Wildwood. *Why this way?*

He didn't know. Couldn't bring himself to comprehend his steps or where they took him.

Does it matter?

Likely not. Here in the Wildwood, or home in the Firelands of the Tawloomez, did it matter much where the worms consumed his burning flesh?

It's so hot. A flame grows inside me. Find the cheos. Open the maw before the snake finds you!

He laughed. How the Teokaka would revel in his predicament. How she'd lick those bloodred lips of hers and bask in his agonized efforts to escape death.

Yet in the end, I thwarted your efforts to end me yourself. Is that not some triumph, at least?

Or did the vile woman credit herself for driving him from the palace? For sending him plunging into the Wildwood to evade her far-reaching grasp?

The sun tilted sideways. How could that distant orb reach into the depths of this jungle? How did it know to peek in and watch Lor's last moments as it scorched his flesh? Did the Teokaka whisper her secrets to that merciless sphere and ask it to come watch Lor's death throes? Would the sun report all it witnessed here?

I'm lying down. The realization dawned like dripping honey. Lor struggled to sit up and shivered. He brought his knees to his chest to contain his body heat. Hadn't he been scorching moments before? Why hadn't he grabbed a cloak before he fled the palace?

Something stirred before him, something large. He tried to move but found his body slow to heed him. Opening his eyes, he spotted a form; tall, very tall, blurry, and topped with green. A tree? It quivered and then bent down to study him.

"It is strange to see someone in the *Ava Vyy.*"

Lor stared at the blurred form, smiling. The tree could talk! It had a heavy accent, but it could talk all the same. What did it mean by *Ava Vyy?*

The tree bent closer still, and a human hand touched Lor's forehead. Did the tree have hands? Perhaps it was part man. The tree-man said something in a language Lor didn't know, and then he felt himself hefted off the ground, cradled like an infant rather than the young man of eighteen seasons that he was.

The tree-man didn't feel like bark, though he did smell of green things. As consciousness slipped, Lor wondered if the tree-man was not a tree at all, but only a man.

———

THROUGH A CLOUD OF FEVER, LOR TOSSED AND WRESTLED against his nightmares. Time stretched into the nether fields of his mind, lost in visions of laughter and lurking shadows. Whispers surrounded him, sometimes low and inaudible, other times howling like the wind had broken free of all its restraints and conquered the world. Thunder boomed around him. Laughter, cold and deep, shuddered through his frame.

The torment endured until Lor had no strength to resist. He could only lie in his bedding and heed the words rushing like poison through his blood.

'You're insane, little prince.'

'You're weak.'

'No one can trust you to rule.'

'You had another fit. It's growing worse each time.'

'Run, Lor'Toreth. Run before she kills you.'

'It's only a matter of time.'

'Only a matter of time.'

'A matter of time.'

'Run, little prince.'

'Run before I get you.'

Lor bolted upright with a scream. Sweat trickled down his face, and he wiped it away as he ran a hand through his long, brown hair.

He found himself on a pallet of woven grasses. A square room surrounded him, small, littered with books piled in stacks, teetering and leaning against one another. The floor appeared to be made of wood and the walls were covered with drawings: circles and strange writing on bits of parchment. Wrinkled up parchment also littered the floor.

In one corner hung a lamp, unlit, swinging in a breeze wafting through a hidden flaw in the corner. The wind moaned beneath the floorboards. Gloom hung over the room, though light filtered in from cracks in the ceiling.

Slipping out from under a woolen blanket, Lor placed his bare feet on the floor and listened for sounds of life. He recalled, as he moved with a wince, the blade he had taken from the traitor who tried to kill him, followed soon by the attack of that emockye. Yet here he sat, alive, mending.

How?

The memory of the talking tree flitted into his mind. *Ludicrous.* He couldn't stifle a soft laugh. Pain throbbed through his side, and he drew a sharp breath.

"Awake, then?" asked a pile of books.

Lor shot to his feet as though struck with a dart. Fresh pain erupted through his body, and he fell to his hands and knees, gasping.

"That was stupid," said the books.

Lor raised his head to stare through his long hair at them, arms trembling. "Who—what are you?"

A rustle sounded beyond the books and a man rose behind them. He *was* a man in appearance, though his short hair was the deep green of a Wildwood tree. His eyes, too, were green, glittering like emeralds. He wore not the garb of a wildman, but finely woven clothes of green and black in a fashion akin to the heathen Kel. He looked well-groomed and his frame was broad.

"Am I a who or a what, have you decided?" the man asked in a soft, wry voice.

"I am uncertain," Lor said, struggling to his feet.

"What makes your decision so difficult?"

"I have never seen such hair as yours."

"You've seen very little," the man said. "If your hair can be brown as the dirt, why can't mine be green like the treetops?"

Lor considered that. "But no one is born with green hair. The Kel are born with blue, but never green."

"But I'm not Kel, and I'm not Tawloomez." The man moved around a precarious stack of books. "I'm something else."

"Are you a god?" Lor asked, wondering why the thought hadn't struck him before. Green was just the color for a Snake God.

The stranger laughed; a sound warm like a crackling campfire. "Me, a god? What would the old man say to that?"

Lor's face heated. "If you're not a god, and you're not a man, what then are you?"

The laughter ceased, but amusement etched across the stranger's face. "You don't think I'm a man?"

Lor hesitated. "You say you're neither Kel nor Tawloomez."

"That doesn't make me not a man." He padded forward, feet covered in stockings. "You must've agitated your wounds a lot, springing up like that. Let's avoid sudden movement in the future." He took Lor by the arm and guided him to a sturdy-looking chair. "I'm Keo, by the way. Your turn. Give me a name."

"Lor'Toreth." He sat, flinching as his side panged.

Keo's brows drew together as he crouched and shifted Lor's vest to prod at his bandages. "Toreth. That was your father, right? He died here."

Lor stiffened. "How did you know?"

"I saw it happen. I tried to intervene, but the *Ava Vyy* will have its way." Nodding, he rocked back onto his heels. "You'll heal if you're careful."

"You have said this thing before, '*ava vyy.*' What does it mean?"

"It's hard to explain. Roughly, it means 'weird wood' or 'unnatural forest,' but *Ava Vyy* sounds more mysterious. Not to mention prettier."

"Prettier? There is nothing pretty about the Wildwood."

Keo snorted and stood up. "Sure there is. But fear makes a man blind. You'll have to stay here for quite some time before you see the grandeur of this unholy place."

"Unholy is more fitting a word." Lor shivered. Of course, he must still be within the Wildwood. "If you are only a man, how do you survive in this place? You say you saw my father die. That was years ago. How could you live so long here?"

"I'm special."

"That explains nothing."

"Which is as much as I care to explain, at present." Keo weaved his way through the piles of books to a covered window. He pulled aside the tattered canvas to let in more light. "You might care to see where I live but mind your injuries. I don't want to bandage you again so soon."

Lor rose, nursing his side with a hand as he weaved along the same path his host had taken to reach the window. He looked out and sucked in air. He had thought to be within a hut on the jungle floor somewhere, but while in a hut he was, it stood on stilts far above the ground. The tops of trees bordered the structure; they swayed in a strong wind carrying the wet scent of a coming storm.

"How does it stand?" Lor asked.

"Very precariously, on its own. I fortify it a little, I'll admit. I'm no architect."

Lor backed away from the window. "How do you climb up here?"

"A woven ladder. It was difficult carrying you up a hundred feet."

"A hundred feet." Lor wobbled. He turned to find his chair, but the floor felt paper thin beneath him.

"You look pale."

"Can your hut hold our weight?" Lor asked, voice pitching higher.

"It has so far." Keo sighed and caught Lor's arm. "Come on." He guided him back to the chair and sat him down. "I don't expect you're at your best yet, but I wouldn't mind a thank you. I saved your life a week ago, or don't you remember?"

Lor blinked, then met the alien green eyes above him. "You did."

"And?"

"And I thank you." Lor blinked again, some of his sense returning as the shock subsided. "I thank you with my whole heart. If I can repay the debt—"

"That's more like it," Keo said, nodding. "We'll speak of life debts later. You must be hungry."

"I am," Lor said, though he wasn't certain.

"Good. You're not a complete idiot, I'm glad of that." A grim smile flitted across his face, then vanished. "Food'll be done in a minute."

Lor rested his hand over his side and stared at the mess of

books, thoughts a tangled heap of words he couldn't capture. Something prodded at his mind. Something urgent.

Think of it later. It will return if you don't try so hard.

Better to rest. Then he could sort out the troubles lying scattered in his fevered head.

.

CHAPTER 18

Huddled in the grass, Lekore tried to ignore the wind spirits whispering around his head. He curled closer to the large rock he'd found for shelter against the rising storm.

'*Rise, Lekki,*' shrieked the wind spirits. '*Aid us. Help!*'

Lekore pushed himself upright and stared into the wrathful heavens. Lightning seared the clouds. He could taste electricity upon the wind. The spirits snatched and tossed his hair.

"Why do you rage?" he whispered.

'*Remember. Don't you remember? Trapped. Ailing.*'

'*Help!*'

Lekore pulled himself to his feet and stared into the lashing storm. *That's right. I left Inpizal to save the trapped spirits. I must go into the Wildwood.*

How had he forgotten?

He lifted his hands against the gale as the scent of damp grass and loam coiled around his nose. "I'm going! Calm yourselves, or I won't have the strength to aid you. Please, be calm!"

'*Do you promise, Lekki? Will you come?*'

"I give you my oath, I will come now. Please still the storm."

The clouds broke apart as the wind ceased its screams and dropped to a strong breeze. The spirits settled into Lekore's hair and clung to his pale blue tresses. He staggered forward, every movement jolting his ragged frame.

He had run as long as he could through the night, until the storm reached an intensity that pushed him from his feet. His muddled thoughts had bidden him to find shelter. Anything more would be too much. But now, wading through the knee-high grass of Erokel, Lekore's mind sharpened in the nippy breeze, and he recalled all that had befallen him in Inpizal.

I will never go back. I cannot face them again.

The wind spirits leapt from Lekore's hair and fluted a warning. Lekore whirled. Pythe rode hard toward him. Four. No, five. One loped far behind the others, out of sight, but not invisible to the wind. Lekore whipped back around and fled before the riders.

"Please wait!"

Lekore faltered. He knew that voice. He had heard it once in the darkness of the Lord Captain's guest chamber. Tossing a glance over his shoulder, Lekore slowed his pace, then stopped and turned. The nearest pythe came into unimpeded view, trotting against the wind. The clouds in the sky broke apart to reveal the glow of first light, gray and silver in the passing storm. Jesh Irothé approached, an arm lifted as though he could stop Lekore's progress from a distance.

Instinct pulsed through Lekore's body, urging him to run. Yet something held him still. The four pythe reached him, one without a rider. Lekore stared into two more familiar faces. One belonged to his rescuer from the dark temple. The other—

Lekore slanted his head. "You have his face." He nodded toward Jesh.

The identical man grinned. "I ought to. I'm his twin."

"Twin?"

"We're brothers," said Jesh. "We shared our mother's womb and were born on the same day. Jeth there is a few hours older than I. Some twins share the same face, others don't. We're among the lucky few."

Lekore looked between them. "Remarkable." Even their

apparel matched, but for the color of their capes: one blue, the other red.

"It certainly is," said his rescuer, leaning forward on his pythe. As Lekore met his eyes, the young man grinned. "I'm Ademas, by the way. After everything, we should be properly introduced."

"I am Lekore. I thank you again for your help." He looked between the three young men on pytheback. "Why have you come here?"

The twins eyed each other. The one called Jeth answered. "Our brother asked us to keep you safe while he sees to a matter south of Inpizal. He knew the Star Worshipers would take an interest in your gifts after you calmed the storm on the city wall. When we first heard the call of your escape from the cathedral, we feared it might be worse than it sounded." He gestured to Ademas. "When we met up with him, he confirmed our suspicions."

"If you'll return with us to Inpizal," said Jesh, shifting in his saddle, "we vow to keep you protected. No one needs to know your location."

Lekore shook his head. "I cannot return. I must see to something." The spirits stirred his hair. "If I do not, the storm will rise again."

"Truly?" asked Jesh.

"Something is causing these storms beyond the whims of nature?" asked Ademas.

"Yes," said Lekore. "It is difficult to explain. I am sorry, but I must be on my way."

"Can we help?" asked Jesh.

His twin nodded. "Yes, let us come with you."

Ademas snorted. "Do you even know where he's going?"

The twins shrugged. "Our vow commits us to stay near Lekore," said Jeth. "I'd rather face the wild Lands Beyond than my brother's wrath should we fail him."

"That is where my journey takes me," said Lekore. "To the Wildwood you call the Lands Beyond."

The twins' faces froze. Their knuckles whitened over their reins.

Ademas laughed. "Bold words, tested so soon. What will you do, Lord Jeth?"

Jeth drew his shoulders back. "I am bound to follow, just as I said, my lord."

A wind spirit settled on Lekore's head and dangled miniature Kel-like feet before his eyes. It tugged on his hair.

"I must go now, and swiftly." Lekore inclined his head. "Please do not worry for my safety. You should return to your duties within your walls."

"Not so fast," said Jeth, and he urged his pythe forward. "We promised our brother. That isn't something you can ask us to break. It *is* our duty to protect you in his absence."

Lekore sighed, chest tightening as annoyance shot through him. "Come, if you must. But do not impede me."

Jeth arched an eyebrow. "We came to assist, not to burden you. Will *this* help?" He tugged on the lead of the riderless pythe, and the omnivorous reptile strode forward, chewing a clump of grass still clinging to its roots. "You'll reach your goal much faster with her as your legs."

Lekore blinked at the pythe.

"Assuming he doesn't just ride the wind," Ademas said.

Lekore glanced at his rescuer, then back to the pythe. "The wind is fickle. It carries me far, only to drop me and run off to sea." He batted the dangling wind spirit from his head. "Perhaps this is the wisest course. I shall ride your pythe, though might I do so without the saddle?"

"Well, I suppose." Jeth scratched his neck. "You might be more comfortable with it on."

Lekore nodded. "I will try it so." He glanced past the riders. "What of your straggler?"

Ademas didn't follow the twins' puzzled glances southward. "I'm certain she'll catch up soon," he said. "Shall we be going?"

"You're coming too, my lord?" asked Jesh.

"Certainly." Ademas grinned. "I relish the opportunity of entering the Lands Beyond to test my mettle, especially if I can help to stop these storms." He adjusted his satin-lined cape to emphasize the chill in the air.

Lekore allowed the wind spirits to lift him onto the pythe's back. He felt eyes staring as he ran his hands across the shimmering green scales of his mount and the stubs where Skye said the species' wings had been five hundred years ago. Then his fingers stroked the beast's coarse black mane. "Let us be on our way." He leaned forward and patted the pythe's head. "Come along." It loped forward as the earth spirits at its taloned feet repeated Lekore's request.

"By the way," Lekore heard Jeth say behind him, "*who* is following us?"

"The princess," Ademas replied. "I figured she would."

The twins groaned, but the wind snatched away words as Lekore's pythe dug its talons into the earth, then leapt forward to race toward the northern mountains and the shadowed realm swallowing their roots. The wind followed him, its spirits dancing and urging him onward.

'Hurry,' they sang. *'Hurry, Lekki. Save them!'*

———

TALANEE SLOWED HER PYTHE.

The streaming smoke of a small fire plumed above the hills surrounding Halathe, whose ruinous walls jutted up like bleached bones under the broad light of the zen-hour sky. She squinted at the bright sun, glad of its company. As she loped into the ruins, her gaze flicked to the faint stains left from the battle not so long ago. Beneath the tower she'd climbed, a company of four crouched before a cook fire, meat roasting above it.

Heads lifted as Talanee approached.

"Hail, Princess," said Ademas with a grin. "Hungry?"

How like him to not show surprise. She tossed hair from her

shoulder. "A little." Her attention turned to Lekore, who hovered closest to the food and eyed it with a considering frown. He looked a grimy mess, from his torn and bloodied sleeve to his smudged breeches and blackened bare feet. *Was he crawling around in a dungeon or something?*

A moment more he shifted the angle of the meat, then at last lifted his gaze to her.

"Hello, again," he said in a soft voice. Something in his manner had changed; the light had dimmed in his eyes; a tension pinched his shoulders in a feral hunch.

A wrenching pain twisted her heart. *He saved my life, but at what cost to his own?* She tried a smile. "I still owe you thanks for saving me."

"That is unnecessary." He dropped his eyes back to the food.

The twins strode to Talanee's side, and each offered his hand. She accepted both and let them help her dismount, then she stepped across the white stones of the ruin, wincing as pebbles bit her bare feet, and stood before the cook fire.

She folded her arms. "What are we eating?"

"Cheos," said a twin. "You should've seen Lekore here take it down. You'd have thought the bird a common thing—none of its fierceness had any effect. And then Lekore conjured the fire from nowhere."

Talanee nodded. "Yes, I've seen him do that before."

"As have I," said the other twin.

"You have?" his brother asked.

Talanee dismissed the Irothé brothers as they discussed an attempt on Lekore's life as he'd slept in the Lord Captain's home. Ademas shifted, giving his full attention to the story. Lekore rotated the meat again, shoulders hunching more.

She stepped to the young man's side and crouched beside him, swiping her sullied skirts away from the threat of embers. "You've had nothing but trouble since you've come to Erokel." Her eyes danced again to his shoulder where his torn sleeve revealed soiled bandages.

She bit her lip, recalling the scissor knife biting into his flesh, then she sighed. "Even before that. I feel responsible somehow."

His fingers pressed the bandages, then fell away. "I chose to come here. I chose to fight the Tawloomez. I also chose to follow the Lord Captain to your city." He turned the bird over. "Now I choose to enter the Wildwood to stop these storms. Afterward, I shall return to my home, and let you and your people make your own choices without me."

"I don't want that for you." The words tumbled from Talanee's mouth, sharp and soft. She grimaced. Too late to keep her peace now. "You're one of us, Lekore. You're Kel."

"And if I do not wish to be your idea of Kel...?" His tones pattered like gentle rain, soft and hesitant. His brow knitted as a faint frown brushed his lips. He dragged his eyes from the cooking cheos and pinned a look upon her, both reproachful and brimming with pity. "I witnessed the murder of children in your holiest habitation, Princess Talanee. The thrill and hunger of your people colored the very air in hues of red. To you, to all of you, those infants mean nothing but an added expense, and a possible threat, if kept alive. Is this not so?"

Heat rushed over her. "They're only Tawloomez."

"No." Lekore's eyes caught fire, but his tone remained low. "Even *you* cannot believe such words. Are they only Tawloomez, or are they your enemy? You cannot brush off their significance in one thread of speech, only to let your hatred for them consume you in a moment of hunger tomorrow. Do their children mean nothing to you beyond a momentary thrill and a means to conserve food, or are they a threat to your people, put down to preserve your way of life?"

She scowled. "You make it sound so shallow. But I won't let you vilify your own people. I'll tell you what they are to us: a blight! A filthy heathen race created by the Star Gods to plague us—and to destroy us if they can. They're a lesser race created by lesser gods. We can do with them as we please, for doing so pleases our gods. Now do you understand?"

He leapt to his feet, nimble as a bird springing from a branch, but his eyes glowed in the sunlight. "No! I do not *want* to understand." He twisted away, shoulders trembling, burying his face in his hands.

Talanee stared up at him. Grit crunched beside her, and she glanced right to find Ademas standing nearby. He studied Lekore, eyes narrowed, knuckles pressed to his lips. A heartbeat passed, then he stepped around Talanee and halted behind Lekore.

"You don't need to understand."

Lekore turned, eyes clouded. He blinked at Ademas. "What?"

Ademas shrugged. "Did anyone require you to understand us?"

Silence settled over the company, but for the whispers of the fire and the sizzle of the bird over its flames. Lekore searched Ademas's face, eyes darting back and forth. He drew a breath, and his shoulders stopped trembling.

"No one did," he whispered. "Yet, always I have felt and understood what I see. The emockye hunts when it is hungry. The cheos kills to protect its nest. The trees stretch their roots to live. The water flows to nourish the land. All things wish only to survive. All things, yet not Kel." He shook his head. "You live for something more than survival. More than to protect yourselves. Am I expected to be thus? Am I to thirst after blood and dominate other life?"

"Did someone request you to conform?" Ademas's voice held only a question, even and direct. Talanee sensed no malice or mockery.

Lekore's shoulders trembled again. "Yes. Your Hakija... He wishes it. Because I would not, he intended to lock me away forever."

Ademas raised his hand and gripped Lekore's arm. "I won't let that happen."

Lekore gazed at the young man's fingers. "Your Lord Captain vowed the same, but there are promises a man cannot keep."

"That's true," said Ademas. "But there are promises a man *can* keep. This is one. And if Lord Captain Nerenoth has made the same oath, you're twice as likely to escape from a life sentence locked in the bowels of the Holy Church."

Talanee rose and stepped closer. "Don't be reckless. The Hakija is much more powerful than you, *Cousin*. He's not an enemy you want to make, no matter your lineage. Don't defy the church."

Ademas glanced at her. "I don't defy the church, Your Highness. I defy only what I feel is *wrong*, as well as those who commit wrong. Do you condone the Hakija's actions?"

She tensed. "What kind of question is that? Don't you dare drag me into this. As the heir of Erokel, I can't become involved. Lekore's fate isn't mine to decide."

Ademas's frown stretched into a faint sneer. "Typical bureaucratic answer. Well said, Cousin. How worthy of the daughter of Netye."

Anger flashed over her like a bolt of lightning. She snarled and threw her hand out to slap his cheek with all her strength—but a hand caught her wrist and pulled her off course.

Heat poured over her, and she jerked back. "Let me go!" Her eyes collided with Lekore's as he held her in place.

"Please, do not hurt him. Please. I will let you go if you promise not to hurt him."

Caught by his stare, shame rolled through Talanee like ocean waves. She offered a curt nod. "Fine. I promise. Even though he deserves it."

Lekore lowered her arm and released her wrist. "Thank you." He staggered back but caught himself. "I do not desire to interfere or disparage your pain, but there has been enough anger...enough hurt...enough..." He swallowed. His eyes flicked to Ademas. "I am very grateful for your desire to protect me from the Hakija, yet that alone is not enough. You cannot safeguard me from all dangers. I do not intend to return to Inpizal unless I am called upon by forces greater than any Kel."

"Aren't you?" asked Talanee, dropping her gaze to the ground. "You summoned fire by the will of the gods. Didn't they send you to save me and my escort?"

"I do not know your gods," Lekore whispered. "I do not think I want to know them." He stooped to turn the bird again. "The meal is nearly ready."

Talanee glanced toward the pythe to find Jesh and Jeth Irothé keeping a respectful distance as they fed handfuls of grass to her tired mount.

No one spoke as Lekore pulled the bird off his makeshift spit and produced a knife to carve the cheos into portions. He offered the first cut to Talanee, and she took it with a grimace as grease covered her fingers. Casting about, she padded to a broken boulder of white stone and sat to nibble at the meager fare. Then blinked. Cheos was a rare delicacy in Inpizal and not one she favored. But somehow this bird tasted savory, and her teeth sank into its flesh with ease. She swallowed and licked her lips.

"It's very good," she said.

Ademas accepted the second helping Lekore offered, then his gaze settled on Talanee. Several moments passed, then he sighed and approached her. "May I sit here, Cousin?"

She glared at him, willing him to feel her displeasure. He eyed her back, unaffected. Then a smile touched his lips, and he sat just the same.

"I need to apologize," he said, juggling the hot bird in his hands. "I lost my temper, and that isn't something I often do. My words were cruel and foolish in equal measure. Will you forgive me?"

Talanee shifted to face him. "I didn't take you for the kind of man who seeks forgiveness."

"Only when I'm certain I'm in the wrong. I assure you, that's very rare." He flashed his amiable smile as his eyes sparkled. "What say you, Cousin?"

"On one condition."

"Being?"

"Never, *never* use my father's name against me, ever again."

The mirth faded in his eyes as his smile dropped. "Ah." He took a bite of cheos. "Oh, that's good. That's really good." He chewed and swallowed. "Very well, Princess Talanee. I promise, never again, or you can hate me forever."

His attention flicked to Lekore, who sat at the fire with the Irothé twins. "Something terrible happened to him in the Temple of the Moon. Something that's shaken him deeply. I want to ask him about it, but I don't want to scare him off. One false move, and I think we'll never see him again." Ademas sighed. "I can't say why, but I want to avoid that at any cost."

———

AFTER THE MEAL, LEKORE SLIPPED AWAY FROM HIS KEL companions to bury the cheos bones while the twins saddled up the pythe. Hidden by the decaying walls of Halathe, Lekore closed his eyes to absorb the bliss of being alone.

So much of his life had been spent alone. He had come to relish it, except in the darkest stretches of night when bad dreams came. *There are other times, too. Do not fool yourself.*

He knelt and dug with his borrowed knife in the dirt. What should he do in company with these strangers? How should he behave?

I thought I was prepared to face them.

"How do you fare, Lekore?"

He gasped and snapped his head up. "Skye! Where have you been?"

The translucent man stood before him in ancient, sharply angled armor that flashed and winked beneath the sun, a red cape draped over one shoulder. Skye's red eyes searched Lekore's face, brow creased. He crouched to level himself with his student. "I must apologize. I did not expect your circumstances to take such a dark turn, and so swiftly. Star Worshipers are rarely as bold as that. I tried to warn you, but the borders of that unholy temple are impossible for me to cross. Even the spirits cannot enter its grounds, nor the dungeons of the Sun Cathedral."

Lekore bowed his head as chills crawled over his flesh. "I

suspected as much, after you called my name. I could hear the wind howling even within the black walls." He rested his hand over the cut on his arm. "I met a dark Hakija. He drew my blood, Skye, and pressed a strange stone to the wound. Its heart flamed purple and made my very bones ache with cold. Even now, I feel a kind of hollowness in my soul." He clutched at his chest. "He told me that they follow you. That you are their founder."

The ghost scoffed. "I'm not their founder, but never let it be said a Kel cannot delude himself into any justification." He sighed. "Do you seek the trapped Spirits Elemental?"

Lekore nodded. "Are you not worried by the black stone and the use of my blood?"

"I am worried. But you must focus on stopping these storms and let me investigate the Hakija of the Night. I will learn what I can, though I fear I already know what his actions will bring about."

"Will you not tell me?"

"I will only if need be. If I can spare you one burden, please let me."

Lekore studied Skye's eyes. Fear filled them like the floods of the Rainy Season pouring into the Vale That Shines Gold.

The ghost offered a faint smile. "Ter and I have done all we know to prepare you for what you now face, Lekore. Be brave. Muster all your strength. Do not flee from your calling."

Lekore dipped his head. "What if I am not equal to what you have foreseen?"

Skye laughed. "Impossible. You have the strength of an emockye pack and the cunning of a cheos mother. You will manage." He rose as his form faded upon the breeze. "Lekore, the Kel are afraid of what they do not understand. If you run from them because they frighten you, you are guilty of the same. Farewell for now. I will return when I can."

The wind scattered the last reflection of his armor, casting prismatic light across the ruins before leaving Lekore alone. He bent and covered the cheos bones.

Finished, he straightened and stared at the white tower where first he had seen the princess of Erokel. "If ignorance makes me afraid, I must educate myself." He shuddered. "Though I do not relish the task."

He set his shoulders and strode back into the ruins.

CHAPTER 19

Rez saluted, still clad in his dress armor and a red and gold cape for Blood Day. "Welcome back, sir. The king requests your presence immediately. All that could go wrong in your absence has."

Nerenoth held in a sigh. "With me, lieutenant. Explain what's transpired."

Together they strode from the garrison building out into the morning glow as Rez Kuaan described the incident at the Rite of Blood, followed by an alarm sounded at the cathedral a few hours before dawn, after someone discovered Lekore had escaped. The Hakija ordered all Sun Warriors and unoccupied soldiers to scour the city in search of him. Dakeer had declared the young man a threat; he must be apprehended at all costs.

Now, upon the front steps of the garrison, Rez sighed as a stablehand raced to the lieutenant's side and bowed.

"Bring our pythe," the Lord Lieutenant said.

The boy sprinted off.

The lieutenant went on. "Somehow, amid all the commotion, Princess Talanee disappeared. According to her lady-in-waiting, the princess thought to follow Duke Elekel's offspring into a less reputable quarter of Inpizal, where she got herself lost. We can't find her or her...uh, cousin. We fear something may have happened to them—something bad. A few priests have accused Lekore of foul play...but honestly, I can't see that."

Nerenoth grimaced at the sun crawling up the sky. "Where is the lady-in-waiting?"

"In the king's dungeon, awaiting judgment for failing to stop the princess."

"Has anyone questioned her?"

"Not beyond her initial confession. We've been up all night searching for an escaped prisoner and two royal persons." Rez blinked. "Oh, this came for you last night. Almost forgot." He dug out a folded note from a pouch at his hip.

Nerenoth accepted the parchment and unfolded it. Jesh's meticulous scrawl had blotted in his haste.

N. We must leave Inpizal to follow your orders. Heading north. Will contact when possible. —J

Folding the parchment, Nerenoth met Rez's inquiring gaze. "We will head first to—"

"One thing more, sir. The Hakija is set to release a public declaration any moment, and from what I can surmise, it won't be good for Lekore."

Nerenoth frowned. "No doubt. Very well, I will answer the king's summons. Head for the cathedral and wait for Dakeer's proclamation to be read, then return and report what he says."

"Yes, sir."

Moments later, the stablehand led two pythe from the stables. Both men swung into their saddles and galloped from the garrison courtyard, pebbles scattering in their wake.

In the courtyard beyond, Nerenoth angled south and guided his pythe into the palace grounds. Guards saluted as he passed. He rode to the wide steps, dismounted, and left his pythe with a liveried servant. Racing up the steps, he weighed the information his lieutenant had presented. He could account for Lekore. Jesh and Jeth wouldn't let Nerenoth down, so they must be near the young man, if not with him. That left the fiasco of finding the princess and her cousin.

Servants scurried out of the Lord Captain's way as he marched along the palace corridors until he reached the throne room. Before he entered, he could hear the king barking out orders.

"—and bring me another goblet of wine. Don't gape at me—off with you, woman! *Where is the Lord Captain? Where is the Holy Hakija?* Don't they know to come when I call?"

Nerenoth inhaled and checked his shoulders as a servant tried to explain to the king that the Hakija was about to make an official declaration.

The guards stationed at the double doors drew them aside at Nerenoth's nod to admit the Lord Captain into the vast chamber. He strode inside, cape billowing, steps clipped and even. Dust from the grasslands coated his armor, dulling its glint, yet he doubted the king would notice. Netye Getaal noticed so little.

The king had been reaching for his fresh goblet but froze as he caught sight of Nerenoth. Relief paled the red of his cheeks as he snatched up the goblet and settled back in his plush throne.

"Where have you been, Irothé?"

Nerenoth allowed his brow to arch. "Putting down the third Tawloomez attack, sire."

Netye opened his mouth to speak over Nerenoth but faltered and finally frowned. "Well. Good, that's excellent. Very good. What was it?"

"An attempt to enter the city through an underground passage in the south to kidnap and murder Lord Barrad's heir. As you can imagine, that would spell disaster for our eastern trade agreements. The warriors sent to accomplish this now lie rotting under the sun. We collapsed the passage."

Netye blinked. "Well." He swirled his goblet. "I'm glad that's tended to. It's about time we showed them the might of Erokel."

"They will try again. If anything, sire, this will anger them all the more. The Teokaka does not like to be bested."

Sipping his wine, Netye snorted into his goblet. "If that should happen, I'm confident you'll beat them again. Meanwhile, things are bad here."

Nerenoth lifted his hand. "I've heard all from my lieutenant. I assure you, sire, I will find your daughter and Lord Ademas."

Netye slammed his goblet down, sloshing wine across his hands and white breeches. "That is *hardly* the most imperative matter right now. Talanee and her foolishness must wait. We've a renegade heretic on our hands! That boy, the one you thought it wise to bring to Inpizal—he's escaped from the cathedral. He's running wild in our streets! The Hakija promised me, he *assured* me he would keep —" He slumped back and swiped a wine-soiled hand over his face, painting his brow the color of blood. "It doesn't matter. See to this, Lord Captain. Find the prisoner and return him to the Hakija."

"I can't do that, sire."

Netye's eyes snapped to Nerenoth's face. "What?"

"It's not possible, Your Majesty. According to my spies, Lekore has already fled the city."

"*What?* How? When?" Netye flung his goblet aside. It landed with a clang, wine sloshing across the dais steps as he leapt to his feet. "Why didn't they stop him if they reported his escape to you?"

Nerenoth stared down his king. "I imagine they tried, yet considering the gifts he has so far displayed, how likely is it that any Kel you know could stop him?"

Blood drained from Netye's face, and he staggered back to land hard against his throne cushions. He pressed his hands to his face. The rings adorning his fingers sparkled as he rubbed his eyes, smearing wine more. "Of course. Of course he escaped. Who could hinder him?" He laughed and dropped his hands to his stained lap. "Yet, that won't stop the Hakija. Not if I know him. That boy will never come back, never. Dakeer will see to it."

Nerenoth stamped down on a nauseating wave of revulsion as he watched Netye Getaal babble, then cleared his throat. "Shall I begin the search for Princess Talanee?"

198

Staring into the abyss before his feet, Netye waved. "Do as you wish."

Nerenoth bowed, turned, and strode across the chamber. *I certainly will, Your Majesty.*

A STREAM OF PEOPLE FLOWED THROUGH THE GOLDEN CATHEDRAL gates across the wide courtyard, returning to their festivities after the proclamation reading, as Nerenoth guided his pythe toward the garrison. Lord Lieutenant Rez waited outside the garrison gate, brows drawn, gaze pinned on the cobblestones beneath his feet. His pythe stood beside him, eating the flowers blooming beneath the garrison's lantern post.

"Well?" asked Nerenoth, as he slowed his pythe.

Rez jumped and clapped a hand to his armored chest. "Sir!"

"What did the Hakija declare?"

Rez's brows pinched closer. "Sir, I'm baffled. The Hakija pronounced Lekore a demon sent by the Moon Throne to deceive and confound us. Yet I saw only—well, innocence and kindness in him. I—I'm not questioning the church—"

"Are you not?"

Rez cupped his hands behind his back. "You're right, sir. It's not my place."

"Perhaps. Perhaps not." Nerenoth nudged his mount past the man. "We have other matters to deal with right now."

"What of Lekore?" asked Rez, following on foot as he led his pythe inside the garrison grounds.

"He's no longer within Inpizal. I have men seeking him."

"Is—Is that wise, sir? I mean, after the Hakija's declaration, should we bring him back or let him alone?"

Nerenoth considered Rez as he halted the pythe before the garrison steps. "Lieutenant."

"Sir?" Rez handed his reins to the stablehand.

Nerenoth dismounted and handed over his reins. "Come with me. There is a matter we must discuss."

"Yes, sir."

The lieutenant followed him inside where the austere white interior echoed with the clamor of pages and soldiers milling about the circular war chamber under a wide domed ceiling. A sergeant at a cluttered table clapped a hand to his breast as Nerenoth strode past on his way to the southern officers' corridor. Several men started toward him, but he lifted his hand, and they halted across the room. Rez trailed after him and shut the door when he entered Nerenoth's private office.

The Lord Captain leaned against his desk, facing the door and his silent lieutenant. He folded his arms and sighed. "Sit, Rez. Please." He gestured to the chair before his desk.

The lieutenant obeyed and stared at Nerenoth. "Sir, you're very grim."

"Can I trust you, Rez? Are you as sincere as you seem?"

Rez's eyes widened. "Sir?"

"I know that your faith in the Sun Gods is sturdy, and that's commendable. Indeed, it lends great merit above all your other accomplishments. But I must ask a personal question, and I need a firm and honest answer...as a friend."

"Yes, sir." Rez shifted in his seat.

"To whom do you bend your knee? To the Holy Hakija and his Sun Priests, or to the Sun Throne itself?"

"Sir, I don't know if I follow."

"Do you lean on the teachings of the church, its modern doctrine, or do you more ardently believe in the Sun Gods, even should they come and rebuke every teaching over the past decade or longer? Where does your heart dwell, Rez Kuaan?"

"With the gods, sir. Always."

Nerenoth dropped his arms to the desk and leaned forward. "Rez, do you swear before the Sun Throne that what I say to you now in confidence will never pass your lips without my consent?

Do you swear to keep this secret with your last breath unless I or the Holy Sun itself declares otherwise?"

"I—yes, yes, sir. I swear it upon the very steps of the Sun Throne."

Nerenoth stood. He turned to the southern window behind his desk and stared out into the gardens beyond the wrought-iron fence of the garrison grounds. Tawloomez slaves weeded the soil beds while a Kel couple strolled along the path meandering beside a stream.

Life goes on, no matter the private storms in people's lives.

He drew a long, fortifying breath. "I have seen a Sun God, Rez."

Air exploded from the lieutenant's lungs. Nerenoth turned around and lifted a hand to keep the questions at bay.

"It was eighteen years ago, on the night King Adelair died. This won't be easy to hear. I've not told a living soul what I saw that night. None of it. If I tell you now, your perspective cannot go back. You will carry this burden with me."

Rez shoved long hair from his face and managed a weak smile. "Sir, you can't leave me dangling after what you've said. Tell me, please. Let me share your burden. I would be honored." His eyes shone, clear and earnest.

Nerenoth's heart swelled. "Very well." He shut his eyes, dredging up the memories. "I discovered the king's body before anyone else, but I chose not to alert the palace staff until I discovered where Prince Adenye had gone. I followed his captor from the palace and into the tunnels beneath Inpizal."

Rez shook his head. "You mean the heir was still alive?"

"Yes. He lives to this day."

"*Sir?*"

"A moment, Lieutenant. That is not the end of my revelations. I have yet to divulge the name of the prince's captor."

"Someone important?"

"King Netye."

Rez shot to his feet.

"Sit down, Rez. I'm not finished."

The soldier dropped into his chair with a clatter of armor. "I... don't understand, sir."

"No, I suppose not. You were quite young. Netye lost his wife shortly before all of this transpired. It...pushed him over a threshold. I believe he lost his mind. All that remained in his view, all that might keep him from succumbing to his grief, was the throne. He had always hungered for it. But Netye had one weakness that remained, even after madness claimed his thoughts. He loved Prince Adenye. He couldn't bring himself to kill the child, despite his callused and cowardly act against his own brother, so instead he led him into the grasslands to abandon him to the wild."

"But you followed him, sir."

"So I did, with every intention of interfering, but I was forbidden to do so."

Rez swallowed as his eyes narrowed. "Forbidden, sir?"

Nerenoth stared at the floor before the lieutenant's chair. "I recall every detail of the Sun God. He was but a child in his form, with hair of golden yellow, and eyes as blue and pure as the cloudless sky. He ordered me to leave the child in his care and to keep my peace. I dared not disobey."

He rested a hand against his brow. "There are times I doubt my own eyes, yet never could I imagine the visage before me. It has led me to doubt much of our priests' rhetoric. If the Sun Gods deigned to rescue the innocent and gentle prince of our people... what can be said of the murderous king who now rules, and those who sanction that reign?" Nerenoth lifted his eyes and lowered his hand. "Lieutenant, the prince once called Adenye is now known as a demon within the walls of Inpizal."

Rez sucked in a breath. "Lekore? *He* is Prince Adenye?"

Nerenoth's stomach knotted. "Remember that you swore you would say *nothing*, Lieutenant. Upon the salvation of your very soul, you swore it. I depend upon your code of honor as I have depended on no one before." He moved from the desk and stepped nearer to the soldier. "Dakeer Vasar knows who Lekore is. He turned a blind eye to Netye's sins eighteen years ago, and now he defies the rightful king of Erokel and calls him heretic and moon-spawn. Yet Lekore—as now he is called—was *raised* by the Sun Gods. Who could better understand their will than him?"

"Sir." Rez licked his lips. "Sir, what will you do? What should we do?"

"My brothers know Lekore's whereabouts. They are near him now." Nerenoth slipped the parchment note from his glove. "I commissioned them to keep abreast of his circumstances in my absence. For the moment, we can do little else beyond search for the princess and Lord Ademas. We must wait." He scowled. "For eighteen years I have waited, and now I must wait on."

"Eighteen years." Rez shook his head. "How have you endured it? Sir, so many think you an unbeliever. So many doubt you have a heart at all. Not me, sir. But I don't know how you've stood against the rumors with such marked indifference."

"I'm not immune to them, Rez, but since I laid eyes upon a Sun God, the opinions of Kel haven't mattered as much as once they did. Do not mistake me: I crave the day when justice will prevail against Netye and his *ilk*. Long have I suffered under the reign of the maddened fool, knowing he struck down his brother and sentenced his nephew to death by starvation or worse. Today, Netye ordered me to find and imprison Lekore, without a thought for his daughter's wellbeing. That man has much to answer for, and Sun Gods willing, I will be there when he does."

His stomach's knots loosened as his muscles eased. He no longer bore the burden of secrets alone.

Rez stood. "I'll reorganize the search for Princess Talanee. We'll comb every inch of Inpizal. But, sir, you needn't join that search. By my way of thinking, if you were blessed to see a Sun God, your place is at the side of our rightful king. Go, sir. Search him out. I'll see to matters here, and I swear on my life, I won't let you down."

CHAPTER 20

Lor curled his hands into fists. "Will you not help me save them?"

The man named Keo looked up from the scribbles he inked across bits of parchment spread over the floor. "Impossible." Ink dripped from his quill.

"Why?" asked Lor.

"Your friends were swallowed up inside that strange building, you said. Well, I can't open it up. Believe me, I've tried. They're absolutely never coming out again."

Lor sank onto his pallet and winced as his side throbbed. "Then they are dead?"

"They will be, eventually." Keo bent to scrawl across a circle of ink. "It's unfortunate, as your actions caused an imbalance not easily remedied."

"What do you mean?"

Keo sighed and plucked up a piece of parchment, studied it closely, then crinkled it up, and tossed it over his shoulder. It landed in a pile of its fellows. Silence resumed its reign in the hut, apart from the moaning of the wind and the creaking of the walls.

"What do you mean?" Lor asked again. He gingerly stood and weaved his way between stacks of books and around discarded candle stubs until he reached the carpet of parchment. "Do not ignore me. Tell me. Please. What did our actions cause?"

Keo lowered his quill and eyed Lor. Seconds passed. "If I tell you, it'll change nothing."

"Yet you mentioned it. Why resist now?"

The man blinked. "Very well, Your Highness. These storms, these frequent outbursts of wind and rain and thunder—you caused them. You and your meddling companions, who couldn't leave well enough alone."

"We sought shelter from the Wildwood."

"Well, now your companions have it indefinitely."

Lor crouched down and searched the man's face. A long scar marred the flesh under one eye. "Why could my companions open the door to that building, yet you cannot?"

Keo's lips curled into a dry smile. "Because those who erected that building are my enemies. I'm barred from that place. And now you've triggered its magic, allowing none to enter." The wind shrieked, and Keo's eyes flicked upward. "Though it seems the Spirits Elemental feel otherwise."

"What do you mean?"

"The storm's requesting help, even as it throws its tantrums. Maybe it's calling the Seer."

"What is that?"

Keo plucked up his quill and dipped it in his inkwell. "The *Ava Vyy* calls him the One Who Sees True. He can see and command the spirit guardians who keep these lands in balance. Now that you've upset that balance, the spirits think their keeper can repair the damage. I'm not sure that's true, but one can always hope."

"A Seer." Lor tapped his fingers to his lips. "Where might I find him?"

"West and a little south of here. He makes his home in what your people call the Valley of Bones."

Lor shuddered and snatched at his snake-bone necklace. "You mean the *Akuu-Ry*? *He* is the Seer who might save my people?"

"If anyone can."

"But he is a demon."

"Who calls him that? Your Teokaka, perchance? The same woman who calls you the mad prince?"

Lor frowned. "Others say he is not a living being. That he is the spirit of a Kel warrior from a past age."

"Interesting. Do they?" Keo shrugged. "Not that this isn't a fascinating conversation, but I have work to do, if you'll excuse me, Prince Lor'Toreth." He bent over a fresh parchment and scratched away.

Lor climbed to his feet and scowled down at the man. "What is so important?"

The quill stopped. "I'm attempting to fortify my home against another gust of wind, so we don't topple to our doom."

"Oh." Lor rubbed his arm and scrutinized the parchment. *Is he mad after all, or can he work magic as the Teokaka can?* He couldn't quite tell. "How long will that take?"

"That depends on how many times you interrupt my concentration."

Lor flushed. "When—when you're finished...when your home is protected...will you help me seek the *Akuu-Ry*?"

Silence. The quill scratched at the parchment. Paused. "Fine. But only if you promise to leave me in peace until I'm done."

A smile bloomed across Lor's lips unbidden. "Yes, I promise. I will say nothing more, no matter how much I am tempted." He tripped his way across the small room and flopped down on his pallet of bedding to watch, ignoring the pulse of pain that rattled up his side. What was pain right now?

CHAPTER 21

Smoke clawed at his lungs, suffocating, burning him from the inside.

He wrenched against the ropes binding him to the well as the stench of rotting flesh assaulted his nostrils. Blood and entrails covered the ground before him, the bright red sheen darkened now to a sickly brown as flies crawled across the corpses. Embers flickered beneath smoke rising like a black scar against the bold blue sky. His gaze drifted across those embers, searching for some remnant of his flame-consumed home.

Anything to keep him from staring at the remains of his family.

His eyes burned. His throat burned.

The world around him burned under the cruel, distant sun.

Why did the gods forsake us?

He slumped against the well. Lank blue hair slid into his eyes as he shifted his feet to avoid the vomit he had retched up yesterzen.

Visions danced before his eyes, replaying the horrors of the Tawloomez attack. He shut them, but the visions brightened against the dark. Blood. Fire. Rape. He gasped out a sob. No tears pricked his eyes. He'd cried his final drops last night. No more would come.

A fly landed on his bare foot. He shrieked and jerked against the ropes as he flailed his foot. The noise caught in his throat until coughs seized his lungs, and he hunched into himself, convulsing until the fit passed.

Why didn't they kill me too? O gods above, why am I left alone?

Footsteps crunched grit.

He lifted his eyes and tried to swallow against the dryness of his closed throat. A figure approached, cloaked in white. The Sun Priest stepped around the rotting remains of fallen Kel, reached the well, and crouched down.

"You poor boy. What is your name?"

"Lekore."

"No," said the priest. "That isn't quite right. Try again."

He held the priest's gaze. "Dakeer Vasar. I am the Hakija of the Sun Gods."

LEKORE BOLTED UPRIGHT. SWEAT TRICKLED IN HIS EYES. HIS skin prickled. Around him, the faint breaths of his companions drifted on the night air. Insects sang in the tall grass surrounding the campsite. His eyes trailed up to the gaping mountain pass shadowed beneath the waning moon as he worked his breaths into a steady, calm rhythm.

He had intended to reach the Vale That Shines Gold by nightfall, but his companions resisted, urging him to turn east and follow the mountain roots into the Wildwood.

At a standstill, Lekore had agreed to decide in the morning, though his desire remained unchanged. Now, he sat up and shivered in the early morning chill. He wiped away his perspiration and watched the nocturnal herd of pythe chase a flop-eared rabbun through the grass. The omnivorous creatures loped and bayed, stubbed wings beating against their scales, disturbing none of the Kel.

Weariness pulled Lekore back down into the grass. He nestled into fitful dreams; fragmented, smelling of smoke and fire; glowing with purple flame, while cheos sang their death songs from the trees.

———

'*It's coming,*' cried the wind. '*Listen. Feel it. It comes!*'

'*Falling. It's falling.*'

'*So bright. It shines!*'

'*Falling.*'

Lekore stood upon Isiltik, the hill wherein his cave dwelt, and looked over the Wildwood and the distant mountain ranges. The grass sang around his legs, and the nearby stream bubbled up as water spirits turned to look up.

Stars hummed. One shone so brightly.

'*Falling.*'

Lekore stared. The star streaked across the velvet sky, glowing bright. Brighter.

'*It's coming, Lekki. Look!*'

He tracked the star as it tumbled downward, blazing, searing hot, heading east. He reached out to stop its descent, but it was too far. Falling toward the Wildwood. It struck the trees; the ground quaked and rumbled. Fire erupted around it.

'*Fell! It fell!*' cried all the spirits in unison.

The wind rose as a storm brewed over the western ocean.

———

Lekore sat up. The eastern horizon glowed with the first rays of morning.

No. He pushed to his feet. It was still too early for dawn.

Thunder grumbled in the west. He turned to find clouds gathering. *What I dreamt happened at the same moment?*

He turned to find the others still slumbering.

"Awaken." He stooped over Jesh. "Please arise. We must make haste."

The young man moaned and turned over. "What is it?"

"A star fell and caught the Wildwood ablaze. We must hurry to put it out." He stumbled to Jeth's side. "Please wake up." He rounded the remains of a campfire to shake Ademas awake, but the young man rolled over and sat up before Lekore reached him.

"Did you say something about a fire?"

"Yes," said Lekore. "A star fell from the heavens. I dreamt it, and now we must hasten there. It fell near the place I must reach to stop the storms."

Jaw tight, Ademas rose. "I'll wake the princess."

Lekore nodded and started toward the pythe but found the twins already rounding them up. One pythe clutched a mangled rabbun in its fanged maw.

Lekore crouched before the glowing embers and reached out his hand. A single flame curled up to caress his fingers, warm and tickling. Lekore smiled. "Let the campfire die out, my friend. Sink beneath the earth and head for the fire that consumes the Wildwood. Please ask your brethren to calm its wrath. I will come as quickly as I can."

The flame sparked, then seeped beneath the embers whose light faded. Lekore straightened up and turned to find Talanee sitting upright, running a hand through her tangled hair.

She grimaced up at him. "You saw a star fall from above?"

Lekore nodded. "I dreamt of it, even as I dreamt of you before and knew to come to Halathe on the day we met." His lips curled down. "Despite our need for haste, we must go first to the Vale That Shines Gold. We will need supplies within the Wildwood, and I have skins I can use to make protection for your feet. We cannot take the pythe into the Wildwood; we must go afoot."

Talanee shifted to let her bare toes peek out from under her skirts. "I won't complain about that. This grass hides prickles."

"You should've said something," said Ademas, crouching. He grasped her ankle and rotated her foot. "Did you lose both slippers?"

Talanee scowled. "*You're* responsible for losing the first. I discarded the other as I raced to catch all of you." She batted his hand away. "One shoe by itself doesn't offer much protection. I'll thank you not to touch me again without permission."

Ademas flashed a grin. "Forgive me, Princess. I didn't think protocol the most pressing concern out here in the wilderness." He stood and glanced toward the twins as he clasped his heavy travel cape on. "Looks like we're ready to depart."

Lekore followed his gaze. Every pythe stood lined up and saddled. "So we are. Let us be on our way."

A STAR FELL FROM THE HEAVENS. TALANEE SHIVERED AS SHE steered her pythe along the mountain pass. *What awaits us where it fell?*

They'd reached the northern end of the mountain pass before dawn. Now Lekore started down the incline into the Charnel Valley, but Talanee stayed put upon her pythe. None of the others moved ahead either. Against the rolling mists in the valley below, mounds huddled in the shadows, and a breeze whispering through Nakoth Pass tugged at Talanee's hair as though to warn her back. *Go back to Inpizal. Leave this place.*

Lekore glanced over his shoulder and reined his pythe in. "Will you come or stay?"

Jesh traced the rising sun before his chest. "This land is forbidden."

"Not expressly," said Ademas. "It's discouraged, but no text has specifically stated we can't enter this place."

Lekore looked ahead, then back at the company. A faint smile dusted his lips. "Wait a moment. We are just in time."

As the mist crawled and wisped over the black earth below, Talanee shifted. Why must they wait? Why couldn't they have gone around the mountains on the southeastern side? Weren't the Lands Beyond dangerous enough without first coming to this gods-cursed place?

Here lay the remains of the fallen from the War of Brothers. The most devout Sun Worshiper and the most ardent Star Worshiper alike said that here, in the Charnel Valley, filled with the bones of Kel and Tawloomez, the spirit of Skye Getaal still walked. He, the founder of the Moon faith—the heretical brother of Erokel the Great—who had cursed the Kel with his dying breath and wandered evermore to fulfill that dark wish.

The mists rose, pale, mournful, reaching for the sky as the last stars faded.

Sunlight ringed the eastern mountains, pooling across their jagged tips, painting them gold. Rays slipped down toward the valley, and the sun peeked its brow above the mountain. Talanee let out a breath. *Blessed Sun Gods, forgive me for being in this place. Protect me from its vile curse.*

Sunbeams touched the valley floor. A flash and sparkle glinted below as the mists burned. As the last wisps of vapor disappeared, the valley caught the light and glowed. All of it, like the flames of the Sun Throne blazing with glory.

Talanee gasped.

"Blessed be the Sun Throne," whispered Jesh nearby.

The other two Kel remained silent, no doubt entranced by the miracle before them.

The valley, blighted only seconds before, looked now like a sea of molten gold. The sparkle of gems—red, green, blue, white—dotted that sea.

All at once, it vanished, swallowed up in shadow as the sun climbed higher toward its zenith. Talanee blinked, and a tear trickled down her cheek.

"I call it the Vale That Shines Gold," said Lekore. "Let us go on."

As the company of five descended toward the valley floor, Talanee pinned her eyes on Lekore's back. What was he? Why had he come into her life; into the lives of all Kel? She'd been so convinced he'd come from the Sun Throne, a divine messenger wielding fire, yet that must be impossible now—for he had condemned and rejected the holy rites of the Kel.

Is he Skye Getaal, come again in corporeal form to deceive us?

Shuddering, Talanee rubbed a hand over her brow to brush back disheveled tendrils of hair. Why had she come here, leaving Lord Father behind, telling no one where she'd gone? How childish. How *stupid*. Now she journeyed with a man unlike any Kel, heading for the Lands Beyond, to find a fallen star.

The slope straightened into a pathway weaving between heaps of bones. Talanee flinched at the grinning skulls but leaned to one side of her pythe to peer closer. *Is that golden armor?*

Some of these weren't Kel, and they weren't Tawloomez. *Erokel the Second described godly messengers who fought in the War of Brothers. Did some of them fall in the fighting after all? It's not a myth?*

The Vale That Shines Gold, so Lekore called it. He truly saw the world differently from other Kel. How did he view these armored skeletons, enemies lying together in forever sleep?

Someone needs to teach him Kel history. He needs to understand.

A howl rose over the valley. Talanee's skin crawled, and she groped for her dagger as Ademas and the twins reached for their swords.

Lekore slipped from his pythe and raced ahead. "Lios, come! Come to me. I'm home."

A yip answered and from the shadows bolted a small emockye, tongue lolling. The gray canine creature bounded to Lekore, green eyes flashing. Lekore crouched to embrace it, laughing. The emockye licked his face and yipped again.

"Yours?" asked Ademas, still clutching his sword hilt.

Lekore glanced at the mounted Kel. "Yes, this is Lios. He is my friend. I never enter the Wildwood without him, nor he without me. Come, my home is only a little farther." He gained his feet. "We must leave the pythe here. They will be safe within my cave."

With Lios trotting at his side, Lekore led the company to a steep slope, and the Kel dismounted to guide their pythe up the rocky incline. Talanee pursed her lips and scrambled up the sharp slope, unwilling to show how much her feet stung as rocks sliced them.

She'd expected Lekore's cave to be primitive and dismal, yet despite its cavernous appearance, Lekore had carved out shelves lined with herbs and clay jars. Everything hung or sat tidily inside his one-man kingdom, and the pleasant fragrance of dried plants lingered in the chamber.

While Lekore plucked up herbs to stow in a rawhide satchel, Talanee roamed the cave interior, glad of the cool, smooth rock against her feet. Lekore's bed consisted of ferns—now dead—and several heavy furs. He even had a pillow stuffed with cheos feathers.

Lekore slipped near. "These hide strips will work well to protect your feet." He proffered them.

Talanee accepted them with a faint grimace. "Thank you."

"Wrap them well."

Her eyes flicked to his new, supple gray boots as he strode back across the cave. Black leather straps crossed at the ankles in a strange design. "Where did you get those, Lekore?"

He turned, then followed her gaze to his feet. "Ter gave them to me."

Ademas looked up from poking through a handful of clay dishes beside a firepit near the cave mouth. "Who is Ter?"

"My mentor."

Ademas's eyes flicked around the cave. "Does your mentor live here?"

"No, he is far away. I have not seen him in several months."

"Ter isn't a name I've heard before. Is he Kel?"

"He is not."

Talanee found Ademas's gaze and arched her brow. Did Lekore mean to suggest Ter was Tawloomez?

Ademas withdrew his hands from the clay dishes and shifted to face Lekore, who'd turned toward a carved shelf to slip more herbs into his bag. Ademas considered him for a moment. "What did this Ter teach you?"

"Many things." Lekore tied his satchel shut and turned to his silent audience as he slung the satchel over his shoulder. "He told me of moons and suns and planets, of magic and the Spirits Elemental, of life and creation." Lekore glanced around the cave. "We would do well to bring light bedding and more water flasks. The Wildwood has changeable weather, and many of its streams are poisonous. Please feel welcome to take from here what is needful."

Jesh and Jeth moved to the heap of folded furs. Ademas strode to the flasks hanging against one wall and took down one for each traveler. Talanee sat to wrap the strips around her scraped feet.

"Please let me help you." Lekore crouched and cradled her ankle in his palm. His fingers moved deftly as he slathered on a smelly ointment and wound the strips over her toes and heel. He lowered her foot and lifted the other. "The cuts are not bad. They will mend soon and leave no scars."

"Did your mentor also teach you healing arts?" Talanee asked.

He peeked up at her and smiled. "He did, though Sk—" His jaw clamped shut, and he bent to his work, long hair sliding into his face.

"What is it?" Talanee brushed her fingertips against his shoulder.

He shook his head and lowered her foot. "That should hold for now. When next we rest, I will check my work." He stood, hair settling around his ankles, and snatched a black cloak hanging from a hook on the rock wall. He draped it over one shoulder. "The day is young, and we will make good time until we reach the boundary of the Wildwood. Let us depart. Leave your pythe."

A WENDING PATH TOOK THE COMPANY AROUND THE CAVE AND along a grassy hill Lekore called Isiltik. At its crest, Talanee and her companions stared down into a narrow pass between the eastern mountain range ending at the dense foliage of the Lands Beyond.

The peculiar forest stretched on for countless miles, interrupted only by a far off, lone mountain scraping the sky. The alien sounds of wild beasts rode the wind, taunting the company of Kel.

Talanee traced the rising sun before her chest. *Gods forgive and protect me.*

Ademas strode up beside her. "Quite the view. I've always been curious about the Lands Beyond."

"I don't know why. They're cursed—what else is there to know?"

"Maybe that's why I'm so curious." His grin flashed brighter than the morning light.

Talanee rolled her eyes. "I suspect you'll die very young, Cousin."

He chuckled. "It's quite possible."

Lekore started downhill. The emockye called Lios trailed after him, tail wagging.

The trek down the narrow pass ended much too soon. As Lekore halted before the tangled wall of trees, the sounds of the Lands Beyond rose like the dooming notes of a dirge. Talanee's heart quickened as she eyed the strange, gnarled trees twisting skyward, vines hanging from the branches, while flowers in strange hues glowered down at the Kel company, petals sharp as daggers, stems pale and thorn ridden.

"Touch nothing brightly colored," said Lekore, pinning a look on each of his companions in turn. "Most are harmful, many are fatal. Follow my steps and make no sudden sounds." He snapped his fingers, and Lios trotted to his side. "Go."

The emockye prowled ahead, movements lithe and silent. Lekore pulled his black cloak on and followed, as graceful and hushed as his wild pet. He plunged into the dense foliage, hair dancing around his ankles but never tangling.

Ademas blew out a breath. "You live but once, right?" He glanced at Talanee and waggled his eyebrows. "Ladies first?"

Talanee scowled. "How comical you are, Cousin. Yet, in case you're confused, I should correct your assumption: Lekore isn't a lady." She whipped past him, skirts rustling, and started for the trees.

One twin slipped in front of her, sword unsheathed. The second twin stood at Ademas's back, shielding the Getaal cousins from all comers.

As the four Kel started forward, Lekore stepped from the trees, eyebrows knitted. "Someone comes." His eyes drifted past the Kel.

The Irothé twins shifted into defensive positions before the company, facing the westward pass, blades gleaming in the sunlight.

A single pythe loped from the shadows of the mountain road, its rider's armor glinting and flashing.

Talanee's heart overturned. "It's Lord Captain Nerenoth!"

The twins were already sheathing their swords and one let out a whoop.

"Hush," said Lekore, striding forward. "Do not forget where we stand."

The twin flushed. "I apologize. That was careless."

The Lord Captain reined up before the company, eyes flicking from one face to another. "Your Highness. I should have guessed you and your cousin were here. I'm heartened to see you all well and glad I caught you ahead of the trees. I feared I'd never find you within that cursed realm." His gaze lighted on Lekore. "Are you well?"

Lekore's eyes searched Nerenoth's face, and a smile stole over his lips, soft and cautious. "I am better than I was. But urgency draws me into the Wildwood for two reasons, and I must travel quickly. Do you come to aid or to hamper our passage, good captain?"

"To aid." Nerenoth swung from his saddle and stroked the dark green scales of his pythe. He unhitched a pack from the saddle, swung it over a shoulder, then slapped the pythe's flank. It loped back up the pass. "He's a smart one. He'll find shelter well enough. Shall we proceed?"

The company turned back to the trees.

"I'm impressed you caught up with us, Lord Captain," Ademas said. "You weren't even in the city when we left."

"He rides like a storm, when he wants," said a twin.

Talanee thought Nerenoth's lips twitched upward.

"We were also rather slow in our progress," the other twin added.

"True, that," agreed his identical brother.

Lekore glanced at them, and the twins closed their mouths. The young man plunged again into the foliage and soon disappeared. With Lord Captain Nerenoth present, the twins followed Lekore, and allowed their elder brother to take the rearguard. Ademas took his place behind the twins. With a grimace, Talanee crossed into the Lands Beyond at her cousin's back.

The rush of the wind through the mountain pass vanished as a cacophony of birdsong and the sweet fragrance of flowers assaulted her senses. Despite the midmorning sun outside the jungle, in here, the canopy of leaves overhead cast a perpetual gloom, as though dusk had settled at her feet. Vines stretched up wide trunks covered in thick mossy blankets; a few vines hung in the narrow path to snatch at her skirts and grab at her fingers. She whipped her hand away and clasped her fingers together.

What am I doing here?

The heavy air scraped down her throat with every breath. Her hair tickled her face as it crimped in the growing dampness.

One twin—Jeth, possibly—halted in his tracks, stopping the progress of the company as he stared at something in the tree beside him.

His twin leaned over his shoulder, gaping. "What is it?"

Talanee tiptoed close. *Oh.*

An elongated, furry sort of creature clung to several vines, its markings blending with the trunk and moss, its squat face naked despite the long fur covering the rest of its slender body. Its tail curled around a branch, while its eyes darted between Kel faces.

"It is a minkee," said Lekore, right beside Talanee.

She jumped and threw a hand over her mouth to stifle a shriek. As she swallowed a growl, she tossed Lekore a narrow glare. "Don't *do* that."

"Do what?" he asked, but as he turned toward the head of the company, his eyes gleamed like Ademas's.

"Minkee," whispered Jesh. Or was it Jeth?

"I've never seen its like," murmured his twin.

The group hurried to catch Lekore and Lios.

Ademas fell into pace beside Talanee, grinning. "You know, I like him."

"Who?" asked Talanee, holding her chin higher.

"You know precisely who."

Talanee tossed Lekore's back a second glare. "You would, Cousin."

"You don't?"

"We've been through this already."

"Have we?"

She hissed as her toes smacked a protruding root. "Let's not talk right now. I need to focus on the dratted path—such as it is."

He chuckled and shrugged. "As you wish, Your Highness."

CHAPTER 22

"Don't be in such a rush, Fire Prince. This stretch of the *Ava Vyy* can kill you through no strenuous effort on your part. See that black bit there?"

Lor stared down at the pool of odorous sludge mere inches from his foot. "Yes."

"Quicksand," Keo said. "One big swallow, that's all it takes."

Lor stepped sideways. "But we must hurry to find the *Akuu-Ry*."

Keo paused under a patch of sunlight along the emockye track. The man squinted up at the sky. "No, I'd say there isn't much hurry. Not yet. We should head north."

"North? But you said the *Akuu-Ry* is west."

"He was. He still is." Keo stepped into the shadows. "We should still go north."

"But—"

"Do you want my help, Lor'Toreth?"

Lor let his shoulders droop. "Yes, of course. But only if you aren't actually mad."

The man with green hair considered Lor for a long, breathless moment. Then he threw his head back and barked a laugh even the Teokaka would deem unholy. Keo dipped his head, green eyes sparking with dangerous mirth. "If you require a sane man on your journey, look elsewhere, but don't hope for too much. What is madness anyway, Your Highness?"

Lor dropped his gaze to stare at the gritty quicksand. "Perhaps it is only a difference in one's point of view." He shuddered as whispers stroked his memory, soft, cruel, so very cruel. His fingernails dug into his palms as he clenched his fists. *I'm not mad. She's wrong. She's* wrong.

"Well?" Keo asked.

Lor blinked at him. "Huh?"

"Do we go north?"

Lor let his thoughts settle into the present, cloaking his ghosts for another time. "Y-yes. North. We will go north."

"Good." Keo brushed past him and stepped onto a narrower path that wound around puddles of pungent quicksand. "It's a more treacherous route, but that can't be helped."

"Will we live?" asked Lor.

"Until we die." Keo chuckled.

They made halting progress as the day warmed. The air pressed down on Lor, rattling through his lungs, as he dragged his feet through dense undergrowth. Sweat stung his eyes. His clothes hung drenched and heavy on his frame. His wound ached with every step. Insects sang near his ears before they sucked out precious blood and left Lor's skin burning.

Keo prowled ahead, oblivious to the torment of the Wildwood. As Lor stared at his back and tried to place his feet wherever Keo stepped, a seething anger grew and simmered inside the Tawloomez prince. None of this was fair. It wasn't right. What great evils had Lor done to deserve an end like this? Had he not tried to succeed his father in a manner the Tawloomez tribes might approve of? Yet it was never enough for them, never enough for the Teokaka, who claimed Lor had fits of madness. That he was unsuited to rule.

He stopped walking. His heart crashed against his eardrums as his body shook and rattled. A hundred pinprick insect bites scorched his flesh, while more bloodsuckers dug in to find another drop of blood. Another tiny feast.

Keo glanced back. His mouth turned down and he strode toward Lor, but the ground stretched out between them. Too far, so far...

A hand fell on Lor's shoulder, weighty, grounding.

"Fight the Wildwood, Lor'Toreth. Don't let it take root, or you'll never come back from its soul."

Lor blinked. His heartbeat retreated into his chest. His bones ceased their rattling as he sucked in air. "W-what was that?"

"The *Ava Vyy* plays tricks on a weakened mind. Drink this." Keo pressed a flask into his hand. "It's strong. Don't drink too much, or you'll vomit it back up."

Lor uncapped it and sniffed. A sharp aroma like sour milk and dirt slapped his senses, and he wrenched it away from his face. "What is this?"

"A medicinal liquor."

Lor sniffed it again and cringed. "I believe you have fermented it too much, though I do not know how you managed that."

Keo chuckled. "Just drink, boy. It's not meant for enjoyment."

Lor wrinkled his nose and poured the liquor down his throat. A sharp, sour tang erupted across his tongue, drawing tears from his eyes. He choked it down and gagged. Worse than spoiled milk, worse than the strongest liquor, worse than visions of the Teokaka. "I think...your warning of drinking too much is...uncalled for. The only danger is drinking too little to cure an ailment."

Keo snorted. "Maybe so. Or maybe the tongues of my people are less sensitive. Back home, this liquor's dearly sought after, and one pays a hefty price to obtain it."

"Then your people are monsters."

Lor expected the strange man to chuckle, or even laugh outright, but sorrow etched lines around Keo's eyes.

"Yes, well, you're not wrong," Keo murmured. "Come, Fire Prince. We've a ways to go yet."

Lor tramped after him, kicking vines aside as he went. He'd

always been proud of his agility, but in the humidity of this place, coupled with his wound, he feared he looked like a clumsy fool compared to Keo's silent, even, comfortable pace.

"Your people," Lor said. "Where do they hail?"

"Elsewhere."

Lor rolled his eyes. "You know much of me, but I know almost nothing about you."

Keo sighed and turned around. "That's true. I know *of* you but not all about you. I know what I've observed, while *you* insist on cheating. Use your eyes a while longer, Lor'Toreth, and determine how much about me you really want to learn." He rubbed his temple. "Such a chattercat I've never met."

Cheeks burning, Lor set his jaw and said no more, even when Keo allowed them to halt for a quick meal. If his silence mattered to the strange man, Keo didn't show it. Once they'd finished eating dried meat and fruit, they carried on. The larger man's pace quickened as they entered a less boggy stretch of the Wildwood, where the thick air still clung to Lor's chest, but it tasted a little less stale, and he welcomed the change.

His wound oozed, mingling with sweat that made his leather top and breeches cling. He said nothing. If he died on this slender trail, so be it.

Growls sang from the trees as they moved, but no emockye opposed them. Odd, considering how aggressive the creatures usually were. Once Keo paused and shot a look into the undergrowth. Did Lor imagine a retreating whimper?

As Keo strode on, Lor let a few more inches grow between them. Perhaps he had been fearing the wrong creatures all along.

The trees grew farther apart as afternoon dipped toward evening. A warm wind engulfed Lor, throwing the faint odor of woodsmoke into his nose. He started to ask Keo if he could smell it but remembered he wasn't speaking to the man and clamped his lips shut.

Keo halted a few yards later in a small clearing and faced west. "We'll wait here. It shouldn't be long."

Lor stared at the trees. Nearby a crowd of minkee shrieked at him, dangling upside-down, their prehensile tails wrapped around tree limbs. He didn't dignify them with a glance. Sweat trickled into his eyes and he wished he could tie his hair back. He scratched a cluster of bites on his forearm. Minutes crawled on.

He sighed. "What are we waiting for?"

Keo grinned. "Your *Akuu-Ry*, of course. He's nearly here. I'm surprised we beat him."

"He's coming here? To this spot?"

Keo nodded westward. "See for yourself."

A rattling sound drifted from the jungle of trees, and a young emockye slipped from the undergrowth, tail wagging. It halted and bared its teeth as a second figure emerged from the dense wood, this one slim, with the red eyes and pale flesh of a Kel. A black cloak wrapped around his frame, tattered hems hanging at his booted ankles.

Lor swallowed and stepped forward, lifting his hands to show he wasn't armed. "Greetings, *Akuu-Ry*."

The Kel stared between Lor and Keo, a frown tracing his lips. He glanced over his shoulder, and Lor stumbled back as more Kel strode from the same line of trees. Two of them. No, three. Four.

Six in all.

As the last Kel separated himself from the dense wood, Lor's legs wobbled. This one, clad in full armor, muscular and tall, with a scar on the bridge on his nose, sent a chill through Lor's bones.

As swords hissed free of their sheathes, Lor staggered behind Keo, fighting for air. "It's him. I know him."

Lor had never seen the Lord Captain of the Kel before, but he'd heard enough to recognize him on sight.

One of the Kel unleashed a sharp phrase. Silence enveloped the trees but for a minkee chattering overhead.

Keo shifted to glance back at Lor. "Are you going to talk to them, or let them cut us down?"

Lor peeked around Keo to find the first Kel—the one with the pale hair and black cloak—standing before his companions, hands stretched between both groups, eyes bright as embers in the gloom. He turned to Keo and issued another phrase, voice soft yet edged like a blade.

Keo said something back.

Lor blinked. Could Keo speak the Kel language? *He speaks my tongue, doesn't he? Don't be a fool, Lor'Toreth.*

"He wants to know who we are and what we're about." Keo's tones fell on Lor's ears like gentle raindrops. "I told him you need his help."

Lor frowned. "Is this the *Akuu-Ry* after all?"

"He is. His name is Lekore."

"I thought he kept apart from the Kel. Why are there so many?"

"A point I'm curious about myself." Keo rattled off more foreign words.

Lor's gaze strayed from the *Akuu-Ry* to his armed companions. All Kel. One female—and beautiful in her pale way. Twins stood near her, swords still held aloft, while another young man looked on with faint amusement haunting his lips, as though it never quite died. The Lord Captain draped one hand over his sword hilt, which remained sheathed, and though his eyes flicked between Keo and the *Akuu-Ry*'s conversation, he held himself with none of the tenseness of his comrades.

"Interesting," said Keo after the *Akuu-Ry* finished speaking. "He says they met in Inpizal and insisted on joining him as he traveled here. He's come to stop the storms, as the wind spirits requested."

Heart skipping, Lor stepped around Keo. "Will you also help my companions?"

The young man called Lekore held Lor's eyes as Keo translated, then spoke a short string of syllables as the other Kel glanced at one another.

Keo nodded. "He'll try."

Lekore spoke again, the resonance of his voice like the even flow of a stream. The emockye padded back to his side and sat, silent, watchful. Lekore stooped to stroke his head.

Keo turned to Lor. "Before he can do anything, he must go northward and find a meteor."

"A what?"

"A fallen star. Apparently, it's caught the *Ava Vyy* on fire, which I'm not eager to ignore myself. Our options are to wait here while he travels north or join him and his fellows."

Lor's eyes darted between the Kel and their weapons. "We had best wait here."

"Are you sure?"

Lekore offered a few more words. Keo nodded and replied, then glanced at Lor. "He gives his word no Kel will bring us harm unless we strike first against them."

Lor scowled. "What is the word of a Kel to me?"

Keo sighed and scratched his jaw. "The difference between your friends' lives and their deaths, I'd wager. This is no normal Kel, Lor'Toreth. He's embraced by the Spirits Elemental and tutored by those with more years and wisdom than you might comprehend in all your days. Choose your course carefully, but make no enemy of the *Akuu-Ry*."

With a sigh, Lor pinned his eyes on the young man before him. Lekore gazed back, hair dancing at his ankles in a private breeze, features smooth and unchallenging. He waited, eyes wielding a keen, clever light.

"Very well." Lor rested his fingertips against his throat. "By the oaths of Teona and the will of the Snake Gods, I agree not to harm these Kel unless first they strike against me. I will join you."

Keo translated, and Lekore nodded, then turned to his companions to speak in soft tones. Low, heated voices answered, the woman most animated of them all. Lekore rebuffed every reply, then shifted his attention to the Lord Captain of the Kel.

Keo inched nearer to Lor. "Fascinating. I don't think the other Kel can quite bring themselves to trust Lekore's decision. They're more of a mind to kill you and me and move on...and now Lekore's imploring one of those who kept silent: The one who frightens you."

Lor hunched into himself. "That is Lord Captain Nerenoth Irothé, one of the Triad of Erokel. He is a ruthless and cunning man."

"Ah, yes. I know about him." Keo's eyes sparkled. "I wonder what compels a man like that to leave his duties and join this ragtag band in this fiendish jungle."

"Who can say? All Kel are mad."

Keo snorted. "That can't be a fair assessment. Why is madness always your answer for people's actions?"

Lor shrugged. "Perhaps it is all I have known for an answer."

"Then it's time to broaden yourself, Princeling. This world is far more complex than you make it out to be, and that's just one sphere worth mentioning."

Lekore stepped forward and spoke.

Keo nodded. "By the Lord Captain's command, the Kel agree to Lekore's terms and swear by their Sun Gods to let you live unmolested—unless provoked. I think it's the best we'll get."

Lor exhaled through his nose. "Very well."

Lekore didn't wait for Keo's translation but rattled off a few more words.

"He's eager to reach the fire," said Keo. "I don't blame him. He asks that we make haste. His speech's very formal, even for a Kel. It's downright archaic." Keo chuckled. "Fascinating."

Lekore moved ahead and slipped into a tangle of northeasterly trees. The Kel woman and one Kel man followed. The twins remained still until the Lord Captain spoke, then they sheathed their swords and plunged into the trees.

"Go on, Lor'Toreth," said Keo. "I'll keep the Lord Captain company and be sure to watch your back."

"My thanks." Lor started into the undergrowth, uncertain how grateful he really was. In this entire train of people, was there a single soul he might trust with his life?

CHAPTER 23

The spirits moved and flowed with him, urging Lekore onward. Trees bent before his touch as the earth spirits, in the forms of birds, minkee, leaves, and myriad other shapes, willed the Wildwood to let him through. Lios stayed at his heels, keeping pace with Lekore's strides—though that wasn't challenging for the lean, lithe creature, especially since Lekore must keep within sight of his traveling companions.

He was glad of Nerenoth's presence—the one living Kel he fully trusted. The man could protect his fellow Kel, even should the Wildwood separate Lekore from them. The Wildwood had its own mind, and it banished all intruders; though it had never succeeded in keeping Lekore away when he must enter the fell realm.

He never relished his trips.

Yet today was different. Though he had come here to still the storms, ever since his dream of the fallen star, his heart sang, and he felt the tingle of *Calir* calling out, reaching beyond its confines.

Strange. *Calir* never grew restless.

Lekore slowed as the earth spirits shifted at his feet. His eyes flicked left, and he glimpsed a hidden pit of quicksand. He swiveled around. "Beware. We have entered a dangerous bog. Follow my steps most carefully."

Ademas and Talanee nodded in unison. Behind them, the twins came into view. Lekore started the slow dance through the mires, keeping a steady eye on the path of the earth spirits until his head throbbed. The stretch of black pools was short, and soon the earth spirits romped ahead.

Lekore let out a breath. He halted until every member of his party had come through the bog.

As Talanee arrived, she scowled at her besmirched gown and shook it. "So many lost jewels. Father will kill me."

Lekore canted his head, weighing the seriousness of her statement. *Kel are bloodthirsty. Perhaps her father truly would kill her.*

He slipped to her side. "Would this help?" He plucked a ruby from a pocket inside his tattered cloak and proffered it. "There are many jewels like these in the Vale That Shines Gold. I am certain the specters there would not mind if you took a few."

Talanee paled a shade as she eyed the jewel. "N-no, I think not. Thank you, but no. I don't want any cursed treasure."

The twins rounded the princess, eyeing Lekore's hovering palm with interest.

The Lord Captain appeared last, a frown resting on his lips. He approached Lekore. "We are slowing you down too much."

Lekore pocketed the ruby. "It cannot be helped. I see best the dangers of this realm—and to leave you alone may be to condemn you to death."

The chattering minkee overhead let out a shriek. Lekore's spine popped as he whirled, fingers tingling. Lios whimpered and crouched close to his heels, ears folding back.

"Emockye?" asked Nerenoth.

"Likely so."

Swords whispered free of their sheathes.

Leaf mold rattled against dancing paws. A flash of pale eyes winked at Lekore through brambles, and hot breath fluttered giant leaves.

Lekore lifted a hand, palm up. "Beware, beasts. We are not so digestible as past meals." Fire sparked in the air above his hand, leeching energy from his bones. The wind spirits blew against the flame until it sprang into the semi-shape of a Kel ablaze.

Growls answered as paws padded backward.

"Do emockye hunt in broad day?" asked Talanee nearby.

"Does it appear like broad day in here, Cousin?" asked Ademas.

"Good point." She pressed closer to him, brandishing her dagger. "Do we stand a chance against them?"

Lekore willed the flame to stay aloft as he lowered his hand. "With our numbers and my fire, they will hang back until we appear vulnerable—or when true night befalls us. We must stay closer than we have. Emockye and quicksand are not our only dangers. Here, the snakes are deadly at a touch."

Talanee cast a narrowed glance toward the Tawloomez. "Perhaps he can pray them away."

"Only if you can pray the sun closer, my lady," said the man called Keo.

Talanee's eyes skirted over the stranger, as though she couldn't quite accept the reality of him. Earlier she and the twin called Jeth had argued that this green-haired man *must* be a demon summoned by the Tawloomez. Lekore had brushed that away with a single word: "Nonsense."

Still, if the Kel gave the Tawloomez called Lor a wide berth, they steered farther away from his companion.

Strange that the color of one's hair could be an anathema. Kel customs were more peculiar and more distressing than Lekore had conceived.

He ran a hand down his cheek, then slapped his thigh. "Come, Lios."

The emockye pup obeyed and trotted ahead as Lekore picked his way over felled trunks and rotting limbs. As the travelers continued north, Lekore caught sight of the emockye pack prowling alongside them in the denser trees. Lios's ears flicked toward the pack now and then, and his tail switched between wagging and tucking between his legs, telling Lekore when the emockye drew nearer.

At his shoulder, the fire spirit waltzed and glided, happy to ride on the surface, so far above its kin in their beds of fire.

The scent of burning wood and acrid smoke teased Lekore's senses as he started up a slope, clutching vines to ease his halting progress. The sounds of over a dozen feet scrambling up behind him clamored in his ears, but beyond that drifted the faint groans of the Wildwood under the barrage of fiery wrath.

Clutching at a vine to keep his balance, he glanced at the fire spirit. "Why is the fire not out?"

'*It is alive*,' answered the spirit with a hissing laugh.

Lekore sighed. "It should not be." He glanced around for water, but its spirits never volunteered to travel with him, always content to make him seek them. *There is no time for that.* He swiped a hand through the fire spirit, letting the wind snuff it out.

A wind spirit settled on Lekore's shoulder and canted its head.

"Please do what you can to contain the fire."

The wind spirit shrugged and sprang up into the air. It took the form of a delicate bird before vanishing in the treetops.

Lekore paused atop the slope to catch his breath. The earth tumbled downward before him, dark and close, hot, tasting of smoke. Again, his fingers tingled as *Calir* called out.

He curled his fingers together. "What do you wish so much to see, my friend?"

"Sorry, didn't catch that," said Ademas, coming to stand beside him. Sweat beaded on his face and in his short, tousled hair.

Lekore glanced at the young man. "Nothing meant to cause alarm, I think."

"What isn't?"

"*Calir* is restless."

"Ka...leer?"

"My sword." Lekore flexed his fingers.

Ademas's eyes flitted to his hip, then back to his face. "You've a sword?"

"Yes. Between spaces."

"Ah, huh." Ademas scratched the side of his head. "I can't decide if you're a lunatic or something else entirely."

"Perhaps," said Lekore, turning to start down the hill, "lunatics often are something else entirely."

So close.

Calir pulsed with every step, yearning to come forth. Lekore resisted, though his fingers burned with the sword's desire.

A full day's travel had brought the company to this spot as dusk settled into night.

The glow of fire rimmed the trees as thin tendrils of smoke curled upon the air. Lekore strode forward, steps soft but quick. The shimmer of wind spirits caught his attention as the tiny creatures attempted to smother the flames by barring the passage of the Wildwood breezes. The spirits let him by, and he asked one in passing to let his companions through as well.

"Give them no mischief," he added, and the wind laughed in his ears.

The fire grappled against wind, but it was dying down just the same, unable to breathe. Trees smoldered, and the lingering terror of fleeing wildlife wisped past, hours old. Lekore clambered over the remains of a magnificent tree and faltered.

The ground ahead had been split apart, drawing a deep, dark mark across the earth. The sky peeked down through the cleared path, dusk-colored in the growing darkness of night. The massive incision spanned the width of a Kel manorhouse and ran out of Lekore's line of sight. He veered left to follow its course, aware of those following behind him. Lios stayed at his heels, tail wedged between his legs, ears pressed against his skull.

Lekore picked his way alongside the giant rut as the fires shrank under his glances. Fire spirits sang and sputtered, willing at last to give up their sport, but not without a few final pops and shrieks. Earth spirits slid up from the ground to round up the stragglcr flames, while wind patrolled above.

Ahead, a hulking mass sprouted up from the trees, marking the end of the black canal. The strange object, larger than any house, as tall as the city walls of Inpizal, blazed white and gold like the Cathedral of the Sun. Heat shimmered off its form, and it lay like a sleeping beast, sleek and graceful despite extensive damage to its body—yet it wasn't alive.

This was no beast, but something crafted like the buildings of Inpizal and the other great cities of Erokel. The bottom of the hulking structure had been torn away, and debris cluttered the surrounding trees.

"By the Blessed Sun Gods, what is this?" whispered Jesh, behind Lekore.

"Can this be a star?" whispered his twin.

"It's a ship." Keo's voice drifted across the air, tones tight.

"I've seen no ship like this upon the ocean," Ademas said.

"It isn't a ship for water," said Keo. "It sails the stars."

Talanee sucked in a breath. "Gods of Flame and Light protect us."

"All of you should remain here," Lekore said, lengthening his strides.

As *Calir* called out again, humming a high note, footsteps followed close. He glanced right to find the Lord Captain at his side.

"Please let me accompany you."

Lekore smiled. "If you wish."

"It is my only wish."

Lekore considered the man's face in profile, then dropped his eyes to watch his path. "When this is finished, good captain, I must tell you of something terrible that happened after you left Inpizal."

A tension rolled over Lekore like the tides of the sea. He glanced at Nerenoth again, but the man's face remained impassive.

Why do I trust him? Why do I not flee? Why does this man feel familiar to me? A jolt stole over Lekore like sparks of flame on a cold night. Could this be Ank? *He came for me. He came. Could he be the man I've long awaited?*

A hissing noise drifted across the wind. Lekore paused and considered the white ship; his gaze traveled across its sleek surface until he spotted a stand of trees that had fallen against it. Here, a square of lines shifted back, forth, back, as though something tried to slide free, but the trees held it shut.

"There." He pointed.

Nerenoth nodded. "That looks like a door."

Lekore trotted closer, wagging his fingers as he summoned the earth and wind spirits. "Help me move these, please."

The spirits tossed trees aside. Freed, the door hissed as it slid to one side, vanishing into a sliver between metal plates.

"Stay here, Lios. Stay. Wait a moment, good captain." Lekore gestured, and the wind carried him aloft, cloak billowing out. He stepped through the opening and stared into the belly of the ship.

Standing within a bright corridor, a slender young man near his age clutched a second figure slumped over his shoulder, unconscious. The young man and his companion both had golden yellow hair, and the young man's eyes shone the same blazing blue as Ter N'Avea. He was clad in ornate raiment of blue and white, torn and spattered with blood.

The young man tried a smile that strained his eyes. "Please, could you help me? My friend's badly injured."

Calir hummed as Lekore's fingers throbbed.

CHAPTER 24

Lekore trotted forward and caught the unconscious man's free arm. "Rest him against the wall, and I shall look over his wounds."

Together they eased the man to the floor and propped him upright. A deep gash ran along his skull, and his skin looked pasty white. One leg jutted out at a bad angle, and blood oozed around his silver breeches.

Lekore frowned. "'Tis bad, but I shall do all I can." He dropped his satchel on the floor, then rose and leaned out the open door.

Nerenoth Irothé stood below, a hand on his sword hilt. "Is all well?"

"I need your assistance, good captain."

A hand fell on Lekore's shoulder, and he whirled to face the blue gaze of the yellow-haired young man. Lekore blinked as he realized the young man's pupils were slitted like Lios's.

"There's a ramp." He gestured to a panel flashing with a rainbow of lights. "The second button in."

Lekore pressed the button and flinched as a faint hiss sounded, and a long, thin bridge slid from beneath the door to span the gap of air outside until it touched ground. Nerenoth raced up the ramp, followed by Lios. As the Lord Captain came level with the doorway, he staggered to a halt and stared at the strange young man.

"Hello," said the stranger. "I'm sorry we've intruded upon you."

Lekore knelt beside the unconscious man. "It does not seem you meant for this to occur."

"No," said the young man. "That we certainly didn't. But I'm afraid we've made a mess just the same." He watched Lekore dig through his satchel. "Are you a healer?"

Lekore shook his head. "It is not my trade, but I know enough to aid this man, I think. I am Lekore."

"Lekore, I'm glad to meet you, especially with your skill. Unfortunately, the section that housed our medical ward was destroyed in the impact. My only recourse was to search for help, but the exit was blocked. I'm called Tora, and this is my friend, Raren." Tora turned to Nerenoth. "And you, sir?"

Nerenoth clapped a hand to his breastplate. "Lord Captain Nerenoth Irothé."

"Lord Captain, an honor." Tora inclined his head. "Was anyone outside injured in the crash? My pilot did all he could to steer away from civilization when the ship malfunctioned, but it charted its own course in the end." Pain brightened his eyes as lines of weariness shadowed his face.

"You crashed in the Lands Beyond," Nerenoth said. "Few living souls dare to breach its borders."

"That's a relief." Tora turned to Lekore. "Yet you found us."

Lekore nodded as he dabbed at Raren's head wound. "I came to this realm for another purpose and witnessed your fall. I knew the fire must be tamed."

"Well, I'm grateful." Tora crouched beside him. "There might be others who need care as well. If your friend, the Lord Captain, is willing," he glanced up, "we could bring them to you?"

"I would gladly oblige, O Lord," said Nerenoth.

"I appreciate it." Tora stood, yellow hair shifting as he moved, revealing pointed ears.

Lekore studied him as *Calir* hummed again. "Do you know of

someone named Ter?" The words tumbled unbidden from his lips as Lios padded close, tongue lolling.

Tora turned to stare. "You know Ter? Ter N'Avea?"

Lekore nodded. "He is my mentor."

The young man let out a gasp. "Thank heavens. We landed among friends. Ter's also my mentor. I've known him all my life."

"As have I." Lekore smiled and turned back to his work. "You remind me of him."

Tora lingered a moment. "This way, Lord Captain."

Lekore glanced up to watch the two men plunge down the corridor, deeper into the ship. His eyes swept over the rich wooden walls and marble floor, the elegant lamps glowing with strange orbs of light, devoid of fire or its spirits. As he turned his focus again toward Raren, he caught the faint glimpse of his own reflection on the wood behind the injured man. He had never seen wood so polished.

Raren looked older than his comrade, with broad shoulders and a fine jaw, but he had the same angular face and defined cheekbones. Lekore brushed a lock of yellow hair from Raren's ear. It angled into the faintest hint of a point, not defined as Tora's, nor as long and twitchy as Ter's.

"You are all a funny lot," he said aloud, smiling a little. His chest warmed at the idea of another person acquainted with Ter.

Calir appeared to agree, for now the sword's song had quieted to a cheery hum, no longer eager to be free, content to remain near. Among friends, Tora had said. Lios nudged Lekore's shoulder, and he absently scratched the pup's ear.

A scream clawed across the sky. Lekore sprang up and raced to the doorway to peer down, Lios growling at his side. The emockye pack surrounded the Kel, and all had their swords out. Lor stood with them, brandishing a slender dagger.

Lekore threw out his hand and summoned fire. The flames around the ship flared up, enlivened by his plea. At the same moment, the man called Keo spread his fingers before him, palm down. Violet strings of light leapt from his fingertips to chase back the canine beasts. As the light struck the nearest emockye, biting pain flared up from the wound the dark Hakija had given Lekore. He hissed and flinched back, bones crusting with ice. Hunching down, he bit back against heightening panic.

Flee, something deep inside cried. *Flee. Run before you are caught.*

Wind stirred his hair, and the tang of lightning pricked his tongue. The sky rumbled. The fire spirits tamed.

The storm is returning so soon?

Flee, the voice urged again.

"I...cannot," he gasped out. His fingers tingled. He threw out his hand. "*Calir*, come to me!" The sword chimed an answering note and rippled into being; it turned solid in Lekore's grasp. Its weight lent clarity to Lekore's mind, and he rose as the chill in his frame thawed.

Footsteps sounded behind him, and *Calir* chimed again, as though greeting a friend. Lekore spun to find Nerenoth and Tora coming fast, wielding swords. Tora's blade pulsed with light and sang out a note harmonizing with *Calir*.

Tora's gaze met Lekore's, bewildered and fascinated.

"What happened?" asked Nerenoth, as he halted.

"Emockye." Lekore pointed outside. "Though I think Keo has handled them." He shuddered as the chill reached out again. "Somehow his magic has made the storm blossom once more. We must hurry to free the spirits, Captain. I do not think I can calm them again...not after such magic has been unleashed."

Tora brushed past Lekore to stare outside, then recoiled. "Kiisuld magic?" He moved to Lekore's side. "What did you see?"

Lekore squeezed his eyes shut. "Flames of violet hue, hungering for my soul."

"Relax," said a familiar voice in the doorway. "I don't want your soul. Nor, might I add, do I want yours, Ahvenian."

Tora whirled, blade lifted against Keo. "Come no closer, Kiisuld."

Lekore caught Tora's shoulder. "He has done no harm here."

Keo raised his hands. "In fact, I just saved the poor souls you left below." He stepped aside to reveal the boy Lor, along with the Kel, clustered together on the ramp, their eyes wide, jaws slack. "I thought we might be safer up here," Keo added. "Especially with the growing intensity of the storm blowing in."

Tora jerked his head toward the interior. "*They* are welcome. You're not, Kiisuld."

As one, the Kel fell to their knees, tracing their fingers before their chests. Their awe thickened the air, bombarding Lekore's senses. Nerenoth alone remained standing beside Tora.

Lekore glanced between them, startled by their responses. *Perhaps they know nothing of life beyond the stars.*

Keo's grin widened, unfazed by the Kel. "I expected as much, to be honest. Ahvenian hospitality would never extend so far. Go on, little Kel. Inside." He spoke again in the Tawloomez tongue, but Lor slinked behind him and shook his head, brown eyes wide, frame trembling. He murmured something.

Keo snorted. "This one doesn't want to stay with the Golden Ones."

Tora frowned. "Yet, I can't let him remain with you."

The wind howled in the doorway, pushing against Keo and Lor as the Kel rose and scuttled inside the wide corridor, their eyes pinned on Tora. Fear rolled over their awe, like they worried they'd be struck down if they moved wrong.

'*Lekki, come,*' cried the wind. '*You promised. Come!*'

Lekore eyed the mounting storm as it wailed and ripped a panel from the ship. "Captain, Tora, I must find the source of the storm. I must go now."

Tora studied the ceiling as the sound of more panels tearing loose shrieked overhead. He dropped his gaze to Lekore. "Please explain what's going on."

He drew a breath. "Many Spirits Elemental are trapped within a space that is wounding them. The other spirits are enraged, especially wind. I have promised to help them, and it seems the Tawloomez also has friends trapped in the same place. I must help him as well." He gestured to Lor.

"You're an Elementalist?" asked Tora, glancing at Lekore, though he kept his sword raised against Keo.

"I am. And I promised."

Tora nodded. "I understand. I'll help you. But first I must deal with this Kiisuld." He cringed as another panel tore free with a wrenching moan.

Keo sighed, green hair whipping around his head in the growing force of the gale. "If I promise to be a good boy and stand in a corner, will that suffice?"

Tora arched his brow. "Do you think I'm stupid?"

"No, but in this moment, you sound a bit paranoid." Keo shrugged. "Tie me up, if it makes you feel better."

The young man narrowed his eyes. "If only it were so simple."

"It could be, if you let me explain myself."

"Oh? Let's hear it. I've no doubt your story will be memorable, at least." Tora's arms trembled. Lekore searched his face and read fear hidden beneath a brave façade.

"I've never heard it called dull." Keo ran a hand through his short hair and sighed. "I was exiled from my people many long years ago."

"If that's meant to instill any trust, your words are having the opposite effect," Tora said. "Kiisuld only exile extremists—and those who offend their royal family."

Keo nodded. "I realize it brings no comfort, but let me assure you, I'm not mad or out of control. It's...complicated, and frankly, none of your business. But I can offer one possible reassurance."

"Do, if you can." Tora's fingers tightened on his sword's grip.

"Ter N'Avea."

Tora blinked. "What of him?"

"He and I are well acquainted, and not as enemies. He enlisted me to serve a specific purpose on this planet." Keo scratched his chin. "I'm a Keeper of Memory."

Breath exploded from the young man's lungs. "Impossible."

"No. Though improbable, I'll grant." Keo shrugged. "Yet here I stand, guardian of this backwater world on the edge of our two borders, aiding the 'good guys' as I keep a history of the unfortunates who dwell here. It's not quite the turn I thought my life would take, but that's pretty typical, isn't it?"

"You're lying."

"I'm not. Ask the Seer; he ought to know." Keo nodded at Lekore.

Tora turned his blue eyes on him. "You're a Seer, too?"

Lekore looked between them. "I suppose I am. My ancestor was, and he taught me all he knew of Sight." His wound from the Temple of the Moon flared up again, and Lekore hissed.

"What is it?" asked Tora as Nerenoth inched closer.

"Magic," Keo said. "Fell magic." His brows knitted together. "When did you get that wound, Lekore?"

So many eyes stared at him. Lekore bowed his head as his heart pounded against his ribs. "I...cannot speak of it now. I must see to the storm first. Please. Or the spirits will tear the world asunder, and we will have nothing to speak of at all."

Tora sighed and lowered his sword. "Time presses me into a decision I'm loath to make. I must tolerate you, Kiisuld, but this courtesy only extends so far, and its time is brief. Don't make any foolish moves."

Keo lowered his arms. "I'm glad you're reasonable. And, strange as this is to say, I thank you for your albeit fragile faith."

"I wouldn't call it that," said Tora. "I'm just desperate." He nodded to Lekore. "Lead on. Let's protect your world."

DAKEER VASAR STOOD ON THE NORTHERN BALCONY OF THE Holy Cathedral of the Sun and watched the massive storm brewing over the Lands Beyond. The clouds swelled to hide the northern mountains, banishing the moon's light as a gale raged through the grasslands around the great walls of Inpizal. Gusts of wind pulled at Dakeer's glittering vestments and long hair, whispering wordless threats to his soul.

He bowed his head. One night ago, he had watched a star fall from the heavens. Now the world stormed. *Gods spare and keep us. Gods forgive and guide me.*

He couldn't sleep. Dreams plagued his nights, digging up memories he had long kept locked away. *My dreams are not responsible. It is that cursed child.*

Adenye Getaal, the heir of Erokel, whom Netye had intended to kill. But the blasted king couldn't manage the simplest tasks, let alone those that mattered.

Once, eighteen or so years past, Dakeer had spoken with the toddler prince, determined to implant a love of the gods early in the boy's life. Adenye had been attentive, even inquisitive. Delighted, Dakeer had planted seeds. Where King Adelair walked a cautious line, unwilling to bring his full force to bear down on the Tawloomez tribes, Dakeer intended to guide young Adenye toward a more certain and stronger future—one where the plague of the heathen Tawloomez was forever purged.

As Dakeer had built his case, Adenye listened. In the silence following his subtle lesson, little Adenye rested a hand over Dakeer's and looked him in the eyes.

"Don't hate them, Dak. Don't hate." He stumbled to his feet on the garden bench and planted his palms on Dakeer's face. "Let the bad go."

Staring into such innocence, such simplistic naïveté, Dakeer's soul blistered. The boy's message, so disgustingly pure, free of reason and experience, jolted the Holy Hakija, unveiling a path no Kel could take. Should this child—so certain already of his answers—ever take the throne, his gentleness would break the foundations of the kingdom. Indeed, he might unravel the tenets of the church and destroy all for which Erokel the Second had sacrificed.

"'Beware the touch of gentle moonlight as on a glassy lake, for the paths of velvet dusk give way to dark defilement,'" whispered Dakeer against the growing storm, quoting Erokel's passage of lamentation. That great man had once loved his brother, and in the end, Skye Getaal betrayed him to the Star Gods. Only divinity's hand had spared Erokel and exalted him as king, Hakija, and Lord Captain of the Kel before the Sun Throne. Skye's treachery had been short-lived, his life ended.

"Not soon enough," Dakeer murmured. Had the vile man not prophesied his return on some future day? Had he not invoked unholy powers of the Night to declare he would undo all his brother had built?

Was Lekore not exactly right to play that role?

I was right to turn a blind eye to Netye's actions. I am right now to banish Lekore from our lands forever. I will be right to end his life should he ever return.

The wind shrieked overhead, and lightning plumed across the black sky.

"Guide and guard us beneath thy eternal flames, O Great Sun Gods." He traced the rising sun before him to ward off evil.

CHAPTER 25

Nerenoth plunged through the tangle of gnarled trees, determined to keep stride with the newly arrived Sun God and his mortal companions despite the wind snatching and shoving in turns.

Overhead, clusters of minkee screamed defiant cries against the storm. Lekore led the way, pet emockye at his heels, and the Sun God called Tora followed behind, while Keo hovered near Nerenoth, with the young Tawloomez at his side. The rest of the company had remained at the Sun Ship, eager to fulfill Lord Tora's request that they tend to his crew.

As a warrior, accompanying Lekore and the Sun God made the most sense to Nerenoth. *Though I doubt I will be of much help to them. These conditions are well outside my skillset.*

Still, he yearned to wield his blade on their behalf, should the situation require it.

They've come at last. Lekore has heralded the return of the Sun Gods, just as I'd hoped.

He glanced at Keo as he sidestepped a rotted log. The Sun God's response to the man jarred Nerenoth's soul. How should the Lord Captain handle this predicament? Lekore hadn't been concerned, but Lord Tora clearly didn't trust the strange being with his peculiar coloring—and Keo recognized the Sun God yet paid no deference.

I understand so little, yet things are transpiring at such a rapid pace.

He must keep his mind clear and take his cues from those he trusted.

A branch swiped at his cheek and drew blood. Nerenoth flinched and strode on, squinting in the sharp wind.

Time lost all meaning against the wrathful elements. Beyond the stretch of reason, a glimmer of light snaked between the fretful trees—but in the black storm, how could dawn appear? *It is likely still hours away.*

"The source lies just ahead," said Lekore, his hair and cloak lashing around him. "I do not know what we will find. Let us tread carefully."

They slipped from the shelter of the trees and stood before a strange, smooth building, not in the angular fashion of Inpizal or its sister cities; this was a wide, tall square, though made of the same white, glittering stone. It glowed against the gray of the storm, lit by a steady stream of lightning striking its flat roof.

"By the Nijaal," breathed the Sun God, lips parted as his slitted eyes absorbed the looming structure. "This is Ahvenian." He slipped forward as his hand lifted from his side. His gloved fingers danced across the air. Before Nerenoth's eyes, the god's magnificent sword slid once more from the air, fine and long, a blue gem sparkling on its delicate golden pommel.

Lekore commanded Lios to stay behind, then loped after the Sun God. The Tawloomez youth followed. Nerenoth started onward, but glanced at Keo, who remained in the line of trees.

"Will you not come?"

Keo grimaced. "If I step foot in there, it could be the ruin of all of us. I'll guard the outside."

Nerenoth frowned. "Is it an evil place?"

The man chuckled. "Depends on who you ask."

"I believe I asked you."

"Right. So you did, but my perspective might be the most

skewed of all. Still, in fairness, I should warn you. It's not a place I would wish on good-hearted souls like those three." He inclined his head toward the young men. "Go with them, Lord Captain. Do what you can to protect them—if anything. And hurry. I fear something worse than the ghosts of this place bears down fast on your world."

Nerenoth searched Keo's face. *This isn't cowardice. It's something else.*

He nodded. "I understand." Drawing his blade, he strode into the full force of the windstorm, but the gale ceased as Lekore reached out and rested his fingers on the strange stone door. Lightning abandoned its tirade.

A breathless pause strummed over the air, thick and befuddled.

Lekore pressed his palm against the barrier as he looked up and down. "How does one open it?"

"Here," said Tora and slid open a hand-span wide panel at chest level to the left of the door. His fingers flew over a series of strange runes within the panel, and the ground shivered as the smooth door slid aside.

A gaping black tunnel stood before them, revealing none of its secrets.

Lekore inhaled and stepped forward.

Tora caught his arm. "Be cautious. While I'm certain my people built this structure, its design and purpose are foreign to me." A frown drew a line between his brows. "Something isn't right."

Lekore nodded. "Yet, we must enter."

Tora withdrew his hold. "So we must."

Lekore lifted a hand, and fire sprang up to hover above his palm. The Sun God matched his pace, and together they entered the unknown. The Tawloomez trailed after them, dark eyes darting around him, his nerves visibly matching Nerenoth's. The Lord Captain drew his shoulders and slipped inside.

The air tasted stale but not dank. The floor clicked like marble under Nerenoth's boots, yet it was slicker, less solid, almost light. *Like armor. Is it some kind of metal?*

The baseless flame wandered ahead of Lekore and sputtered in a faint breeze made by the open door behind them. A corridor stretched on into hazy darkness, revealing nothing beyond the same polished black plates adorning Inpizal's oldest halls, set at eye level in wide intervals.

Tora moved to one, pulled a silver glove from his hand, and rested his splayed fingers over the plate. Nothing happened. "It must be on backup power." He lowered his hand and started forward again to catch Lekore, who hadn't stopped.

The Tawloomez youth froze in place, and Nerenoth circled him to offer a questioning scowl. The youth ducked his head and stared at the floor.

"*What is it?*" asked Nerenoth, using the halting tribal words he'd learned over the years.

The youth's head whipped up. He stared, jaw slack, then licked his lips to wet them. "*You speak the Fire Tongue?*"

Nerenoth pinched his gloved fingers together. "*Very little.*"

The young man raked a hand through his thick brown hair. "*My people—trapped—should be—*"

Nerenoth held up a hand. "*Slow. I do not follow.*" Footfalls sounded ahead, and the Lord Captain glanced over his shoulder to find the Sun God and Lekore eyeing them, firelight dancing across their faces.

"I can translate," said Tora.

The Tawloomez rattled off words so fast, Nerenoth caught none of them. He glanced at the Sun God to find him blinking.

"I see." He shifted his focus to Nerenoth. "His people are trapped somewhere in here. It's been over a week, and he's worried about them if there's no food available. Yet, he feels they would have kept a watchman near the door no matter how deep they plunged for sustenance. He's alarmed they didn't do so."

"Ah." Nerenoth nodded and sighed. "All we can do is search."

Tora repeated the words without switching tongues, but Lor understood, judging by his nod.

Lekore turned and started back along the corridor. Striding closer to the young heir, Nerenoth searched Lekore's face, noting the spark in his eyes. *He is fixed upon his goal, much as his father always was.*

The firelight revealed a wall ahead, where the corridor ended. No sign of trapped Tawloomez. No indication of anything further.

Tora strode forward. He tapped a metal plate on the left, and another panel slid aside to reveal more runes. These he pressed, but a red light flashed as a piercing note sang across the air. The Sun God frowned. "Odd. The master password worked before..."

A faint click sounded overhead, the light flashed green, and the wall slid aside. No rumble this time. Merely a whisper as air washed over the company, clean and crisp. Lights flickered into being within glass orbs set along the wall, to reveal a passage beyond, this one bearing the golden heraldry of Sun Gods rather than the stark surfaces of before.

"I didn't do that." Tora frowned. He scanned the corridor beyond, then stepped over the threshold and into the light, which bathed his yellow hair in golden hues. He glanced around. "It doesn't answer the question of how your people got through, Prince Lor'Toreth."

Nerenoth wheeled to stare at the Tawloomez youth. *This ragged enemy was the crown prince of the Tawloomez tribes? I thought their prince was mad.*

Lor'Toreth said something, his tones hasty and tense. As Nerenoth considered the youthful royal, he weighed what he knew against what he saw. Reports declared Lor'Toreth a slight young man, about eighteen years of age, and sickly. Yet, while a nervous flinch attended the prince's movements, his eyes burned with earnestness, not a lunatic gleam. His shoulders hunched under a shoulder wrap woven to resemble snakeskin, yet he sought to rescue his people.

He's been downtrodden and likely abused, but he's no madman.

Nerenoth's heart throbbed. Strange to feel compassion toward a prince of the Tawloomez. His eyes flicked to Lekore, who gazed around at the orb-like lights, awe easing the burdens that had painted shadows on his face. *Are they so different? Betrayed by those they should most trust...*

He sucked in a breath, forcing his thoughts into the presence. He stepped nearer to the Sun God. "Forgive me for speaking out of turn, my lord."

Tora's blue eyes landed on him, steady and bright. "Certainly—Nerenoth, isn't it?"

"Yes, my lord." He dipped his head. "The man called Keo refused to enter this abode, claiming his presence might threaten our survival. I heard the ring of truth in his words. But even without him, this place makes me uneasy." He hesitated and raised his eyes. "Do you know what might threaten us?"

Tora shook his head. "I wish I did, but this facility is a mystery to me...though others of my race definitely built it. That makes sense, since what brought me to your world was an Ahvenian distress signal." He glanced between the Kel and Lor'Toreth. "I don't imagine my explanation makes much sense to any of you. Am I right in supposing the only ships you use are sea-bound?"

"Yes, my lord." Nerenoth shifted as Lekore started down the corridor. "Forgive me, but it looks like we're moving on."

A smile played at Tora's lips. "So it appears." He started after Lekore, Nerenoth beside him, Lor'Toreth trailing in their wake.

As he walked, Lekore reached out and ran his fingers against the polished wall made of a sparkling marble veined with a subtle rainbow of colors. His hair rippled around his ankles, feet sure and purposeful. His head tilted to one side as though he listened to silent voices guiding his steps.

"He's quite special, isn't he?" whispered Tora, gaze pinned on Lekore.

Nerenoth's heart swelled. "Yes, my lord."

Tora nodded. "A Seer *and* an Elementalist. I've heard of such gifted souls before, but outside of Raal Corenic I've never seen them—although Ter mentored him, so I suppose it amounts to the same thing." He smiled.

"Raal Corenic, my lord?"

"Yes. It's a training ground for most gifted people in the Universe. It's an entire world devoted to their education, in fact." Tora sighed. "Perhaps I shouldn't explain so much. My arrival on your world is more than enough to swallow, I suspect."

Hunger burned through Nerenoth's veins. "No, my lord. I will keep afloat. I don't mind learning."

The Sun God's smile deepened. "Fair enough, Nerenoth. Considering my people have been here before, perhaps it's arrogant of me to withhold knowledge from yours."

The lights flickered as Lekore's even steps faltered. He glanced back. "Something terrible lies behind this wall." He gestured to faint lines running in a square, indicating a nondescript door like those hidden in the palace of Inpizal or the Sun Ship.

Nerenoth's hand caught his hilt, flesh tingling.

Tora slipped forward. "Can you tell what we might expect?"

Lekore shook his head. "It feels cold and dark, that is all I know." His eyes flicked to Tora's sword, then back to the god's face. "Will it open?"

"I can bypass most Ahvenian codes—unless it opens on its own again. Be prepared for anything."

Lekore lifted his hand, and his flame danced back to his palm, like a pythe loping toward its master. He stepped away from the door and let Tora access a panel. Again, the red light flashed, and a noise echoed along the corridor. The light flashed green, and the door slid aside.

The sickly-sweet metallic scent of blood and rot rolled over Nerenoth, stinging his eyes as he sought its source. Bodies. A heap of them, indistinct in the gloom of the chamber. The buzz of insects hummed on the putrid air.

Lor'Toreth threw his hands over his face as foreign words escaped his lips. Probably names.

Nerenoth crept into the chamber, gripping his hilt. Smears of dry blood stretched beneath the Tawloomez dead, and the gleam of shadowed gore suggested their throats and stomachs had been sliced open. He stepped back and took Lor'Toreth's arm to move him away from the sight. The Tawloomez prince allowed himself to be steered, tears falling from his eyes.

The lights flickered again.

Lekore eyed Tora, face pale. "I must go in there. It is the path the spirits guide me to pursue."

The Sun God frowned and looked into the dim chamber. "I can't let you go alone." He glanced toward Nerenoth. "We must assume some*thing* or some*one* lives in this facility—and it's malevolent in nature. I hate to make Lor'Toreth travel deeper, but I loathe the idea of splitting up."

Lor'Toreth murmured something.

Nerenoth glanced down at him and spoke in halting Tawloomez. "*If you mean to remain here alone, I cannot allow it. We are better off staying together.*" A writhing guilt coiled in the Lord Captain's stomach, born from years of fighting the Tawloomez tribes, and from his recent losses in Erokes. Should he really be helping the prince of his enemy?

Yet this was barely more than a child, his bandaged arm feeble in Nerenoth's grip, frame quivering.

Lor'Toreth lifted his red-rimmed eyes to stare at Nerenoth. The Lord Captain blinked. *He is much like Jasu'Hekar.* The former slave of Nerenoth's plantation estate had become a kind of friend as he risked his life spying for the Kel once the Lord Captain had freed him.

Nerenoth had always attributed his fondness for Jasu'Hekar to the man being raised among Kel rather than part of some heathen tribe; those who pillaged and burned the northernmost villages of Erokel and carried off the women and young Kel children to sacrifice them to their Snake Gods or enslave them in the Teokaka's palace. Yet, this prince didn't look bloodthirsty. He looked weak and forlorn.

"*I will come,*" said Lor'Toreth. He drew a quaking breath. "*It is better to face truth than run to a lie.*"

Jasu'Hekar often said the same thing. Was it a Tawloomez adage?

"Very well," said Tora. "Let's hurry." The Sun God turned to Lekore. "Lead on."

Lekore stepped into the dim chamber and circled the bodies. Tora slipped inside next. Nerenoth guided Lor'Toreth forward and whisked him into the darkness. As he strode over the threshold, a piercing alarm screamed across the air, and the door slid shut behind him.

Lekore's flame guttered in the center of the wide room, the company's only source of light.

Tora padded to the door and fingered the panel on the wall. It didn't slide open. He gritted his teeth. "We're trapped."

Chills swept over Nerenoth's flesh as he glanced between the Sun God and Lekore, both mere shades in the semi-darkness. Beside him, Lor'Toreth shivered.

"This way." Lekore strode on, his flame following. He reached another wall, and it slid aside with no prompting.

"Ah, so it leads us deeper," Tora murmured and stepped around the bodies to follow Lekore. "Keep alert, everyone."

Nerenoth pulled Lor'Toreth along while he kept his free hand on his sword.

"TELL ME YOU SAW HIM, TOO."

Talanee glanced to her side, a soggy rag in her hand. Her eyes met Ademas's before he looked down to dab at the wound oozing on the Sun God's leg.

"Saw who?" she asked.

Ademas twirled his wrist. "You know, the *Sun God.*"

A shiver sprinted through her frame, even as her chest warmed.

She wiped at the perspiration on the unconscious being's brow. "Of course I did. What do you call this one?"

"Half dead." Ademas sighed. "You know what I mean. Did you see...?" He worked his mouth. "I don't know how to explain."

Talanee nodded. "I saw." She too had recognized that indefinable quality, that superior blending that made up the beautiful young god who had pitted himself against the dubious man called Keo. She had also seen his trust in Lekore.

What do I make of it all?

"Is this a servant, then? To be wounded so. Can gods bleed?" Ademas rested the poultice Lekore had left for them upon the man's jagged wound.

"They fell from the heavens, for Light's sake. He must've been wounded in a divine battle." Talanee frowned. "Right?"

"I...don't know." The creases of his brow ran deep. "I never quite believed in the gods."

She shot him a startled glare. "*What?*"

Ademas shrugged. "They just seemed so far away, and frankly, too consistent with church doctrine."

"Of *course* the Sun Gods are consistent with church doctrine. It's the church!"

"Calm down, Princess. What I mean is, with every rising Hakija, the gods seemed to alter to accommodate his private agendas. Are gods changeable like that?" He shrugged one shoulder. "My mistake was assuming that meant the gods might be complete fabrications, instead of real, divine beings whom we fallible mortals misunderstand and misconstrue. It only makes sense we would. We're finite, after all. They're infinite. It's impossible for us to comprehend them. Meanwhile, we must look like silly little ants worth poking a stick at now and then."

"You're very odd. I hope you know that." Talanee resisted an urge to inch away from him, lest she be struck down in proximity. *We're helping a god. Surely that counts for something.*

Ademas chuckled. "I don't profess to be otherwise."

"Even so, you ought to be branded with some kind of warning."

Her eyes flicked to the pendant chains around his neck, tucked beneath his green tunic. "You're not really a Star Worshiper, are you?"

He tracked her eyes and pulled a pendant free. Its face flaunted a starburst. "You're referring to this."

She hissed and glanced at the sleeping god. "Put that away before you offend the Sun Throne, you fool."

He shrugged and slipped it under his shirt. "It's just a tool, Talanee. It allows me to travel into the more questionable sectors of Inpizal and learn what I must."

"To what end? What are you looking for?"

He met her eyes. "Answers."

"To what?"

"That isn't something you need to know just now."

"Why? I'm your princess—and kin. Shouldn't I know?"

"No. Not yet. Can't you be satisfied with knowing your gods are real?"

Talanee scowled. "My gods, not yours?"

He sighed. "Of course, my gods, too. I just mean, isn't all this enough?" He gestured to the unconscious figure just as the god moaned.

Heart leaping, Talanee leaned close to the Sun God. "Holy One, can you hear me?"

The man's eyes fluttered open, revealing irises of fiery orange. Talanee's breath caught as his slitted gaze met hers. "Who—" His voice, deep and resonant, drove thrills dancing over her skin. His eyes widened as his jaw clenched, hand diving for his ornate sword. He leaned forward. "Where is the prince?"

Talanee inhaled a sharp breath but shook off her shock to press him back down. "Be still, Holiness. If you seek the one called Tora, he's hale enough, and had to leave on an urgent matter. *You*, however, are in no state to follow, and with all due respect, I beg you not to move yet. Your wounds are severe."

"Tora, yes. Of course." The Sun God leaned back and closed his eyes. "I thank you for your kindness, my lady."

Talanee's cheeks warmed. "I'm humbled, Holy One."

The god sucked in air and cracked one eye open. "What of the crew?"

Ademas shifted. "Two of our companions are searching your ship to help those they can find."

"Good. Again, you have my thanks." He shut his eyes. "Please wake me when—when Tora returns."

"As you wish, Holy One," said Talanee. She waited until the man's shoulders slouched and his breathing deepened, then let out a sigh. "My head is storming with questions. There's so much I want to ask, to know! If only the Hakija were here."

"It would certainly prove interesting," whispered Ademas.

She glanced at him and found his eyes speared on the Sun God, brow drawn. She pinched her skirts. "Don't you see the blessing in all this, Cousin? These messengers from the Sun Throne—indeed, the very *prince* of the Sun Throne—will pour light over all our concerns. Everything will be made clear as a cloudless day."

"True, that. I can hardly stand to wait." He bent to his work on the god's leg.

Talanee stood and rolled her shoulders to loosen her muscles. "Stay with him. I'll help the twins—"

Thunder exploded overhead, and the ground shuddered. Ademas sprang up and sprinted to the open doorway of the ship to stare out into the storm, his short hair flailing in the furious gale. All at once, the wind died. He drew back inside and turned around, frowning, eyes bright in the glow of the light orbs. "Something is out there. I—I don't know what it is."

She straightened up and whisked to his side, jeweled skirts rustling. Her feet throbbed as she moved, but Lekore's wraps had spared her worse pain, so she refused to complain. She leaned outside, and the forming night mists caressed her cheeks.

Darkness enveloped the jungle, apart from the faint remains of fire from the shipwreck, but they were mere coals defying death.

"I don't see—" A feeling crept over her flesh like a thousand spiders pattering over her arms and legs, and she stepped backward as her heart clattered in her ribcage. "By the gods, what is that?"

Nothing moved in the stillness. No emockye, no minkee, nothing beyond the mist...and the intangible, horrible feeling of something lurking in the dense trees.

She sucked in air and leaned out the door to peek up at the night sky. No sign of stars or moonlight. Just the wrathful clouds louring down on her, whispering nameless threats. She stepped back and met Ademas's gaze. "Can we close this door?"

He stepped to the panel. "I can try." He pressed on a circular button and the door hissed shut. "Ah, there. That was easy."

"Can we bar it somehow?"

He shrugged. "There are too many options. I don't think we should risk pushing these to figure it out."

"No, I suppose not." She shivered. "This is a holy ship. We'll be safe, right?"

He shook his head. "I don't know, Talanee. It crashed. That doesn't just happen. Which means there was an enemy up there, and I can't think of a reason it wouldn't come down here to finish what it started."

CHAPTER 26

The fifth door along Lekore's course slid open to reveal a vast, well lit chamber, faint whirring sounds filling the air, a few blinking lights spread over surfaces like stone desks. Lekore slipped inside, letting his flame die, Tora at his heels.

"Ah, this must've been the command center." Tora strode to a desk in the middle of the room. He leaned over its slanted face, eyes darting across the switches and buttons. "This is the main console. I suspect this may also be related to my ship malfunctioning." He tapped a flashing amber light. "The distress signal originates here. If nothing else, I need to deactivate that, to avoid further casualties."

Lekore padded to his side and stared at the console. "Might this also supply a method for our escape?"

"It might at that. I'll need a few minutes to override the controls." Tora's fingers flew over a series of buttons laid out in rows. "It's an outdated system. At least eight hundred years old, maybe more. Strange that I've heard nothing of your world. It didn't even show up on my star charts."

Lekore watched the foreign runes scrawl across a kind of window set above the rows of writing Tora's fingers tapped. He shook himself. "Please hurry, if you can."

Tora nodded. "I understand your anxiety. Whatever murdered those people is still here somewhere, and my instinct insists they mean us no goodwill."

"Indeed, not." Lekore turned as something flickered in his periphery. A single wind spirit waved at him from a dark corner. He turned and strode to stand beneath the flitting wisp as it motioned to a box set into the wall near the ceiling. He glanced over his shoulder. "What is this?"

Tora glanced up. "An air duct. I think we've been gradually traveling underground. Something I can confirm if only..." He trailed off as his fingers flew faster.

Lekore looked up to watch the wind spirit tug on the box. "What does an air duct do?"

"It regulates temperature—and purifies the air, in this case, to prevent us from suffocating." Tora's fingers faltered. "Why?"

"The wind is trying to open it. I wonder..." Lekore lifted his hand. "Please come." The spirit flitted to his finger as it morphed into the shape of a small bird. "You must tell me. I cannot guess your thoughts."

'Trapped. Trapped inside.'

Lekore nodded. "I will free them."

'Dying. Trapped. Sick. Dying.'

"I understand. I will—" Something split his vision, a kind of warping as reality tipped. A translucent hand snatched his wrist and dragged him toward the wall. The arm attached to it slithered from the wall itself. Lekore shouted as he tugged against the grip.

A blade swung through the wrist. The limb faded into nothing, releasing Lekore from its otherworldly grip.

Sweat pricked his neck, and he glanced right, expecting to find the Lord Captain. Instead, his gaze settled on Tora, whose slitted eyes were mere pinpricks, almost feral in the chamber's glow. Behind him stood the Lord Captain, his own blade drawn, the Tawloomez at his side, pale and trembling as he clutched his bone dagger.

"I've never seen anything like that," Tora said, pushing his fair hair from his face.

"I have." Lekore's voice was a mere whisper. He tried again. "It was something dead. I do not think the Spirits Elemental are trapped by anything innocent or even mortal. I fear they have been used to lure us here."

Tora rubbed his chin, brow drawn. He studied the wall where the arm had been. "I don't—"

The lights died.

Lekore lifted his hand. *Fire, please come forth.* Flames sprang up from his palm as his blood ran hot, answering the summons, bathing the chamber in orange light, revealing— "Look out!"

Tora spun, swinging his sword before him. The blade bit air as the spectral figure Lekore had glimpsed faded into darkness mere inches from Tora's body. A drifting breath rippled over the air, deep and guttural, washing over the company until gooseflesh danced up Lekore's arms.

"We know one thing," Tora said into the silence. "While my sword can't strike a fatal blow, it appears to have some slight effect upon our—*host*."

"Does that comfort you?" The voice crackled from the ceiling, loud and disembodied.

Tora looked up. "Who are you? What is all this?"

Faint laughter drifted across the air. "A game, perhaps. It has been ages since last I encountered an Ahvenian of flesh and blood. My goals were different, but I'm adaptable. Welcome, boy. What is your name?"

Lekore dropped his gaze to find Tora's face. The scowl he wore might well wither a garden of flowers.

"Tora, ambassador of the Sun Empire of Ahvenia. What is yours, captor?"

"So bold, you are."

A faint smile brushed Tora's lips. "Whatever tricks you're attempting to play on our minds, and whatever this place is, of one thing I'm certain: You're no ghost."

A sigh issued forth from some hidden space above. "No, I'm not. Though it isn't much longer until I will join my fellows in their—should I call them graves? Perhaps, final rest? It matters little, I think, when you're the last."

"The last of what?" asked Tora.

Lekore flinched as flickering memories poured through his mind, too rapid to comprehend beyond the feelings that lingered in their wake. Regret. Anguish. Hatred.

"The last of a cause, that is all I will say."

Tora stepped toward the voice, sword still clutched in one fist. "Do you know what happened to this facility? What it was? Are you Ahvenian as well?"

A chuckle. "So inquisitive, and so young for an ambassador. Does the Sun Court now indenture mere youths to fulfill its agendas?" Another sigh. "It matters little. Not any longer. Our cause ended so long ago, I've forgotten the span of time I've been in this realm, upon this backwater world with its petty squabbles. What of the Universe is left for me?"

Tora's expression softened. "Can I take you from this planet and bring you to your home?"

The snigger sounded again. "Oh, no. I'm tied to this place, and all that's left for me is to thwart the dooming cry of that accursed man."

"What man?" asked Tora.

A tingle tracked up Lekore's spine. He whirled as fingers slipped from the wall. Hands. Arms. Reaching for him. He staggered back and thrust out his hand. *Calir, come!* The sword formed in his fist, heavy and sure as it rang out a chiming note. The arms in the wall paused.

Laughter bore down on the chamber. "No matter your power, little Seer, there's nothing you can do. You'll remain trapped in this fortress until you surrender yourself to me."

"What do you want with him?" asked Tora.

"Fear not, Ahvenian lord, I have room enough to wish your demise as well, and I've no love for the Kel or Tawloomez either.

You will each fall, one by one. You'll be sacrificed, just as those who entered this building before you."

Tora raised his voice. "Sacrificed to what end? We're not here for your amusement."

"Amusement? No. This is vengeance."

The arms in the wall pushed forward again, and a body appeared, its features indistinct, shimmering like moonlight on a black pool. The fingers of its right hand flexed and curled into a fist, and a slender sword formed, a translucent black hue. The figure stepped away from the wall, tall, broad-shouldered, faceless. Lekore lifted *Calir*.

Tora stepped next to him, his blade hoisted as well, sword humming a note to match *Calir*'s chime.

"Captain, please protect Lor'Toreth," Lekore said.

"As you command."

Nerenoth's words startled Lekore, but he dropped the feeling as the ghost swung its blade. The immortal material struck *Calir* and Tora's weapon with a deafening peal. Lekore's fingers stung as he stumbled against the impact, Tora falling back with him.

"Lekore, stand aside!"

He glanced over his shoulder, heart soaring. Skye appeared beside him, red eyes ablaze with a fire that burned in his soul. The ghost held the memory of *Calir* in his hands, its curved blade brighter than the chamber could account for.

Lekore shifted his blade to let Skye stand before him. "An ally has joined us."

Tora shot him a startled glance. "What do you—"

The ghostly stranger swung again, and Skye lifted *Calir*'s twin to counter the blow. The same pealing tone rippled across the room like a fierce wind, snatching up hair and clothing.

Tora gaped, then threw a look at Lekore. "Who?"

"My ancestor and mentor, Skye Getaal."

"Ah, at last!" boomed the voice above. "I knew he'd come for his heir. At last, I have you, accursed one. You'll not leave—and I'll make your kin pay for your transgressions!"

Skye forced the faceless ghost back, their swords locked in a discordant note. He grinned. "Has not enough time passed yet for you, Talajin? Why do you harbor the same bitter blindness? Did Erokel and his *gods* not draw enough blood?"

A frigid laugh descended. "Ah, Skye. Should the Ahvenian Empire fall, should the Kiisuld leech life from every planet in this Universe, it would not be enough to satisfy me—until you are cowed. Until you beg for mercy—and I deny it!"

A grimace stole over Skye's face. "Your madness has tarnished your soul to its depths, Talajin." He glanced at Lekore. "Tell them to stay back. I must muster full strength to fend off Talajin's pawn."

Nodding, Lekore paced backward. "We should move away from the fight. Skye needs room."

Tora withdrew at once, following Lekore across the chamber to stand near the center console. Nerenoth had already brought Lor'Toreth there, sword still in hand, his other hand gripping the Tawloomez's shoulder. Nerenoth met Lekore's eyes with a question but said nothing.

"Lekore," said Tora. "Why can I see one ghost, but not that of your ancestor?"

Lekore shook his head. "I'm uncertain. Perhaps it is because the one is chained by someone."

"Necromancy?" Tora flinched and turned back to the fight.

Skye's blade flashed as he danced around the imprisoned specter, pushing the faceless ghost toward the far wall.

In the gloom, only the light of the ghosts and Lekore's hovering flame illuminated the chamber in an eerie, pulsing glow. Shadows rose like tendrils from the floor, and Lekore gasped as Tora raised his blade.

The Lord Captain shoved Lor'Toreth between him and the metal desk as the young man let out a foreign curse.

Five faceless specters slid from the floor to surround Skye, ethereal blades lifted. As one, they stabbed inward to pierce the ghostly flesh of their enemy.

"Skye!" Lekore's voice rang out over the chamber, flames bursting around him, scattering shadows.

The ghost of his ancestor screamed as the swords plunged through armor and cape, into his otherworldly frame. A pulsing wave of glee washed over Lekore from the circle of specters even as he stared, shaking.

Where the blades met Skye's form, his shape faded. Skye craned his head toward Lekore, eyes lined with pain. He offered a faint smile. "They cannot slay me, Lekore. Find me, free me before it's too late." His body broke apart into a misty haze, wisping upon the air.

A tear leaked from Lekore's eye, and he bowed his head as a menacing laugh hammered down upon him like the rains of a flash flood. The flames ebbed as his shoulders sank. The specters slid back into the floor, leaving only the fire elementals behind to light the chamber.

Gentle fingers brushed his shoulder. "What happened?" asked Tora.

Lekore drew a breath. "He has been wounded and captured. I must find him."

"Oh, yes, little Seer," said the voice above. "Find him if you can. Find him and keep him from his fate."

A clicking sound echoed throughout the chamber. A surge of fiery wrath shook Lekore's frame, sparking the fire spirits. Flames engulfed his body, licking at his flesh and dancing along the tendrils of his hair. He glowered at the ceiling, letting the flames burn inside him, letting them purge his soul of any doubts, any fears, until all that remained was raging certainty: He would save his mentor, his friend, his ancestor.

"We'll help," said Tora. "I suspect this building is immense, but between your skills and mine, it won't be impossible to seek him and the caged Spirits Elemental out." He stepped before the console and fingered the many buttons and switches. "Our greatest challenge may be the chained souls and their otherworldly blades. I've never fought anything like them before."

Above the console, a shimmering square of light flared into being, painting pale colors across the faces of all assembled. Lekore studied the image and blinked. "This is a map, is it not?"

"It is. A map of this structure, in fact." Tora pressed a few more buttons. "It's not as large as I feared, but there's still a lot of space to cover."

Lekore searched the lines and turns of the map. *Such detail. I've seen no other map like this.* He reached up to touch the image and his finger passed through the shimmering light. "It is just like Skye."

"Not so complex as a spirit," said Tora, flashing a smile. "This is made up of wires and lights and—well, a few other things."

Lekore nodded and returned to the map. "How many levels does this structure encompass?"

Tora clicked a few buttons. "Six, each deeper than the last."

Lekore chewed the inside of his cheek as his eyes danced over the tiny hallways and chambers represented on the map. "We must go to the lowest."

"I was afraid of that." Tora brought up a different image, this one showing a miniature of stairs and corridors lined in red. "This is the most direct route using stairwells. Considering the nature of these chained spirits, I'd prefer not to take any elevators." His lips crooked into a smile. "Though I suppose none of you know what those are."

Lekore shook his head and Nerenoth echoed him. Lor'Toreth mumbled something, eyes staring at the ground. A pang shot through Lekore's heart, and he slipped to the Tawloomez's side.

Lor'Toreth jerked backward. "*Hequt, Akuu-Ry!*"

Lekore lifted his hands. "I mean no harm. *Jyit gasha'hatu.* No harm."

"He meant to comfort you, I suspect," said Tora.

The Tawloomez ducked his head, long brown hair hiding his face.

Lekore frowned and sought Tora's gaze. "It is possible that his dead companions are now chained—perhaps they are even those who stabbed Skye to bind his soul. We must free them somehow."

Tora sighed. "Do you have experience with necromancy?"

"No, none."

"Nor do I." Tora fingered his sword. "We must go on nevertheless." His blue eyes flicked to Lor'Toreth. "I wish you could remain safely behind, but that's foolishness."

Lor'Toreth glanced up and rattled off something fierce.

Tora smiled. "I don't doubt your bravery at all. It isn't that. This circumstance is beyond any of us—but we're here."

Lekore started across the room, fingers tingling where he clutched *Calir*. The blade hummed again, and Tora's sword replied, like songbirds greeting one another at dawn. He glanced back at the yellow-haired young man, curiosity nudging against the worries of his heart. Tora held his gaze.

"Something to speak of later, I think," the young man said.

Lekore nodded and turned toward the door barring his way. He drew his cloak closer as flames flitted along its black folds. "I have seen no sign of the spirits I came to rescue. They must be below as well."

Tora slipped past him to play his fingers over the panel. The door slid aside, and lights flickered into life to illuminate their path. "This is a game to our host, despite what he says, yet I feel it's a twisted sport. He could easily kill us now. I fear what he has in mind instead."

"Agreed." Lekore's throat tightened as his arm throbbed where the Star Worshipers had drawn blood. This was different, but it carried the same malice, the same dark hues of lurking hunger. Lekore strode through the doorway, his companions close on his heels. "If this man knew Skye Getaal as a living man, he is old indeed."

"How long ago did Skye live?" asked Tora.

"Five hundred years, my lord," Nerenoth said.

Lekore glanced over his shoulder to consider the Lord Captain. Fear raked fingers of doubt over his heart. *Those in the Temple of the Moon knew Skye. They revered him. Does the Lord Captain consider him evil like the Hakija does?*

Nerenoth found Lekore's eyes. Held them. His lips curled upward in a humorless smile. "I don't pretend to understand most of this, but I little doubt that my knowledge of Skye Getaal is tainted by the opinions and agendas of Kel these past five centuries."

Lekore's heart quickened as his muscles relaxed. He nodded, then padded along the corridor, drawing his thoughts back to the matter at hand. He mustn't let his fears distract him.

Despite the silence wrapping its limbs around the group, a kind of hollow note climbed across his mind, toning until it reached an earsplitting crescendo.

Shivers rippled over his soul like a thousand pebbles thrown into a black lake. Fleshless fingers pawed across his mind, then plunged into his heart as ice lanced up his legs. He gasped and staggered forward as he caught a flash of shimmering hands jutting like stalagmites from the floor to clutch his ankles. His knees smashed against the hard floor, the flames of his cloak flickering before they extinguished.

He tightened his grip on *Calir* and contorted to slash his blade through the spirit's wrists. The fingers gave way, and he stumbled loose, then sprang upright as hands reached from the wall to snatch at his arm. He fended them off with a second swipe, but his eyes snared on more hands coming from the walls to surround their party.

Fire, please help!

The fire spirit sputtered and tried to reform but faded. Lekore shuddered as the warmth in his body snuffed out like a candle.

He slumped against the wall as the Lord Captain danced away from another faceless specter. Hands caught Lekore's throat from behind, pinning him against the cold stones.

His body trembled, frost climbing his bones.

He reached for wind. Silence answered.

Earth!

The ground held its breath.

Water, he must find water. But the surrounding structure

barred the outside world, and water rarely answered his summons, anyway.

His vision shimmered and darkened. Breath rattled through his lungs, echoing like some distant gale in his ears. His arms slackened.

Fight this, Lekore. What of the Lord Captain? What of Tora and Lor'Toreth?

It couldn't matter now.

Not even the frail hope that Nerenoth Irothé might be Ank lent any strength.

Silence deafened his senses.

His eyes closed.

CHAPTER 27

T he ship's door burst open.

Shards of charred metal sailed across the air to land around Talanee's and Ademas's feet. One shard bit Talanee's jaw, drawing blood. Her heart jumped into her throat, but she wrestled her expression into something approaching calm derision. She lifted her chin to punctuate the effect.

A figure stood in the doorway, lithe and lean, shadowed by dust swirling before the entrance. It stepped through the miniature whirlwind. Talanee sucked in air as she slid back a step and sent a metal scrap skidding across the polished floor.

Ademas jabbed his sword ahead of him as his eyes flashed a warning.

The Tawloomez woman paused, brown eyes narrowed, her tongue sliding over bloodred lips. She tilted her head and flashed white teeth in a grin that stretched up until her dark eyes lit like a mad flame.

"Ah," she said. "Kel nobles. That I did *not* expect."

The cadence of her voice, free of any foreign stumbles, marched chills up Talanee's arms. Somehow, though she'd never seen the woman before, Talanee knew who stood before her.

"Depart, Tawloomez, and I'll let you live," said Ademas, his face as calm as Talanee hoped hers remained. "This is neutral ground, and I've no private quarrel with you."

The Tawloomez woman chuckled. "What generosity from the pampered descendants of Erokel." Her eyes flashed over the lavender locks in their hair. "There is no neutral ground, little Kel. The Wildwood belongs to my tribes, and you are trespassing—but that is what Kel are wont to do. You claim the fertile southern lands for your own, yet those, too, belong to us." She strolled forward, every move a kind of simpering slither.

"Ademas," Talanee whispered.

"I know, Tala."

She blinked. Then understood. *He knows this is the Teokaka herself, and he doesn't want to reveal who I am to her.*

Noble status wasn't something they could hide. That they were royalty was an altogether, far more dangerous threat, best kept secret.

The Teokaka halted mere yards away, a snug, green, snakeskin gown shimmering in the even lighting. "Are there any survivors, Kel?"

Ademas frowned. "None we've found."

"How do they look?"

He shrugged. "Dead."

The Teokaka's mirth slipped a little on her lips. "Do not test my patience too far, little Kel. Are they the Golden Ones? Let me see."

Ademas caught Talanee's wrist, and he drew her aside and offered passage to the Teokaka. "We gathered them into the large chamber just there. Do what you please with the corpses but let us be on our way."

The woman paused before the chamber beyond and angled her head until her glinting brown eyes met Ademas's face. Her lips curled into a viperous grin. "So many demands." Her finger stroked the panel beside the chamber door, and she glanced inside as the door slid open. "Ahhh. Such luscious destruction." Her body quivered. "Mahaka, come."

Movement seized Talanee's eyes, and she watched a second figure peel away from the shadows of the ship's entrance. He was a tall, muscular man, draped in glistening snakeskin and leather armor, hair shorn off but for a ponytail at the side of his head. He clutched a scissor knife in one hand. His sunken, dark brown eyes resembled the hollow pits of the skulls in the Charnel Valley— though he wore no grin to speak of.

"Search the ship for survivors," said the Teokaka. "When you are finished, return to me. I must take my slaves to their new home." She licked her poisonous lips.

Talanee stiffened. She and Ademas had hidden the wounded god and several other survivors among the bodies of the fallen Sun Gods Jesh and Jeth had gathered into the large chamber. Would Mahaka find those who still lived?

I can't risk it.

She must also distract the man from finding the twins, who had gone into the levels below to seek any remaining divine souls.

Seizing the dagger hidden in her skirts, she spun and sprinted into the chamber as the Teokaka barked out an order. Talanee flew to the first corpse she spotted, flung herself beside it, knees smarting, and rammed the dagger between the woman's ribs.

Footsteps halted behind her.

"Why did you do that, Tala?" asked Ademas, wrenching her wrist away. "They might not have noticed her."

Talanee hid a smile. *At least my cousin is no fool.* She brushed long hair from her face. "I would never condemn a Sun Goddess to the cruelty of a Tawloomez heathen. Better to kill her now."

Rough hands snatched her arms and lifted her up. The man in snakeskin turned her to face the unholy beauty of the Teokaka, and Talanee held her chin high before the viperous smile.

"Clever girl to hide her among the dead. Still more clever to destroy her." The Teokaka's eyes swept over the room littered with the bodies of over two dozen crewmembers. All silent. All still. "Come, Mahaka. They've done our work for us, it seems. Best to let the Wildwood claim this vessel now." She drifted from the

279

room as Mahaka leaned down to drag Ademas upward. He guided Talanee and Ademas from the chamber, and the door slid shut with a faint hiss.

Mahaka led them toward the broken doorway. Mist curled inside to swirl around the Teokaka standing with her back to them, eyes searching the darkness beyond.

Staring at the tinted skin of her captor, Talanee shuddered. *This is truly happening. I'm being taken to the Firelands of the Tawloomez. I'll never see my home again.*

Her eyes darted to Ademas, and he met her wild gaze with perfect calm.

No. Not calm.

His eyes blazed. His lip curled up in a faint smile. Not a flicker of fear crossed his countenance.

He's not giving up. Well, neither am I!

She squared her shoulders as Mahaka's large hand tightened on her arm, his palm damp through the cloth of her stained gown. The Teokaka strode near, eyes like pits of mud. Her fingers wrapped around Talanee's wrist, cold, dry like parchment.

Tingles raced up Talanee's arm, and the world tilted, then righted itself, as dawn stretched over a distant horizon and a wave of heat crawled over her skin.

In the mere blink of an eye, the ship had vanished. She stood now in Tawloomez lands. Young mountains of red stone hugged the western sky beyond a wall of the same red rock. Across a courtyard of twisting trees wilting under the dry heat of early morning, the Tawloomez palace stood, made of the same red hues.

Talanee's eyes climbed northeast to the peak of Fire Mountain, hazy with smoke, painting the lightening sky in shades of blood where its maw gaped open to reveal its blistering wrath.

The mountain that broods but never bleeds, so Erokel the Second had called it. Ever did it hiss and sputter, but only once had the volcano erupted in the past thousand years.

Mahaka shoved Talanee toward the palace proper, pushing Ademas at the same time. They trailed after the Teokaka, whose gown dragged behind her as she swayed along the path cobbled in bloodred stones.

Talanee caught Ademas's eye. He shook his head.

To fight and flee now, here, so far from home would mean only death.

Every step thundered through Talanee's body, but her mind flittered away from the fact of her capture, unwilling to settle on it. This couldn't be real. She must have fallen asleep in the Lands Beyond—or perhaps in Lekore's strange cavern dwelling.

Perhaps I never left Inpizal at all.

The wind wafted through her hair. Her lungs hitched on a dry breath.

Dawn's light drifted over the looming palace, reducing the scarlet hues of stone to an orange-red color, revealing the cracks and crumbling angles of the ancient edifice. Or perhaps it wasn't age that scarred this royal house, but the wear of something crafted by mortal hands, unlike the hallowed Cathedral of the Sun and all else the Sun Gods had gifted to the Kel.

She dug her nails into her palms and willed away the thundering fear that probed at her heart. *I am a proud princess of the chosen Kel. I have seen the Sun Gods for myself. I am not forsaken yet!*

Apart from the murmuring wind and the scuff of feet against stone, silence filled the air. Ademas kept his eyes forward. Talanee glanced at him twice before they reached the edge of the courtyard where steps ascended to an open doorway. The Teokaka reached the entrance and turned to face her captives.

"Take the young man to the pits, Mahaka. The girl will serve me here."

Talanee stiffened as Mahaka released his grip on her shoulder. He led Ademas away from the steps, along a narrow path leading to a patch of shadows against the palace wall. Ademas glanced over his shoulder and offered up a grim smile, eyes still aflame.

Talanee trembled and willed her leather-bound feet to stay rooted. *Gods go with him. Light protect him. There's nothing you can do, so don't be a fool. Bide your time. The Sun God and Lekore will come for us.*

"Is your will to fight already extinguished, Kel?"

Talanee turned to the Teokaka and tossed a lock of hair over her shoulder. "Is that what my silence implies?"

The Tawloomez offered a sneering smile. "This way, slave. There is work aplenty to be done." Her eyes dropped to Talanee's hands. "I do so *long* to ruin your dainty little fingers. Come. *Now.*"

Talanee drew a long breath and stormed up the steps. As she neared the Teokaka, the woman snatched her hair and dragged her close until Talanee could smell her musty breath. The Teokaka pulled tighter, and Talanee's scalp burned as hairs ripped free.

"I will break you, little Kel."

Talanee narrowed her eyes even as her stomach churned. "*Try.*"

The woman released her and shoved her inside the palace. Strange lamps hung from the low ceiling at intervals, illuminating the corridor where Talanee found herself. The air curled around her limbs, cool compared to the courtyard.

Down the corridor came the faint scrape of footfalls. Shadows stretched long over the stone floor until cloaked figures appeared, candles flickering in their hands, their flames reflecting off the sheen of snakeskin robes. They halted and bowed low, hiding the shadows of their cowled faces.

The Teokaka strode past Talanee to face her entourage. "This is my latest acquisition. Dress her appropriately, and put her to work, then gather my people. We must celebrate the blessed destruction of false idols."

The cloaked figures quivered, perhaps with pleasure, and Talanee lifted her lips in a snarl. *Heathen scum!*

One figure parted from the group and approached, bearing no candle. It was a slender little creature, shorter than Talanee. As the lamplight fell across its face, the flame banished shadows enough to reveal the dark skin and brown eyes of a Tawloomez girl, no older than eleven or twelve years. They stared at each other.

"*I'tete,*" said the girl in a soft, melodic voice.

Talanee let the girl take her wrist and lead her past the Teokaka and horrible, snakeskin-clad worshipers. She had braced herself for a wrathful Lady of Maids or a commanding slavedriver to lead her into the halls of her captivity, but against this birdlike child, Talanee had no defense. No defiant utterance.

She followed the heathen girl down several channels, pausing as the girl halted to pour oil into a lamp that sputtered more than the rest, or straighten a tapestry of brilliant colors. Once, the girl halted to stare at a blank wall.

"*Stataj*," she murmured, then crouched down. She cupped something in her small hands, straightened, and moved to a window overlooking the blushing gardens at dawn. Strange, yellow-red flowers unfurled with the promise of light as the girl tipped her hands on the windowsill to release her eight-legged captive, then watched it scurry out to freedom. She turned back to Talanee, smile radiant as the picturesque morning. She flitted near, took Talanee's wrist again, and pulled her onward.

The child took Talanee into the very bowels of the heathen palace, where the heat from outside had no province, and cool, clammy air embraced her as she entered a room of gray stone. A heap of rags claimed one corner. The girl flitted to the corner and dug through the heap until she wrenched loose one tattered gray garment from the rest. She returned to Talanee's side with the grace of a hopping bird intent upon a worm.

Pressing the garment into Talanee's hands, she rattled off a series of words, then danced from the room. The door snipped shut behind her. A single lamp lit the room.

Talanee grimaced as she held aloft the ragged, shapeless dress. *Bide your time. Submit for now. There will be time to fight soon.*

Sighing, she stripped off the remains of her ruined scarlet gown and slipped into the dank-smelling tatters. The dress hung loose and lumpish on her slim frame, devoid of clasps or ties, a perfect testament of her predicament. A burning sensation climbed Talanee's throat and pricked at her eyes, threatening, impulsive. She choked it down and dug her nails deeper into her palms.

You will not cry, you foolish girl. What good comes from such weakness?

Erokel the Second had despised all weakness, most of all tears. When his wife had died far too young, he'd penned a lament condemning his own grief.

"'Behold me not, O Glorious Light,'" Talanee whispered, dredging up the words she'd memorized years ago for the Week of Bitter Starlight, "'for I am stricken by darkness in my weakness. Turn away thy Beaming Countenance, that I perish not from the shame of my mortal confines. Tomorrow will I become strong again, and rebuke myself most wretchedly for this damning pain. None know better than I what befalls him who allows grief and greed to remove him from truth and salvation. I am overwrought and blind in the shadows of night.'"

Surely, Talanee's situation wasn't so heartrending as when that great man lost his love and his muse. Surely, she could endure this trial, even to death itself, should the Sun Gods require it.

The door creaked open, and Talanee turned to find the Tawloomez girl haloed in the light behind her. She rattled off another sentence or two and tiptoed into the room.

"I can't understand you," Talanee snapped, glad her flash of temper banished the last threat of tears.

The girl blinked at her, but her smile only grew. She tapped her collarbone and said in slow tones, "Khyna." She tapped again. "Khyna."

"I assume that's your name." Talanee ran a hand down the side of her face. "Fine, I'll play along." She tapped her collarbone. "Tala. Taw-luh."

The girl flashed white teeth in a grin. "Tala." She pointed. "Tala." She turned the finger on herself. "Khyna."

Talanee rolled her eyes. "Very well. Khyna."

The girl nodded but wrinkled her nose. "Kai-nuh."

Talanee adjusted her tongue to try again.

Khyna nodded. "Good, Kel." Her accent was thick enough, it took Talanee a moment to realize she'd spoken in the Kel tongue at all.

Relief sent breath exploding from her lungs, and she snatched

Khyna's shoulders, digging her fingertips into the girl's bony flesh. "You speak the Kel tongue?"

The girl shook her head and answered in a string of fluent Tawloomez. She finished with, "Very little, Kel. Little."

With reluctance, Talanee released the girl. "A little is better than nothing." She pushed her hair aside. "Now what happens, Khyna?" She considered the slight figure with the heathen face. "What now?"

"Work." Khyna tugged on Talanee's ragged clothes. "Come. Work." The girl ducked her head. "Stay low. Clean. Stay safe, Tala."

Talanee let Khyna lead her from the barren little room. "Why are you protecting me?"

The girl glanced at her and pressed a finger to her lips. "No speech. Sacred place."

Talanee scowled but kept her feelings to herself. This poor heathen wretch couldn't know she served false gods.

Khyna led her from the sparse, silent halls beneath the earth and up into a bustling, clambering realm filled with Tawloomez in shabby garb much like Talanee's new apparel. Some carried bundles; others carried platters; all flowed hither and thither on their own private quests.

The servants eyed Talanee with a cold, aloof arch in their brows, like they might scrutinize a speck of dust that had escaped their last inspection. One sneered, and Talanee answered with a glower.

The girl stopped beside a brightly colored tapestry on the wall, to offer Talanee a goblet, and, parched, Talanee drank from it. The liquid tasted bitter on her tongue.

After that, Khyna led her to a vast chamber filled to bursting with dried herbs, bottled elixirs, bones of snakes and other animals, barrels, and jars. The odors of earth, spices, and the iron tang of blood haunted the close air. Talanee gagged on the scents as Khyna drew her to a grime-caked window and forced it open a crack, then motioned to a chair before a table laden with the dried remains of animal innards.

"Bottle," Khyna said.

Talanee stared. Shook her head. Backed away, flesh prickling. "I won't be part of any heathen rites. I won't."

Khyna pushed her toward the chair. "Bottle."

"No."

The girl's brow creased, and she murmured strange words. As if she'd issued a command, something seized Talanee's limbs, and she found herself walking to the chair. She sat against her will. Her fingers plucked up a vial and a tiny animal heart and forced the organ into the glass container. She let out a shriek, but her hands kept working, regardless of her will.

Wild-eyed, she found Khyna watching her with a somber expression. "Stop this. Make it stop!"

Khyna murmured again, and the hold fell away. The little girl pointed to the animal parts. "Bottle."

Talanee bent to her work, tears rolling down her cheeks.

CHAPTER 28

The *Akuu-Ry* slumped beneath the clutches of the faceless ghosts, and his sword vanished as it slipped from his grip.

Lor backed up, terror hacking away at the last cords of rational thought. *Escape, escape, escape.*

A hand snatched his arm and dragged him near. He stared into the face of the Lord Captain of Erokel. Lor faltered. Against the barrage of fire blazing in the man's red-eyed glare, he had no strength to resist or flee. He let his shoulders droop and lowered his gaze to the man's powerful hand. A sword shone there, ordinary, yet reassuring.

This man is Kel. Why does he protect me?

A flash of gold snared Lor's focus, and he watched the Golden One dance among the countless specters pouring in through the walls and from the ceiling, white clothes radiant in the darkness. Oily hands slipped up from the floor to snatch at his ankles, but the figure called Tora dodged all in his efforts to reach Lekore. Sword flashing and swinging, he arced over dozens of groping fingers to land beside the *Akuu-Ry*, then knelt to check for a heartbeat.

"He lives," Tora declared, "but his flesh is icy cold. We must escape these—" he broke off to swipe at a slithering hand "—these horrors." His blue eyes flitted through the onslaught of bodies, questing, until he narrowed on something beyond Lor's view.

"Is this how you want us to end, you coward?" asked Tora. "Is this satisfactory enough, to tear us to pieces, never to understand what we've done that demands such cruelty?" He slashed at more groping hands.

A clicking noise jolted the air and sent sparks of fear up Lor's arms.

The voice from before drifted down. "It's a fitting end, Ahvenian. Yet, you're right. I've never been a coward. I will face the Sun Throne one last time before my end."

The specters fell still as the limbs jutting from the floor slipped back into whatever abyss they came from.

Tora caught Lekore by his arm and shoulder and dragged him upright as Nerenoth guided Lor to their side.

"What of Lekore?" Tora asked the ceiling. "Can you wake him?"

"He fights a separate battle, Ahvenian," said the voice. "There is nothing anyone in this sphere can do for him now. He alone must conquer or die within a realm of spirits."

Something flashed in the Golden One's eyes, cold, tinged with frost, then Tora looked at the Lord Captain. "We must go on. Should I carry Lekore, or should you?"

"I shall carry him." Nerenoth sheathed his blade, hoisted Lekore, and draped him over one shoulder, showing no sign of strain. He drew his sword again and nodded. "Let us delay no longer."

Tora led the small company along the corridor, steps firm and wide, sword bright in his hands. Nerenoth urged Lor to follow the Golden One, and the Lord Captain took the rear, boots clicking against the floor in an even, solid gait.

Lor tried to absorb the courage of his fellows, but each step toward the bodiless voice sent tremors through his frame. His mind revolted against his course. Couldn't they find a different way out?

His people were dead. Slaughtered like animals in one of the Teokaka's rituals. He flinched away from the memory and the taunting odor of decay lingering in his nose. They had been servants, not friends, yet Lor had relied upon and loved them better than his own kin. When he had fled for his life, these few brave souls had come with him, only to suffer the torments of the Wildwood, and end up trapped in this gods-forsaken hole.

Why have I been spared so many times, when all around me run to death's summons at the first note of a dark dirge?

First, Mother. Then, Father. Loyal Nananu, foolish Retak, and now his last supporters. Teokaka Susunee had taken them all from him, one by one. She, too, must take responsibility for those lost here in this fell prison—for she had driven Lor from the palace and all he knew, at last determined to end the line of kings that had existed since before the Snake Gods came. Back when the kings worshiped the land and all its quiet treasures. Back when the line of Lor's forefathers retained respect and power across the tribes of ancient days.

Not anymore. Now, the Teokaka held all the power, for she had been born of a Snake God and had lived since the War of Brothers five hundred years ago. Since her rise to power, the kings had become a formality upheld in the name of tradition and by a fit of mercy Susunee had bestowed upon one of Lor's ancestors.

Lor'Toreth's pride had been brittle in his earliest years. Now, he wielded it like a shattered sword in bloodied fingers, a fading memento to honor his fallen father and all who came before, though it wounded him to clutch the memory.

And now, I tread strange paths beside the enemies of my people, seeking out death or a worse end. Will my ancient gods forsake me here, as the Teokaka's gods did long ago?

He studied Tora's back; his strange, elegant clothes spotted with blood; the golden locks that fell against his neck.

Strange times forge strange alliances, is this not so, my dead sire? But do I betray my soul in this action? Will I stand condemned for associating with one of the Golden Ones and the Akuu-Ry? What else might I do instead?

He walked on. *Best not to think so much.* His thoughts only grew more tangled with each question he granted life.

The trek drummed deliberations from his mind, until he walked in a sort of lethargy, unwilling to comprehend further the ending of his steps and all it would signify. His mind drifted between bitter, voiceless fears, and a kind of chilling numbness.

The ground fell away before smooth steps leading into a dark abyss. Lor stared. *What are these for?*

The Golden One took them, and Lor blinked as sense settled back in around the dust of his aimless thoughts.

Oh, we're going down. Yes, of course. We must find the voice that killed my servants.

Fire lanced through his veins, reconnecting feelings. He set his jaw. *They meant nothing to that fiend, yet the voice killed them. I must seek justice for their spilled blood.*

So Father would have done. So the gods of old would have required.

He shifted his footing and stalked down the stairs, each step firmer than the last. Teokaka Susunee had always called him a coward. He had begun to believe it, and then he'd embraced it, somewhere along the way. Well, no longer. He was a proud son of kings, and he wouldn't let anyone dispute that anymore. Not Kel, nor spirit, nor the Teokaka herself.

Nothing halted their progress as they plunged deep into the earth. Lights flickered into being ahead of them, illuminating the way, leading to whatever doom lurked in wait. As soon as they passed by the strange, flameless orbs fixed into the walls, those lights gave out, dousing their path of retreat in darkness.

At last Tora stopped before a smooth door and eyed the seam running down its middle. "Ready, Captain?"

"I am," answered the Kel in soft tones.

Tora lifted his hand, but before he could touch the panel beside the door, it slid apart from the middle, admitting them into the chamber beyond.

THE WORLD LOOKED GRAY.

Lekore stood among shadows and wisps whispering nonsense in his ears. Ahead of the shades, separate from the cold slithering through his spiritual frame, he glimpsed a flash of colors: red flame, blue water, lavender wind, green earth—and a fifth. Something new. Something very, very old. It shone white and silver.

Is it Skye?

His heart flinched. *I must reach them.*

He started forward but stumbled as the wisps clutched his ankles to hold him still. He scowled and summoned *Calir*. The sword hummed into being, bright in its spirit form, comfortable in his translucent hand. Lekore sliced through the wisps. They recoiled with faint hisses. He strode toward the colors, passing through the looming shadows that might be walls in the mortal sphere.

As he crossed one threshold, the specters slipped up from the black ground—but now Lekore could see the features of their angular faces. He stared. The contortions of pain and hatred that drew lines across their eyes and mouths threw chills along his soul.

"Successor of He Who Hears The Wind, born to work his final will, we will not let you leave this realm." The voices rose in unison around Lekore, and he whirled to find the ghosts of yellow-haired men and women surrounding him, hatred flowing from their beings to become the very shadows and wisps.

He staggered under the growing force of wrath. "I have done nothing to you."

The voices rang out. "You exist. This is enough."

"Your judgment is wrong."

Wisps curled around Lekore's ankles and shot toward his wrists. He parried them with *Calir* and cut himself loose, then reached for the Spirits Elemental but met the restraints that held them captive.

He found the slitted eyes of one specter. "You would cage the essence of the world to lure me here and declare that my existence is enough to justify your actions! Well, I am here. Let the Spirits Elemental depart."

"Would you subject yourself to our will in exchange for their release?"

Lekore bowed his head. Must he? Would it be right? "Will you release Skye as well?"

"Never!" thundered the voices.

Lekore gritted his teeth. "What of my companions? Those who remain in the mortal sphere. Will they be allowed to leave?"

"No," the voices said with a laugh. "They will not escape *him*."

"Yet you have no right and no cause to hold the spirits here. Release them."

"Only if you agree to remain. It is fair. It is best."

A discordant note struck behind the tones of their unified voice. Lekore scowled. "Lies. This is not just, nor is it well." The high note sounded again in their silence, pouring forth an assault of images Lekore couldn't understand. "Is it Skye who is to blame for your pain and present condition? Is it he who commands you and holds you in this fell realm? I think not!"

"Enough!" cried the voices, and they swelled in upon him like a great tide.

Lekore lifted *Calir* to block them, but the barrage of ghostly figures struck him with a force too great to fend off. A hundred hands reached claw-like fingers to rake at him, to tear him into shreds. The sword in his hand sang out a long, sorrowful note.

The distant white-silver light answered, crying out in his mind: *FORGET NOT YOUR PROMISE, O FAIR ONES.*

Lekore screamed as the fingers pawed and ravaged his spirit.

FORGET NOT.

FORGET NOT.

O FAIR ONES.

FORGET NOT.

He opened his mouth to scream, but the words tumbled out instead. "Forget not your promise, O Fair Ones!"

Warmth exploded through his limbs.

Light burst from his fingertips, his toes, and silvery flames engulfed *Calir*.

The specters shrank and screamed before the light.

"Lekore!"

The voice sent thrills through him. "Skye, where are you?"

"Let the light in. Let it swallow you. Do not be afraid. Give way to it."

Lekore drew a breath to drink in the savor, letting it fill him up, casting away all the cold. When he opened his eyes, he found himself sitting upright, his hands cupped before him. The dark souls writhed on the ground. Upon Lekore's palm stood a tiny Kel-like figure effused with silver-white light, wisps like hair dancing around its form.

"What are you?" he asked.

'*A Spirit Elemental,*' it answered like a musical note.

"I have never seen your kind before."

'*Oh, but you have,*' said the spirit.

"What are you called?"

'*I am the Spirit of Spirit, that which breathes life into all others.*'

"Why do I see you only now?"

'*You needed to see me only now, but always have I been near, O Seer. Shall I release the Spirits Elemental and Skye Getaal?*'

Lekore blinked. "Yes, please."

'*Stand. Command me, and I shall obey.*'

He stumbled to his feet. A thousand hurts throbbed along his soul, and he trembled but kept his unsteady footing. "Spirit of Spirit, unchain your fellow spirits, and release the soul of Skye Getaal."

Off the flaming figure flew like a graceful bird trailing sparks of purest white. The caged colors brightened as the bird approached them across the plains and cliffs of darkness. *Calir* hummed as the Spirit of Spirit glowed bright, brighter—and infused all surrounding it with blinding white. Lekore flinched and turned away, even as his soul felt the chains breaking beneath the will of this new Spirit Elemental.

It has always been; it is not new.

The light faded, and Lekore turned back. His heart soared as his eyes found the spirits of wind, water, fire, and earth coming toward him, riding upon the winged Spirit of Spirit.

He lifted his hands and caught the Spirits Elemental as the silvery spirit dropped them. Fire shifted from its flaming form to peck his cheek, while water pooled into droplets on his open palm. Earth took the shape of a bird to light upon his shoulder. Wind caressed his face as it shed its shape. Lekore laughed, then grinned as Skye strode into view, his translucent armor glinting in the fire glow.

"We must leave this realm," said Skye. "Otherwise, your body will soon expire." His smile faded. "There are more enemies to face than these pitiable spirits trapped by the will and greed of another."

Lekore nodded. "How do I return to the mortal sphere?"

"Command it of the Spirit of Spirit. It has answered you, and thus you are worthy."

Lekore glanced up to find the silvery bird wheeling close. "Please return me, and all of us, to the realm of the living."

'As you command, O Seer. But know that within that realm, my reach cannot extend so far. You must count upon your strength above my own.'

"I understand."

'Breathe.'

Lekore obeyed. Cold surged through him, and his limbs tingled. *Calir* toned a note, then vanished from his fingers.

His mind hammered and wobbled.

Am I hanging upside-down?

He exhaled and heard someone draw a sharp breath.

"He's waking." Nerenoth's deep, reassuring voice, hope-filled. "Set him down."

Lekore's stomach fluttered as hands swung him upright, then

PRINCE OF THE FALLEN

rested him against a cool surface. He peeled his eyes open, and the world teetered until color bled into his vision.

Nerenoth crouched before him, sword in hand, concern bright in his red eyes. "Are you well, Lekore?"

He shook his head. "I do not quite know. I have returned to my body, that much is good news to me." He reached up, fingers tingling, to scrub at his face. "I found them, Lord Captain. The Spirits Elemental are free." He could feel them lurking nearby even now, curious, grateful. "He had captured all of them."

"Will the storms cease?"

"Those of that caliber, yes."

"Not for long," said a voice, familiar now, but rather than coming from the ceiling, it drifted through an open doorway, from a bright, sparse chamber beyond.

Swords clinked as Nerenoth sprang to his feet and Tora angled himself to face the door. From its bright maw stepped a man, muscular, broad-shouldered, with golden-yellow hair tinged white, and eyes of pale blue. He clutched a sword in one hand; its blade glinted in the light. His apparel was a simple white thigh-length overcoat and breeches, trimmed in gold and silver.

Tora's sword trembled. "You *are* Ahvenian."

"I was, once," said the man. "I forsook my race in ages past—but that doesn't mean I won't impart one last blow in the name of my failed cause." He spread out his arms. "Do you still call me a coward, Ambassador?"

"I don't know what to call you."

"Ah. True, that. I am called Talajin—so my name once was." His smile held the rime of the tall peaks above the Vale That Shines Gold. His eyes flicked to Lekore. "You freed Skye Getaal. This is unfortunate for all of you."

"Hadn't you intended already to kill us?" asked Tora, tones wavering between heat and quavering doubt. A pulse of emotions swept over Lekore; the young man didn't want to fight one of his own kind. Curiosity flickered between resolve and conflict, pinning Tora in place.

Yet Talajin is evil, Lekore wanted to say.

A wan smile touched Talajin's lips. "So I did and still do."

"Why?"

Talajin sighed. "It's a long tale. I'll not bore you with details you wouldn't value. In short, Ambassador, we settled this world to create weapons strong enough to destroy the Royal House of Ahrutahn."

Tora's eyes narrowed. "I already suspected that. You built this facility to contain the components for biological warfare."

"Correct. That jungle out there was once ground zero for our experiments. It's fascinating to see how it's grown, isn't it?"

"You risked destroying this world and all its inhabitants." A rumble tremored through Tora's voice.

Talajin's smile stretched wide and cold. "Small consequence to reach our goal. The two races inhabiting this world are primitive and negligible. Only one man born upon this rock caused us any trouble—and still attempts to thwart me, even in death." His eyes speared Lekore. "I don't appreciate his descendant carrying on the tradition."

Lekore frowned and dragged himself to his feet. The Lord Captain aided him and held him steady when he wobbled. "Talajin, you cannot condemn a ghost for wrongs committed against you after holding the Spirits Elemental captive. Your corruption outweighs anything he might have done."

"You're wrong. He ruined all our work. All our efforts. That man is responsible for the destruction of my colleagues and our project."

"It seems Ahvenia owes Skye Getaal our gratitude," Tora said.

Talajin's eyes glittered. "It's not over yet, young one. We'll not rest, alive or dead. My colleagues remain even in death to help end the reign of Ahrutahn."

"*Why?* What has the Royal House done to you?"

"They stole the throne from the rightful line."

Tora scoffed. "Preposterous. The line of Ahrutahn has ruled for millennia."

Runes and whispers filled Lekore's mind. He staggered under the weight of foreign words and the power behind them. Nerenoth held him upright.

"Yes, and usurpers all that time," said Talajin. "But it hardly matters now, not for you. This facility is your tomb, Ambassador, and none of you will escape. Your souls will remain, and I'll bind you all to my life until my last breath leaves this failing frame. After that, I'll work beyond the grave to end the line of usurpers."

"What did Skye do to you?" Lekore asked.

Talajin scowled. "Why explain it? What difference does it make now?"

"Enough that you are obsessed with capturing him even so long later."

"A fair point, and yet..." Talajin turned his back on the company. "Yet, I grow weary at the thought of explaining all that transpired. All we suffered because that *fool* couldn't leave well enough alone. He even allied himself with our greatest enemy, only to betray them, and us, and even his own brother in the end." The man ran a hand over his eyes. "Now his heir has come, just as he declared." Talajin slid his hand from his face and let his arm fall to his side as he turned to meet Lekore's gaze. "How loathsome you are to me, Seer."

"I cannot help how you feel," said Lekore. "Let us go, Talajin. Have you not wasted enough years on what is already dust?"

"Never. Your ancestor invoked prophecy to bring you about. This he did to exact his revenge, and I'll return his spite for spite. You'll not leave. All that Skye Getaal proclaimed will come to nothing—so I've sworn on the blood of my fellow scientists."

Tora shifted, knuckles whitening against his sword hilt. "Did your colleagues agree with your view, or was their blood shed unwillingly to enact your vengeance, Talajin?"

Talajin's lips lifted in a tight smile. "Ours was a brotherhood, Ambassador. We did nothing unless all agreed."

"Yet, you alone live?"

"Unfortunately." Talajin sighed. "In the end, I was chosen to live. The rest offered their blood to give me the power necessary to capture Skye and to leave this tomb." His eyes danced from the ceiling to the walls. "Now, I must depart and leave *you* to die in this laboratory, for justice."

"Untrue," said Lekore. "We are not to blame for the sins of our forebears, nor the choices of our race. I should not be condemned for what my ancestor may have done to you—whether or not his actions were conscionable. Nor should Tora pay for the disagreement between you and his king's house. If it were otherwise—if we must pay for the sins of the past—surely you, too, are guilty of another's crime from some past hour. Using such logic, no one is innocent, and all must suffer endlessly."

Talajin chuckled. "How much like Skye you sound, young one. How contemptible in your self-righteousness." He flicked his wrist.

Specters sprang from the walls, blades raised, malignant magic pouring from their hate-filled souls. Lekore lifted *Calir* as Nerenoth slashed through the nearest ghost. The Captain's sword passed through it, useless, but Tora's sword hummed as it followed the same path—and the ghost shrieked and faded away.

Lekore caught the blade of one specter and dodged the thrust of another. He cast a glance at Talajin. The man's eyes were narrowed, lips pinched together as anger colored his face. Before him, Skye materialized. Talajin let out a cry and stumbled backward. The specters turned as one, abandoning Lekore and his companions. They charged Skye.

"We must help!" Lekore darted forward, *Calir* clutched before him.

Tora matched his steps, and they flung themselves into a fight against a dozen or more spectral shapes. Where their swords met ghostly flesh, the specters vanished, but more poured in from the walls and floor.

A hasty glance their way revealed that the Lord Captain and Lor'Toreth had disappeared. Lekore's heart flinched, but he couldn't stop to find them. He must protect Skye; he must defeat Talajin.

If he could, he must free these souls from their captivity.

A flash of silver-white light glinted above him. He glanced up and found the Spirit of Spirit flickering in and out of a Kel-like form. Its voice tumbled into his mind like chiming notes: *'Forget not your promise, O Fair Ones.'*

A heartbreaking ache flooded Lekore's body, and he stumbled. Hands seized him. Would the words set him free if he used them again?

'Forget not your promise, Fair Talajin.' The words chimed louder in Lekore's mind. *'Say them. Declare this truth!'*

He found the man locked in combat against Skye.

"Talajin!" Lekore shouted.

The man scowled at him. "Keep out of this. I'll come for you next, Seer!"

"F-forget—" Lekore blocked another specter. "Fire! Wind! Earth!"

The ground trembled. Fire shot up around Lekore's feet, and the wind hurled it around him, fanning out his cloak as he danced clear of Tora. Talajin yelped and fell backward, as the specters lurched away. The man struck the wall behind him and lifted his arms to fend off the heat.

Lekore marched through the fire, unharmed, and lifted his hand. The Spirit of Spirit settled onto his palm, its shape now like a silver flame. Lekore met Talajin's blue eyes. "Forget not your promise, Fair Talajin!" His voice rang with strange power, and as his words curled over the air, cords of wrathful light revealed themselves, running from Talajin's heart and into the soul of every specter.

'Sever them,' whispered the Spirit of Spirit.

Lekore slashed through the cords as *Calir* hummed. Otherworldly wails sailed over the air as the specters hunched into themselves. The inky shadows faded from their frames to reveal pale skin and yellow hair.

Tora sprinted to Lekore's side. "The ghosts are gone."

"No, they remain, but they are free of their chains." Lekore turned to Talajin, who crouched against the wall, arms wrapped over his face. Sobs escaped his lips as he shook.

"W-what have you done, Seer?" Talajin whispered. "What agony is this?"

Lekore frowned. "I know not."

Skye strode to loom before Talajin. "An ancient oath long broken now condemns thee, Talajin Kinslayer."

Voices filled Lekore's mind as faceless ghosts draped in white and silver called across the wind from a distant shore: *'Forget not thy promise, O Fair Ones. Forget not thy promise, O Fair Ones.'* The chant climbed louder, higher, sweet yet mournful. *Calir* hummed a low note in counterpoint.

The weight of the vision pressed Lekore to his knees. As the images faded, he lifted his head and stared into Talajin's eyes. "What have you forgotten?"

The man shook his head, white-yellow hair slipping into his eyes, lips trembling. He set his jaw. His eyes narrowed. "I won't fail!" He lunged forward and stabbed his sword through the air.

Tora swung his blade and knocked Talajin's weapon from his hand. It clattered to the ground, and Tora kicked it away. "Enough." He set his sword tip against Talajin's throat. "Surrender, and I'll spare your life."

Talajin swallowed and glared up at the Ahvenian. "To stand trial before the Ahrutahns? I refuse. Kill me."

Tora's muscles tightened, and he shifted his grip on his sword. Then paused. Hesitation, regret, fear pulsed out from Tora's soul to wash over Lekore.

"Allow me." Nerenoth's voice came from behind Talajin, near the entrance to the room beyond the corridor. He shoved his sword through Talajin's back, through heart and ribs, until the blade emerged through the man's chest. Red blood bloomed like a rose against his white coat and dribbled down his chest as he gurgled. Nerenoth wrenched the sword free, and Talajin slumped forward with a few last, gasping breaths. He fell still at Tora's feet.

Tora stared down at him, then shut his eyes. Sorrow flowed from his soul.

"Forgive me," said Nerenoth. "I didn't think mercy should extend so far, after all he has done. Nor do we have the means to take him with us if we can escape this place. It would be too hazardous."

"You're right," Tora said. "Thank you, Lord Captain." He turned to Lekore. "Let's find a way out of here, and we'll then try to unravel the mysteries you've presented."

Nerenoth motioned to the chamber he'd come from. "Lor'Toreth and I sought a means of opening the doors, but we're ignorant of your craft."

Tora started for the room. "Give me a moment and—"

"I can open the doors," said Lekore, pushing to his feet. He swayed. "The earth and wind spirits will aid me to break open the doors, now that they are free."

Nerenoth trotted to his side and caught his arm. "Then let us be on our way."

CHAPTER 29

The front doors of the laboratory rolled open with a shrieking protest as earth and wind spirits wrenched them apart. Lekore stepped out into the early glow of morning and spotted Keo and Lios standing within the line of trees. A stillness had settled over the Wildwood in the aftermath of the rising storms.

Keo padded forward, his strange green eyes flicking between every man who slipped through the doorway. "I can't believe you're all still alive."

Lor'Toreth sprinted ahead, brown hair streaming behind him, and halted before Keo. He rattled off words in his native tongue, hands flying as he spoke. His narrative dragged on for several long minutes until Keo raised a hand to cut him off.

Keo looked at Nerenoth. "You killed Talajin? That's...impressive."

Nerenoth shook his head. "He had already been defeated. I only claimed the final blow."

"Still." He glanced at Lekore, then Tora. "Are we safe to leave this inhospitable hellhole?"

"Yes," Tora said. "We should hurry. I want to check on Raren and any other survivors and then return here with reinforcements.

This lab needs to be taken apart stone by stone until I know what transpired here, then I'll destroy its foundations."

Keo's lips twitched upward. "I don't blame you. It's unwholesome, even by my old standards."

Tora eyed him for a long, silent moment. He sighed. "Let's head back to my ship."

Lekore whistled, and Lios trotted to his side, gray and pink tail wagging. He patted the emockye's head, then straightened up, relieved he kept his feet without the Lord Captain's help. Even so, he welcomed the nearness of Nerenoth, just in case his strength gave out.

The company tromped into the trees, leaving the eerie, hunching structure behind. Lekore glanced back once, but the dense foliage had swallowed the building up.

It is better left alone for now. He never wished to return to the facility reeking of blood and hatred.

AN HOUR OR LONGER BROUGHT THE COMPANY TO THE EDGE OF the trees, and Lekore's gaze settled on the scar across the earth where Tora's ship sprawled like the broken carcass of a giant, pale pythe. Tora moved ahead of the rest, his steps fluid and nimble, until he faltered. Panic punctured the air.

"The door's been blasted." He sprang ahead, booted feet flying over the ground, touch light as feathers. Lekore darted forward to catch him, the others on his heels.

Tora reached the ramp, leapt up, and landed at the doorway. Lekore charged the wind to carry him up, and he struck the strange floor as his hair fluttered down to settle around his arms and ankles. Within the ship, twin faces stared back at him and Tora, red eyes wide and nervous.

"Thank the Sun!" cried Jesh.

"They took them, Holy One!" Jeth added.

"Who?" asked Tora.

Nerenoth trotted up the ramp behind Lekore and slipped past him to move inside. "Who took whom?"

"Her Highness and Lord Ademas," said Jesh. "Tawloomez took them away."

Lekore inched forward. "Tawloomez do not enter the Wildwood."

"These did," Jeth said. "I can't be certain, but one of them carried herself like..."

"Like the Teokaka," Jesh finished. "We saw them drag Princess Talanee and Lord Ademas to the door. Then they *vanished* into the very wind."

"Figures," said Keo. "This ship drew a lot of attention, and the Teokaka knows what it really is."

Tora looked between the twins and Keo. "Who is this Teokaka? And Tawloomez?"

Lor'Toreth tugged on Keo's sleeve and murmured something. Keo translated for him, then looked at Tora. "Short version? The Tawloomez are a race of semi-nomadic earth worshipers. Lor'Toreth here is their prince—though they banished him. Their spiritual leader is called the Teokaka. Her given name is Susunee. She's...unpleasant, on her best days. Historically, the Tawloomez and Kel are the bitterest of enemies."

"I see." Tora's frown gathered shadows around his eyes. "Then your companions are in considerable danger."

"Yes, my lord," said Nerenoth. "I'm surprised they didn't kill them outright."

Jeth moved closer. "They didn't use their right names. Ademas called the princess 'Tala.' And she tricked the Teokaka into thinking she'd killed the last surviving—" his gaze danced to Tora "—last surviving of your people, Your Eminence. The Teokaka left without harming anyone."

"I'm grateful for your princess's quick thinking." Tora rubbed his chin, then lowered his hand. "How many of my people have survived. Do you have a count?"

"Yes, Your Eminence," Jesh said. "Five, including yourself. The other four are injured, but not fatally."

Tora turned away, and Lekore braced against the onslaught of sorrow pouring off the young man's soul. Moments passed, then Tora turned back to the company. "I'm glad of that, though it grieves me that so many died. Forgive me. We need to rescue your companions. There will be time to mourn afterward." He looked at Lor'Toreth. "We must enter your lands. Will you guide us? I give you my vow, no harm will befall you, Your Highness."

Lor'Toreth eyed him as tremors of fear pulsed over his frame. Lekore caught flashes of pain, terror, and heartbreak, but the Tawloomez prince nodded and said something softly.

"Good." Tora turned to Keo. "What will you do?"

"Come, I suppose. But don't expect me to aid you, Ahvenian. Not against the Teokaka."

"I would never expect or welcome your aid, Kiisuld." Tora's blue eyes flashed like lightning.

Waves of animosity rolled between them, and Lekore found himself moving into the clash of emotions. "Let us go. We waste time if we squabble amongst ourselves. The journey into the Firelands is not a short one."

Tora sighed and wiped his brow, as though that would wipe away his enmity. "We won't have to journey on foot. I can take us the same way this Teokaka did."

"Not quite," said Keo. "She used the Hollow."

Tora glanced at the doorway. "Yes, I see that well enough. But I can trace its destination if it's on-world."

"What is this Hollow?" asked Nerenoth.

"The fabric between space and time," answered Keo. "Or, rather, its underside. Dark beings use it to travel over distances. Its lighter side is called the Void by most. The more powerful beings of the Universe can tap Void or Hollow to hop between worlds. The rest of its wielders can go shorter distances."

Silence met Keo's words like a wall. Lekore glanced at his

fellow Kel and found them blank-faced. Jesh's lips parted, and he mouthed something that might have been "worlds."

The concept was familiar to Lekore, though Ter had only touched on it once or twice.

"I think that was too much," Tora said. He glanced at Lor'Toreth. "Are you familiar with the Void or Hollow?"

The Tawloomez prince shook his head.

Tora frowned. "How then does your Teokaka know of it?"

Keo shrugged. "That's easy. She's a half-Kiisuld."

Tora sucked in air as he paled. He shut his eyes and let out a long breath. "That complicates matters a bit."

Keo snorted. "Just a bit."

"It doesn't change what we must do." Tora angled his gaze to Lekore. "Will you help me?"

"Yes." Lekore's fingers tingled as he stretched his senses toward *Calir*. "I am prepared." His soul throbbed, his mind ached, but he mustn't let his discomforts keep him from helping the few Kel who had shown him kindness.

"We're coming, too," the twins said.

"As am I." Nerenoth stepped up beside Lekore.

Tora smiled grimly. "I'd expected as much. They captured your princess. Take hold of one another, and we'll go." He glanced past the twins. "I worry for Raren, though."

Lekore whistled and Lios padded to his side. "Stay here and guard those aboard this ship. Let none harm them."

Lios let out a huff and padded toward the open door down the corridor.

Tora's smile warmed. "Thank you. Now, let's depart."

Keo waggled his fingers in a halfhearted wave. "See you on the other side."

Lor'Toreth grasped his arm and spoke in earnest tones.

Keo eyed him with a crooked smile and spoke softly as he pried Lor's fingers free, then vanished like a wink.

Tora breathed out. "All right, everyone. I'll count to four, and we'll arrive in the lands of the Tawloomez. Be on your guard. One."

Lekore grasped Nerenoth's shoulder and caught one twin by his arm.

"Two."

Rustling cloth.

"Three."

Sharp inhalations.

"Four."

The world tilted, then righted itself. The smell of sulfur haunted the wind, and the sky glowed red. Lekore glanced around him. He stood with his companions in a walled courtyard whose trees twisted toward the sky, leafless and dry as bleached bones.

Footsteps crunched to his right. Lekore turned as someone gasped.

Nerenoth charged the Tawloomez servant draped in white and green before the man could dash away. The Lord Captain pressed a sword to his chest, and the man lifted his hands in surrender.

Tora sprinted to Nerenoth's side. "Don't call for help, Tawloomez. We'll cause no trouble if you tell us where the Kel prisoners brought here today were taken."

The Tawloomez's jaw slackened, and he stared at Tora with growing wonder.

Nerenoth shook him. "Speak."

The Tawloomez flinched, then let out a shriek before Nerenoth clamped a hand to his mouth. The twins rushed forward, swords drawn.

Wind whispered through the courtyard, but no one came to answer the servant's cry.

Lekore sighed. He lifted a hand to let a wind spirit light upon his fingers. "Seek out Talanee and Ademas. They resemble me and them." He motioned to the twins and Nerenoth. "Find anyone with blue hair."

The spirit soared off, raking a breeze over everyone.

Tora turned his attention back to the servant as Lor'Toreth strode close and rattled off a few barking words. The servant's eyes widened more.

Lekore looked between the three men clustered around the servant, then the twins standing like sentinels before the palace looming overhead. Fire spirits rode the wind in droves, born from the embers of the distant Fire Mountain.

Skye materialized beside Lekore and gestured. "I found the princess. She's within the palace on the east end. It will be difficult to reach her undetected. I've yet to locate Ademas, but I'll continue my search." The ghost vanished.

Lekore yearned to ask his ancestor a dozen questions about Talajin and all that had transpired five hundred years ago, but that must wait. He looked at his companions. "Skye is seeking Ademas. He has found Talanee. She resides within, eastward." He nodded toward the palace. "We will not be able to remain discreet."

Keo wandered from the sparse shadows of a copse of brittle trees, twirling a twig around his fingers. "She'll have been made a slave, and likely she's kept in the lower levels. Lor and I can make our way there, if you want to find Ademas. I'd guess he's with the warrior slaves near the pits." He glanced at Lor'Toreth and rattled off a question.

Lor'Toreth nodded. "*Thatu kret.*"

Keo shrugged. "Shall I?"

"I don't savor the idea of splitting up," said Tora.

Keo rubbed the back of his neck. "Once we're discovered, we'll want to get out of here as quickly as possible. I'd prefer to avoid a confrontation with the Teokaka. Wouldn't you?"

"I—" Tora whirled, and two heartbeats later, the clatter of boots struck stone.

"New plan," Nerenoth said. "We fight our way through."

Tora drew his sword from the air before him. "So it seems. Try not to slay the innocent."

"I understand." Nerenoth strode to his brothers, captive servant still in his grip. "Refrain from harming servants. Focus on warriors and the Teokaka."

"Understood," the twins said.

Warriors with painted faces poured into the private courtyard, snakeskins shimmering in the morning's light. Spears, scimitars, and scissor knives glinted and flashed.

At a foreign command, the enemy charged. Nerenoth unhanded the Tawloomez servant, and he and his brothers lunged into the fight, but Lekore raised his arms and let the fire spirits wreathe above his open palms until they formed a vortex.

Shouts ripped through the Tawloomez warriors. "*Akuu-Ry! Heden Akuu-Ry!*"

"Tell them to stand down, please," Lekore said, spearing Lor'Toreth with a glance. Keo translated, and the Tawloomez prince reeled forward, lifted his hands before him, and shouted in rapid Tawloomez speech.

Weapons clanged to the ground. A few warriors sank to their knees, gazes riveted on Lekore's flames, while others bolted.

A voice cut across the air. "Cowards! Hold your ground." A woman slithered into sight, draped in silks and shimmering snakeskins, hair coifed and bejeweled. Bloodred lips lifted in a cold smile while brown eyes twinkled with cruel mirth.

Skye had warned Lekore to stay far away from this woman, this *creature*. "She is an unholy monster born of greed and bred of malice," the ghost had said.

Seeing her, *feeling* her malevolence like the dark Hakija's malice in the Temple of the Moon, Lekore's instinct screamed at him to flee. He spread his feet wide to anchor his body and his nerves, and directed fire to encircle his companions without singeing them.

Lor flinched away from the wreathing flames, but Tora eyed them with a faint smile, and the twins turned looks of wonder on Lekore. Jesh traced something across the air as Jeth pinned the captured servant at sword point. Nerenoth held his ground, gaze fastened on the Teokaka as she approached despite the wrath of the spirits.

"Enough, *Akuu-Ry*," she said. "You cannot sustain this forever, and I can wait until you tire. Or we can end this now. Lower your shield of flames and let me see the Golden One you have brought into my realm."

Lekore narrowed his eyes. "Under the watch of Fire Mountain, I need not sustain these spirits. They come as they will and shall protect us even as they burn down your palace. Return the Kel you have taken, and we shall leave all unharmed."

"You declare war upon us by your actions, Kel!"

Nerenoth pointed his sword at her through the fire. "You have already declared war, Teokaka. Your warriors decimated Erokes and attacked our sacred ruins of Halathe. We have endured your violence far too long, and I say: Enough."

The woman's brown eyes settled on Nerenoth, and her lips curled into a devilish grin. "Lord Captain, ah! How honored we are by your presence. Yet, where is your army?" She glanced at the twins. "Here? How...terrifying. My. Your sun gods must be so proud." She leaned close to the flames. "It makes one wonder *why* you've entered my lands. *What* could compel you to risk life and limb over two little Kel slaves?" Her tongue darted out to lick her lips. "Are they important?"

"They are important to *me*."

She laughed and danced back as the flames stretched out to scorch her. "Well, then, Lord Captain, take them from me—if you can." She whirled around and waved her arm. "Bring the boy."

Two warriors in snakeskin and leather armor strode forward, dragging Ademas between them, dressed in simple gray breeches alone. The young man hung his head but lifted it as he approached. Blood stained the edge of his mouth and the side of his face. One eye sported a deep purple bruise.

He offered a limp smile. "Hello, Captain. Beautiful morning, isn't it?"

A warrior rammed his fist into Ademas's exposed ribs, and the young man doubled over and coughed up blood.

"Cease that!" Nerenoth threw himself at the flames, but Tora caught his arm.

"No, Captain. Think."

Lekore inhaled and slid through the flames to stand free of them.

The Teokaka eyed him from where she stood near Ademas. She tossed her head like a pythe. "What now, *Akuu-Ry?*"

He summoned *Calir.* "You will let him go and bring the young woman here as well. Release them, and I will spare you."

The Teokaka laughed. "You make demands, even as I hold the Kel hostage? What of the other slaves, *Akuu-Ry?*"

He froze. "What other slaves?"

"All the other Kel, boy. We have hundreds of them, didn't you know?"

He swallowed down bile. "You enslave *people?*"

She scoffed. "Do not condemn me, Kel. Do not your people do the same?"

Lekore took a step. "It seems that is so, but that does not lessen your sin." Flames curled around his shoulders and down his right arm. "Release all your slaves, Teokaka Susunee. Every Kel will go home this day, and when I return to the lands of the Kel, I will speak with their leaders and free your people as well."

The Teokaka threw her head back to belt out a wild laugh. "Ah, *Akuu-Ry!* You're just like your ancestor: stubborn and idealistic. What a fool!" Her laughter pitched into hysterical mirth.

Lekore whipped fire at the warriors holding Ademas. They stumbled backward and dropped him. Ademas struck the ground with his knees.

The Teokaka's mirth died. "Pick him back up!"

The warriors eyed the flames dancing and writhing above Ademas. One shook his head and protested in his native tongue. The Teokaka flicked her wrist. Threads of violet light wrapped around the warrior's throat and tightened. He gasped, then gurgled as he slumped to the ground.

Lekore flinched, stomach churning. "You're a monster."

The Teokaka chuckled. "Aren't we all, *Akuu-Ry?*"

"No."

"Lekore," said Tora through the flames, "let me come through. I'll help you defeat her."

"Ah, yes!" The Teokaka extended her arms. "Let the Golden One come forth. How I've yearned to see another of his race after so long."

Skye appeared beside Lekore. "Be careful. The connection between Ahvenians and Kiisuld is tainted. He will suffer a most excruciating torment if she shackles him."

"I will let no one else become a captive," Lekore said. His eyes flicked to Fire Mountain. "Teokaka Susunee, release all your Kel slaves. This is your last warning."

She bared her teeth in a grin. "Or what, little Kel?"

He closed his eyes and issued a request to the earth spirits beneath the ground. He sent the same request to the fire spirits upon the air. Wind laughed and tossed his hair around his legs.

The ground rumbled. Fire Mountain let out a groan like drumming thunder.

The Teokaka whirled to face the volcano. "No. You wouldn't dare! It would destroy us all!" She spun to face him. "Your merciful heart wouldn't risk the lives of so many."

"What is a life of slavery, Teokaka?" asked Lekore. "Death is a mercy for one who cannot be free."

"Liar!" She grinned. "You're too soft, just like your ancestor."

The ground before him cracked. The courtyard walls shuddered. Black clouds marshaled overhead as smoke spewed from the mountain.

"Stop, STOP!" screamed Susunee.

"Release the Kel prisoners, Susunee, and swear an oath to keep peace between your people and the Kel."

She shrieked. "I won't! I will not! You're lying."

Lekore's eyes narrowed. "Test me, Susunee, if you dare."

Flames burst from mountain peak as fumes belched against the reddening sky. The world rumbled.

Susunee trembled and clutched at her scalp, jewels spilling to the ground as her hair loosened and slid free of its coif. "Fine! I swear, I swear! Take them. Take all the Kel and begone, spawn of the *Reka-Ku*! Calm the mountain's wrath."

"Send for the young woman you captured," Lekore said. "And bring all the slaves together." He glanced at Tora. "Will you be able to transport them as you did us?"

Tora nodded. "If all are touching, yes. But we'll need to arrive in a place where they can stand on level ground, somewhere wide enough to contain several hundred people. Preferably an uninhabited location, or we'll trample a few bystanders."

Nerenoth spoke up. "Perhaps outside the walls of Inpizal, my lord. It is wide enough, and less alarming if we're appearing from the very air."

Lekore stepped toward the Teokaka. "Call for the slaves. Bring them to a place wide enough for all to stand together. *Now.*" The earth shook with his last word.

The Teokaka angled her head. "Release the slaves! Take them to the main courtyard and unshackle their limbs."

The nearest warrior bowed as his brown eyes darted between his leader and Lekore's flames, then Fire Mountain.

"GO!" screamed Susunee.

The warrior sprinted off, barking orders. Other warriors followed him, while the rest stood in helpless silence.

The Teokaka lifted her head until she met Lekore's gaze, wisps of hair fluttering before her wrathful eyes. "I will not forget this humiliation, *Akuu-Ry*. I will—" she gasped.

Lekore turned to follow her gaze and found Keo standing beside him.

"You!" The Teokaka sneered. "Curse you, *Jatve!*"

A tight smile touched Keo's lips. "Easy now, Susunee. I'm not to blame for all this. *You* banished your prince, and he found me. *You* captured the noble Kel from the Ahvenian craft. I'm just along for the ride."

Susunee's attention slid to Lor'Toreth within the protective flames. "First a coward, now a traitor." She spat on the ground.

"You are damned, and the Snake Gods will soon come to claim your soul."

Lor'Toreth hunched behind the twins, a ragged figure in his tattered leather and bandages.

"Be silent, you hag," Jeth said. "Best consider your own fate now. You stand before a Sun God."

The Teokaka glared at Tora. "Lies. Deceptions. Your people shall soon answer for your meddling."

Tora glanced at the twins, then narrowed a look on the woman. "No more than you, half-Kiisuld."

"Nerenoth!" Talanee's tones rang out across the courtyard, and the fire spirits sparked up as she raced through the cowed Tawloomez warriors. She halted before the ring of fire. "Gods be praised, I feared I'd dwell here for the rest of my days." She rubbed her hands across the lumpish gray dress she wore and turned her radiant smile on Tora. "Blessed be the Sun Throne forever and ever, Your Holiness." She curtsied low.

Tora's smile looked strained around the corners of his mouth. Lekore caught shame and horror dancing across Tora's heart, but the young man didn't contradict Talanee.

Talanee glanced at those within the circle of flames, then at Lekore and Keo. "Where is Ademas?"

"Here," he whispered behind her.

She whirled and trotted to his side, ignoring the Tawloomez surrounding him. "They've beaten you!"

He grinned. "I told them no once or twice."

"Take him into the fire, Talanee," said Lekore.

She nodded and swung Ademas's arm over her shoulders, then helped him to stand.

"Talanee?" The Teokaka barked a single, harsh laugh. "Of course! You're the princess. Why else would the Lord Captain risk all to come here?"

Talanee guided Ademas toward the fire but wobbled as the ground shook again. Black smoke and flame vomited from the top of Fire Mountain, and embers painted the sky in red and gold.

The princess stared at the mountain. "We'll not make it."

"We'll be fine," said Tora.

Talanee blinked, then beamed like a starburst. "Forgive me, Holy One. My fear blinded my reason." She reached the flames, and Lekore willed the fire to part. The two Kel entered its safety, and the fire closed its wall behind them.

Minutes stretched on. The Teokaka lapsed into silence as she glowered between Lekore and those within the flames, her hands clenching and unclenching. The mountain sputtered and shook, but the fire spirits remained content to let Lekore hold them at bay. The churning rage of the magma within Fire Mountain begged to break free, but the spirits cooed and coddled it, and fiery death held its peace.

A warrior raced from the palace and bowed before the Teokaka. "*Vestesh kess'ku, Teokaka.*"

"There, it's done," she said, venom lacing her voice. "Go your way, *Akuu-Ry*, but remember this is not an ending for us. I will meet you again when the Snake Gods return from on high to ravage your Kel lands!"

Lekore conjured fire to corral the Teokaka and all her warriors, then let the flames around his companions die. "Lor'Toreth, lead us to the main courtyard, if you please."

Keo moved to the prince's side and repeated Lekore's request. Lor'Toreth nodded and strode ahead of the company, shoulders drawn back, head high. Perhaps for the first time in his life, the Tawloomez prince could stand proud and safe before his people.

Nerenoth helped Ademas to walk, careful of his bruised torso, and Talanee hovered close to assist as she might. Tora fell into step beside Lekore, who walked just behind Lor'Toreth. The twins fanned out to guard the company, while Keo strode along in the rear, hands in the pockets of his long tunic, a dry smile on his lips.

The company strode the palace corridors, stirring tapestries in their wake, as Lor'Toreth led them toward the western end. Servants never surfaced, nor did warriors halt their progress. The Teokaka's man had been thorough, it seemed.

At length, Lor'Toreth pushed open heavy doors leading to a grand landing above wide, red-stone steps. At the base of those steps, a vast courtyard spread out, this one adorned with red and yellow flowers in patterns weaving among the cobblestones and tinkling fountains. The trees here held sparse leaves of sickly white.

Over four hundred Kel stood among the flowers and knobbled trees, most hollow-cheeked and draped in gray rags like Talanee's apparel. Some dressed in worn leather armor sported scars or open wounds along their arms and legs.

Lekore's heart clenched as he stared at the gaunt figures, and they stared back. "Is this all of them, good captain?"

"Likely. My spies claim that few Kel captives are kept as slaves, and usually only for death sport or palace service. They're never allowed to breed." The Lord Captain passed Ademas off to the twins and strode to the ledge of the first step.

He lifted his sword until every red eye found him. "My Kel comrades, today you are liberated! By the will and grace of the Sun Throne, we will return to Erokel and offer you peaceful sanctuary all the rest of your days." He shifted and motioned to Tora. "Behold, the Sun Gods have returned!"

Skeptical, worn eyes flicked from their Lord Captain to the yellow-haired newcomer adorned in elegant white and blue clothes. Those same eyes widened, and gasps and whispers rippled through the flood of bodies. Someone let out a cheer. More followed. Hands lifted, groping the air far below Tora.

"Praised be this glorious day!" someone shouted.

Tora's brow creased, and he turned a glance toward Lekore, who stared back.

Tora is not a god. Why do they think he is?

Neither said anything. Better to offer hope to these miserable souls until they reached Erokel. After that, Lekore must flee to his home. He couldn't remain in Inpizal, but he would see his fellow Kel brought to their lands before he vanished forever.

Tora stretched out his gloved hands until silence rolled over the crowds. "I will bring you to your country now. Everyone, take hold of the person beside you. Let no one stay behind."

Hands clasped. Teary eyes turned upward again to stare at Tora. The young man swept his gaze over the crowd and nodded. "Let's depart before we have any trouble."

Lekore glanced at the fire spirits. "Calm the volcano once we have vanished. Do not let harm come to the Tawloomez."

"That's a pity," muttered Jeth. His twin elbowed him.

The company moved down the steps to connect with the crowd, then touched one another's sleeves, and waited for Tora to send them home. Tora eyed Nerenoth. "Think of the place we must reach. Imagine it with as much detail as possible. We won't be very precise, as I've never been there, so you'll need to direct our course."

Keo sighed. "I'll do it."

"No." Tora scowled. "I can't travel your way."

"I realize that. Let me take the Kel. I've been to Inpizal before. *You* return to your ship and gather your crew. Then, follow my pathway, and you'll reach Inpizal with no clumsy mishaps. Blind travel's never a good idea."

Tora's scowl deepened. "I don't trust you, Kiisuld."

"I trust him," said Lekore. "He means no harm."

Tora considered him. He brushed his yellow hair away from his face and sighed. "Very well. Will you come with me, Lekore? I'll need a little help, and you've left your canine with my crew. Better to have you there to call him off." He offered a smile.

Lekore nodded. "Gladly." From there, he could go home and avoid Inpizal altogether.

"Let us come, too, Your Holiness," said the twins. "We can help."

"They'll be no trouble," Nerenoth added.

Tora nodded as Lekore's heart sank.

Perhaps I can still slip away.

Keo snatched the hem of Nerenoth's cape as the twins and Lekore stepped away from the departing crowd. Doubts clouded the eyes of the nearest Kel slaves, but then the crowd, the Lord Captain, Keo, Lor'Toreth, Talanee, and Ademas evaporated in a single blink.

Tora let out a low breath and tried a smile as the ground trembled. "Let's be on our way."

CHAPTER 30

The ground shuddered again as Lekore caught Tora's brocaded sleeve. The twins clamped their palms on Lekore's cloaked shoulders, and the world tilted then righted itself.

They stood upon the ship's threshold. Lios let out a growl, then padded forward to lick Lekore's fingers, green eyes bright and pleased. Tora traipsed down the corridor, boots clicking upon the polished floor. The twins trailed after him, and Lekore followed with Lios at his side. Tora entered the massive chamber where his colleagues lay dead. Heartbreak rolled off his frame like pounding waves.

The twins passed him and moved to a pile of bodies across the room.

"We hid the living here, Your Eminence," said Jesh. "The princess and Lord Ademas thought it best to cover them up, as they sensed something evil in the darkness outside."

"That was well conceived," Tora said, crouching to help them tenderly lift the corpses and set them down, away from Raren, and the breathing crew members in blue and silver uniforms.

Lekore paced near, eyes lighting on the faces of the fallen. "Talajin caused this, did he not?"

"He did, it seems." Tora glanced around the wide, ornate room.

"I'll need to switch off the pulse he used to cause our ship's malfunction, or any attempt to rescue us will end the same tragic way." He turned back to Raren, who stirred at a gentle word.

"My pr—"

"Careful," Tora said over him. "You've had quite the ordeal, *Raren.*"

The man blinked. His orange gaze roved over the twins, then Lekore, and he moaned. "How many did we lose?"

"Nearly all. You, I, and three others survived."

"Are you hurt, Tora?"

The young man shook his head. "Minor bruises. You spared me worse."

"I'm glad." Raren shut his eyes and swallowed hard. "My leg is bad, it seems."

"Yes. And we're stuck here until I can shut off the pulse that destroyed our systems. Raren, Ahvenians once inhabited this world. Corrupt Ahvenians."

Raren's eyes snapped open. "That's not possible."

"Unlikely, I'll grant you, but it's possible. And it happened." Tora leaned back on his heels. "I don't know the details, but I'd guess they've done more than a few horrible things to the natives here."

The twins exchanged mystified glances, while Lekore inched closer to the yellow-haired strangers.

"The Lord Captain knows an excellent healer," said Lekore. "He could see to your fellows."

Tora glanced at him with a weary smile. "That would be wonderful. Thank you."

"How does one heal a god?" Jesh whispered to his brother. "Or even manage to wound one in the first place?"

Jeth shrugged. "Must've been quite the battle. Can you imagine it?"

A grimace crossed Tora's face as he leaned closer to Raren. "If I use the Void, the pain will be terrible. But the alternative isn't acceptable, I'm afraid. We're in a jungle and far from civilization."

Raren shifted and hissed out a breath. "I...suppose that makes my mind up for me. Void it is."

Tora looked up at the Kel. "We'll need to touch again."

Jesh and Jeth circled Lekore and bent to aid two of the three Ahvenians resting beside Raren in his blood spattered brown and silver outfit. Two women, one man. None of them stirred.

Lekore crouched beside Tora. "Why will using this Void hurt your friend?"

Tora's slitted eyes lifted from Raren to meet his questioning gaze. "When you step outside of time, all mortal issues are suspended. To re-enter space will cause injuries to flare up—almost like the moment Raren received his wounds. It can be deadly if the pain is too intense."

Lekore grimaced. "Is there no cushioning that we might manage?"

"No, sadly. Not that my people have found." Tora turned back to Raren. "Ready?"

"No. Help me anyway."

Lekore helped to lift Raren to his good leg, and Tora ordered the man to lean on him. Lekore stooped to claim the last unconscious of the yellow-haired Ahvenians: a woman dressed in a blue and silver uniform. She moaned as he lifted her into his arms.

Skye stood near Lios at the doorway. "Don't forget your promise to the Teokaka."

Lekore canted his head. "My promise?"

"You said you would free the Tawloomez slaves within Erokel."

Lekore frowned. So he had, and so he must—but he couldn't see how. *Back to Inpizal I must go after all.* He drew a breath, reached for Tora's sleeve, and took it in ginger fingers. He felt very sorry for himself, and he couldn't shake the dread or pity.

He never wanted to see Inpizal or its denizens again.

Jesh caught Lekore's hair, while Jeth pinched Tora's other sleeve. Lekore glanced at the doorway. "Go home, Lios. I'll return soon. Go home and stay safe."

The emockye whimpered.

Through his weariness, Lekore summoned a fire spirit. It danced across the air before him. "Please accompany Lios to my cave. See that no harm befalls him."

The fire spirit guttered and bowed, then flitted to Lios's side. The emockye tucked his tail, then huffed a resigned sigh.

A wave of dizziness pressed against Lekore's mind, and the world settled under his feet, bright and warm under the midday sun hovering above Inpizal's great wall. The Ahvenian Lekore held writhed in silent agony as her wounds bled afresh.

He lowered her and wrapped his black cloak around her shoulders to stave off a little of the bleeding, then glanced at the wall towering mere feet away. Had Tora not needed to first return to the land of the Tawloomez to follow Keo's pathway? He eyed the yellow-haired man, but Tora's gaze had settled on the crowd gathered before the gates. Nerenoth Irothé stood at their head, Lor'Toreth tucked behind him, while Talanee spoke to a cluster of slaves. Ademas leaned on the princess. Keo was nowhere in sight.

Tora inhaled, then let out a breath, and squared his shoulders. "Raren, brace yourself."

Jesh and Jeth started toward their brother, supporting the last two Ahvenians. Lekore lifted the woman and followed, Tora joining him as Raren limped at his side.

"You seem different from your people, Lekore," Tora whispered.

"I was raised apart from them."

"I see. And do you consider me a god?"

Lekore shook his head. "No."

"That's something, at least." Tora sighed. "I'd hoped to avoid this scenario in my life."

Raren chuckled. "Yet it was inevitable at some point, Your Hi —ah, Lord Tora."

Lekore glanced between the two men. "If you do not wish to deceive others about your mortality, why have you said nothing to correct them?"

Tora's brow creased. "Doing so goes against strict Ahvenian

protocol. We're not to interfere with the culture of other worlds. Revealing the truth could undermine your people's entire theological system. If they believe us to be their Sun Gods, and we refute that, it might have disastrous consequences. Your people demonstrate astonishing faith. I don't want to discourage such devoutness...especially if I'd be to blame for its collapse."

That made sense, yet Lekore's experiences with the Kel hadn't given rise to any desire to protect their faith or culture. He wished only to escape both.

But do they understand their own cruelty? Their own malice?

They owned slaves.

His people, the Kel, owned slaves. Worshiped cruel idols. Condemned any who believed otherwise. Wished to destroy Lekore for reasons he didn't understand.

Ank is one of them. If Lekore fled, he would never discover Ank or learn why the man had left him alone for so many years. *And Skye told me to educate myself, not to cave to fear.*

Lekore halted before the Lord Captain and met the man's gaze. *Is he Ank? He came for me. He protects me.*

"Where is the Kiisuld?" asked Tora.

Nerenoth frowned. "Keo vanished as soon as we arrived. He said nothing." The Lord Captain rested a hand on Lor'Toreth's shoulder. "I will keep his charge safe, nonetheless."

The Tawloomez prince glanced up at Nerenoth, then at Tora, then Lekore. His eyes were wide as the moon at full strength.

Tora shifted Raren's weight. "Lekore said you know a master healer, Lord Captain. May we enter your city?"

"Of course." Nerenoth strode to the wall, Lor'Toreth falling into step behind him. "Watchman!"

A man in armor suspended his head over the wall, blue hair trailing in a high breeze. "Sir! Where have you been?"

"Never mind that now. Open the gates."

"Sir, yes, sir!" The man slipped out of sight.

Moments later, the gates rumbled open as trumpets sounded. The Lord Captain led the procession to the road, then turned and raised his arms. "Remain here, and I will send out food, blankets, and tents until we can organize accommodations. Be patient."

Kel eyes roved toward Tora, and no one protested the Captain's directives. While the freed slaves remained behind, Nerenoth led the rest of his company into the city proper. Soldiers stood at attention. Onlookers gazed through the columns of watchmen as words wafted over the air, and wind spirits danced to the din.

Lekore lowered his head, skin prickling, heart hammering. *Run! Run!* He quelled his instinct with every ounce of willpower he could muster and shifted the weight of his unconscious burden. He was not some child prone to fly at the first sign of a threat. He must face it. He must do the right thing.

Yet, he felt the probing questions rolling over him. Hungry eyes lingered on the company, questing, ever questing for what might give them satisfaction. As Tora and Raren passed under the shadows of the gate and stepped into sight of the crowds, the feelings shifted. Gasps and cries raced over the Kel.

The twins carried the other Ahvenians into view. Gasps turned into tears and prayers.

The clatter of talons on paving stones echoed against the buildings and city wall as gold-armored Sun Warriors on pytheback forced their way to the fore of the throng.

Lekore flinched back, stamping harder against his desire to run away.

The cluster of pythe halted before Nerenoth. The frontmost Sun Priest, draped in white and gold vestments, scowled down at him, eyes flashing. "Lord Captain, where have you been? Why have you opened the gates? By order of His Majesty the King and Hakija Dakeer Vasar, these gates must remain closed. The star-touched demon you brought to Inpizal has captured the princess—"

"That's not true," said Talanee, marching forward, commanding despite her lumpish dress. The shirtless Ademas limped right behind her. The princess slapped a hand to her collarbone. "I'm here, and I'm safe."

The priest's pythe backed up a pace or two as its rider drew his reins. "Your Highness!" His eyes stuck on Ademas. "*You*. Reports declared you were in league with the one called Lekore."

Ademas quirked a smile. "That's not entirely wrong."

"There is much to explain," Nerenoth said, "but first, priest, look a little better." He stepped aside to reveal Lor'Toreth, Tora, and Raren. The twins waved beyond them, still supporting their yellow-haired burdens.

Last of all, the dumbfounded priest found Lekore, tattered and blood-caked, cradling the cloaked woman. The wonder, the disbelief, hardened into revulsion. The priest traced the rising sun before him. "The Holy Hakija must decipher—" His gaze darted back to Tora and Raren. Tendrils of doubt and awe weaved around the priest's soul, combating for supremacy.

"They're real, priest," Nerenoth said.

Leather creaked as the other priests dismounted. As one body they knelt, hands tracing the sun symbol over the air.

The first priest shuddered, then joined his fellows upon the ground. "Forgive me, O Holy and Bright Gods of the Sky." His voice cracked, and he bowed his head.

"Please rise," Tora said. "What we need right now is a healer."

The priest jumped to his feet. "Of course, Holy One. Let us escort you to the Cathedral of the Sun, where you will find comfort, healing, and protection from your battle in the sky."

Strain touched Tora's mouth again, but he nodded. "I thank you, priest."

The priest inclined his head, then gestured to his pythe. "Please, Holy God, use my beast of burden."

Tora guided Raren to the pythe. "Thank you once again. Raren needs to get off his feet." He glanced at the twins. "And if my companions might also...?"

The priest motioned, and four more pythe were guided forward. Lekore brought the unconscious woman to the nearest pythe, where a priest peeled back the cloak, took one look at her, then swung up into his saddle. "Hand her up," he said, and Lekore complied.

As he stepped back, hands seized his arms.

"Lekore Star-touched, you are under arrest by proclamation of the Holy Church of the Sun," boomed the voice of the first priest.

Fear seared Lekore's insides, and he called for the wind. Spirits swooped toward him as Tora's voice rang across the road. "Leave him be! What's his offense?"

The wind stilled at Tora's voice.

Hands retreated. The first priest bowed his head low. "Forgive me for this display, O Holy Sun God, but this—this Kel is a blasphemer. We must take him to the Sun Tribunal for—"

"Are you daft, Zanarin?" asked another priest in a loud whisper. "You're questioning a *Sun God!*"

The wind spirits perched on Lekore's shoulders, fluting questions. Lekore ignored them, intent upon Tora and Priest Zanarin.

The priest bowed lower before the young man on his pythe. "Forgive me, Most Holy Light. I—I'm under orders..." His mouth worked, then he looked up. "What would you have me do with the star-touched Kel?"

Tora eyed Lekore. "Let him stay with me."

"As thou wilt, O God of the Sun," Zanarin said, backing away. He whirled on Lekore. "You've been granted a fathomless gift, unworthy one. Walk beside the Sun God and reflect upon your second chance."

Lekore slipped to the pythe and smiled faintly up at Tora, who nodded back. The Lord Captain had moved close, Lor'Toreth beside him.

Zanarin let out a stifled gasp. "What defilement is this, Lord Nerenoth?"

The Lord Captain followed the priest's finger. "A Tawloomez, priest, what else?"

"You bring a Tawloomez warrior into Inpizal?"

Tora lifted a hand. "He, too, comes with me, lord priest. This

Tawloomez performed a service for me, and I intend to protect him." Danger lit in the strange blue gaze, and Zanarin folded beneath it to kneel upon the ground.

"Forgive my ignorance, Great Sun God!"

"Please rise and lead me to your healers."

Zanarin sprang up and assisted Jesh and Jeth to mount their borrowed pythe, Ahvenians slouched before them. The priest moved to the head of the Sun column, where he walked between the parting crowds.

Not a single Kel spoke; they looked on, silent as Lekore had never seen one. Nerenoth strode beside Lekore, one hand draped over his sword hilt, eyes keen. Lekore let himself relax a little.

For the moment, with Nerenoth and Tora so close, he would be safe.

CHAPTER 31

The Cathedral of the Sun sparkled under the brilliant sky. Lekore shrank back, recalling the blood sacrifice of Tawloomez infants; the icy prison beneath the posh heights; the hatred of Dakeer Vasar and his past suffering, so profound and horrific.

"Please," he whispered. "I do not wish to enter this place."

Nerenoth rested a hand on his shoulder. "Be brave. Stay near the Sun God or myself, and no harm will befall you. I vow it."

Lekore glanced into the tall man's eyes and found only truth there, though a secret lay on Nerenoth's lips. Yearning burned in Lekore's chest. *Ask, ask!*

He snared the Lord Captain's cape. "Are you Ank?"

Nerenoth's eyes widened. His brows knitted together. Slowly, he shook his head. "Would that I could say I am, for your sake."

Tears muddled Lekore's vision as he turned away and dropped the Captain's cape. "I see."

They walked into the cathedral grounds. The crunch of pythe talons and Kel boots over gravel rattled through Lekore's mind as his heart hung limp and throbbing in his chest.

The cathedral doors boomed open. Lekore stumbled backward, but Nerenoth's gauntleted hand caught his arm. Down the wide front steps, the Hakija and High Priest Lithel stormed, robes flying in their haste. Dakeer's eyes pinned Lekore in place, but a gasp from Lithel brought the Hakija up short, and when the High Priest flung himself to the gravel, the Hakija searched for a reason. Wonder bloomed across his features, mouth falling open, as he spotted Tora and Raren on the foremost pythe, their silver threads shining in the bright morning light.

"Glory be to the Sun Throne." He lowered himself to prostrate beside Lithel. "It is the dearest honor of my life to welcome thee to thy holy house, O Wondrous Sun Gods."

Tora shifted, and Raren's head snapped up from slumber. Both eyed the Hakija with blank faces as tension mounted in their shoulders and spines. Raren whispered something in Tora's ear, and the young man nodded.

"We thank you for your hospitality," said Tora. "My companions need healers immediately, if possible."

The Hakija rose. "At once, Holy Light. Bring them inside, and they shall be tended to straight away." He issued a string of orders to Lithel and the surrounding priests and commanded the cathedral gates be shut to the crowd gathered at its threshold.

No one protested. No one whispered or even dared to cough.

Priests guided the pythe to the cathedral steps. Tora slipped from his mount and helped Raren down. The injured Ahvenian pressed his lips together and inhaled hard as he moved his broken leg. Priests fluttered around the yellow-haired strangers, along with Jesh and Jeth, and conducted them up and into the cathedral while Nerenoth held back, keeping Lor'Toreth and Lekore close.

Talanee sat atop a pythe she'd commandeered from someplace, Ademas behind her in the saddle. Sun Warriors stationed at the latched gates stared straight ahead, unmoving, unhelpful.

"Best we go inside," Nerenoth murmured.

"Must we?" asked Lekore.

Talanee nudged the pythe forward. "My cousin requires treatment as well, and there's nowhere safer for you and the Tawloomez than with the Sun God. We should go in."

Footfalls brought every head back to the cathedral stairs. Priest Zanarin inclined his head as he reached the bottom step. "Lord Captain, the Holy Gods request the presence of all here." He looked up, but his gaze skirted away from Lekore and Lor'Toreth.

"We shall obey at once," Nerenoth said. He turned to the pythe and offered a hand. "Princess?"

Talanee smiled and allowed the Lord Captain to help her down, then Nerenoth guided Ademas to the ground. The company followed Zanarin inside, and Lekore's heart struck his ribs like the tolling zenbells he'd sometimes heard across the grasslands. Now and then, the wind spirits carried the sound to the top of Isiltik, his hilltop near the cave. How he'd longed to come nearer to Inpizal, to watch the cathedral bells on Zendays, as Skye had described them.

Now, he wished only to vanish and never return.

I must keep my promise.

Instead of the chapel or the room where Lekore had stood trial, Priest Zanarin led his charges up a flight of grand stairs that ended at a wide corridor lined with polished wooden doors. Zanarin strode to the farthest and entered a grand bedchamber where Tora stood beside the curtained four-post bed. Raren lay upon the coverlets, yellow hair sprawled over the silken pillows. Several gold clad Kel hovered over the man, holding instruments and water bowls as one of their order examined Raren's leg.

The Hakija stood at the end of the bed, Lithel beside him. The latter held an unblinking stare on Tora, even as Dakeer turned a glance upon the Lord Captain. His eyes flicked to Lekore and stayed there, brow wrinkling as his lips pulled down in a frown. He wrenched his gaze away.

"Welcome, Lord Captain." The Hakija glanced at the princess and Ademas. "Your adventure must be a very compelling one. I'm eager to hear it in full."

Nerenoth nodded. "I've no doubt of that, Your Holiness. Perhaps later."

The Hakija nodded. "Yes, after things have quite settled down.

I sent a message to King Netye. He's been very anxious about your disappearance, Princess."

Talanee made a noise like a cough, doubt coiling around her heart. "I'm certain he has."

"Where are my brothers?" asked Nerenoth.

"I ordered them to bathe before returning to the presence of divinity," said Lithel, as he turned to face the company. "Likewise, I'd ask each of you to do the same—if you please, Your Highness. Lord Captain."

The Hakija opened his mouth to add something, but his gaze landed on Lor'Toreth and he stiffened. "You bring Tawloomez filth into the presence of Sun Gods, Nerenoth?"

Tora slipped away from the bed and glided nearer. "Please —*Hakija*, is that right? This Tawloomez aided me."

Dakeer's head whipped around to stare at Tora, eyes bright. The man trembled. "You...wish to spare his life, Holy Light?"

"He is under my protection."

A crushing agony hammered into Lekore from Dakeer's frame. The man rocked back, perhaps against his will or knowledge. "As... as you wish." The Hakija bowed his head, then retreated to stand beside the healers.

Against the onslaught of confusion and betrayal emanating from Dakeer, Lekore caught a wave of opposing emotions: triumph, satisfaction, pride. He glanced up and found Nerenoth's face as stoic as ever, despite the roiling feelings beneath his calm exterior. What delighted him so?

Time slipped from Lekore's thoughts as he applied his focus to the healers' deft fingers at work. When the fingers withdrew, voices murmured around Lekore, indistinct. He didn't wish to hear. Didn't wish to face the task before him. And yet...his soul balked against the very concept of slavery. How could the Tawloomez and Kel justify such behavior? How could they imprison life?

I must save the slaves.

The door slammed open. Lekore spun to find a man with

thinning hair and rich green and gold apparel standing at the chamber threshold, a wild look in his red eyes. The man entered, familiar, so familiar. He drew breath to speak—then let it out in a rush as he found Tora and Raren.

"Holy Gods, forgive the king for his shock," said Dakeer, striding close. "Though we knew you would one day return, we didn't expect it on the very eve of our Sun Day celebration. He is overwhelmed in your presence."

The king grunted, then arched his back in a bow. "I am...indeed most humbled and gratified, H-Holy Gods."

"Thank you, Your Majesty," Tora said. He inclined his head. "I'm called Tora, and this is my companion and protector, Raren. Three more of my people rest in the next room. We're grateful for the help and hospitality we've received from those in your fair city."

The king's eyes darted between the Ahvenians, then Dakeer, then the Lord Captain. He found Lekore and his shoulders slumped. "What is *he* doing here?"

Dakeer circled the company to stand beside the king. "I suppose we cannot delay longer in addressing the emockye in the room, but perhaps a drink first, sire?" He gestured and a healer moved to a cabinet, poured red liquid from a crystal decanter into a goblet, and brought the goblet to the king. Bowed and backed away.

The king sipped, but his gaze never strayed from Lekore. He lowered his drink and licked his lips. "All right, Dakeer. Explain. I thought he'd been labeled a Star Worshiper."

"And so he is," said the Hakija, turning toward Tora as he spoke. "If you would listen a moment, Holy God, it is my burden to explain the blasphemies of this tainted soul."

Lekore's heart dropped as his mouth turned dry. Nerenoth's hand fell on his shoulder, firm but kind. The Lord Captain said nothing.

Dakeer Vasar launched into an explanation of Lekore's arrival in Inpizal, of calming the massive storm, of interrupting the blood ceremony in the cathedral, and of his escape. "It is unpleasant to recount his sacrilege. Worst of all, Holy One, this creature has allied himself with the very Star Worshipers of this city. My informant has assured me that Lekore aided the cultists in a blood rite to summon darkness itself."

Lekore's arm ached with the memory. "It's not true." Eyes settled on him like boulders crushing his limbs. He looked up. "They took me to their temple against my will. Never would I ally myself to such ills—not of the Sun or the Moon. However, if my *willing* actions blaspheme against your faith, and if that makes me guilty of some terrible evil, I must accept that label. It is better than embracing the execution of babies and the enslavement of people."

Lithel marched forward, vestments billowing, jabbing a finger at Lekore, hatred roiling through his limbs. "Sacrilege! Blaspheming heathen." He reached out like he wanted to grab Lekore and shake him—but Nerenoth stepped in the way, sword scraping as he drew it several inches from its sheath.

"Stand down," the Lord Captain said.

Lithel blinked. "You would dare to defend a heretic?"

"Please stop this." Tora moved forward, hands raised like a barrier. "I don't wish to interfere, but I can't stand by while you threaten the life of this man." He glanced at Lekore. "For my part, I agree with his view on these subjects."

"No!" The king flung his hands to his sparse hair and wrenched it from his circlet like he might rip it loose. "That can't be! Dakeer, you said the Sun Throne sanctioned my reign. Sanctioned my actions. You said—"

"Be quiet, you fool." The Hakija's voice snapped over the air like a whip, and the king recoiled, blood draining from his face until he stood colorless and small before the wrath of Dakeer Vasar. The Hakija sighed and ran a palm across his face. "Help us understand thy will, O Sun God. Do you mean to condemn our actions against the Tawloomez?" His hand shook as he lowered it to gaze into Tora's blue eyes.

"I think he means to condemn you for more than that," Nerenoth said. "Say all, Dakeer. Let us hold nothing back now."

"What do you mean, Lord Captain?" asked Talanee. At some point she'd bathed and changed into a silken pink gown, and now sat on a settee beside Ademas, whose wounds were bandaged. He also wore fresh clothes of deep green and gold. He eyed the proceedings with keen, bright eyes.

"Just what I say, Princess," Nerenoth answered. "Long has the Holy Hakija abused his authority, declaring that the gods have led his actions—but they have been the actions of a frightened, prejudiced man determined to provoke the genocide of the Tawloomez race, no matter the cost to his people and to his soul."

"Not so," said Dakeer. "The gods moved me to do as I have done."

"Which gods?" asked Nerenoth. "Surely not those in this chamber."

The Hakija flinched.

Netye moaned and bowed his head into his hands. "Doomed, Dakeer. What am I to do?"

"Your Majesty, don't—"

"Don't interrupt him, Dakeer." Nerenoth stepped closer to the king. "Say on, Netye Getaal. What are you to do about *what?*"

The king lifted his head, hands stretched before him like a beggar. "Do?" His eyes shifted out of focus, and he smiled a broken smile. "I won't. I can't. No, no, no." He shook his head. "I've paid too high a price to merely let my kingdom fall around my ears now. No, Lord Captain, you shan't..." Tears leaked from his eyes.

Sorrow, guilt, and a hundred secret pains crashed over Lekore, oh so familiar. Could it be? Dare Lekore believe his heart? He gasped and bolted to the king, hair floating after him. "Ank! Ank?"

Netye sobbed out a groan. "Oh, child. Little child. Why do you live?"

Lekore caught the man's wrists and stared up into his wild eyes. "Ank, is it you? Have I found you?" His throat burned as longing and heartache scorched his chest. "Oh, Ank. Where have you been? I've waited such a long, long time." He released the king's wrists and touched a tear on the man's cheek. Traced his finger down his face. "Ank, do you know me?"

The king moaned a long, horrible noise, curling into himself, hunching down to his heels in a pool of green satin. "No. No no no no no. You're dead. I left you for dead. Dead, you're dead."

Someone gasped. Confusion, horror, bloomed up around the chamber like poisonous flowers in the Wildwood.

"Not dead." Nerenoth's tones rattled with suppressed rage. "Though you left him to be the feast of emockye, he lived—for the gods willed it so. I witnessed your transgression, Netye Getaal. I saw a Sun God appear to spare his life. The god commanded that I keep my peace, and I watched him take young Adenye away, to be raised as the Sun Throne would have it."

Shivering, Lekore searched the Lord Captain's face as his mind grasped at fleeting memories. Adenye. He *knew* that name. Somehow, he knew it. "You saw Ter?" he asked, recalling the gentle fae hand reaching for him. Calling him Lekore. Guiding him to his cave within the Vale That Shines Gold. Ter had come often after that, bringing supplies Lekore needed to exist in the wilds.

"Ter intervened?" Tora's blue gaze lanced Lekore. "Is that how you met him?"

"Yes, and he taught me to survive," said Lekore. "He and Skye Getaal."

"Skye!" Dakeer blinked, perhaps startled by the vehemence of his own voice. "Skye was a traitor and a heretic."

Lekore frowned. "Not so. His brother Erokel murdered him, then stole his wife, his unborn child, and his title. His spirit remains upon this world until his descendants right the wrongs committed against him and fulfill prophecy."

All eyes stared at Lekore.

"Lies," wheezed Dakeer.

"No." Lekore shook his head. "Truth."

"It can't be," said Lithel, despair lacing his voice. "The founder of our faith was no covetous heretic! His pen has guided our course these five centuries. You're deceived."

Lekore scowled as fire danced across his emotions. "Why am I deceived? Because I see differently from you?"

"Enough." Dakeer lifted a hand and claimed every gaze. "These are weighty matters, not to be discussed like a common debate at court. We stand in the presence of Holiness. Let us learn truth and wisdom from its source—but first, let those who have traveled far rest. There is time enough to sort out what is right and what is wrong."

Relief scored Lekore's blood like water poured over an open flame. He let out a sigh.

"I think not, Hakija." Nerenoth's voice hummed, low and soft.

"Captain, please—"

Nerenoth raised his hand against the Hakija's protest. "On matters of theology, I know better than to debate. But more has been dropped here than issues regarding Skye Getaal."

"Agreed," said Ademas. He rose, tugged his tunic straight, and limped forward to join the circle of men. Talanee followed him, her brow creased, lips a thin line, face colorless. Ademas looked squarely at the king. "I want to know more about Adenye Getaal and what the Lord Captain says he witnessed eighteen years ago." He glanced at Lekore. "Is *this* the lost heir of House Getaal?"

Lekore blinked. "I do not understand."

King Netye moaned. "Dakeer...it is over."

"It's true, Lord Father?" Talanee whispered.

Lekore searched the king's face, reading the lines of guilt and sorrow. "Ank, please. I do not understand what is going on."

Netye moaned again, wringing his hands. "It's not my fault. Dakeer Vasar led me to do what I did." He looked up from the floor to stare hard at Nerenoth. "Believe me, Lord Captain, I was but a tool—"

Ademas bent and caught the king's collar. "The Hakija *led* you to murder your own brother, abandon his heir, and steal the throne for yourself?"

Lekore weighed those words against his heart. A note of truth rang through them, harrowing...like a dream he'd long harbored but never explored.

"You called him 'Ank'," said Nerenoth, "because you couldn't pronounce 'uncle.'"

"I did *not* lead you to make the choices you did, Netye," Dakeer said into the heavy silence. "Nor did I encourage you to leave the heir to the mercies of the wilderness."

Netye jerked his eyes to the Hakija. "You would abandon me in this? Indeed, you would... The church will never soil its own hands."

"Yet," Nerenoth said, "truth cannot be hidden behind a cloak. We stand in the presence of the very Sun Gods."

Bodies shifted to include Tora in the tightened circle around the king. Lekore ignored them all; he gently pried Ademas's hands from the king's raiment. Ademas acceded and stepped back. Tears shone in the king's weary eyes. The lines of his face cut deep grooves, revealing sleepless nights and weighty sorrows.

"Oh, Ank," breathed Lekore. "How tired you are." He stroked the man's face. "Shed your burden, and I will care for you. It matters not what you have done."

"Perhaps not to you, Your Highness," said Ademas, "but he must pay for his crimes. He killed your father the king. Murdered him in the dead of night."

"That's not true." Talanee let out a sob. "He's not a kin killer."

"It is true, Princess," Nerenoth said. "I witnessed his flight after pushing King Adelair through his study window. He took young Adenye with him. He left the boy upon the grasslands to die."

"How could you keep this silent?" asked Lithel, staring hard at the Lord Captain.

Nerenoth glanced at him. "I believe I already answered that."

"But..." Lithel turned to Dakeer. "Your Holiness, surely you knew nothing about this."

"I knew." Dakeer's voice was a quiet rumble. His eyes hardened as he turned them on Lekore. "Not all. Not at first. Netye acted on his own in a fit of madness...yet he confessed all to me in the days that followed. I had been...concerned with the crown prince's behaviors and deemed it best to leave matters as they laid."

"That's a lie," gasped out Netye. He rose and danced around Lekore to face the Hakija. "You spoke often of the prince before I killed Adelair! You—you spoke of how dangerous he would be once he took the throne. You all but suggested I do as I did!"

Dakeer's eyes flashed with the light of an inner storm. "I spoke of the danger from a place of great concern for the welfare of Erokel, but I *never* suggested you kill your own kin. That sin rests upon your soul, Netye. Not mine."

Netye covered his face and let out a despairing cry that stabbed Lekore to his center.

He wrapped his arms around the king. "Oh, Ank. Please do not suffer alone. I am here. I will care for you."

"He must stand trial," said Ademas with vehemence.

Netye's head snapped up and he wrenched back. His breaths shortened. He snatched a dagger from a sheath at his hip and set it against Lekore's throat.

Lekore flinched, then fell still. His heart twisted in his chest as despair swallowed his soul, pressing in, dimming color. "Oh, Ank. Please do not betray me now."

"This ill fate belongs to both of us, little Nye," gasped out the king. "We began this journey together, and so we will end it. No one approach, or the boy dies sooner!" His eyes, red-rimmed, darted toward the Lord Captain. "Stay there. Don't you try anything, Nerenoth. Adenye is mine. Let us depart the cathedral."

"You've lost the last of your wits," said Dakeer Vasar. "Have you forgotten the Holy Gods in our presence, Netye?"

"I don't care. I don't care!" Netye released a high, mangled laugh. "Long have I known the state of my soul. It matters little. Adenye understands me, don't you, little Nye?"

Tears burned Lekore's eyes. He shook his head, and the knife bit at his flesh. He swallowed. "No, Ank. I do not understand you.

I do not understand why you left me alone, why you broke your promise, why you keep slaves and murder children... I do not understand any of you." A tear rolled down his cheek.

Netye paused. His chest rose and fell as he wheezed out breaths. "Ah, little Adenye. I knew this life would be too cruel for you. I meant to spare you. Spare you from the hatred, from all the sorrow and regret... I didn't want you to see what I'd become. I didn't want..." His fingers slackened, and the knife clattered to the floor. His shoulders hunched.

The Lord Captain rested his sword against the king's chest. "You're under arrest, Netye Getaal, for conspiracy, murder, treason —and, if I do not overstep myself, heresy." He glanced at Tora, who remained still, watchful, silent.

"You do not overstep yourself in this," said the Hakija. "Please escort him to the cathedral dungeons, Captain. I think it would be best not to cause a scene outside, on the very heels of the Sun Gods' arrival."

"Agreed." Nerenoth slipped behind Netye and seized his wrists. "Come."

Netye nodded, then lifted his gaze to meet Lekore's. "I loved you, Nye. More than anyone, except my beloved Naveena."

"A pity," Nerenoth said. "You had a daughter much like her, but you were too blind to find healing where it dwelt." He nudged Netye toward the door.

Lekore tracked them from the chamber. He bowed his head, heart bleeding in his tightening chest. How long had he waited for Ank to return? To make right all that had felt wrong? To offer the shelter and love Lekore had longed to receive?

He left me to die. He never meant to return for me.

Never had the truth hurt so much. Never had he ached so much to flee and hide away.

"You're the rightful king of Erokel." Ademas's voice cut across the soft murmurs drifting around Lekore. Cloth rustled. Lekore turned and found Ademas kneeling on the ground, a fist clamped to his heart, head bowed. "Your Majesty," the young man said.

A sob sounded behind Lekore. He whirled and found Talanee withdrawn from the circle of bodies, eyes lowered, hands clutching at her pink skirts. Shame and terror, anguish and longing pulsed from her frame. Lekore abandoned Ademas's deference and stepped to Talanee's side. He caught her hand and pressed it between his fingers.

Talanee looked up, eyes bright with tears. "Please don't execute him," she whispered. "Please."

Lekore flinched as chills raced over his flesh. "I could not."

"Thank you." She slipped her hand free and twisted away.

Lekore swallowed and turned back to the crowd. Every eye watched him. He shook his head. "I do not wish to be king."

"Yet, you were born to lead us," Ademas said, still kneeling.

"Such eagerness," said Lithel. "I didn't take you for a sycophant, Lord Ademas."

The young man shrugged. "This isn't about politics. This is about blood. If this man is truly Prince Adenye Getaal, he must rule. He's our king by divine appointment."

Lekore's skin crawled. A whispering compulsion pulsed through his blood: escape, escape, escape.

I must stand firm. I must do the right thing.

He planted his feet. "I did not return to Inpizal to steal another's crown. I came to beg the release of Tawloomez slaves. I came to right that wrong. All the Kel slaves have been freed from the Tawloomez lands." His gaze flicked to Lor'Toreth, who huddled outside the circle, wide-eyed and ignorant of all that had been said.

Dakeer Vasar jolted and followed Lekore's gaze to the Tawloomez prince. "Is this true?"

"It is, Hakija," whispered Talanee.

"So it is," said Tora. "Though I'm afraid it upset the Teokaka. She swore vengeance."

The Hakija stared at the yellow-haired young man, then let his head drop as a sigh escaped his lips. "Praise be to the Sun Throne. Your generosity is unequaled, Holy God."

Tora lifted a hand. "I can't take credit for Lekore's work. He insisted upon their freedom and summoned fire to lend weight to his request." Tora's eyes sparkled. "It was quite something to witness. Lekore is uniquely gifted."

Alarm flickered over Dakeer's face as guilt and confusion churned inside him. "Does...does your Holiness sanction the rule of this—unconventional Kel?"

Tora shifted his feet, a frown crossing his lips. "I won't interfere in the affairs of your people, Hakija. But I *will* stress that I owe Lekore for his aid and won't let harm befall him, no matter any political strife."

Dakeer inclined his head, reverence choking out the doubts cluttering his heart. "As you command, so shall it be."

The door opened. The Lord Captain stepped into the room, Jeth and Jesh on his heels, both cleaned and groomed. Relief pounded through Lekore's blood.

Nerenoth crossed the floor and placed himself beside Lekore, his wrist draped over his sword hilt. "My lieutenant met me on the way to the dungeons. He is seeing the king properly deposited there. I thought my place should be here."

The twins took up positions on Lekore's other side.

The Hakija chuckled, though his eyes cradled no humor. "Fear not, Lord Captain. Greater forces than even you might conjure protect your charge. The Sun Gods shine their favor upon the rightful heir." He plucked the miter from his head and ran fingers through his light blue hair. "As for my fate, I leave that in the hands of thee, O Glorious Light."

He bent to his knees before Tora. "My sin is not regicide, but in turning my eyes from that action. I feared what King Adelair and his heir would do to our people...yet I wonder now if my prejudice blinded me to the will of the gods. If I have erred in promoting thy will, my anguish shall never end."

Tora considered the Hakija with a thoughtful frown. He crouched before Dakeer and rested a hand on his shoulder. "I'll not be your judge in this. That isn't my place. Do you *feel* you have been wrong, Dakeer Vasar?"

Silence enveloped the chamber. Emotions roiled within Dakeer like bubbles rising to boil over the edge of a pot. Lekore closed his eyes to shutter his soul against the writhing feelings.

"My blindness has been willful, O Holy One," said Dakeer.

Tora nodded. "Do you still desire to blind yourself?"

"...No. I wish to understand." Dakeer lifted his eyes as the press of his guilt ebbed in the wake of desire. "I have ever longed to serve the Sun Gods, and if I have misunderstood your will, I would repent."

Tora blinked as he recoiled an inch. Slowly, he stood. "If you wish to understand truth, I encourage you to see beyond what you think you know. That's all I'm able to say on that."

"It is enough, Holiness." Dakeer straightened to his full height. "For now, I think it wise to leave your companion to his rest. Lekore— No, forgive me. *Adenye* should be taken to the palace. Arrangements must be made to inform the people of the changes..."

"There is one more matter to discuss," said Nerenoth. "I think it is best done before the Sun Gods."

Lekore caught a scowl flit across Dakeer's face, but though annoyance fluttered through his feelings, he held no malice. "Yes, Captain?"

Nerenoth turned toward Ademas. "Forgive me if I've timed this ill, but should you not reveal yourself in all this, my lord?"

Ademas's lips quirked in a smirk. "I hadn't guessed that you knew."

Nerenoth lifted his armored shoulders in a faint shrug. "I am among the few who knew of your existence."

"What are you talking about?" asked Talanee.

Ademas's smile slipped into a lopsided grin tinged with dry humor. "Oh, well, I might have steered you astray upon our meeting, Princess. You asked after my connections. I didn't precisely lie, but nor did I correct your assumptions." He shrugged. "Maybe that's not right. Elekel and I agreed to lead the masses wrong. It gave me cover without causing me to lose influence."

"What are you talking about?" Talanee repeated, eyes flashing with renewed fire.

Lekore looked between them, curious despite his aching heart. Despite the barrage of emotions slithering about the room.

"It's simple," said Nerenoth. "Lord Ademas is *not* Duke Elekel's illegitimate son."

Talanee blinked, then a snarl touched her lips. "You're not my cousin? Why make such a wild claim if—"

Ademas lifted his hands, palms forward. "Easy now. I *am* your cousin. My only misdirection was in hinting at a false parentage. My father was King Adelair Getaal, and my mother is Queen Zanah."

Lithel gasped. "But—but the queen died in child..." His eyes widened.

The fire in Talanee's eyes faded. She shook her head, emotions rising like a flood: betrayal, heartache, disbelief. "Why lie?"

Ademas barked a laugh. "*Why?* Because I came to ruin your father. So my mother raised me. She's a strong, fearless woman, but she had to hide my existence or Netye would've hunted us down before I was skilled enough to take the throne back."

"So." Dakeer shook his head. "Both children lived after all."

"That we did, Hakija," said Ademas, and his gaze flicked to Lekore. "I hadn't expected *that*, but it changes very little."

"Doesn't it?" Talanee spat. "You aimed for the throne, but now your elder brother has returned from the dead. Both you and I are displaced."

"Wrong. We are now placed right where we should have been, before my father met his dreadful end. The way I see things, everything is being mended." Ademas's eyes darted to Tora. "And small wonder."

Lekore glanced at Nerenoth. "I'm not certain I understand."

Nerenoth smiled. "Put simply, my king, Ademas is your younger brother. Do you understand the word?"

Lekore glanced at the twins. "Family," he whispered.

"Yes." Nerenoth shifted to eye Ademas. "Though, I must ask if you intend to support your elder brother's birthright, Prince Ademas. Treachery does run in your blood."

Ademas's crooked smile softened. "A concern well warranted. But have no fear on that account, good captain. My lady mother taught me two things above all others. The first was what my uncle had done to his brother, and all that his actions broke. Revenge was my foremost education, and Zanah was nothing short of obsessed. But her second lesson, she hammered harder even than the first. She spoke of my brother, Adenye, as a priest might speak of the Blessed Naal, Holy Queen of Erokel. I never envied that, though I knew she loved me second best."

He beamed at Lekore. "In truth, I longed to know you. I wished to meet that wondrous boy who caused such dissension or adoration in all who knew him. Perhaps she painted you as more than you are, or ever were, but even so I came to love Adenye. I told myself if ever he had been king, I would have served my brother most faithfully—unlike Netye, who betrayed my father to his death. Treachery among brothers is a vile sin, by my mind." His smile flashed into a grin that showed teeth. "To think, Adenye lived. Mother will—" He swallowed. "Mother will want to meet you, Lekore. You can't know how much."

Lekore tilted his head to one side. "You accept me even as I am?"

Ademas shrugged. "And what are you?"

"I am not Adenye. At least, that is not my name now. I am Lekore."

Ademas nodded. "Whatever, *whomever*, you wish to be, you're my liege lord." He knelt and pressed a hand to his heart. "I pledge to you my life, my heart, my very soul, brother."

Lekore knelt before him. "I am not a king. I do not wish to be a king. But I will gladly accept you as my brother. You saved my life and helped me to escape—and that you did without knowing we share the same blood. I am indebted to you, Ademas."

"So, it was you who broke him free of the cathedral dungeons?" asked Lithel.

Ademas stood as Lekore straightened. "No," Ademas said. "He'd already been dragged from there by the Star Worshipers into the Temple of the Moon. I helped him flee from there."

Dakeer took several steps nearer. "The Star Worshipers? They truly took you by force, Lekore?"

Lekore nodded. "I did not at first understand...but then they made me afraid..." He clutched at his torn sleeve, trembling with the memory. "They stole drops of my blood to summon their gods."

"They took *your* blood?" Dakeer hissed.

"Was magic invoked?" asked Tora, striding near, eyes bright with panic. "Could you tell?"

Lekore willed himself to explain all that had befallen him within the unholy temple, and he described the black stone and violet flame.

Tora's face paled several shades. "The violet flame. Did it resemble the malignant force the Teokaka used to kill her warrior in the courtyard?"

Lekore flinched. "It...felt similar."

Fear danced over Tora's soul, sharp, deep. "Then whatever these worshipers entreated, it can't be wholesome. There's so much about your world I must come to understand." Tora rubbed his chin. He turned to Dakeer. "Is there a private room where Lekore and I might converse?"

"Of course, Holy One." Dakeer motioned to the door. "Follow me, please."

CHAPTER 32

"May I see your sword?"

Lekore summoned *Calir* and rested the blade on the polished stone table before him. Tora reached from his place opposite Lekore and brushed his fingertips over the firestone embedded in *Calir*'s pommel.

They sat in the Hakija's study, surrounded by shelves of tomes and scrolls. A few books cluttered one edge of the square table, and candles guttered in gentle breezes as wind spirits flirted with the fragrant flames. All had left them alone, though the Lord Captain's presence lingered just beyond the door where he kept guard.

Still fingering the gemstone, Tora used his free hand to slide his own blade from thin air. *Calir* toned a note of greeting, and the other sword answered.

Tora set his weapon beside Lekore's. "Its name is *Calisay*. Several years ago, it chose me as its wielder, though it'd slumbered for two thousand years or more within a secret chamber where I live. I've never found craftsmanship to rival its design. Now, though the shapes of these blades are different, somehow, they resemble one another. They call to each other as twins might."

"They are forged from the same master," said Lekore, as the

353

words fluted through his mind. "I do not know how or when or by whom. But *Calir* confirms these swords are brothers."

Tora smiled. "And so *Calisay* tells me. Yet, that's only one mystery we must solve." He leaned back in his chair with a sigh. His blue eyes flitted about the study. "This place. This city. What do you know of its construction?"

"Only what Skye has told me." Lekore rose from his seat and padded to the study's single, wide window. The sun bore down on Inpizal as it blazed a path toward its tor. Rooftops glimmered under its influence, while Kel lingered at the cathedral gates, just visible from Lekore's vantage point.

He turned from the sight to study the palace and its domed turrets. "Long, long ago, men and women with golden hair descended from the very heavens and constructed this city, and several others like it. Skye and the rest of the Kel hid within the Wildwood before it became a tainted realm, but at last the golden-haired Ahvenians discovered them. Hurt them. Used them in horrible ways as they poisoned the forest."

He turned to face Tora. The young man stared back, pain lining his features.

Lekore let out a soft breath, long hair slipping to cover half his face. "Then the Kiisuld came."

Tora sprang from his chair. "The *what?*"

"Kiisuld. Skye called them that. They came...and everything grew worse. They corrupted Skye's people, most notably his elder brother Erokel. Erokel made a pact with the Kiisuld in order to take Skye's wife for himself. What he offered in exchange, I know not." Lekore's arm throbbed, and he rubbed it. "In the end, Skye gave his life to stop the destruction of Kel, Ahvenians, and Tawloomez."

Tora searched Lekore's face, then he sat down and rubbed his eyes. "This is worse than I feared. If Kiisuld were involved... But I suppose I should've made the connection sooner. Keo lives here, and he called the Teokaka a half-Kiisuld. I'm just so tired."

He lowered his hands. "Forgive me, Lekore. My people worked

hard to destroy your world once already, and now we've come again. While I mean no harm, the faith your people place in me and my companions can't remain for long. I fear the repercussions of telling them the truth, but to deceive them is equally untenable. It's quite the quandary."

He rested his elbows on the table, laced his fingers together, and propped his chin over his knuckles. "I'm lost in this matter. Raren might offer some solution I can't find, if only he weren't so injured..." He glanced at Lekore. "You said you know Ter. I don't suppose he's here somewhere?"

Lekore shook his head. "I have not seen him in several months. He might not return for another fortnight or longer."

Tora nodded without lifting his head. "That sounds like Ter." His eyes dropped to the swords. "Nearly everything I've learned about this world unnerves me, yet these..." He slid his hands apart to finger the blades. "I can't believe mere coincidence brought these twin swords together again." His lips twitched toward a smile. "I suspect Ter is responsible somehow, and if that's the case, he has the answers we seek."

"He usually does," said Skye, materializing at the window.

Lekore glanced at the ghost. "Where have you been?"

Tora followed his gaze. "I assume you're not talking to me."

Lekore shook his head. "Skye is here."

"Is he well?"

"Yes, he is much improved."

Tora straightened up and studied the air near the spot where Skye stood. "You've conjured all five types of the Spirits Elemental, and you can see the dead, Lekore. Your gifts are rare enough on their own, let alone joined within one soul. No wonder Ter mentored you."

Skye drifted to the table. "Lekore, I came to warn you. I've seen him—he's coming."

"Who is coming?" asked Lekore.

"The one who caused the Kel to fall—he who answers the

summons of your blood. Prince Vay-Dinn of the Kiisuld will arrive in four days by starship."

Chills raced over Lekore's skin. He met Tora's gaze as his heart clenched. "Skye comes with a warning. He says the prince of the Kiisuld is coming here from the stars. He will reach us in four days."

Tora shot to his feet, chair clattering behind him. "The *prince?*" He snatched his sword and sheathed it in the air. "Is Skye certain of this?"

Lekore nodded. "He is."

Fear, panic, rage, coursed across the air currents surrounding Tora. The young man frowned at the tabletop, candlelight flickering in his eyes. "Keo must have summoned him."

Lekore tapped *Calir*. The sword vanished. "No. Skye said it was my blood which called him to this world."

"But why would that—?" Tora shook his head. "Questions later. Right now, we must fortify your city. Kiisuld seldom leave bystanders alive. If he came before, and let the Kel thrive, it won't happen a second time. A Kiisuld's whimsy shifts in a mere blink." Tora's eyes danced across the study. "The pulse that caused my ship to crash is still active. If the Kiisuld arrive before I deactivate it, they'll crash as well. Such a landing might destroy their crew, but never the prince or his traveling partner."

"Does their magic prevent that?"

Tora nodded as Skye mirrored him. "Yes," said the Ahvenian. "Kiisuld born of nobility are devilishly hard to kill. No crash would do it. At least, not permanently." He ran a hand through his golden tresses, and Lekore caught the flash of a deep scar running partway down Tora's forehead.

"What do we do?" asked Lekore. "Return to the Wildwood?"

"No. Not right away." Tora strode to the door and opened it. "Lord Captain."

Nerenoth turned and clapped a hand to his armor. "Your Holiness?"

"Would you say the palace is the largest structure in your city?"

"Yes, though the cathedral comes close."

"I must go to your palace. Will you escort me?"

"Gladly." The Lord Captain gestured. Lord Lieutenant Rez, who stood across the corridor, snapped off a salute and sprinted down the hall, red cape streaming behind him. "He will prepare a carriage, my lord. Though the palace is just across the Sun Square, this will spare you from the eager masses."

"Thank you." Tora moved down the hall. "Let's start that way. Time is precious."

Nerenoth nodded as the three marched along the passage after Rez. Lekore let himself take in the portraits and paintings hanging from the walls. Skye faded in and out beside him, silent, perhaps lost in memories as he often was.

Dakeer Vasar appeared ahead of them from an adjoining corridor. "Your Holiness?"

"I'm glad you're here," said Tora. "We're heading for the palace."

"Ah."

"Please accompany me." Tora motioned for the Hakija to join their procession. As Dakeer fell into step beside him, Tora spoke on. "A powerful enemy of my people is descending upon your world. We have only days to prepare for his arrival, or we'll be annihilated faster than you can dream. If your city is designed like Ahvenian settlements on other worlds, it will have a shield I can activate. That will spare your people from any aerial assaults. If not, I'll need the chance to build one, if possible. That's our priority. Depending on the strength and reach of the shield, you might need to offer sanctuary to any of your people dwelling outside the walls. I'm hoping it will extend further than that but be prepared to receive refugees."

"We're already prepared for that, my lord," Nerenoth said. "We'd been expecting a siege from the Tawloomez."

Tora's frown deepened. "There's the matter of their safety, as well." He glanced at the Lord Captain. "Where's Lor'Toreth?"

"With my brothers at my private estate."

"Very good." Tora looked ahead as he started down the steps. "Once we assess the shield, I'll need to deactivate the pulse that brought my ship down and boost the distress signal to reach my father. He'll already be seeking me, as I'm overdue to arrive home. The signal will bring his armada here, and we'll stand a chance against the Kiisuld invaders. But only if that shield holds. The Kiisuld will arrive in four days. If we're lucky, they'll number only two with a small crew onboard. At worst, we could be talking dozens of Kiisuld. At that point, we'll have no chance at all of surviving until the Ahvenian armada reaches us. That will take at least a week."

A grim sort of energy charged the air, emanating from Nerenoth and Dakeer. Tora's soul pulsed with fear tinged by defiance.

Lekore's arm panged, and he swallowed down a surging desire to escape. No matter how dark, how horrible, the magic caught in the dark Hakija's stone, and what it signified, he wouldn't abandon Inpizal to save himself.

The party reached the first level of the cathedral and marched toward the front doors. As priests pushed the doors aside, Lekore squinted in the bright light. A silhouette stood like a black cutout against the sun.

Tora flinched. "*You.*"

Lekore blinked until the features of Keo's face sharpened into sight.

The man smiled grimly. "Hello, Ahvenian. It seems I'll be aiding you against a coming threat."

Tora scowled. "Why would you help?"

Keo shrugged. "You might call me a fugitive of justice. Kiisuld justice, mind you. I'd rather not get caught. You work on activating the city shields. I'll see about protecting the Tawloomez. I just wanted you to know I'm not working against you. Right now, in this, we're allies."

"I can't trust you," said Tora.

Keo's smile turned dry as dust. "So you already said. Just give me the chance to earn it. That's all I ask." He vanished on the spot.

"He speaks the truth," Lekore murmured. "He means to help."

Tora's brows knitted, and he started walking again. "We'll see."

A carriage rolled across the gravel, drawn by two pythe.

Tora's grimace softened. "I didn't expect pythe to live on this world, too. I assume my people brought them here." His blue eyes darted to the stubs. "They're wingless, though. Poor things."

He slipped into the carriage, and Lekore followed. The Lord Captain came next, and Dakeer settled in last. The Lord Lieutenant rode with the driver, as the carriage bounced and rolled to the gates, then out into the square.

The fountain flashed and winked in the brilliant sunlight, but Nerenoth drew the carriage curtain before Lekore found any Kel faces staring up at him. *That's probably best.*

"Are Star Gods the enemy we must soon face, Your Holiness?" Dakeer asked.

Tora frowned at his hands folded on his lap. "I call this enemy Kiisuld. I don't know if it's the same as Star Gods... Though if I can guess anything about how my people and theirs have influenced your world, it seems likely. Tell me about the Star Gods."

"They are dark and cruel. Lovers of night and the vile moon." Dakeer sighed. "Two descended from the Moon Throne many ages ago. They tainted the Tawloomez into the snake-worshiping heathens they now are. Even many Kel were deceived by their lies, Skye Getaal among them."

Lekore opened his mouth to protest but stopped himself. *He will not listen to me.*

"That story might be false," said Tora. "I've had the chance to interact with this Skye Getaal, in a way, when he helped me against a foe. He was wronged by his brother, Hakija. I hate to fracture your doctrine, but I can't ignore the plight of an innocent man condemned to wander your lands in spirit until justice is done."

Dakeer's eyes widened as Tora spoke. He bowed his head. "Have *we* been so deceived?"

"There is truth in our faith, Dakeer," said Nerenoth. "But just as you let prejudice sway your heart, so too, other Kel before you have altered the tenets of our religion to suit their ends. We are not an infallible people. What we must do now is uncover the truth, so that we are worthy of those who have descended from the Sun Throne."

Dakeer stared at his palms. "Yes. You are correct, Lord Captain. I must learn to *see*."

Lekore studied the Hakija's face, sensing no lies in his countenance. Was it possible for this man, and for the rest of the Kel, to change their ways? He shifted and reached out to brush his fingers across Dakeer's arm until the Hakija looked up.

"Will you free the Tawloomez slaves?" whispered Lekore.

Dakeer released a long, weary breath. "That is not my province, O Prince. That is yours. But I will not argue against your actions. You are..." Pain lit in his eyes. "You are chosen of the Sun Gods to lead us into enlightenment. I will not stand against you in anything you do."

Lekore settled back against his seat as the carriage rocked to a halt. Nerves clawed at his soul. *Must I be king? Dare I accept such a burden?*

Tora stepped from the carriage, and Lekore followed, though his feet felt weightless and far away. His mind hung suspended above the sights and smells of reality. He moved through space like he moved against a strong current, each breath a struggle.

The palace loomed before him. As he started up the steps leading to its front doors, wind spirits threw the fragrance of flowers at him. The scents, so familiar, clung to his mind like fond, faraway memories. *I lived here once. I lived here and was happy.*

"Nye," a voice had called from a garden. "Come, see the flowers."

Memories floated into his thoughts. The flow of water, whose spirits rippled and danced across a pond lit with golden light from

360

the setting sun. The laughter of leaves as the wind spirits whispered secrets from the distant sea. The tumbling joy of earth spirits at play with the garden's insects. The contented fire spirits dozing in their lanterns. A Spirit of Spirit hovering at the garden wall, observing, smiling, relishing a moment caught in precious remembrance forever.

Tears pricked Lekore's eyes. He'd stopped walking, and Nerenoth stood with him, waiting. Lekore looked into the Lord Captain's face. "This is my home."

Nerenoth smiled. "Yes, my king. Welcome back."

Lekore's eyes traveled to the high dome of the palace. *At last, I am home.*

Now I must defend it.

Lekore's story continues in...

BOOK TWO: RULE OF THE NIGHT

.

DEAREST READER

You're holding in your hands my first-ever imagined fantasy novel. Back in January 2002, Lekore was my original inspiration for this story. He and the story have come a long, long way since then, but the heart of the tale remains the same:

Being different isn't bad.

I felt very alone back then, in a community that didn't accept me or my family, until I found belonging in fantasy books and worlds.

So many years later, Lekore still resonates with that young writer's lonely heart, and his journey heals me a little more with each new book in this series.

If Lekore speaks to you as he does me; if he makes you feel less alone; not so much of an outcast; a little more loved because he has so much love to give those like you and me, then I've done something right.

Thank you so much for reading!

If you've enjoyed this first installment in the *Record of the Sentinel Seer*, please consider leaving an honest review online to support my efforts to bring more of Lekore's story into the world.

You may also enjoy reading the prequel novelette, *Way of the*

Spirits, which is available for free to anyone who signs up for my newsletter.

Visit my website at www.mhwoodscourt.com to learn more! And never forget, you're worthwhile just as you are.

Kindest regards,

M. H. Woodscourt

GLOSSARY

CHARACTERS

Adelair Getaal [*odd-eh-lair get-TALL*] – King of Erokel and brother of Netye and Elekel Getaal.

Ademas Getaal [*odd-eh-moss get-TALL*] – Self-professed cousin of Princess Talanee, from the island of Ra Kye.

Adenye Getaal [*odd-en-ī get-TALL*] – King Adelair's son and heir.

Barrad [*bawr-odd*] – A Kel nobleman with strong eastern trade connections.

Carak [*kair-ack*] – A soldier in the Royal Army of Erokel.

Dakeer Vasar [*duh-KEER vuh-SAHR*] – The Holy Hakija; head of the Sun Church. One of the Triad of Erokel.

Elekel Getaal [*ELL-eh-kel get-TALL*] – A prince and the youngest brother of Adenye and Netye Getaal.

Jasu'Hekar [*jaw-soo hek-ahr*] – A former Tawloomez slave turned spy working for Nerenoth Irothé.

Jesh Irothé [*jesh ee-RAW-thay*] – Twin of Jeth Irothé and younger brother of Nerenoth Irothé.

Jeth Irothé [*jeth ee-RAW-thay*] – Twin of Jesh Irothé and younger brother of Nerenoth Irothé.

Keerva [*keer-vuh*] – Princess Talanee's handmaid.

Keo [KEE-oh] – A strange hermit living in the Lands Beyond.

Krett [kret] – A Star Worshiper.

Khyna [*kī-nuh*] – A Tawloomez servant.

Lanasha Jahaan [*luh-NAW-shuh juh-HAWN*] – Nerenoth Irothé's noble-born betrothed.

Lekore [leh-KOR] – A strange Kel who lives in the Charnel Valley (or the Vale That Shines Gold).

Lios [*lee-oh-ss*] – An emockye pup and Lekore's friend.

Lithel Kuaan [*Lith-ELL koo-awn*] – High Priest of the Sun Church and Dakeer Vasar's righthand man.

Lor'Toreth [*lor TOR-eth*] – The prince and heir of Tawloom.

Mahaka [*muh-HAWK-uh*] – Seenth of the Teokaka. A Tawloomez warrior.

Naal Getaal [*nawl get-TALL*] – The Blessed Lady, married to King Erokel the Second five hundred years ago.

Naveena Getaal [*nuh-VEEN-uh get-TALL*] – Deceased wife of King Netye Getaal.

Nerenoth Irothé [*NAIR-eh-noth ee-RAW-thay*] – Lord Captain and military leader of Erokel. One of the Triad of Erokel.

Netye Getaal [*net-ī get-TALL*] – King of Erokel. One of the Triad of Erokel.

Raren [RAIR-en] – A Sun God.

Rez Kuaan [*rez koo-awn*] – Lord Lieutenant of Erokel. Nerenoth Irothé's righthand man.

Skye Getaal [*skī get-TALL*] – Lekore's mentor. Also called the Voice of the Stars or the Heretic.

Susunee [*soo-SOO-nee*] – The religious leader of the Tawloomez.

Talajin [taw-luh-jin] – An Ahvenian scientist.

Talanee Getaal [tuh-LAWN-ee get-TALL] – Princess of Erokel and daughter of King Netye Getaal.

Teon Keela [*tee-awn kee-luh*] – A warden in the Sun Cathedral's dungeon.

Ter N'Avea [*tair NAW-vay*] – Lekore's mentor. A Sun God.

Tora [TOR-*uh*] – A Sun God.

Vay-Dinn [*VAY-din*] – Prince of the Kiisuld.

Zanah Getaal [zawn-uh get-TALL] – Wife of King Adelair Getaal.

Zanarin [*zuh-NAW-rinn*] – A priest of the Sun Church.

CREATURES

Cheos [*chee-oh-ss*] – A carnivorous bird native to Erokel and the Lands Beyond.

Emockye [*ee-mock-ī*] – A canine animal similar to coyotes, though larger, with venomous claws and teeth.

Minkee [*meen-kee*] – A lemur like animal native to the Lands Beyond.

Pythe [*pīth*] – A reptilian/equine cross between a dragon and a Pegasus. The pythe of Erokel have lost their wings through scientific devolution.

Rabbun [*rab-boon*] – A rabbit like animal native to Erokel and the Firelands.

PLACES

Cathedral of the Sun – The cathedral of Inpizal in Erokel, where the Kel worship the Sun Gods.

Charnel Valley (Also called the *Vale That Shines Gold*, the *Valley of Bones*) – A valley filled with the bones of those who fell during the War of Brothers five hundred years ago.

Erokel [*air-oh-kel*] – The kingdom of the Kel.

Erokes [*air-oh-kess*] – A fortress city in Erokel.

Halathe [*huh-LAYTH*] – The holy ruins where Kel perform the sacred Lighting ceremony.

Inpizal [*inn-piz-ALL*] – The Royal City of Erokel.

Isiltik [iss-ILL-tik] – A hill above the Charnel Valley.

Lands Beyond (Also called the *Wildwood, Ava Vyy*) – A massive jungle filled with deadly plants and animals, the Kel and Tawloomez alike avoid passing its borders at all costs.

Nakoth Mountains [*nuh-KAWTH*] – The mountains between Erokel and the Charnel Valley.

Ra Kye [*raw kī*] – The southern islands in the Kingdom of Erokel.

Sun Court – The court of the Sun Gods.

Wildwood (See *Lands Beyond*)

RACES

Ahvenian [*ah-ven-ee-ehn*] – Another name for the Sun Gods.

Kel [*kell*] – The people who dwell in Erokel.

Kiisuld [*kee-sool-d*] – Another name for the Star Gods.

Tawloomez – [*taw-loom-ehz*] – The people who dwell in Taloom (more commonly called the Firelands).

TITLES AND TERMS

Hakija [huh-KEE-juh] – The holy leader of Erokel's Sun Church and Voice of the Sun Throne.

Keeper of Memory – A historian.

Lord Captain – The leader of military affairs in Erokel.

Moon Throne – The holy throne of the Star Gods.

Snake God(s) – Deities worshiped by the Tawloomez.

Spirits Elemental – The guardian elementals in charge of protecting and defending the Elements of the world: fire, wind, water, and earth.

Star God(s) – The gods who rule the Night. Kel who worship these fallen gods are considered heretical by the rest of their race.

Sun God(s) – The gods who rule the majority of the Kel and their faith.

Sun Throne – The holy throne of the Sun Gods.

Teokaka [*tee-oh-kaw-kaw*] – The holy leader of Tawloomez's church and Voice of the Snake Gods. Literally translated to *Holy Voice*.

TAWLOOMEZ TERMS & PHRASES

In order of usage:

Akuu! Nu jas Akuu-Ry! – Demon! Here comes [the] Demon Child!"

Akuu-Ry – "Demon Child."

Tauw-Nijar – "Honored Warrior."

I'tete – "Come."

Stataj – "Wait."

Thatu kret – "That is likely."

Akuu-Ry! Heden Akuu-Ry! – "Demon Child! It's the Demon Child!"

Reka-Ku – Dark Seer

Vestesh kess'ku, Teokaka – "It is accomplished, Holy Voice."

ACKNOWLEDGMENTS

First, I must thank my family, always. They've had to put up with this specific story, in all its incarnations, for nearly twenty years— and they've been super about it. THANK YOU, ALL! In particular, I offer my heartfelt gratitude to Heidi and Tawnee, Lekore's first allies, both of whom have plowed through my endless drafts and rewrites of this series, especially this first book. Somehow, they still love the story, anyway.

I also want to acknowledge Audrey Juhasz: Though we've lost touch over the years, I'll never forget your early support of this story. Also, Brian Jarvis, though we've long lost contact: Thank you for enjoying Lekore way-back-when. I wish you the very best. To Brett Starks, who discovered Lekore years later and supported his story with just as much enthusiasm as the others, thank you.

To Megi Perkins and Madeleine Ethridge: Your friendship gave me the courage to pursue my dream. Thank you for believing in me during those fragile adolescent years. Also, to my high school class at ILA, thanks for putting up with my endless chatter about Lekore and other stories; especially you, Rinda Goff, Trevor Vandever, Stephanie Shah, and Craig Simmerman.

A huge shoutout to my amazing alpha and beta readers: Laura A. Barton, Sonya Bramwell, Elvira Foster, Mandi Oyster, and Heidi Wadsworth. Thank you all for your tireless efforts to beat this novel into submission. Your tough love made all the difference!

And an enormous thank you to my phenomenal editor, Sarah B., who came out of retirement to work her magic and help me polish my novels one by one. You're amazing!

I suspect I've failed to mention others who have also raised the banner high and helped me muster my forces to write, write, write! Know that I'm grateful; that I'm touched and honored by our paths crossing, no matter how briefly. I hope you're all well.

Finally, but not least of all, I thank my Father in Heaven for blessing me with the determination to dream, write, and never give up—and for opening doors I didn't bother to seek, then shoving me through them. I'd be lost without You.

ABOUT THE AUTHOR

Writer of fantasy, magic weaver, dragon rider! Having spent the past 20 years devotedly writing fantasy, it's safe to say M. H. Woodscourt is now more fae than human. This is her sixth published novel.

All of her fantasy worlds connect with each other in a broad Universe, forged with great love and no small measure of blood, sweat, and tears. When she's not writing, she's napping or reading a book with a mug of hot cocoa close at hand while her quirky cat Wynter nibbles her toes.

Learn more at www.mhwoodscourt.com

facebook.com/mhwoodscourt
twitter.com/woodscourtbooks
instagram.com/woodscourtbooks

ALSO BY M. H. WOODSCOURT

WINTERVALE DUOLOGY

High Fantasy/Young Adult

The Crow King

The Winter King

PARADISE SERIES

Portal Fantasy/Humor/Young Adult

A Liar in Paradise

Key of Paradise

OTHER TITLES

Crownless

A stand-alone YA/High Fantasy Novel

October Cove

A YA/Urban Fantasy Novella

Printed in Great Britain
by Amazon